D0968143

She could claim his fortune,
but never his heart . . .

Lust, he told himself as he drew her toward the door, pausing to claim another kiss. Lust was all he felt for the Gypsy. His blood blazed out of control because she had refused him, taunted him for weeks. Until now.

Near the carved archway of the door, the chatter of voices intruded on his feverish state. Quickly he pulled Vivien back into the gallery, holding her flush against his body, out of sight of the corridor. He put his finger to her lips and then kissed her again.

The laughter and talk had faded away by the time he could drag his mouth from hers. Only then did he guide Vivien to the empty doorway.

"Where are we going?" she asked drowsily.

"To my chamber."

Awareness dawned on her slumberous face. "To . . . your bed?"

"Yes," Michael said, tortured by the knowledge that she alone could transport him to paradise. "I'll give you more joy. Just let me love you, Vivien."

Her eyes widened, expressive with wonder. "*Could* you truly love me, Michael?"

Her literal interpretation mystified him. He couldn't imagine how she could mistake his intent. "Come upstairs with me, please," he urged, not caring that she'd reduced him to begging. "I'll love you as I did a few moments ago. I'll do so again and again until we're both satisfied."

Abruptly, Vivien tore herself free. "No," she said, a catch in her voice. "Curse you, Michael. I'm not like your mistresses. I won't be your whore."

Passionate Praise for Barbara Dawson Smith, "One of America's Best-Loved Authors of Historical Romance!"*

Romancing The Rogue

A SELECTION OF THE DOUBLEDAY BOOK CLUB

Seduced by a Scoundrel

"Barbara Dawson Smith uses her consummate skills to bring a powerful story to life and leave readers breathless . . . as love triumphs over scandal. As always, Ms. Smith manages to touch the heart and soul of readers with an unforgettable romance brimming with sexual tension and deep emotions. A must-read of the season."
—*Romantic Times,* K.I.S.S. Award and Top Pick of the Month

"Barbara Dawson Smith offers a tantalizing historical romance that pits a prude against a notorious rake . . . and it's wonderful. Theirs is a glorious story of two people who try hard not to like each other. The reader will find tons of angst and great seduction scenes to make this a memorable read."
—*The Oakland Press,* 5 hearts rating

"Refreshing . . . [A] sensual historical romance."
—*Publishers Weekly*

"SEDUCED BY A SCOUNDREL shows why fans think Barbara Dawson Smith is one of the genre's top historical romance writers . . . Ms. Smith imbues the plot with plenty of sexual tension, a move that will elate Regency readers who love a touching tale with a lot of spice."
—Harriet Klausner, *Painted Rock Reviews*

"From the first page, Barbara Dawson Smith hooks the reader . . . A remarkable storyteller. Sensual, exciting, tight plot, and characters with a purpose combine to create a novel that satisfies and entertains. Ms. Dawson Smith has a pipeline to excellence that brands each of her books, making fans eager for more."
—Kathee S. Card, *Under the Covers Book Reviews*

"Barbara Dawson Smith has once again crafted a story of romance, love and internal conflict, interwoven with intriguing mystery and adventure. The plot is fast-paced and the characters will win your heart, both because of and despite their fears and foibles. It's little wonder Ms. Smith is considered one of the stars of Regency historical romance."
—CompuServe Romance Reviews

Too Wicked to Love

"In TOO WICKED TO LOVE, Barbara Dawson Smith makes magic, bringing unlikely people together in a dance of love that is exciting, mysterious, and altogether joyous. Savor this delicious, delightful masterpiece."
—*Romantic Times,* K.I.S.S. Award and Top Pick of the Month

"Take your time to savor TOO WICKED TO LOVE, Barbara Dawson Smith's latest creation that will keep you laughing . . . This book is wickedly wonderful . . . The love story is so adorably sensual . . . Oh boy! Don't miss this story for anything. A 5★ read. Once you read a book by Barbara Dawson Smith you will raid the bookstores for her backlist, and be on the lookout for her next one. Her books are all on my keeper shelf! Miss Smith is a superb storyteller."
—*The Belles and Beaux of Romance*

"Ms. Smith is heading back to the familiar grounds of best seller-dom with this riveting Regency romance."
—Harriet Klausner, *Painted Rock Reviews*

Her Secret Affair

"Fast-paced, intricately plotted and filled with intriguing characters . . . Smith blends the elements of romance and mystery well. But most of all, the warring wills and sexual tension between Justin and the sensuous Isabel sizzle throughout."
—*Publishers Weekly*

"Barbara Dawson Smith cleverly merges old-fashioned Gothic suspense with a seductive romance all packed into an alluring setting . . . This one will keep you up all night, and you'll see why Ms. Smith is so respected for her ability to create a new and different story each and every time."
—*Romantic Times,* Exceptional Rating

"Ms. Smith's books are always a pleasure to read. She conjures remarkable characters and a wondrous love story. I was most impressed with the honesty of thought, word, deed, and sexual desire between the hero and heroine . . . Ms. Smith's name on the cover is synonymous with spellbinding reading."
—*Rendezvous*

"HER SECRET AFFAIR is Regency romance at its most inventive."
—CompuServe Romance Reviews

"The brilliance of Barbara Dawson Smith imbues this terrific tale with freshness."
—*RomEx Reviews**

Once Upon a Scandal

"ONCE UPON A SCANDAL is a marvelous love story . . . This future classic is a keeper that is destined to be re-read many times, especially when the reader needs an emotionally uplifting experience."
—*Affaire de Coeur*

"Barbara Dawson Smith is an author everyone should read. You'll be hooked from page one."
—*Romantic Times,* Exceptional Rating

"Barbara Dawson Smith is one fabulous writer of stories that stay in the heart."
—*Bell, Book, and Candle*

Never a Lady

"It's time for the rest of the world to discover what Barbara Dawson Smith's fans have known all along—this is a can't-miss author."
—*RomEx Reviews*

"A treasure of a romance . . . a story that only a novelist of Ms. Smith's immense talent could create. Barbara Dawson Smith continues to be a refreshing, powerful voice of the genre. A must read."
—*Romantic Times,* Exceptional Rating

"Once I started NEVER A LADY, I didn't put it down until I read the very last page. Loved it!"
—*Belles and Beaux of Romance*

A Glimpse of Heaven

"Superb reading! Barbara Dawson Smith's talents soar to new heights with this intense, romantic and engrossing tale."
—*Romantic Times*

"Fascinating storytelling!"
—*Atlanta Journal & Constitution*

St. Martin's Paperbacks Titles
by Barbara Dawson Smith

A Glimpse of Heaven

Never a Lady

Once Upon a Scandal

Her Secret Affair

Too Wicked to Love

Seduced by a Scoundrel

Romancing the Rogue

ROMANCING THE ROGUE

Barbara Dawson Smith

St. Martin's Paperbacks

ROMANCING THE ROGUE

ISBN: 0-312-97511-2

Printed in the United States of America

St. Martin's Paperbacks edition / September 2000

St. Martin's Paperbacks are published by St. Martin's Press, 175 Fifth Avenue, New York, N.Y. 10010.

10 9 8 7 6 5 4 3 2 1

Contents

Romancing the Rogue

Chapter one

The Three Rosebuds

Devon, England
August 1810

"I have wonderful news," Vivien told her Gypsy parents by the campfire after breakfast. "I've decided to take a husband."

Striving to look joyful, she clasped her hands to her yellow blouse. The words had been more difficult to say than Vivien had expected. Even harder was her effort to show a happy expression, the smile of a woman in love.

Her parents exchanged a glance that was more disbelieving than delighted. Reyna Thorne stood clutching a stack of tin plates, her knuckles gnarled with the rheumatism that had pained her of late. A short man with the build of a bear, Pulika Thorne sat on an overturned crate, his crippled leg stretched out before him.

The yellow and blue caravan at the edge of the camp gave them a measure of privacy from the band of *Romany*. A short distance away, children ran laughing past the painted *vardos* with their tall wooden wheels, past the men who sprawled by the sun-dappled brook, past the gossiping women who gathered up the dishes and pots. The aroma of spices and cooking drifted on the summer breeze. In a nearby orchard, apple trees hung heavy with fruit, the branches drooping over the stone wall beside the narrow dirt road.

Her father struggled to his feet with the aid of a thick oak stick. Watching him, Vivien felt a familiar helpless constriction in her breast. The horrifying injury to his leg the previous year had sapped him of strength, though his spirit hadn't dimmed. He could still spin enthralling tales, his wide mouth smiling, his teeth glinting. He could make Vivien shiver at his stories of enchantment and laugh at his jests until her sides hurt.

But his eyes weren't twinkling now. A puzzled concern on his weathered features, he regarded his daughter. "A husband, you say? But only Janus has been courting you."

Vivien brightened her smile. "Yes, Janus," she said, forcing her tone to savor his name when she wanted to spit it out like a bite of green apple. "He wishes me to be his wife. Isn't it wonderful?"

Her mother released a little sound of distress. "Oh, Vivi. That one?"

"He's a swaggering fool," Pulika said flatly. "You told me so yourself when he joined our camp."

"That was before I knew him," Vivien said with a romantic sigh. "Just look at him. He's so very handsome."

She turned her starry gaze to the stocky man who stood in the meadow among the picketed horses, currying a dapple-gray mare. As always, she ignored a crawling sensation on her skin. Everything about Janus repelled her, from his cocky manner to the gold buttons that flashed against the gaudy red of his vest.

A fortnight ago, their wandering band had met up with his group, and Janus had persuaded them to travel south to Devon. Each evening, in a circle of some forty caravans and tents, the dark-eyed Gypsy had singled her out for attention. He liked to talk about himself, to hoard all the attention, to challenge the other young men to feats of strength. Vivien had spurned his attempts to impress her with his prowess. She had no interest in his games, only in the ancient epics and legends being told around the fires.

Until she'd discovered Janus owned something none of her other suitors had possessed. A sack of gold guineas.

In a swirl of purple skirts, Reyna set down the plates on the wooden step of the caravan. "That one is trouble, mark my words. He boasts only of his own importance."

"Listen to your mother," Pulika said. "She's a good judge of a man."

"Look at who she married," Vivien teased.

But for once her father didn't smile. Nor did Reyna, who moved closer to her husband and regarded Vivien worriedly.

Reyna Thorne was small-boned and dark-skinned, no bigger than a fluff of eiderdown, Pulika often said. When Vivien had grown to be a head taller than her mother, taller even than her father, she had hunched her shoulders, feeling awkward and unfeminine beside the daintier girls of the *Rom*. But Reyna had told Vivien to stand proud, for she was like a beautiful willow among the more common reeds.

Reyna had always been her staunch advocate. Until now.

Now she looked so distressed that Vivien fought the urge to shift her bare feet in the sun-warmed grass. Always, they had been closer than other families, for she was their only child, the daughter born to them in middle age. Because they were so much older than other parents, she felt the fierce desire to provide for them all the things they couldn't afford since her father's injury—meat for the cookpot to give him strength, a brazier to warm the caravan during the winter so that her mother's joints wouldn't ache, new clothes and more blankets and soft pillows.

"Why did Janus not come to me himself?" her father demanded. "He shouldn't hide like a coward behind your skirts."

"I wished to talk to you first," Vivien said. "I feared you might object."

"Might?" Pulika hobbled forward a few painful steps and leaned on his makeshift cane. "Of course, I object. Am I to give my beloved daughter to a man who cannot make her happy?"

"Janus *will* make me happy." Or rather, she would be happy to know of her parents' comfort, Vivien thought resolutely. "I wish to marry. To know the happiness of having a husband and children."

"You are but eighteen summers," Reyna said. "There is time yet to choose."

Vivien shook her head. "I'm much older than the other girls. Were you not fourteen when you and *dado* wed?"

"Indeed so," Reyna said softly. She and Pulika exchanged a look of affection that somehow made Vivien feel left out, lacking in some vital part. If only she could find such a love herself.

A dream slipped past her defenses, the yearning for a hero like the one in the *gorgio* book she had once found in a rubbish heap, the pages tattered and stained. Her father had taught her to read signposts and handbills, and she'd deciphered the tale of knights and fair maidens. But that was only a story, Vivien knew. Reality was pledging her life to Janus, cooking for him and mending his clothing, letting him touch her in the dark of night. . . .

Reyna placed a gentle hand on her daughter's shoulder.

"Love is a fire in the heart. And you, I think, have not found that with Janus."

Those wise almond eyes saw more than Vivien wished. "I've found everything I want," she insisted. "Don't forget, you gave me the right to choose my own husband."

"We thought you had the sense to choose wisely," Pulika chided.

She touched his fingers curled around the stick, feeling the warm sinews and rough skin, the hand that had soothed her when she'd scraped her knee and whittled toys for her as a child. "Oh, *miro dado,* you wouldn't trust any man who would take me away from you and *miro dye.*"

Pulika scowled. "You're right, I don't trust Janus. Tell me, where did he get that sack of gold he flaunts before everyone?"

"At the fair; his horses brought a higher price than anyone else's."

"Bah. He likely stole the gold from the *gorgios*. That's why he insisted we hasten southward."

Vivien had wondered uneasily about that very thing, but she refused to consider it. "Should we roam a thousand roads, I wouldn't find a better husband," she said. "Janus has agreed to take me without a dowry, and to share his gold with both of you. You'll want for nothing in your old age."

Pulika's face went rigid. Gripping the stick, he straightened, though putting weight on his leg must have pained him. "So that is what all this talk of marriage is about. You think me a helpless cripple."

Reluctant to injure his pride, Vivien hastily said, "I didn't mean that. Yet no longer can you climb the apple trees at harvesttime or find odd jobs in the villages we pass. It grows difficult for you to rise in the morning to see to the horses. If you and *miro dye* had enough money, you could live easier—"

"No. You will not sacrifice your life for us."

"It's no sacrifice. I'm happy to wed Janus. I want to have children, to give you grandchildren." She turned beseeching eyes to her mother.

But Reyna's plain, careworn face looked troubled. "Your father is right. We cannot bless such a marriage."

Refusing to accept failure, Vivien resolved to act the besotted bride-to-be over the coming days. She would make a show of being in love with Janus. Though her insides curdled at the prospect, she would cater to his whims, hang on his every word, gaze adoringly into his lustful eyes. She would do it for the sake of her parents, for she knew no other way to provide for them.

A sudden cacophony drew her attention. The half-wild dogs of the *Rom* rushed out of the camp, snarling and barking as they did whenever a *gorgio* merchant on horseback or a farmer with a wagon laden with hay passed by. Today, an elegant black coach drawn by four white horses rattled down the dirt lane. A coachman in crimson livery perched on the high front seat, and two footmen clung to the back.

Vivien stiffened. Carriages were seldom seen on these winding back roads; the wealthy *gorgios* kept to the main thoroughfares where traveling was easier and inns more prevalent. Should they encounter Gypsy wagons, they drove swiftly past, disdaining the *Rom* as if they did not exist.

But this coachman drew on the reins, and the carriage halted near the encampment. Vivien wondered angrily if their wagons were trespassing on property belonging to a local landowner. She despised the *gorgios* for claiming all land as their own. They asserted their right to the very air and water and fruits of the earth, as if God had created the world for them alone.

She also had a fierce, unforgiving reason for hating the *gorgios*. One of their kind had set the deadly trap that had lamed her father.

A footman leapt down and lowered a step. With a flourish, he opened the door of the coach. An old lady with a halo of white hair emerged, small and dainty in a gown of sky-blue, her wrinkled face bearing a gentle smile.

In her wake appeared another woman, her round figure encased in yellow silk and lace, her face plump and rosy, and her eyes merry beneath the yellow turban crowning her head.

Lastly, a dignified woman stepped to the ground. Tall and elegant, she had a pinched mouth that looked as if she'd bitten into a crab apple. Her fingers were curled clawlike around the ivory knob of a cane.

They were ancient, these three *gorgio rawnies*. They stood like a row of statues in the lane, the breeze fluttering the ribbons on their fancy hats and wafting their perfumes with the richness of cultivated flowers.

Men abandoned their discussions, women ceased their gossiping, children stopped laughing. For a moment, only the shrill yapping of the dogs broke the silence. Baring their yellowed teeth, the animals formed a ragged line separating the ladies from the Gypsies.

Three pairs of *gorgio* eyes surveyed the gathering. Vivien found herself standing up straight and rigid, glaring at the outsiders. They gazed with disdain at the large circle of caravans, the iron cooking pots bubbling over the fires, the half-naked children creeping forward for a closer peek at the magnificent carriage. She would never flinch from these—

Then she did flinch.

In a flash of movement, the tall woman swept her cane toward the snarling dogs. "Be gone!"

Though the stick failed to make contact, the pack scattered in an instant. Recognizing her authority, they lowered their barking to a growl and slunk away to the outskirts of the camp.

Vivien bristled. Who was this stranger to frighten their dogs?

She parted her lips in fury when a big hand closed around her arm and she looked into the unnatural paleness of her father's face. "Stay here," he said in an undertone. "Wait with your mother."

Vivien emphatically shook her head. "These *gorgios* don't belong here. I'll tell them so—"

"This is a man's business. For once, you will hold your tongue."

His unexpected harshness raised rebelliousness in Vivien, yet something in his haggard features alarmed her. Now was no time to provoke him, anyway, not when she had to convince him to approve her marriage to Janus. Her throat taut, she nodded, watching as her father limped away.

Too small to see over the crowd, Reyna climbed onto the caravan step. Striding to her mother's side was a husky man with bulging muscles and a swarthy, overconfident face with an elaborate drooping moustache.

Janus.

Regarding Vivian with a smoldering intensity, he lifted his bushy eyebrows as if to ask if she had spoken to her parents yet about the marriage. She answered him with a noncommittal shrug.

A fire in the heart. Turning away from him, Vivien subdued her unfulfilled yearning for a storybook love. She must be practical about marriage, rather than chase after dreams.

At the front of the throng, the tall lady gazed down her nose at the Gypsies. "I am the Countess of Faversham," she said in a voice that pealed like a church bell. "Is there a man here called Pulika Thorne?"

Mutterings of surprise and curiosity swept the crowd.

Puzzled, Vivien glanced at her mother, but Reyna watched the ladies intently. What could this *gorgio rawnie* want with her father?

The multitude parted, and he hobbled forward until he stood face-to-face with the countess. He bowed, the red kerchief at his brown throat waving in the breeze. "I am Pulika. We will speak alone."

Lady Faversham nodded crisply. "Come, ladies."

As she led the procession to a spreading oak tree across the lane, she hardly used her cane at all, in sharp contrast to Pulika, who leaned heavily on the rough oak stick, his slow gait piercing Vivien's heart anew. That *gorgio* woman probably didn't even need a cane. She used her fancy walking stick as a frivolous complement to her long, skinny form.

The footmen hastened to bring three stools from the coach, which they placed in the shade for the ladies to sit. Pulika remained standing proudly, and it enraged Vivien that they didn't offer a seat to a crippled man. Lady Faversham planted the tip of her cane in the earth and began to talk to him. Giving a sharp shake of his head, he said something back. Vivien couldn't discern their words, but it didn't appear to be a friendly discussion.

"What do you suppose they're saying?" she whispered to her mother. "*Dado* hasn't done anything wrong. Perhaps Zurka stole another chicken for his stewpot."

"Mmm," her mother said distractedly.

Reyna's face had gone pale, her brow crinkled with something oddly akin to fear. Her gold bangles chiming musically, Vivien caught her mother's brown arm. "*Miro dye,* what's wrong?"

"Go inside," she whispered, indicating the *vardo*. "Quickly."

"But if that lady is accusing *dado* of a crime, I won't allow it."

Janus took hold of her elbow. "Such a spirited filly needs a husband to tame her."

Vivien recoiled, for a man was forbidden to touch an unmarried girl, even his betrothed. Then a suspicion struck away all other thought. "It's *you* they're after. You'll let my father take the blame for gold that you stole."

Grooming his thick moustache, Janus laughed. "These *gorgios* have no quarrel with me. Perhaps you should go and see for yourself."

Was Janus telling the truth? There was amusement in his gloating black gaze, a sneering enjoyment she didn't understand . . .

A loud voice interrupted them. Beneath the oak tree, Lady Faversham rose to her majestic height and shook her cane at Pulika. "You, sirrah, are nothing but a lying Gypsy!"

Angry mutterings rippled through the crowd. The men milled uneasily; the women whispered. Reyna moaned, her hand clasped to her mouth, and her distress made the volatile emotions inside Vivien burst forth.

"Don't speak to him that way!" she cried out.

She started forward, disregarding the glares directed at a girl who dared to flout the laws of the *Rom*. In her haste, she stepped on a pebble, but the pain was a mere nuisance. Hurrying across the rutted lane, she brushed past her father and confronted Lady Faversham.

Up close, the elderly countess had eyes as cold and gray as ice. For once, Vivien had the rare experience of not being the tallest female present. "My father is no liar," she declared. "Nor has he stolen anything."

Those frosty eyes widened slightly. Lady Faversham glanced at Pulika, then in a rather quiet voice, repeated, "Your father?"

"Yes." Vivien gave a toss of her black braids. "I know his character far better than you do. He would never tell a lie."

Lady Faversham did not reply. She merely stared at Vivien, her gaze piercing, as if she searched for some truth in Vivien's dark features.

"Child," Pulika said with a strange, hoarse urgency, "return to your mother. *At once.*"

He gave her a little push, but Vivien stood unmoving, her bare feet rooted to the earth. She was determined to protect him against these accusations. All three women subjected her to an intense scrutiny, making her keenly aware of the contrast between herself and these outsiders—her shabby green skirt and faded yellow blouse, the gold bangles that clinked at her wrists, the dark braids that fell to her waist.

The small lady with the white curls rose from her stool to take Vivien's hands in a warm, surprisingly firm grip. "My dear girl," she crooned in a soft and vibrant voice. "Is it possible . . . is your name Vivien? Vivien Thorne?"

Wary, Vivien pulled free. "Yes. Why do you wish to know?"

"My stars, it's *her*!" the plump one said. She clapped her hands, her rosy cheeks glowing. "What a bumblebroth there'll be when the neighborhood hears the news!"

Lady Faversham turned sharply. "The neighbors will hear nothing. Do you understand me, Enid? This is not fodder for your gossip mill."

Lady Enid frowned. "Of course, Olivia. I shan't breathe

a word. But people will ask, and I must tell them *something*—"

"Send the busybodies to me. I'll set them straight."

"Oh, bother your quarreling," the white-haired lady said. "Here's our sweet girl at last, all grown up. 'Tis quite astonishing, isn't it?"

Were they all mad? Bewildered, Vivien regarded her father. "What are they talking about? Why did they call you a liar?"

An inexplicable fear haunted Pulika's eyes. " 'Tis nothing. A mistake."

"It is no mistake," Lady Faversham said with a sniff. "This is the girl you were given eighteen years ago."

The girl you were given.

A shadow dimmed the brilliance of the day. It was merely a cloud passing over the sun, yet Vivien felt a chill climb the stairs of her spine. She glanced wildly from her father to the watching ladies. "I don't understand. What are you saying?"

The diminutive woman in blue patted the back of Vivien's hand. "We haven't made ourselves very clear, have we? I'm Lucy, Lady Stokeford, and we're the Rosebuds. We've come to take you back where you belong."

"Back?"

"Yes. You were born of a noblewoman and spirited away as a newborn babe. So you see, you are not a Gypsy at all. You are one of us."

The hot summer air draped Vivien like a suffocating shroud. She heard the rustle of the oak leaves, the snort of a horse, the drone of a bee. Unable to move, she stared down at the frail white hand resting on her sun-darkened skin. These ladies were claiming her as one of them. A *gorgio.*

Impossible.

Her heart banged as hard as a blacksmith's hammer,

and she struggled to draw a breath into her starved lungs. "No," she whispered, backing away. "My mother is Reyna. Not a noblewoman."

"She was a governess, Miss Harriet Althorpe," said Lady Stokeford in her soft patrician voice. "Eighteen years ago, Harriet taught my three grandsons. Since she had no other relations, she was like a daughter to me."

"I don't believe you! What sort of woman gives away her own child?"

"It was her lover who gave you away," Lady Faversham said.

"While she was ill," Lady Enid added, "he wrested you from her arms."

Lady Stokeford's clear blue eyes held sympathy and kindness. "It's the truth, my dear," she said gently. "Ask the man who adopted you."

Frantic for reassurance, Vivien jerked herself around to face her father. He would scorn this absurdity. He would explain that these women had played a monstrous trick to amuse themselves at her expense.

But Pulika's dark eyes shone with torment. Like a cornered bear, he watched her, his thickset form hunched over the walking stick.

"*Dado?* Tell me they're lying."

"Your mother and I always feared someone would come for you," he said heavily. "Always at the edge of our minds was the fear."

"No. *No* . . ."

He held out one hand to her, his broad palm turned up. "We didn't steal you, Vivi, I swear it. May a thousand curses be upon me if I am lying. You were given to us by a *gorgio* servant."

Sweat dampened her palms. She rubbed them on her skirt. "Servant? Whose servant?"

"We didn't know his name. We were told to take you

away . . . to never tell another living soul how you came to us. And so all these years we've loved you as our own daughter." Tears trickled down his leathery cheeks.

Reyna appeared at his side, bracing him with her small arm. Her stricken gaze on Vivien, she murmured, "We weren't blessed with a child of my womb . . . and we were so overjoyed to have you, Vivi, that we asked no questions. We never meant to hurt you."

But Vivien did hurt. A hole had been ripped in the fabric of her life, and she couldn't think of how to mend it. *Gorgio* blood coursed through her veins. With a dizzying lurch, she understood why she was taller than the other girls, why a hint of copper tinted her black hair, why she had a secret, shameful interest in books and learning.

She hated the *gorgios* . . . the shopkeepers who tried to sell them bad meat . . . the mothers who shooed their children away when Gypsy caravans passed by . . . the rich landowners who set traps like the one that had maimed her *dado.*

Yet she was one of *them.*

Quietly weeping, her father and mother watched her. They were old and stooped, shabbily garbed, with strands of silver dulling their dark hair. She wasn't the miracle of their middle years. She had been *given* to them. How could they have kept such an earthshaking secret from her?

The child in her wanted to cry and wail, to rebuke them for their deception. Yet she also wanted to feel their comforting embrace. Vivien grasped the thought like a lifeline. They were her parents. If not in blood, then in love. She felt nothing for the *gorgios* but hatred.

"This has been a terrible shock," Lady Stokeford said. "But if you'll gather your things, you'll feel much better once you come home with us."

Come home?

Horrified, Vivien regarded the three aristocrats. Lady Enid fanned her plump, flushed face. Lady Faversham stood tall and proud. Lady Stokeford smiled as if granting Vivien a gift. They clearly expected her to leap at their offer, to abandon the only life she had ever known. To step into their carriage and ride away with them, never to look back.

Resentment surged and clamored for release. Vivien parted her lips in a fury; then out of the corner of her eye, she saw Janus standing at the edge of the throng, his feet planted apart, his fists on his hips, his gloating gaze a vile reminder that she belonged to him. That she needed his money . . .

Or perhaps not.

A daring idea sprang into her mind. A plan that would free her from the necessity of marriage and yet provide her parents with all the luxuries they could ever desire. Buoyed by desperation, Vivien addressed the trio of ladies. "All right, then, I'll go with you. For a price."

London
September 1810

A fortnight later, Michael Kenyon, the Marquess of Stokeford, stared blandly into the face of death.

The mummy was a rather shriveled specimen. Light from several candelabra flickered on leathery skin drawn taut over the aquiline features of the dead woman. Oiled strands of hair clung to the desiccated skull. Stringy arms were folded across the bosom, and for modesty's sake, the yellowed wrappings remained in place over the lower portion of the anatomy. Bits of crumbling cloth were strewn over a basket on the floor of the drawing room.

Lord Alfred Yarborough held up a lapis amulet that had been nestled in the folds of linen. The artifact was no bigger than his thumb. "Behold another talisman of Her Majesty, Queen Shepset."

He bowed to a smattering of applause from the privileged group of aristocrats. Ever since Napoleon had conquered Egypt, and England in turn had subdued the Corsican, the *ton* had been fascinated by the ancient land of the pharoahs. Furniture and clothing showed an Egyptian influence. The rich collected amulets and scarabs and other trinkets. Some even acquired the mummies of kings and queens and other dignitaries, all for the purpose of exposing the remains to a hedonistic throng of gawkers.

With an air of aloofness, Michael watched the proceedings. Though he usually enjoyed decadent amusements, for once he couldn't share in the glee. He pictured the mummy as a living, breathing, flesh-and-blood woman. And he found himself wondering if she had been loved . . . or hated like Grace.

Fighting the dark memories, he gritted his teeth. It served no purpose to resurrect the past. He far preferred to live in the present, to pursue pleasure with single-minded recklessness.

A hand brushed his thigh. "Charming, isn't she?" Lady Katherine Westbrook drawled in his ear. There had been gasps and squeals from the other ladies present, but not from Katherine. His mistress regarded the proceedings as she regarded life: with worldly amusement.

His gaze lingered on her fine white breasts. "Frankly, I fancy my women a bit more hot-blooded."

Her fingers danced closer to his groin. "And I fancy my men handsome and virile."

The stirring scent of her musky perfume drifted to him.

Katherine was everything he liked in a woman: cool, clever, cultured. She would make a suitable wife for him, Michael knew, and recently he had decided to legalize their union. He had no doubt she would agree; more than once, she'd hinted at a desire for a more permanent liaison. He had only to ask her.

"I've a question for you," he murmured. "But this isn't the place for it."

Her blue eyes assessed him. "I'm yours to command, my lord."

They were seated at the rear of the semicircle of chairs, and with the rest of the assembly still intent on the mummy, they were able to slip away easily, their footsteps silent on the plush rug. As always, he enjoyed the sway of her bottom, the familiar brush of her hips. His loins tightened with anticipation of the pleasurable night ahead. Yes, he would like having a woman in his bed without the bother of arranging discreet meetings.

Then his gaze fell upon the tall, long-limbed man who lounged against the gilt door frame. His cravat was untied, and he held a drink in his hand. The light from a wall sconce cast shadows over his harshly hewn features and dark brown hair. A half-moon scar brought up one corner of his mouth in perpetual, sinister amusement.

Michael cursed under his breath. They'd once been friends, he and Brand, growing up on neighboring estates in Devon. But that scar gave testament to the rift between them. He hated no man as much as he hated this one. "Faversham," he acknowledged with a curt nod.

The Earl of Faversham bowed to Katherine. "Quite a sight," he said, nodding at the mummy. "But hardly one for a lady."

Her lips curved into a coy smile. "Or for an ill-fated queen."

A gleam in his gray eyes, Faversham chuckled. "So

you say." Rather than ask for an introduction, he said conversationally, "Gypsies are said to be descended from these ancient Egyptians."

Michael tightened his hold on Katherine's waist. "I wouldn't know."

He started out the door, but Faversham stepped into his path. "Thieves, liars, and fortune-tellers the Gypsies are," the earl went on. "They are adept at fleecing the unwary and, in particular, preying upon the elderly."

Clearly, Brand had a purpose; he always did. "Make your point, then."

"All in good time. You haven't been to Devon of late, have you? Not since Grace's death." The earl clucked in sham sympathy. "Do forgive me for mentioning that unfortunate event. Perhaps instead I should ask after your daughter's health—the Lady Amy, I believe."

White-hot anger stabbed Michael. He burned to kill the earl as he should have done long ago. For the past three years, Michael had exiled himself from his ancestral estate for reasons no one knew. Not even this man. Aware of his mistress, who was watching with shrewd interest, he controlled his rage. "We were on our way out. Perhaps you and I can chat another time."

"You'd be interested to know about the letter from my grandmama."

"Letter?"

"The one I received just yesterday. She had quite the fascinating tale to tell of *your* grandmama."

Michael waited in rigid silence while Brand tossed back a swallow of wine. Despite his distaste for Brand's sport, he had to know what mischief Grandmama had embroiled herself in this time. "Tell me, then."

"It seems Lady Stokeford is threatening to rewrite her will. Again."

Relaxing marginally, Michael shrugged. "So which one

of my brothers does she favor this time? Gabe or Josh?"

"Neither. She wants to leave all her money to her new companion." The scar beside the earl's mouth quirked in sly amusement. "A filthy Gypsy fortune-teller."

Chapter two

A Hard Bargain

"Use your silverware, dear," Lady Stokeford suggested. "Lest you send Enid into another swoon."

Vivien started to lick the gravy from her fingers, saw the three ladies watching in scandalized disapproval, then remembered to use the little cloth in her lap that they called a *serviette*. It seemed a shame to soil the fine white damask, and worse, to waste such a delicious sauce, but the *gorgios* had many peculiar customs and this was the least of them.

Picking up the heavy fork, she speared a ladylike portion of roast beef. The tender meat melted in her mouth, a masterpiece from Lady Stokeford's French chef. Never had Vivien dreamed that the rich dined on meat at every meal along with a dizzying abundance of side dishes. She felt disloyal for comparing this fancy cooking to her mother's plain, wholesome fare.

A pang of melancholy threatened to steal her appetite. How she missed her parents. But for their sake, she must play this game to the hilt.

"Miss?" Holding a silver dish, a white-gloved footman appeared beside her. "Would you care for more *pomme de terres soufflées*?"

Stoically, Vivien focused on the ladylike manners she had learned over the past fortnight. "Thank you, Mr. Rumbold," she said, helping herself to the golden puffed potatoes. "How is the carbuncle on your leg today?"

A blush pinkened his freckled face from his stiff white collar to the tips of his big ears. "Much better, miss," he mumbled before scuttling back to his position by the sideboard.

Across the table, Lady Enid Quinton nearly choked on a swallow of wine, and her brown eyes twinkled in her well-fed features.

"Vivien!" Thinning her lips, the Countess of Faversham frowned from her chair at the end of the linen-draped table. "It isn't suitable to converse with a servant at the dinner table. Nor to ask questions of such a personal and disgusting nature."

No slurping. Sit up straight. Don't saw your meat. Vivien's head swam with all their silly rules. Though she knew she was breaking yet another one by talking back, she said defiantly, "When I saw Mr. Rumbold limping yesterday, I fixed him a posset of burdock-root tea and I only wanted to know if—"

"Enough." Lady Faversham bristled like a hedgehog. "We do not address footmen as *mister.* We also do not need a description of your Gypsy remedies. If anyone in this household requires a physician, we shall summon Dr. Green from the village."

Vivien refrained from saying tartly that if the countess continued to rant, she would need a dose of herbal oil for constipation. Assuming a look of wide-eyed innocence, she murmured, "But this very morning, you told me it was the duty of a lady to see to the smooth running of her household. That surely would include tending to those in her employ."

Lady Faversham harrumphed. "You know what I meant, and don't pretend otherwise."

"Pretend, my lady? But I only wish to understand your many strict laws of behavior."

Determined to win this battle of wills, Vivien held her chin high. Having left behind everything she held dear—though only for a short while—she felt compelled to bend a few of the rigid rules in this strange *gorgio* world. She would not be discouraged by one ill-tempered snoot.

Lady Stokeford smiled, her finely wrinkled face merry in the candlelight. "Oh, do admit Vivien has a point, Olivia. It's a lady's right to minister to her staff. She only thought she was behaving as she ought."

"I'll allow the girl has made remarkable progress," the countess said with a regal nod. "Though it will be some time yet before she is presentable."

"What do you mean, presentable?" Vivien asked.

"Why, you must be prepared if you're to associate with society," Lady Stokeford said. "You've been working especially hard on your social graces. You're a very bright girl."

"She's a beauty, too." Lady Enid nodded vigorously, her multiple chins jiggling and a few faded ginger curls sticking out of her turban. " 'Twill be great fun to watch as the young squires and gentlemen farmers in the neighborhood meet her. They're bound to be smitten."

The elderly women nodded, murmuring to one another. Even Lady Faversham ceased glowering, and her cool gray eyes thawed a little. She and Lady Enid had come to visit each day, helping Lady Stokeford to teach Vivien all the complicated details of being a lady.

Her fancy gown of sea-green silk rustling, Vivien shifted uneasily in her chair. Was that their plan, to marry her off to some arrogant *gorgio*? Little did they know, she wouldn't be here for long. "I don't wish to meet anyone else," she stated. "I'm content to live here at the Dower House with you, Lady Stokeford."

"My dear girl, that's very sweet of you," the marchioness said. "Yet I shan't be around forever. Heaven knows, I might die next week."

Vivien dropped her fork, heedlessly splattering her silk bodice. "Are you ill, my lady?"

"I'm fine," Lady Stokeford said. "Yet when one is old, one never knows. You, however, are young and lively and ought to be wed. Surely you wish to be more than a companion to a rather settled old woman."

"Oh no, I enjoy your company very much. I especially like to listen to your stories." It wasn't a lie. In spite of her mistrust of all things *gorgio*, Vivien had taken a certain delight in the Rosebuds, as they called themselves. She stretched her arm across the white-draped table to grasp the dowager's blue-veined hand. "I entreat you, please don't make plans for me to marry a strange man. I won't do it."

Lady Stokeford laughed, a delicate chime that echoed through the cavernous dining chamber. "There's no need for dramatics. When the time is right, you'll choose a husband from among the local gentry."

" 'Twill be a love match, and you'll live happily ever after," Lady Enid declared. "Why, that's exactly what dear Harriet would have wanted for you."

At the mention of her natural mother, Vivien swallowed hard. Even after so many days, the truth of her past still throbbed like an unhealed wound. But she hadn't asked more than a few cursory questions about the woman who had given birth to her—or the unknown man who had sired her. Somehow, wanting to know more seemed a betrayal to her *dado* and *dye*.

So did the pleasure she'd taken in this *gorgio* life.

In accordance with her plan, Vivien had allowed the

Rosebuds to fuss over her like hens, arraying her in fine clothing, rubbing lemon juice on her skin to lighten the effects of the sun, and teaching her how to act in what they called "polite society." To her guilty surprise, she'd found she loved the hot baths, the plentiful food, the softness of silk on her skin. She loved hearing Lady Stokeford speak of times gone by and the pranks her grandsons had played. Most shameful of all, she discovered that she couldn't hate these *gorgio* ladies, for they were kind and well-meaning, with a startling similarity to the women of the *Rom.*

Lady Enid reminded her of old Shuri, who liked to giggle and gossip. Lady Faversham was like peevish Pesha, critical and yet compassionate. Lady Stokeford was most like Reyna Thorne, sweet-tempered and smiling.

That last comparison galled Vivien. How could she favorably compare any *gorgio rawnie* to the loving woman who had raised her?

Seized by a clamor of conflicting emotions, she thrust back her chair. Just in time, she remembered her manners. "Please, may I be excused?"

"But you haven't finished your dinner," said Lady Stokeford, dismay in her sky-blue eyes.

"We've plum cake for dessert," Lady Enid said. "It's your favorite—and mine, too."

"I told the footman to make your tea stronger, the way you like it," added Lady Faversham.

"Thank you . . . all of you . . . but I'm really not hungry anymore."

Turning her back on them, Vivien fled the dining room and hastened down the corridor. Sudden tears pricked her eyes. She didn't want kindness from the Rosebuds, nor did she want to like living in this lavish house. She felt dizzied by its endless array of rooms and confined by these walls with their many paintings. Odd how the *gorgio* preferred to hang pictures of landscapes rather than live outside and experience nature in its full glory.

Her quick footsteps echoed in the grand foyer. The facets of the crystal chandelier caught the last rays of sunlight through the tall windows, sending rainbows dancing over the walls. At another time, she might have been enchanted by the sight, but now she could think only of escape.

She hurried to the front door and ran out into the dusk, down the broad steps of the verandah and across the neatly cropped lawn. Men with long, curved scythes had cut the grass that afternoon, and the lingering fresh scent saddened her, for the *gorgios* didn't seem to understand that nature was meant to grow wild, not to be trimmed and tamed. Nor did they comprehend that she had a free spirit that chafed at their rigid rules.

How she longed for the woods and the open road, for the smells and sights and sounds of the encampment. She longed for her parents, for their easy laughter and familiar conversation. She missed the lulling motion of the *vardo* as they journeyed toward an unknown destination.

Drawn by the musical sound of the river, Vivien headed toward a thicket of rowan trees. Across a stone bridge, an even more palatial mansion loomed in the distance, but she stopped at the embankment, breathing in the scents of water and vegetation.

Defiantly kicking off her slippers, she wriggled her stockinged toes in the grass. Then she plucked the tortoiseshell pins from her tight chignon, releasing her hair to tumble freely down her back. Turning around, she lifted her face to the evening sky, her soul seeking solace in the layers of deep cobalt blue, the pinks and purples of sunset.

She wondered if at this very moment her *dado* and *dye* were gazing up at the first stars, too, and thinking of their daughter. The daughter who was not of their blood.

In a flood of pent-up emotion, tears scalded her face. Vivien took deep lungfuls of cool air to ease the constriction in her breast. Why was she weeping? Though she'd uncovered a weakness in herself for *gorgio* luxuries, she intended to return to her family as soon as she had earned enough money.

She had struck a hard bargain with the Rosebuds. For every month she stayed with Lady Stokeford, she received the princely sum of one hundred gold guineas. At her insistence, the old ladies had advanced ten guineas to her father. He had tried to refuse it, but Vivien had reminded him that the alternative was marriage to Janus, and at last he had given in.

'Tis only right that you learn the ways of your blood, he'd told her. *Perhaps you'll wish to stay there.*

She had protested vehemently, vowing to return. Two months, she'd told him. Two hundred guineas. Then she would be free to rejoin the *Rom.*

Though the Rosebuds didn't know it, that was her plan. They naïvely believed that once she'd had a taste of wealth and comfort, she would renounce her life with the *Rom.* They thought she would wed one of their kind and live among them forever.

A fire in the heart.

Remembering her mother's words, Vivien dashed the last of the tears from her cheeks. The Rosebuds were dreaming. She'd never find happiness with an arrogant *gorgio* nobleman. She could never fit into a world where people would always view her with suspicion, where evil landowners set traps for unsuspecting Gypsies.

Yet a blessing of fate had brought the Rosebuds to her. She would pretend to cooperate for the allotted time. The money was a mere trifle to them, so she mustn't regret the need to trick them.

"My dear girl, you move far too swiftly for this elderly lady."

She spun around to see Lady Stokeford slowly making her way toward the river. In the twilight, her snowy hair shone with an almost ghostly glow. An airy white mantle draped her dainty shoulders.

"My lady," Vivien said in wary surprise. "You shouldn't be out here. You'll catch a chill."

"I was afraid we'd upset you." Peering closely at her, the dowager clucked her tongue in her kindly way. "Poor dear, you've been weeping, haven't you? Come now, talk to me. Think of me as your dear old auntie."

In short order, Vivien found herself seated on a stone bench facing the river, Lady Stokeford patting Vivien's cheeks dry with a lacy handkerchief. "There, there now, darling. We should not have badgered you so. This life is all so new and complicated to you, isn't it? Our customs must seem very strange to you at times."

Despite her earlier desire for solitude, Vivien felt in desperate need of company, for she missed the long talks she'd shared with her mother. "It's odd to spend so much time within walls," she found herself admitting. She thought about her narrow escape from Janus, and her resolution firmed. "But I'm determined to learn the ways of the *gorgios*. I'll uphold my end of our bargain." *At least for two months.*

Lady Stokeford smiled. "I'm sure you will. You're rather like your mother in that respect. A very proud young lady she was."

Vivien crumpled the damp handkerchief in her fist. Was she a traitor to Reyna to wonder about her *gorgio* mother? Yet surely Lady Stokeford would expect questions from her. Taking a deep breath, she said, "Tell me more about my . . . about Harriet."

"She was a sober, capable woman whom I hired as

governess to my three grandsons. Even with that rambunctious lot, she showed great dignity." The dowager laughed a little. "Why, I remember one night when Michael, the eldest, draped himself in a sheet and commenced a ghastly howling to frighten her. Unfortunately for him, it was a warm night and my windows were open, and so I ran upstairs to the nursery and caught him just as Harriet sat up and ordered him back to bed, as calm as you please."

Vivien smiled, trying to picture the stately Harriet in her surroundings. "The nursery. That is where you keep children, is it not? I haven't seen any such place at the Dower House."

"No, I moved here after my son died and my grandsons left for good." Misty-eyed, Lady Stokeford pointed at the palace far across the river, barely visible through the dusk. "Back then, we all lived together there at Stokeford Abbey. What wonderful days those were, even though my son was too often muddled by drink. And his wife—my daughter-in-law—spent most of her time in prayer." The dowager made a sour face. "She would have been content to let those boys run wild, as if litanies alone could civilize them. But I made certain they learned to mind their *p*'s and *q*'s."

So Lady Stokeford had raised her grandsons. Vivien set aside an unwarranted curiosity about them in favor of a more pressing matter. "What happened then?" she asked. "To Harriet."

"One morning, poof! She was gone. She left a note saying that she preferred the fresh sea air and she'd found another post on the Isle of Wight. I thought those mischievous boys had finally managed to terrorize her, so I punished them soundly."

"Surely you knew she was with child."

The dowager sadly shook her head. "No, I didn't, else

I would have gone after her and brought her home. You see, she was like a daughter to me. I was so very hurt by her abrupt departure."

"How did you find out . . . about me?"

"After her death last year, her solicitor found a letter among her effects, addressed to me. In it, Harriet confessed to having had a lover, then going away to give birth to a daughter. To you, my dear."

Vivien's fingers dug into the folds of her silk skirt. "She renounced me easily enough."

Lady Stokeford reached out to touch her. "No! You mustn't blame Harriet. While she lay ill with childbed fever, her lover gave you, his own daughter, to the Gypsies. Harriet was desperate to find you, but she was sickly and alone, without anyone to help her."

Vivien burned with rage at the man who had so callously misused Harriet. The man whose seed had given life to Vivien. "Who was he?" she demanded. "This man who tore me from my mother's arms?"

Lady Stokeford scowled into the gathering shadows beneath the rowan trees. "I wish I knew. I should like to twist off his . . ." Then the fierce expression on her face vanished, and she again looked like the tenderhearted matriarch. "But never mind him, dear. All that matters is that you're here, when for eighteen years, we didn't know you even existed."

Vivien swallowed a host of questions about the unknown *gorgio* who had fathered her. He was an evil man, and he meant nothing to her. Nothing mattered but the two hundred gold guineas. "How did you find me?"

"Why, I hired a Bow Street runner, of course."

"A . . . what?"

"An officer of the law all the way from London. He made a few discreet inquiries for me. Though the trail was old, we were greatly aided by having the names of the people who had taken you in, from Harriet's letter." Lady Stokeford smiled reassuringly. "And now we Rosebuds are your family."

Vivien regarded her curiously. "What is this flower name you call yourselves?"

The older woman laughed. "It has naught to do with flowers, my dear. But it's a long story, and one for another night. For now, we thought you might enjoy practicing one of *your* customs for a change."

"What do you mean?"

In the fading light, an impish smile made the dowager's eyes sparkle like stars. "Why, come inside and find out!"

Chapter three

Lucy's Plan

In the doorway of his grandmother's candlelit boudoir, Michael stood thunderstruck by the scene within.

He was saddlesore, gritty-eyed, and hungry. Rather than stop at the Abbey, he'd come straight here to the Dower House. While peeling off his leather gloves, he'd heard from the butler that Grandmama and her new companion were huddled in consultation, and so he had stormed upstairs, intending to evict the conniving Gypsy before he sat down to enjoy his supper.

Instead, he stood riveted in the doorway. The carpet must have muffled his footsteps because the three Rosebuds didn't look up. Like awed admirers, they clustered in chairs around a ravishingly beautiful, dark-haired girl.

For a fleeting moment, he was puzzled, glancing at the pink-frilled boudoir with its elaborate hangings and white French furniture, its fragrance of powder and perfume. Where was the shifty-eyed crone with a wart on her nose whom he had envisioned a hundred times on the long ride here? The sly swindler who had finagled her way into this house? She had to be hiding somewhere, perhaps rifling through drawers in the dressing room while his grandmother was distracted.

Then he realized it was *her*. This gorgeous creature was the Gypsy.

Arrayed in a gown of sea-green silk, she perched on an ottoman in the center of the semicircle of chairs. Her unbound hair flowed in lavish waves to her waist, skimming curves that made a man think about tumbling her to the sheets. The hearth fire gilded fine features dusky from exposure to the sun. She had high cheekbones and rosy lips, and a charming way of tilting her head as if totally absorbed in her task.

Cupping his grandmother's hand in hers, the Gypsy peered intently at the palm, tracing the lines with her fingertip. "You will live to a very great age," she said in a lyrical tone. "In truth, I see much adventure yet to come for you."

The Rosebuds twittered among themselves. His grandmother looked delighted. "Do tell me more, dear. What sort of adventure is this to be?"

Lady Enid leaned forward, her bosom like the prow of a ship. "Does it involve a gentleman?"

The Gypsy smiled mysteriously. "Adventure often does. Yet there is only so much a palm reveals."

The anger that had sustained Michael on the long ride came surging back. This Gypsy wasn't content merely to pick a pocket. She had gone for bigger game, spinning lies for his gullible grandmother, taking advantage of a gentle old soul while plotting to rob her of a fortune.

"The wench is a fraud," he said from the doorway. "You'd do well to lock up your valuables, Grandmama."

With a gasp, Lady Stokeford jerked back her hand. But he ignored her and the surprised squawks of her friends, keeping his stony gaze trained on the Gypsy.

She stared back at him, her large doe-brown eyes rimmed by an abundance of dark lashes. Her lips parted slightly, and she returned his look with a bold, unblinking interest.

As if in a reverie, she lifted her clasped hands to her breasts. Lush, womanly breasts.

His blood heated. Perhaps he'd turn her game to his own advantage by taking her straight to his bed.

"Don't stand there staring like a mooncalf," Lady Stokeford said. "Come and greet me properly, and I'll consider forgiving your rudeness to my companion."

His attention snapped to his grandmother. Though it galled him to be treated like a callow boy, Michael crossed the room and bent down to kiss her wrinkled cheek. Only then did he notice her air of fragility and the new lines engraved on her patrician features. He wondered uneasily if he'd been wrong to ignore her letters, if his informant had been mistaken to report her in excellent health. "Grandmama. How are you?"

She caught him in a perfumed embrace. "Why, Michael, darling. You're the last person I expected to walk through my door." Then she drew back, daintily waving a handkerchief at her nose. "Phew, you reek of horses."

"Forgive me," he said tersely, his bow encompassing her elderly cronies. "I just arrived. I started out at the crack of dawn, my coach broke an axle, and I was forced to ride the rest of the way on a nag that threw a shoe." Not to mention that he'd given up a lusty night in Katherine's arms.

The other two ladies chirruped nervously, but Grandmama regarded him blandly. "Ill humor is no excuse for bad behavior. Now, may I present my new companion, Miss Vivien Thorne." The dowager turned a tender, too-trusting smile on the Gypsy. "Vivien, dear, this is Michael Kenyon, the Marquess of Stokeford, and my eldest grandson. The callous one who seldom comes to visit . . . except when he wishes to berate me."

Ignoring the gibe, Michael focused his hard gaze on the Gypsy sitting on the ottoman. For a female her age—

and she couldn't be more than eighteen—she had a brazen stare that lacked the blushing modesty of well-bred girls. Over the years, many women had flashed him that come-hither look, but none so blatantly. Clearly, this one was a trollop.

He inclined his head in a mocking bow. "Miss Thorne. Alas for you, I know all about your kind."

She didn't seem to hear him. Her lips moved. In a voice so low he thought he misunderstood, she whispered, *"A fire in the heart."*

He frowned. Was she daft, then? No, her aura of dazed bewitchment was part of her pretense. She was hoping to hedge her bets by charming him.

"Eh, what was that?" Lady Enid said, cupping a dimpled hand to her ear. "You must greet him properly."

"Address him as 'my lord,' " Lady Faversham whispered, nudging the Gypsy with the ivory knob of her cane. "And don't forget your curtsy."

Like a dreamer awakening, Vivien Thorne blinked at the Rosebuds. Then slowly she rose from the ottoman. She was taller than he'd first thought, full-breasted and narrow of waist with long legs that could wrap around a man's hips as he rode her. She needed to lift her gaze only slightly to meet his, and again he felt the sizzle of her sultry attraction. She sank into a graceful obeisance, her hair rippling around her like an ebony veil.

A woman never wore her hair loose except in the bedchamber, and then in front of no man but her husband.

Or her lover.

As she stood up again, she spoke with the trace of an exotic accent. "It's a pleasure to meet you, my lord."

"Forgive me if I don't return the sentiment," he said coldly. "It would be *my* pleasure to see you depart this house at once."

"Michael!" Lady Stokeford exclaimed.

He paid his grandmother no heed. Nor did the Gypsy. The entrancement left her velvet-brown eyes, and she stiffened slightly, arching her chin high. "You know nothing about me."

"I know that you won't defraud my grandmother. Not so long as I'm here."

"Defraud?" she said, tilting her head to the side. "What do you mean?"

"You Gypsies call it grifting. So don't pretend innocence."

"What is the meaning of this appalling behavior, Michael?" Lady Stokeford made a chiding motion of her hand. "Apologize to Vivien at once."

"You've always been too kind for your own good," he bluntly told his grandmother. "You've taken in vagrants and given them work in your household without checking for references—"

"If you're referring to Rumbold," she interrupted, "I gave shelter to a frightened boy who'd run away from a cruel father."

"Last year, you donated a hundred guineas to that sham orphanage in Bristol. You didn't realize you'd been duped until I did a little investigating."

Unfazed, she glowered at him. "I would sooner be generous and discover I'm wrong than be as stingy and mistrustful as you are."

"Good show," said Lady Enid, clapping her hands.

"I quite agree," Lady Faversham added.

His gaze flicked over her avidly watching friends. "Grandmama, perhaps we should speak alone."

Those patrician lips pursed in a familiar stubborn manner. She shook her head, the firelight shimmering on her white hair. "The Rosebuds can hear whatever nonsense you have to say. And do sit down, young man. You're giving me a dreadful crick in the neck."

Rather than fetch a chair, he hunkered down beside her, gently grasping her thin, wrinkled hand, the hand that had once soothed a young boy's brow when he'd suffered from a fever and embraced him when his mother had been preoccupied by her own salvation.

"Miss Thorne is an impostor," he said with great patience. "She's taking advantage of your soft heart."

"Balderdash. She's a dear, sweet girl." Lady Stokeford's mouth turned downward. "Surely you understand why I need a companion—you and your brothers have abandoned me. What's a lonely old woman to do?"

Michael subdued a twinge of remorse. "There are far more appropriate companions to be found. Miss Thorne intends to fleece you of your wealth."

"Pish-posh. I can leave my possessions to whomever I choose," she said with a sniff. "And at present, that lucky person is *not* you, Michael."

"Be that as it may, she's not fit company for the dowager Marchioness of Stokeford. She is a Gypsy."

"I'm well aware of that. I found her in their camp myself, and thank heaven I did." Her silvery brows drew together quizzically. "But who told you about her? If one of the servants dared to be so indiscreet . . ."

"It was Brand. He received a letter from Lady Faversham."

The crones turned to glare at the countess. She gave them a guilty look, then lowered her gaze to her hands, folded around the knob of her cane.

"Olivia, really!" Lady Enid said in a shocked tone. "All these weeks I've been careful to not so much as *breathe* a word, and it's *you* who lets the cat out of the bag! You, who claim to be the pillar of discretion."

"I thought it only right that the marquess should know," Lady Faversham said stiffly. "Lord Stokeford is, after all, the head of their family."

"I would have told him in good time," Grandmama said with a trace of censure. "But what's done is done." She returned her gaze to Michael. "Did the letter also explain that Vivien is a gentlewoman by birth? She was given to the Gypsies as a baby."

So that was her game. Springing to his feet, he stepped toward Vivien Thorne, forcing her to raise her head to view him. The unguarded interest had been replaced by a veiled look he couldn't fathom. She had secrets, all right. Secrets he intended to expose to the world.

"Given to the Gypsies, were you?" he mocked. "This sounds like a scheme to prey upon the wealthy."

"It's the truth, dear." Grandmama leaned forward, lowering her voice to a conspiratorial whisper. "She's the love child of Miss Harriet Althorpe."

Althorpe? He wracked his brain before remembering the tall, strict, and proper woman who had been his governess until he was twelve years old and ready to go away to school. She had been aristocratic to the bone, one of those unfortunate penniless ladies forced by circumstance to labor for a living. Nothing like the lushly sensual Vivien Thorne.

"Miss Althorpe had blue eyes and brown hair," he said. "She had principles, too. I can't imagine her engaging in an illicit affair."

His grandmother snorted. "Of course you can't. It's always difficult for a child to imagine that his elders could be swept away by passion."

"It's not that," he said, cringing at the unlikely image of that prim old tabby caught up in the throes of desire. "I'm referring to her character."

"Character, bah. When a woman fancies herself in love, she sets aside all inhibitions."

"Surely she was far too old to carry a child."

His grandmother smiled with sly tenderness. "The truth

is, she gave birth to dear Vivien when she was one-and-thirty."

Dumfounded, he reassessed his memory of Miss Althorpe. That dried-up prune had been . . . his age?

" 'Tis a long sad tale," Lady Enid piped up.

"But one you should hear," Lady Faversham added.

"Indeed," said Lady Stokeford. The Rosebuds nodded and murmured to each other. Then his grandmother proceeded to tell him a fantastical story about Harriet Althorpe bearing a daughter by a secret lover who had given the baby away to the Gypsies.

Michael didn't believe a word of it. Quite clearly, Vivien Thorne had somehow found out about Harriet Althorpe's connection to his family and devised the tale as a means of establishing herself in this household. He had to give her credit for cleverness. "Melodramatic nonsense," he stated when Lady Stokeford was through. "The letter was clearly a forgery."

"I'll show it to you, then," Grandmama said. "Olivia kept it, but she'll bring it round tomorrow."

Lady Faversham nodded. "You'll see for yourself that it's genuine."

"I'm sure the letter appeared genuine," Michael said testily. "Gypsies are experts at counterfeiting and other crimes."

"She's telling the truth," Vivien Thorne said suddenly. "Don't badger her."

He pivoted toward her. "You've no right to speak. Be silent."

"No. Believe whatever you like of me, my lord. But I will not keep still while you show disrespect for an elder of your family."

She sat upright, her gaze insolent and her manner superior. As if she had the right to be lady of the manor. He snapped, "Then I'll badger you, Miss Thorne. You'd gain a tidy fortune by swindling my grandmother."

Her dark eyebrows winged together, and before she could spin another falsehood, he pressed home his point. "Tell me the truth. How much money have you wheedled out of my grandmother already?"

She sat stubbornly silent. But he saw guilt flash across her fine features.

"How much?" he repeated in a dangerous tone.

"Ten guineas," she spat back. "And a hundred for each month I remain here. It isn't for me, but for my parents who raised me."

Enraged, he seized her arm and yanked her up from the ottoman. She stumbled a little, and for one burning instant as her soft bosom brushed his chest, his body surged with unholy heat. As badly as he wanted to toss her out on her ear, he also wanted to haul her into the nearest bedchamber and make her acknowledge him as her master.

The elderly women sputtered and gasped as he pulled a squirming, protesting Vivien Thorne toward the door of the boudoir. If he hadn't been so furious, he might have taken more notice of the fact that his grandmother made no attempt to stop him.

"Kindly comport yourself like a gentleman, Michael," she called after him. "And do remember, you are in the Dower House. You have no authority to dismiss my companion."

"Oughtn't we go after them? Stokeford is in a terrible fury," Enid whispered as the angry footsteps faded down the corridor. "It's all Olivia's fault," she added, glaring at the countess. "You shouldn't have written to Brandon. You *knew* he would delight in telling Michael."

"Oh, save your scolding." Her lips compressed, Olivia glanced worriedly toward the door. "Right now, all that matters is that the marquess should not be alone with Vivien. They must be chaperoned."

She leaned on her cane as if to stand up, but Lucy put out a hand to forestall her. "No. Leave them be."

"But she'll be ruined if they're found alone together! She'll lose all prospect of making a decent marriage. All our hard work will be for naught."

Feeling the tingle of secret excitement, Lucy smiled at her friends. "Oh, I wouldn't be so certain of that."

At first, she had been aghast to see her grandson stride into the room. Like most men, Michael could be pigheaded, and she had wanted to ensure Vivien's future without suffering his interference. But then she had glimpsed something between them, something interesting . . .

"Did either of you notice the way they looked at each other?" she asked.

Enid nodded. "His lordship glowered rather savagely. As if he wanted to . . . to spank her." Rather than act appalled, she heaved a romantic sigh. "What a rogue he is. With those fierce blue eyes and that coal-black hair, he's far too handsome for his own good. Why, it makes me long to be young again."

"Don't be a ninny," Olivia said rather severely. "It's Vivien who concerns me. While we sit here chatting, her future could be in jeopardy."

"Wait," Lucy said. "Listen to me for a moment. Ever since Grace's death, Michael *has* turned into a rogue. He's been seduced by the vices of London, taking mistresses, wasting his time and money in idle pursuits, horse racing and drinking and wenching." She pursed her lips in a grimace.

"The poor boy did suffer," Enid said, shaking her turbaned head. "He was devastated by the loss of his wife."

"Grace was so young and beautiful," Olivia added, her

pinched features softening. "Their poor daughter was left motherless."

For a moment, the only sound was the crackling of the fire on the hearth. Aware of the familiar burden of sadness, Lucy reflected on the horror of that dreadful night. Then she gave herself a stern shake. She had learned long ago the futility of wallowing in the past.

Reaching out, Lucy touched their hands in turn, old hands now, spotted by age, as withered and wrinkled as hers. The other Rosebuds bore the marks of experience, and they would surely accept the wisdom of her idea. "More than anything in the world, I should like for Michael to be happy again," she said. "I want him to resume his rightful place at Stokeford Abbey. Vivien may just provide him with a reason."

The ladies stared uncomprehendingly at Lucy.

"You mean you wish him to ravish her?" Enid asked, goggle-eyed. "But she can't be his mistress. That wasn't our plan."

"She will be settled as the wife of a gentleman farmer or squire," Olivia concurred, punctuating her statement with a thump of her cane. "We all agreed that such a union would be appropriate for a woman of her . . . unusual credentials."

Lucy shook her head. They were her dearest friends, but good heavens, they could be buffle-headed at times. "You misunderstand me, Rosebuds. I don't want Vivien to be Michael's paramour. I wish him to *marry* her."

Chapter four

A Bribe Rejected

Vivien had never been so alarmed in all her life. Not even when a flash of lightning had startled the horses and the *vardo* had gone careening down a steep hill with *dado* hauling futilely on the reins. Not even when she had stumbled into a bee's nest while playing in the woods and her screams had brought her mother running to her rescue.

Now she had only herself to rely upon. Lady Stokeford clearly did not know how dangerous her grandson could be.

But Vivien knew. The cold fury in the marquess's blue eyes chilled her. His fingers bit into her arm. In her narrow skirts, she had trouble keeping up with his lengthy strides down the shadowed corridor.

What did this *gorgio* lord mean to do with her? After her father's encounter with the trap, she knew too well the cruelties of the English nobility.

"Release me," she demanded again, trying to dislodge his firm grip. "You've no right to touch me."

He snatched a candle from a shell-shaped wall sconce. In its wavering glow, he scowled like a demon sorcerer. "I have every right. So long as you're deceiving my grandmother."

"I've taken only what she's freely given—"

"Save your excuses for someone more gullible."

Shouldering open a door, he hauled her into a darkened chamber and kicked the door shut. The candle cast a small circle of light that failed to penetrate into the murky depths of a bedchamber. A stale, shut-up odor pervaded the air. Spying the large four-poster bed in the shadows, Vivien felt another stab of fear. When he pivoted away to set the taper on a round oak table, she lunged for the brass handle of the door.

In a flash, his muscled body trapped her against the white-painted panel. She struggled fiercely, panting with effort. Had she been turned toward him, she might have clawed his face, but his size and strength thwarted her. With every breath, she inhaled his scent of horses and leather and something feral, something that set off a pulse-beat low in her loins.

"Be still," he commanded. "I've no intention of hurting you."

With diabolical tenderness, he brushed a strand of hair from her face. His warm breath blew on her neck, raising prickles over her skin. She went limp, needing all her reserves to control a bone-deep shiver. Her heart surged faster than it had when she had first beheld him, looming in the doorway like a hero of legend, broad of shoulder and darkly handsome in a coat, white shirt and doeskin breeches, his blue eyes burning into her. She had been seized by a great longing, a deep inner warmth, as if her body had recognized its mate.

A fire in the heart.

Impossible. She could not be destined to love this brutish lord.

His fingertips trailed over the whorls of her ear. "Now that's better," he said silkily. "I like a woman who's warm and willing."

"I'm far from willing," she snapped. "I curse you. May you die in agony and the crows eat your stinking carcass."

He chuckled softly in her ear. "Such venom from lips that were made for kissing."

At the thought of his mouth on hers, a curious quivering ran through her. She felt its effects in her breasts and loins, and all the way down to her toes. "If ever my lips meet yours, it will be to draw blood."

He laughed again, then went on in that stirring tone. "This scheme of yours will never succeed, Miss Thorne. I suggest you work your wiles on me instead. I'd pay handsomely for your services." Then he settled himself more snugly against her bottom so that she felt the unmistakable pressure of his male part.

For one searing moment she could think of nothing but the shameful ache that throbbed low in her belly. She knew what it was from hearing the whispered talk among the women of the *Rom*. It was the need of a woman for her husband.

Then his meaning struck her like a slap. Lord Stokeford desired her in his bed without benefit of marriage. He wanted her to be his whore.

With all her might, she thrust her elbow into his abdomen and stomped on his instep. "Filthy *gorgio*. Get away from me!"

Swearing, he leapt back, bringing her with him. He thrust her deeper into the musty room so that she stumbled on the plush carpet.

She scanned the darkened bedchamber, seeking another escape route, but there was no connecting door, no other way out except the windows at the far end of the room. She would never have enough time to wrest open the casement and scramble out in this close-fitting gown. Let alone climb down the stone wall in these flimsy silk slippers.

She was trapped.

Vivien spun around to face her adversary. Crossing his arms, Lord Stokeford leaned against the door and watched her in that unnerving way of his. He looked like a man of dubious reputation, his dark hair mussed and his eyes gleaming with secrets. Man-woman secrets.

She pressed her fingers into her damp palms. "Do not ever touch me again."

His smile mocked her. "You've a skill for acting the outraged virgin."

"Why do you see everything I say or do as false?"

"Because I know women. And because I know the sort of people you come from."

His superiority made her bristle. The *gorgios* were the wicked ones! But like so many farmers and villagers and landowners, Lord Stokeford despised the Gypsies. When their band passed along a road, men crossed themselves against the evil eye. Women hurried to take down their clothes drying on the line or to shoo their geese into the barnyard. Their foolish *gorgio* superstitions had always been a source of amusement for the *Rom.*

"You know nothing of my people," Vivien said scornfully. "No man of the *Rom* would dare to touch a woman as you just did, a woman who didn't belong to him."

He laughed derisively. "If you're so noble a race, then explain why Gypsies have stolen chickens from my tenants and apples from my orchards."

"We of the *Rom* don't recognize boundaries of property. The fruits of the land belong to all of God's creatures."

"That's an excuse for petty thievery. Even as children, Gypsies pretend to be blind or crippled, begging for handouts in the village."

"Bah. You rich *gorgios* would rather pretend that poor children do not exist." Her senses alert, she paced slowly through the shadowed bedchamber. Somehow, she had to find a way to force him to let her go.

"I despise deception in any form," he said. "And there's the matter of inventing fortunes for naïve old ladies. Great adventure, indeed."

Vivien cast him a cool glance. So what if she let people believe she possessed special powers? Since girlhood, she had learned the art of evaluating a customer at a glance, gathering clues from their manner and appearance about what they hoped to hear. She liked to think that in exchange for a coin or two, she could make people happy with her harmless, sunny predictions.

But admitting so to Lord Stokeford would only swell his conceit.

Hoping to lure him away from the door, she strolled farther into the gloomy chamber. "I didn't read the Rosebuds' palms for money. It was my gift to them."

"In the hopes of being named as Grandmama's heir."

His insulting accusation made it easier for her to subdue the clamor of guilt. "Believe what you will. Her ladyship and I know the truth."

As she'd planned, he prowled after her. "Allow me to make a prediction of my own," he said. "Your plot will not succeed."

"As this plot exists only in *your* mind, my lord, you are certain to be proved correct."

With a lurch of excitement, Vivien spied something on a dainty writing desk in the shadowed corner. She whirled to face him, keeping her hands hidden behind her while she nimbly palmed the treasure.

In four long strides, he crossed the chamber. "What was that you picked up?"

"Why, nothing. You have a very suspicious nature."

"I saw you steal something."

Stopping mere inches from her, he seized her forearm

and pulled it forward. She resisted only a little, her gaze caught by the steely contours of his face, his jaw dark with bristles. What was it about this man that made her heart leap and her body weaken? Then he drew her hand from behind her back, and his look of triumph soured.

In her palm lay a gray-feathered quill pen.

"Truly, my lord, you are too miserly," she said. "Would you begrudge me the loan of this pen?"

"You'll only use it to forge another letter." He snatched the implement from her and tossed it back onto the desk.

She took the chance to step away from him, gliding on a meandering, ever closer path toward the door. "I'll find myself another pen," she said breezily. "After all, in case you do manage to thwart my *plot*, I may just write to the Prince Regent and convince him that he's my father."

Lord Stokeford let out a snort. "If that's your idea of sarcasm, then don't think yourself too clever. You won't make a fool out of me."

"I'm sure you can manage that well enough on your own, m'lord marquess."

His mouth quirked, and in the meager light, she could not tell if he smiled or grimaced. Then he stalked her again, his steps as unhurried as a wolf certain of his prey. "Enough of this nonsense, Miss Thorne. I want you out of this house. Without another tuppence from my grandmother's purse."

"You should show more trust in her choice of companions," Vivien said, stepping neatly around a stuffed chair. "She's a far better judge of character than you are."

"I'll make it worth your while to leave here, then. Three hundred guineas in your pocket right now, and you disappear forever. I won't even send the magistrate after you."

For the barest moment, Vivien was tempted. That was more riches than she'd planned to give to her parents. She could leave this *gorgio* house immediately and return to her people. Yet as she met the marquess's chilly gaze, something curdled inside her. He believed her a thief. But she would take only the *gorgio* money she earned as payment for being a companion to Lady Stokeford.

"Keep your bribe," she snapped. "I've made an honest bargain with your grandmother."

He scowled. "If you don't agree to my terms, I'll have you arrested for fraud. If you're lucky, you won't be sentenced to hang. You'll be transported to a penal colony in Australia, halfway around the world, never to return to England."

His threat gave her pause. Did he truly have the power to see her imprisoned on trumped-up charges? Would she spend the rest of her days malingering in a dank cell or forced to do hard labor in some wild, unknown land across the seas?

Swallowing hard, Vivien tightened her fingers around the object hidden in the folds of her skirt. She mustn't let this puffed-up nobleman frighten her into leaving. "I've done nothing wrong," she stated, edging a few steps closer to the door. It was almost within her reach. "Lady Stokeford will not permit you to have me locked up."

"I'll find the evidence against you, then. Criminals always leave a trail."

"Search if you like. You'll be wasting your time." Insulted for the last time, Vivien made a dash for escape. This time, she managed to wrest open the door before the marquess caught her.

He pushed his body against hers—this time, breast to chest. There was no mistaking the power of the muscles beneath his fine coat, or the heat of his anger. His gaze scoured her, and in spite of herself, she felt the effects of his animal allure. Curse him, he could make her shiver with just a look.

In a harsh tone, he said, "Running out on me, Miss Thorne? You're not leaving this room until we resolve this matter. To my satisfaction."

"No, your lordship, to *mine*."

In one swift move, Vivien drew her hand out of her skirt and thrust the small blade in between them, pressing the tip against his groin.

He reared back, though maintaining his hold on her shoulders. "What the devil—!"

She took fierce delight in the surprise that chased the arrogance from his too handsome features. "It's a knife you *gorgios* use for sharpening pens. You see, you ought to have checked *both* my hands." Vivien tried not to gloat at his look of consternation. "Now, step back slowly. This blade might be small, but one slip and it could geld you."

Lord Stokeford complied with great care, releasing his grip on her and then retreating, his hands upraised, palms open. Those breathtakingly blue eyes studied her with guarded interest, from the knife in her hand to the defiance on her face.

Then to her amazement, he smiled, lowering his hands to his hips. "Touché, Miss Thorne. You've won this round. But it isn't the end of our battle."

It was useless trying to convince him of her innocence. "I've no interest in your games," she said. "I'd advise you to return to London lest you wake up one night to find this knife at your throat."

"If ever you enter my bedchamber, it won't be for purposes of murder." The curve of his mouth deepened, a smile of devastating promise. "Should you decide to pay me that visit, you'll find me in the west wing of the Abbey, second floor, at the end of the main corridor. My bed is more than large enough for two."

"You are *despicable*. I would sooner lie with a . . . a *snake*."

He chuckled, and a certain animal alertness in his manner made her uneasy. "You and I shall be closer than you think, my pretty Gypsy. So be forewarned. Henceforth, I'll be watching your every move."

The next morning, groggy after a night of restless dreams, Vivien slipped into Lady Stokeford's apartments only to find the boudoir empty and the draperies still closed against the sunny day. No maidservants bustled about, bringing out various gowns for her ladyship's inspection or fetching shoes and shawls from a dressing room far larger than any Gypsy caravan.

Vivien frowned. Her ladyship liked for her to visit each day at the hour of nine sharp, and although Vivien still could not fully fathom this *gorgio* need to regiment time, she had learned to decipher the mysterious movements of a clock.

Perhaps today she had misread the device. Or perhaps the gentle old woman had been distressed by the events of the previous night. Had she overheard her grandson's quarrel with Vivien?

Silently cursing the marquess, she tiptoed to the doorway of the dim bedchamber. "My lady?" she whispered.

"Yes, dear, I'm awake." The thready voice came from the huge bed with the elaborate pink silk hangings and carved gilt doves. "Come closer. I've been waiting for you."

Vivien hastened forward to see Lady Stokeford clad in a frilly white nightcap and lacy nightgown and reclining against a mound of feather pillows, the embroidered satin coverlet tucked to her small bosom. In the half-light, her dainty features appeared drawn and pale.

Sitting down on the edge of the bed, Vivien reached for the dowager's hand. It nested in her palm like a little wren. "Oh, my lady. Are you ill?"

" 'Tis the ravages of old age, my dear." Lady Stokeford released a wispy sigh. "But don't let me worry you. I'm a bit weary, that's all."

"Did you sleep poorly? I hope you haven't been fretting."

"Fretting? Oh, you mean about Michael." The dowager's face brightened with interest and she leaned forward. "Tell me, what exactly did that rascal say to you? It was quite a long while before we heard him tramp downstairs and leave the house."

Vivien bit her lip. Against her will, she remembered the heat of his muscled body pressing into her, and the caress of his fingers on her skin. Other men had desired her and, like Janus, they had cast her looks of lust. But no man had ever touched her like *that*. She'd been so shaken by the encounter that she hadn't returned to the Rosebuds; she'd slipped outside for a long walk in the darkness.

Now, she hoped the flush in her cheeks didn't show. "He . . . repeated his suspicions about me. He tried to convince me to leave here, but I refused, of course."

Lady Stokeford pursed her lips. "Well, don't let him trouble you. Men like to bully and bluster. They remind me of little children sometimes."

Vivien smiled, though an anxious thought disturbed her. "Do *you* doubt me, my lady? Because I didn't falsify that letter, I swear it. If I'm lying to you, may my soul be cursed to wander forever in darkness."

The dowager patted Vivien's hand. "Why, my dear girl, you mustn't distress yourself with such thoughts, not even for a moment! You're charming and innocent, and in time, Michael is bound to realize his mistake."

Vivien scowled at the bedside lamp with its painted roses on the glass chimney. The dowager didn't know that she planned to leave here after two months. "I don't care what m'lord marquess thinks of me," she said. "But I do care if he upsets you." It was true. Somehow, she'd come to like this *gorgio* lady. She was kind, at least.

"I know how to handle men," her ladyship said. "Despite his pigheaded behavior last night, Michael is a fine, admirable gentleman. A bit of a rogue now and then, but perhaps that's due to the tragedy . . ."

Surprised, Vivien returned her gaze to the dowager. "Tragedy?"

"The death of his beloved wife three years ago. You see, one night during a wild rainstorm, her coach overturned on a road near London. Leaving their daughter motherless." Lady Stokeford sadly shook her head. "Michael took the loss dreadfully hard. He settled in London for good, taking my sweet little great-granddaughter with him."

The marquess had a child? Vivien couldn't imagine him as a father. Fathers were warm, jolly, comforting creatures. "How old is she?"

"Amy is now four years of age, though I seldom see her. Michael, I fear, has spent his time drinking and gambling and doing whatever else men do to forget their sorrow."

Vivien sat unmoving on the edge of the mattress. She heartily despised the marquess, yet she found herself wondering about him. *Was* he still grieving for his wife? Had misfortune turned him into a harsh, unfeeling tyrant?

That was no excuse for his petty arrogance. She would prove him wrong about her. She would earn every pence of her two hundred guineas by being an excellent companion to his grandmother.

Vivien hopped off the bed. "Such talk will only tire you, my lady, when you need cheering up. The room is stuffy, don't you agree? Fresh air and sunshine always make me feel better."

"A splendid notion, dear." Lady Stokeford languidly waved her hand. "If you wouldn't mind . . ."

Vivien hurried across the sumptuous chamber to throw back the draperies. After a brief tussle with a window that resisted her attempts to open it, she felt a cool breeze eddy inside, blowing away the mustiness and somehow easing her tension.

Her ladyship inhaled a deep breath. "Ah, you're right, that's quite invigorating. And yet . . ."

"What is it, my lady? Does your head ache? I could fix you a willowbark tea."

"No, no," Lady Stokeford said, sinking deeper into the pillows. "I'm merely fatigued. I do believe I shall spend the day right here in bed. It would be quite pleasant, though, if you would read to me."

Eager to fulfill the request, Vivien started for the door. "You'd like the story of *Gulliver's Travels* that Lady Enid lent to me. It's full of excitement and adventure about giants and little folk."

The dowager sighed, fretfully plucking at the coverlet. "Forgive me, but I'm not in a humor for fairy tales. There must be something more interesting in this house."

"I saw a book of sonnets downstairs in the music room. And there's the Bible in the drawing room. I've read many fine stories in there—"

"Pish-posh, poems are too often maudlin and I hear enough sermonizing on Sundays. I had in mind something a trifle more . . . fun." As if lost in thought, Lady Stokeford stared down at her folded hands. "Ah, I know just the thing. There was a book I read as a young lady that I should like to hear again. *Moll Flanders*."

"Where is it? I'll be happy to fetch it."

"No, never mind." With a shake of her head, the dowager closed her paper-thin eyelids. "I couldn't ask you to go to any trouble on my behalf."

"Please, it's no trouble."

The dowager slitted her eyes. "Are you quite certain? I fear you would have a bit of a walk."

Vivien laughed, her spirits soaring at the notion of escaping these confining walls. "I love to walk. In truth, you'd be doing me the favor."

"Well, if you insist, then. You shall have to go across the river to the library at Stokeford Abbey." A slight smile touching the corners of her lips, the dowager added, "I fear you'll have to see my impertinent grandson again."

Chapter five

The Mantrap

Cantering down the slope overlooking his ancestral mansion, Michael spied the Gypsy.

He had slept heavily and awakened early, contrary to his city habits where ofttimes he stayed out till dawn and slumbered past noon. Plagued by restlessness, he had ridden the bay gelding hard at first, the pounding rhythm driving out all thought save an awareness of the woods and pastures and farms that belonged to him by right of birth. After months of riding the symmetrical pathways of Hyde Park, he'd nearly forgotten the pleasure of galloping over the rolling hills and dales of his own land.

Invigorated by the cool morning air, he'd visited a few of his tenant farmers. They'd acted reserved, doffing their caps and lowering their eyes, but he was pleased to see the harvest had been excellent. All in all, the morning had turned out to be far more satisfying than he had anticipated.

Until now.

Reining in his mount, he shaded his eyes against the bright sunlight. Tension gripped his muscles. There was no mistaking that willowy figure or that uninhibited stride.

The breeze tugged at Vivien Thorne's tawdry turquoise gown and ruffled her upswept black hair. She wore no hat, of course, another mark of her unrefined nature. No lady would venture outside without a bonnet.

She paused on the circular drive, her head tilted back in a slow survey of the ivy-covered stone, the tall mullioned windows, the archways that had once been part of an ancient monastery. With ill-bred swiftness, she marched up the steps to the covered porch with its huge pillars, where she glanced furtively in both directions. Without knocking, she pushed open the door and vanished inside the house.

He felt a rush of anger. Why the devil would Vivien Thorne sneak like a thief into his house?

Because she *was* a thief. A virago who would cut off a man's bollocks.

Nudging the gelding with his heels, he rode quickly down the slope and to the front drive, where he leapt off the bay and looped the reins over a post. As he entered the massive foyer, a footman scurried forth from a corridor beside the curving staircase.

"M'lord! Praise heavens you're here. There's a rather unusual person on the premises—"

"Where is she?"

Huntley blinked. "Er . . . it's Lady Stokeford's companion. She wished to view the library, so I took her there. I hope that was permissible."

"She's there alone?"

"Why, yes." The young man's face turned a dull red beneath his formal white wig. "She asked so politely, m'lord, I didn't see as it would do any harm."

Michael cursed under his breath. He couldn't take Huntley to task for being fooled by the Gypsy's pretense of civility. Vivien Thorne had a knack for charming her way into the homes of unsuspecting people.

"Have a groom see to my mount." He tossed his leather gloves toward the servant, who caught them to his crimson-liveried chest.

Boot heels ringing on the sand-colored marble, Michael headed straight for a passageway that led to the rear of the house, where the library overlooked the formal gardens. If he weren't in a fury, he might relish the sight of these familiar walls, the tall Ionic columns and classical statues in niches, the echoing corridors where he and his brothers had played chase, much to the consternation of their grandmother. He might remember Grace gliding toward him on their wedding day, draped like an angel in palest blue, her arms held out to him like a loving wife . . .

Clenching his teeth, he returned his mind to the Gypsy. At this very moment, Vivien Thorne could be looting his collection of rare books or pocketing the household cash from the strongbox in the bottom drawer of his desk. He wondered grimly if she'd crept into his house before today. He must order Mrs. Barnsworth to tally the silver.

But when he stepped through the great arched doorway of the library, the Gypsy wasn't cramming coins into her pocket or secreting currency down her bodice. She stood in the center of the long chamber with its many shelves of books, turning in a slow pirouette while gazing up at the balcony that contained a second floor of volumes. Her feet were bare, and she held her slippers in one hand, clasped to her bosom. Her lips were parted in rapt wonder. She looked like someone who had just been transported to heaven.

Not at all like the wildcat who had thrust a knife to his groin. That unpleasant memory still scorched his pride.

Stalking toward her, he said, "Miss Thorne!"

She spun around, and a smile brightened her features so that she glowed with an inner joy.

She ran a few steps in his direction, the gold bangles

on her wrist chiming musically, then stopped to gaze around the library again as if she couldn't bear to look away for more than a moment. "M'lord marquess! I never dreamed there were so many books in the world. Are they all yours?"

"I own every rock and brick for miles around," he said coldly. "And you are not welcome here."

She lowered her lashes slightly, veiling the light in her eyes. Dipping a flamboyant curtsy, she mocked, "Pardon me for intruding on your kingdom, sire. Your grandmother asked me to come here."

"Why? If you mean to tell my fortune, I'm not interested."

"I know what lies in store for you, m'lord." After dropping her slippers to the floor, she dramatically pointed one finger at him. "Your hair and teeth will fall out, your muscles will wither, and a pox will shrivel your manly parts. Women and children will flee screaming at the sight of you."

Throwing back his head, Michael laughed. "If that's a curse, you'll find I don't frighten easily. Now, what message does Lady Stokeford send to me?"

"She didn't sleep well, and she's feeling poorly. Truth be told, she was greatly disturbed by your quarrel with her last night."

Was she? He hadn't meant to distress his grandmother, only to protect her from being exploited. "*You* instigated that quarrel," he said. "If you cared a brass farthing for her, you'd return to the Gypsies where you belong."

A subtle change altered Vivien Thorne's fierce expression. Her velvety brown eyes went blank, her lips compressing into a downward curve. "*You* should return to the devil, where *you* belong."

"For someone so quick-witted, you seem unable to

grasp one fact: I will not tolerate your presence in the Dower House."

"Nor will *I* tolerate your badgering her ladyship. She deserves your respect, not your bullying."

"Then I'll be sure to reserve my bullying for you," he said smoothly. "Run along now and tell Lady Stokeford I'll call on her after luncheon."

As he reached for her arm, intending to steer her out the door, Vivien Thorne nimbly eluded his grasp. Stepping behind a stuffed leather chair, she bumped into a pedestal. She turned, her gaze riveted to the small globe that perched on the carved wooden stand.

"Develesa," she whispered reverently, holding out her hand in awe. "What is this wonderful thing?"

"Surely you've seen a model of the Earth before." Yet he could believe in her naïveté this once, and he found himself adding gruffly, "Touch it if you like. It spins."

Her bracelets tinkling, she gave the sphere a tentative push. When it twirled, she laughed in delight, a sparkle lighting her dark eyes. Something stirred inside him, a warmth that plumbed deeper than sexual desire.

Thrusting out his hand, he stopped the globe. "How foolish of you to try to distract me."

"How tiresome of *you* always to mistrust my actions," she said with a toss of her head. "Now, if you can trouble yourself, where is England?"

Those lively eyes challenged him, and reluctantly he pointed out the British Isles to her. "There."

She touched the area with a solemn brush of her fingertips, and then tracked a path halfway around the sphere. Her brows drew together in a frown. "This is . . . the Bering Sea . . . and China. Not . . ."

Catching her meaning, Michael chuckled darkly. He stepped behind her, placed his hand over hers, and guided her finger down to the Southern Hemisphere. "Here's your future home. The penal colony of Australia."

He should have moved away then, but he didn't. She stood with her back to him, her attention focused on the globe. He wanted to touch the fine downy hairs on the nape of her neck. To inhale her exotic scent. How he would relish kissing the defiance out of her, tasting his fill of her burnished skin, her lush mouth. Her hand felt slim and strong beneath his, and he imagined those fingers caressing him, gliding downward . . .

She ducked beneath his arm and whirled around to face him. "You will not send me there," she stated as imperiously as a queen. "I will not go."

It took him an instant to pick up the thread of conversation. "Then leave here while you can. Because the moment you take tuppence more from my grandmother than she's already given you, I'll have you clapped in irons and shipped out on the next transport."

The Gypsy lifted her chin. "If any coin is stolen, it will be done by you, m'lord marquess. And I will not stand by while you falsely accuse me of the crime."

He almost choked on a glut of outrage. "You dare to suggest . . . I would deliberately incriminate you?"

"I do indeed dare. I warn you, Lady Stokeford would be hurt to discover your true nature."

"*My* true nature."

"Yes." Her lips pursed, Vivien regarded him as if he were lower than a maggot. "She speaks far too highly of you. I couldn't bear for you to destroy her illusion."

There was something about the way her forehead was furrowed, her dark eyebrows winging together, that brought a startling reminder of the stern Miss Althorpe.

No, he thought, hardening his jaw. *That* was the illusion. Vivien Thorne was no more well-born than a trollop selling herself on a street corner.

"Enough of this nonsense," he said testily. "Out with you now."

He reached for her arm, and again, she deftly sidestepped him. "I must fetch a book. Lady Stokeford asked me to read to her from one called *Moll Flanders*." Her eyes dark and shining, Vivien glanced around the library. "You must show me where to find it."

"Are you saying *you* can read?"

"Of course. We Gypsies are cleverer than you think, m'lord."

Michael ground his back teeth. He should send the Gypsy away and deliver the book himself, but perhaps this time Grandmama truly *was* ill. She had appeared frail the previous evening, frailer than he could remember. It would be churlish to refuse this simple request.

"Works of fiction are shelved near the windows." He snapped his fingers at Vivien. "Follow me."

She snapped her fingers right back at him. "I am not a dog to be brought to heel, m'lord."

"I beg your pardon." He made an elaborate bow. "I forgot you were pretending to be a lady."

She coolly looked him up and down. "I've been told a true gentleman always shows respect toward women." With a twitch of her turquoise skirts, she marched past him, heading toward the far end of the library, where the tall windows looked out on the concentric green pathways of the garden.

Forced to trail in her wake, Michael grimaced. Damned cheeky vagrant. He'd like to toss her out of here on her shapely bottom.

No. He'd like to press her down onto one of the long oak tables, push those ladylike skirts up to her waist, and caress her until she went wild for him, panting and begging. Only then would he give vent to his lust, plunging into the velvet clasp of her body and knowing the fierce pleasure of—

"Well? Shall we search on this side of the windows or that side?" Poised near the farthest bookcase, her hands on her hips, Vivien Thorne stared at him in that brazenly forward manner of hers. "Of course, if you're too busy to help your grandmother, I'll be happy to seek out the book myself."

"And leave you alone in my house? I think not." Disciplining his base impulses, he pointed to a column of shelves near her. "You look there. I'll take the section over here."

She tightened her lips as if to toss another sour comment at him, then tilted her head to the side to scan the titles. A lock of curling black hair tumbled down her neck, but she didn't appear to notice. Within moments, that look of total absorption returned to her face, and she touched each volume with her fingertips as if to assure herself the books were real. Her lips moved slightly, and he could just hear the hushed tone of her voice as she whispered the name of each book.

He watched, fascinated in spite of himself. He couldn't imagine any lady of the *ton* being enthralled by his library, for God's sake. Katherine would cast a languid glance around, offering a jaded comment or two, her fair features reflecting a worldly disdain.

Not that Katherine had ever been to his estate. He preferred to conduct his affairs elsewhere. Upon taking an abrupt leave of her the night of the mummy unwrapping, he'd promised to join her at her house in Kent as soon as possible. He intended to ask her to marry him.

Sourly, he scanned the Gypsy from the top of her unruly black hair down to the tips of her bare feet, wondering how her bold dark beauty could arouse him when he had always preferred cool, elegant blondes like Katherine, sophisticated ladies who knew how to please a man. Vivien Thorne was a liar and a fraud, a female so mercenary she would befriend and manipulate an old woman in order to steal a fortune. One hundred guineas a month, indeed. A proper companion didn't earn that much in a year.

Yet he couldn't reconcile the greedy swindler with the earnest girl standing a few feet away, engrossed in his books.

He jerked his gaze to the shelf before him. He resented being made to realize that he took this library for granted. It had been his refuge while growing up, and he could remember times when he'd curled up in a chair on a rainy afternoon or hid up on the balcony to evade his mother's pious preaching or his father's drunken melancholy. Here, he had learned about barbarian invasions into ancient Rome and studied volcanoes and other geological formations.

Here too as an adolescent, he'd discovered a volume of carnal drawings concealed high on a shelf behind some other tomes. He'd secreted the forbidden book beneath his shirt and thence proceeded up to the attic, to a cobwebby old priest hole that his younger brothers hadn't yet discovered. He'd spent several glorious hours examining by candlelight a series of naked men and women engaged in the most astonishing positions. It had been a boy's erotic heaven—until Grandmama had caught him.

His lips quirked. The dowager always seemed to know when he was hiding something. That was one of the reasons he'd stayed in London after Grace's funeral, not returning until now. It would serve no purpose for Grandmama to find out the truth about what had really happened on the stormy night of his wife's death. The past was best left buried.

He shifted his attention back to Vivien Thorne. She was bending over to examine the books on the bottom shelf. As he watched, she drew out a book and leafed through the pages with almost worshipful attention. If she were to pivot toward him just a bit, he'd be able to see down her bodice. It was a juvenile impulse, but he edged a little closer.

She stood up before he could get more than a glimpse of those tempting breasts. To his disappointment, she clasped the opened book to her bosom. "I suppose," she said, lifting her gaze to him, "it would be too much to ask if *I* might borrow a book, too."

"If it will occupy your time so that you stay away from my grandmother, then go ahead."

She gave him a keen stare. "Five books would keep me even busier."

"Two," he countered irritably.

"Four."

"Three, and that's my limit."

"Why, thank you, m'lord marquess. Perhaps you're a gentleman after all." Flashing him a saucy smile, she whirled back to the bookshelves and proceeded to make her selections.

Bloody hell. The seductive baggage had manipulated him. Likely, he would never see those books again. Well, knowledge was power. It was time he found out all he could about her, the better to prove her a fraud.

He snatched a leather-bound volume off the shelf. "Here's the novel my grandmother wants," he said, handing it to her and watching as she tucked it with the other books she held so carefully to her bosom. "How is it that you can read? Gypsies are uneducated."

"In formal schooling, yes." She cast him a sly glance. "However, there's always a need for someone with the skill to forge letters and other documents."

Blast her wit. "Then did you attend school for a time?"

"No. School is for dullards who can't figure things out on their own."

"Someone must have tutored you."

"My father—my Gypsy father—can read a little, enough to get along with the *gorgios*." She glanced away, but not before Michael noticed a flash of nostalgia in her eyes. "To keep me amused as a child, he would point out letters on signs along the road. It was a game to see if I could make out the words. He showed me newspapers and handbills, too. Then later, when I found a book lying by a rubbish heap, I figured out the rest on my own."

Her childhood had been radically different from his privileged upbringing with the very strict Miss Althorpe, who had taught him and his brothers everything from Latin and Greek to algebra and geometry. "You're exaggerating," he said flatly. "No one can simply open a book and commence reading with so little instruction."

"Perhaps not *you*. Only those who possess a superior mind."

Despite his resentment, Michael found himself chuckling at the outrageousness of her insult. "What about ciphering? You must have a talent for counting money."

"I've never owned more than a few coins."

"You already weaseled ten guineas out of my grandmother."

She whirled to face him. "The money is for my father," she said with sudden fire. "Last year, his leg was caught in a mantrap on the estate of a duke. Now he's crippled and unable to work. He's fortunate he didn't die at the hands of you *gorgios*."

Struck by her outburst, Michael grimaced inwardly. A mantrap was a ghastly device with sharp iron teeth, easily hidden in a pile of leaves, and used by callous landowners to guard against poachers—often Gypsies. "I'm sorry. I abhor such cruelties. But your father's injury doesn't give you the right to rob my grandmother."

"I'm not stealing. Lady Stokeford offered me money to live with her. I agreed only to keep my family from starving."

"At a hundred guineas a month, they'll eat strawberries in winter and ice cream in summer. And live in a fancy house, too."

"My father prefers to live in a caravan. But even if he did own a great mausoleum like this one, he'd never set up fences and gates and mantraps. The land should belong to everyone."

"Don't pretend you're so virtuous. You want jewels. Fine clothing. More gold bracelets."

"Bah! Possessions don't bring happiness to a person." She looked him up and down. "They haven't made *you* happy."

Her words slapped him with undue force. How dare she presume to judge him? He was bloody damned pleased with his life. Or he would be, if only he could rid himself of *her*.

Seething, he took a step toward her. "So what makes you happy, Vivien Thorne? A sackful of gems to show off to your Gypsy cronies?"

She held her ground. "You wouldn't understand."

"Tell me anyway," he said, knowing she would never admit the truth.

"All right, then." Her eyes bright, she glanced away. "What I treasure is . . . the trill of a lark at dawn. The sound of a child's laughter. The warmth of a campfire on a cold night." Holding the leather-bound volumes like a shield, she looked at him, defiantly tilting her chin. "And yes, books. But I needn't *own* them to appreciate them."

"Come now, Miss Thorne. Everyone covets something.

If nothing else, you Gypsies need coin to gamble among yourselves."

"Don't judge me by your wretched *gorgio* standards. I'm not like *you*."

Goaded, he closed the distance between them, stopping so close he could see each curling black lash that rimmed her expressive eyes. "Perhaps you've a greedy lover, then. A man who set you up to rob a kindly old lady."

"No!"

She did a fine imitation of outrage, and his pulse surged with the anticipation of exposing her lies. If ever a woman had needed taming, Vivien Thorne was the one.

Reaching out, he trailed his fingertips over the smooth, warm skin of her throat. In a husky murmur, he said, "The truth now, Vivien. How many men have you bedded? Does one of them make you steal for him?"

If he hadn't been standing so close to her, if he hadn't been lowering his mouth to those delectable lips, he might have seen the blow coming. Her fist flashed up and connected solidly with the underside of his jaw.

The impact sent him stumbling backward into a row of bookshelves. He caught the balcony ladder to steady himself. Flummoxed, he glowered at her. She'd struck him. Vivien Thorne had delivered an underhook as tooth-jarring as any rendered by a skilled pugilist in a bout of fisticuffs.

He rubbed his throbbing jaw. "What the devil was that for?"

Flexing her fingers, she glared at him. "That was your answer, you stinking maggot. You may be master here, but you aren't *my* master."

With that, she turned and marched out of the library with an armful of his books.

Chapter six

The Forged Letter

"There you are, Vivien." Like a hawk homing in on its prey, Lady Faversham made her way across the cavernous kitchen. Her gray gown swished around her spare form, and her cane thumped with each step. "What is this nonsense about having no time for your lessons?"

Vivien sat at the long trestle table, her quill poised over a sheet of Lady Stokeford's beautiful cream stationery. The portly French chef stopped in the middle of a story he was relating, his wooden spoon frozen in the air and his little black moustache quivering with indignation.

The scullery maid, who had been clinging dreamy-eyed to her broom, resumed her industrious sweeping of the slate floor. The lower cook, who had been leaning his elbows on the table, hastily began rolling out a lump of pastry dough.

Vivien hid her annoyance at the interruption. "Lady Stokeford is ill today. That means my lessons have been canceled."

The truth was, Vivien couldn't bear another tedious afternoon of instructions in the finer points of etiquette. Not after her unsettling encounter with Lord Stokeford that morning. He'd accused her again of conspiring to trick his grandmother. He'd even dared to suggest that Vivien had had many lovers. He was too blindly arrogant to realize why she'd lashed out at him like an ill-tempered witch. She was still amazed at how much her hand ached from that impulsive blow.

You should return to the Gypsies where you belong.

He made her so angry she could spit. He also made her weak at the knees, fluttery in her heart, and she *loathed* him for that.

Lady Faversham clapped her hands. "Come," she said. "Lucy may be a trifle under the weather, but two Rosebuds are more than sufficient."

"Later," Vivien demurred. "Monsieur Gaston was just telling me a wonderful tale about a scullery maid who's transformed by magic into a princess and goes off to a ball in a pumpkin coach—"

"This is no time for childish stories," the countess broke in, her upper lip curling. "A gentlewoman does not hobnob with the staff. Nor distract them from their duties."

"Bah," Monsieur Gaston grumbled, stirring a pot on the big black range. "Never would I allow ze soup to burn. It is a pleasure to tell ze tales of *ma mère* to Mam'selle Thorne."

Lady Faversham raised an eyebrow. "Monsieur, we will take tea in the drawing room. Vivien, it is poor manners to keep Enid waiting. You'll have me thinking you don't appreciate Lady Stokeford's kindness in taking you in."

Though Vivien bristled, she knew she had to humor the Rosebuds or risk losing her monthly payments. Rising from the chair, she curtsied to the chef in his immaculate white apron. "I'll return soon to hear the ending."

"We shall see what happens to *la petite* cinder girl at

the stroke of midnight." Monsieur Gaston flashed her a conspiratorial wink. "She is much like you, no?"

Vivien smiled tactfully, turning away to carry her papers, pen, and inkpot to a cupboard for safekeeping. Little did the cook realize, she had no wish to meet a haughty prince who would have scorned his dance partner if he'd known the servile life from whence she'd come. No woman should have to hide her true self in order to win a man's love.

As they walked into the corridor, Lady Faversham gave Vivien a critical scrutiny. "Shoulders back, my girl. Chin up. A lady walks with dignity. Ah, that's better. Your fingers are smudged with ink, but I don't suppose that can be helped."

Vivien rubbed her thumb against her forefinger, succeeding only in smearing the black stain. Of all the Rosebuds, this countess irked her the most. Trying not to wince at her sore knuckles, she curled her fingers into a loose fist. "Lady Enid won't mind. She would have encouraged me to finish recording Monsieur's story."

"Enid is a featherbrain. She doesn't always know what's best for you."

"Nor do you," Vivien said. They were the same height, and she looked straight into the countess's chilly gray eyes. "I'm a grown woman, not a puppet on strings."

Lady Faversham frowned, and a ray of sunlight from the foyer showed the fine lines of age on her proud face. Surprisingly, her angular features softened a little. Slowing her steps, she gave Vivien a considering look. "I'm aware of your independent nature, my dear," she said in a moderated tone. "Please understand that I wish only to guide you through the treacherous waters of society. To help you find a place for yourself in this world."

Every now and then, the countess unbent enough to show a glimpse of caring, and it made Vivien long for a mother's embrace. How absurd. Lady Faversham was nothing like the gentle Reyna Thorne with her warm arms and soothing manner. Even in her better moments, this *gorgio* lady had an aloof, touch-me-not air.

The older woman motioned for her to go into the drawing room. To the footman stationed at the door, she said, "When the marquess comes downstairs, ask him to join us later for dinner."

"Yes, my lady." Making a formal bow, Rumbold took up a stance by the grand staircase.

Vivien halted just inside the doorway. Her heart flipped in her breast. "Lord Stokeford? He's *here*?"

Lady Faversham smiled, a mere twist of her thin lips. "How remiss of me not to mention him. He's upstairs, visiting with Lucy."

Vivien hadn't put much faith in his promise to call on his grandmother. A *gorgio* rogue like him couldn't be bothered with a sick old lady. Better he should return to his wastrel friends in London, far away from here. "I must go to Lady Stokeford, then. He cannot be allowed to upset her."

"Don't be absurd," Lady Faversham said, her cold, bony fingers propelling Vivien into the formal gilt and green drawing room. "Lucy can handle the boy."

Boy? He was a man, Vivien thought spitefully, all arrogance and aggression. She couldn't forget how he'd cornered her by the bookcase, how her pulse had sped so fast she'd felt dizzy . . .

Perched on a sofa, Lady Enid Quinton looked up from her London news sheet, her brown eyes huge behind a gold-rimmed lorgnette. On her ginger hair, she wore a rich purple turban that matched her voluminous gown. "Olivia, do listen to this news! Lord M. has been wed at Gretna Green to a Miss T. B. Why, it must be Montcrieff and that coal merchant's daughter, Theodora Blatt." She tut-

tutted, shaking her head. "I'd pity him, having to marry that horse-faced ninny. Yet 'tis *her* I pity, for that gamester will soon run through all her papa's gold."

"Never mind your gossip," Lady Faversham said impatiently. "Here's Vivien at last. I was assuring her that Lucy will keep Michael well in hand."

As they walked closer to the ring of chairs by the hearth, Vivien glanced worriedly at the doorway. She couldn't help being concerned about the dowager. "*I* was saying I should go upstairs and see what he's about."

"Ah, Michael." As Lady Enid lowered the lorgnette, a merry smile spread over her round face. "A handsome one he is, with those wicked blue eyes and that dissolute smile. Were I younger, I'd be dashing up there, too, to have another look at him."

"That isn't why I wish to go upstairs," Vivien choked out, appalled at the older woman's error. "I need to protect her ladyship from his bullying."

The Rosebuds exchanged a glance that held both amusement and something else, something secretive.

"More likely, Lucy will bully *him,*" Lady Enid said. "So you see, there's no need for you to play Joan of Arc."

"You'll sit right here with us." Lady Faversham guided Vivien to a gold-striped chaise and gracefully sank down beside her. "There, now. You mustn't misjudge Michael. You and he started off badly, that's all."

"It's more than that," Vivien said, her muscles rigid with the hope that he would strut in here at any moment. She could endure his presence if it kept him from berating Lady Stokeford. "He believes me far beneath his exalted self. He's called me . . ."

"Called you what?" Lady Faversham said in an outraged voice that encouraged Vivien.

"A thief, a liar, and . . . and an unchaste woman."

"Unchaste?" Lady Enid leaned forward in her chair,

her generous bosom shelved on her knees. "Did you give him cause to think so? Did you allow him to kiss you?"

"Enid!" Lady Faversham scolded. "Vivien knows better than to permit such an impropriety." Yet her gray eyebrows clashed in a worried frown.

"All girls of the *Rom* guard their chastity," Vivien said fiercely. "Should Lord Stokeford dare to touch me, the stallion will find himself a gelding."

Lady Enid choked out a cough, though her eyes twinkled.

Lady Faversham gave Vivien a curt nod. "It's admirable that you prize your innocence. However, I hardly think it necessary to be quite so . . . picturesque in your description. Michael is, after all, a gentleman."

"He's a beast," Vivien countered, not caring if she offended them. "Even a horse with the finest bloodline can have a devil's nature."

"Quite so," the countess said. "Yet you'll encounter many like him in society. People who will judge you by your past and find you wanting. It's best you learn how to handle them."

"Perhaps you could try winning him over gently," Lady Enid suggested. "Use your allure, my girl. That's what men like."

Gripping the arm of the chaise, Vivien shook her head emphatically. "I could never lure *him*. Nor would I ever *want* to do so."

"Don't be too hasty now," Lady Faversham said, a gleam thawing her frigid eyes. "Enid has put an excellent notion before us. If ever you are to win the acceptance of society, Vivien, you must proceed to the next step in your education. You must learn the wiles of a woman. Who better to practice your charms on than Michael?"

The suggestion jolted Vivien. *The wiles of a woman?*

Surely they were jesting. They couldn't expect her to entice that swaggering lord.

Horrified, she glanced from Lady Faversham's thin smile to Lady Enid's earnest nod. "But I could never . . . I wouldn't know how . . ."

"Bat your eyes at him," Enid said, fluttering her faded ginger lashes. "Men are flattered by a lady's flirting."

"It would be a wasted effort," Vivien protested, though a forbidden thrill tingled through her. "His lordship despises me as much as I despise him."

"Quite the contrary," Lady Faversham said sagely. "His attraction to you was obvious last night."

"He's smitten for certain," Lady Enid said, waving the folded newspaper like a fan. "Oh, what smoldering looks he cast at you! Why, the sight nearly sent me into a swoon."

"Those were looks of disgust," Vivien said, clenching her hands in her lap. "When we were alone, he made his ill opinion of me quite plain."

The two older women exchanged an intent glance.

Lady Faversham patted Vivien on the knee. "My dear, we're not suggesting that you be *serious* in your attentions to him. This is merely an opportunity for you to rehearse your social skills."

"We Rosebuds learned long ago that men can be maneuvered," Lady Enid said with a wink. "You must smile mysteriously, make him wonder at your thoughts. 'Twill be excellent practice for you to romance the rogue."

Vivien felt backed into a corner. Was this what she must do to humor the Rosebuds? To seek out the company of that arrogant *gorgio* lord? "It won't work," she argued. "He'll see right through me."

"Have faith in yourself," the countess said with a heartening smile. "You're clever and spirited. Surely you can get the best of a mere man."

As Rumbold wheeled in the tea table and Lady Faversham rose to pour, Vivien gripped the soft folds of her skirt. Something in her responded to the challenge set before her. Why was she doubting herself? Janus had been easily taken in by her compliments and smiles. Though the marquess was a more hostile and dangerous man, surely he could be fooled, too. She let herself imagine him enraptured by her wit and beauty. How satisfying it would be to see his fine-and-fancy lordship fawning at her feet, begging for her attention. How delightful to watch him behave like a babbling simpleton.

Yes.

Absorbed by the fantasy, Vivien sat up straight. Like the cinder girl, she could transform herself into a tempting woman. Instead of quarreling with the wretch, she could play him for a fool. She could use all of her newly acquired *gorgio* charm to entice the rogue. She could make Michael Kenyon, the Marquess of Stokeford, fall madly in love with her.

And then, when she left here, she would laugh in his face.

"Open the window a bit more, will you, darling?" Lady Stokeford said. "There, that's better."

Michael turned from the tall window to see his grandmother settling more comfortably against the pillows in her four-poster bed. Her white hair was styled in a sleek knot. The afternoon sunlight bathed the fine seams of age on her face. A hint of natural color touched her high cheekbones, and her blue eyes were bright and watchful. He'd always regarded her as omnipotent, immortal, a permanent fixture in his life. Now, it shook him to consider the fact of her mortality. She wouldn't be around forever.

But was she truly ill . . . or was this merely another bid for attention?

Walking toward her, he said, "I'll send for a physician from London. You should have a thorough examination."

"Pish-posh," the dowager said with a hint of her customary spark. "There's nothing a doctor can do to cure the effects of old age."

"He might prescribe a tonic or remedy to ease your symptoms." Resting his hand on the carved bedpost, he watched her closely. "By the way, what *are* your symptoms? Have you been wheezing again?"

"I'm weary and my bones ache, that's all. Not that I expect any sympathy from *you.*" She stared keenly at him. "If you cared a whit for my welfare, you wouldn't have stayed away for three long years. Or kept my only great-grandchild from me."

Michael tensed. He had shunned Stokeford Abbey for reasons she couldn't know—reasons he intended to guard forever. "I haven't kept Amy from you. You're welcome to visit us in London whenever you like."

"Bah! You know how the air in town affects my lungs. The last time I came to visit, I spent a fortnight in bed and scarcely saw the dear girl."

He tightened his fingers on the wooden post. "I prefer the city to the country. I've explained that to you many times in my letters."

"There was a time when you took pride in this estate. A time when you wouldn't have run from your responsibilities."

"My steward reports to me in London every quarter," he said stiffly. "That's more than sufficient."

"It isn't sufficient reason to keep my great-granddaughter from here. This is her home, too. Her heritage."

He gritted his teeth so hard the ache in his jaw worsened. He had kept Amy safe from scandal, and that was more important than any other consideration. "Amy stays with me. And I stay in London."

The dowager shook her head, pain in her eyes. "Think, Michael. Think of what you're denying me . . . and her. She needs a woman in her life, a mother. It isn't right to keep a four-year-old girl in a bachelor household."

"Amy is firmly attached to her governess, Miss Mortimer. And to me." He paused, wondering if he should mention Katherine, then decided against it. His grandmother would find out his marriage plans in due course.

"Why did you not bring Amy with you, then?" she asked.

"She's starting her schoolwork, and I won't have her uprooted."

"She can learn her letters here as well as there. I'd be happy to tutor her myself." Tears shimmering in her blue eyes, Lady Stokeford held out her hands. "Please, Michael. Don't deny me the dear girl. I miss her sorely."

Her tears struck him as hard as that blow to his jaw. Her letters, alternately pleading and imperious, he'd been able to answer with cool detachment. But it was another thing entirely to come face-to-face with his grandmother's unhappiness.

Perhaps he was being overly cautious. Perhaps he could bring Amy here for a brief visit. If he took care, no one would discover the secret that had shadowed his life for three long years.

Moving to the bedside, he kissed the back of his grandmother's hand. It felt small and dainty, as if her flesh and bone had shriveled. "It shall be as you wish, then. We'll come for the Christmas holidays."

"Send for her *now,* Michael. There's no need to wait."

He firmly shook his head. "I won't have my daughter near that Gypsy. However, if you were to send away Vivien Thorne, I might reconsider."

The distraction worked, but not in the way he intended. Drawing her hand back, his grandmother made a huff of impatience. "Must you persist in your dislike of Vivien? You don't even know the girl."

He placed his fists on his hips. "I know her kind. She's adept at lying. She's abusing your trust."

"Nonsense. Vivien has behaved like a daughter to me. And I must say, she's far more attentive than *you* are."

"Of course she's attentive," he said, anger deepening his voice. "She wants you to change your will in her favor."

But Lady Stokeford wasn't listening. Frowning, she leaned forward and subjected him to another close scrutiny. "For goodness' sake, Michael, is that a bruise on your jaw?"

Clamping together his teeth, he rubbed his still tender face. Much as it would prove his case about the Gypsy's low breeding, he couldn't admit he'd been drubbed by that female. "This? It's nothing."

"You've been fighting. I thought you'd outgrown such childish actions."

"I practice often in the pugilist's ring in London," he said glibly. "All the gentlemen do."

"Men punching one another." She made a snort of disapproval. "I only hope people realize *I* didn't raise you to be a bloodthirsty heathen."

"It's merely a form of activity, Grandmama. It isn't important." Irked, he turned the conversation back on course. "What *is* important is your well-being. Not only your health but your choice of companions. I shouldn't have to tell you that a Gypsy woman isn't suitable company for a marchioness."

An unexpected smile bloomed on the dowager's face. "My, you sound stodgy, Michael. Quite as stodgy as your grandpapa, God rest his well-meaning soul."

Stodgy! To hide his chagrin, he turned to pace the fine Aubusson carpet. "There's nothing stodgy about my desire to protect you. Vivien Thorne inveigled her way into your good graces with this fantastical tale of being aristocratic."

"On the contrary, *I* sought *her* out. She knew nothing of her heritage."

"She knows exactly what her heritage is *not*," he muttered, prowling to the far end of the bedchamber.

On a table beside a chaise lay the book, *Moll Flanders*. Michael picked it up and by impulse, brought it to his nose. Along with the stale scent of paper and leather binding, he caught a whiff of her musky perfume. Lust seared his loins as he remembered Vivien holding the book to her bosom.

"Have a look at Harriet's letter if you don't believe me," Lady Stokeford said. "Olivia brought it this morning and left it on my desk."

"Why the devil didn't you say so sooner?" Dropping the book, Michael wheeled around and strode to the dainty writing desk. He snatched up the letter, unfolded it, and found himself staring down at . . .

Harriet Althorpe's handwriting.

He knew that stiff, precise penmanship. He'd read enough of her notes on his schoolpapers, meticulous corrections on his essays, his Latin and Greek assignments, his mathematics exercises. Though at the time he'd resented her high standards, he supposed she'd made a better scholar of him.

Swiftly he scanned the missive. *Many years ago, while I lay ill with fever, my cruel lover took my darling babe and gave her away to the Gypsies . . . I implore you, my lady, find the Gypsy named Pulika Thorne, bring dear Vivien home, and give her the life of a gentlewoman . . .*

"Melodramatic nonsense," he muttered. He took the

letter over to the window and examined it more closely in the sunshine. To his gratification, he spied a few inconsistencies. "This isn't her writing. This is a forgery."

"Balderdash," his grandmother scoffed. "You can't know that."

"Miss Althorpe often wrote on my schoolwork. She used proper form with two exceptions. Her *r*'s and *s*'s had a certain little curl that isn't here."

Lady Stokeford harrumphed. "Perhaps she changed her penmanship over the years. Or perhaps your memory isn't up to snuff."

"Or perhaps Vivien Thorne is a clever forger," he said flatly, tossing the letter back onto the desk. "Your proof is right there."

His grandmother settled back against the pillows. "You may bluster all you like, darling. I shan't forsake dear Harriet's daughter."

The letter had only firmed his conviction of the Gypsy's guilt. "I'm not blustering. Vivien Thorne is milking you out of a hundred guineas a month, with an eye for more. I won't allow it."

"Alas, you've no choice in the matter." Smoothing the coverlet, she slid a calculating glance at him. "By the by, you should be the first to hear my news. I've decided to give a weeklong house party a fortnight from now."

Taken aback, he frowned. "But you're ill."

"All the more reason to invite my friends and neighbors for a nice, long visit. That way, I'll have a chance to see them all before I die."

His chest tightened even as he eyed her suspiciously. She was merely trying to manipulate him. Wasn't she? "You aren't about to die."

"When one reaches my advanced age, one never knows when the end might come." On that nebulous statement, she aimed an imperious stare at him. "You will hire additional help from the village, air all the bedchambers at Stokeford Abbey, and have the ballroom dusted and polished."

He strode to the bedside. "I most certainly will not. You aren't strong enough to plan a party, let alone to entertain a crowd for a week."

"Nonsense, the very thought of it invigorates me. I'll be up and about before you know it. The Rosebuds will help me with the arrangements."

He grimaced. "This was their idea, wasn't it?"

"They're in agreement with me, of course." She cast another challenging glance up at him. "You see, we've decided it will be the perfect opportunity to introduce Vivien to a select group of the *ton*."

For a moment, his throat choked with rage. He had underestimated Vivien Thorne. She'd spun her web of deceit far more completely than he'd imagined. "Have you gone mad?" he burst out. "She's a pariah. People will scorn her. They'll scorn *you*."

"They shan't dare," his grandmother countered in a steely tone that had once made him quail in his youth. "Vivien cannot help the circumstances of her past. I shall see to it that no one treats her ill."

Reaching down, he seized her hand and strove for equanimity. "Think, Grandmama. The *ton* will never accept her. Even if they were to swallow her ridiculous story, they'd condemn her as a bastard."

"She's charming enough to overcome any obstacle. I must say, it's uncharitable of you to believe the worst of an innocent girl."

"Innocent." Remembering her bold manner, he gave a harsh laugh. "She's no better than a harlot strutting her wares along the Strand."

"Michael, I've heard quite enough. If you believe such nonsense, then you've been in wicked company for far too long." Lady Stokeford thinned her lips. "Have a care lest I think you an unfit father for little Amy."

His grandmother's sharp voice still had the power to silence him. Though he knew she had no legal right to take his child, she made him face the doubts in himself, the fear that he would fail to raise his daughter properly. *Amy.* He pictured her elfin face, the freckled cheeks and inquisitive hazel eyes. With an unmanly wrenching in his chest, he missed her sunny smiles, her warm hugs, even her incessant chatter.

Lady Stokeford went on. "I won't have you ill-treating Vivien at my party. Thusly, I insist you spend some time with her over the coming weeks, so you might realize just how pure and kindhearted she is."

Like bloody hell, he wanted to retort. He shifted his thoughts to the Gypsy, to the vixen sway of her hips, the impudence of her gaze, the ripeness of her curves. He knew of only one use for a woman like her. Only one way he'd care to get close to her . . .

He narrowed his gaze at his grandmother. It would be futile to reiterate all his objections. Despite her frail appearance, Lady Stokeford had a backbone of steel. But if she wanted proof of Vivien Thorne's low moral character, then he would give it to her on a golden platter.

"All right, then," he said. "I'll seek out her company."

The dowager smiled, her expression softening. "Bless you, my boy. Perhaps London hasn't spoiled you, after all."

He flashed her a cool smile. Little did his grandmother realize, he would do more than befriend Vivien. He intended to use his considerable charm to woo her into a sense of false security.

Then, when he had the Gypsy fully in his power, he would seduce her.

Chapter seven

A Dangerous Game

At dinner that evening, Vivien set out on her campaign to bewitch Lord Stokeford. The surprise was how swiftly he responded to her efforts.

When she'd smiled at him upon entering the dining chamber, he had greeted her without a hint of rancor, bantering pleasantries with her as if she were a lady he admired and respected. He had even complimented Vivien on her daffodil-yellow dress, though his gaze caressed her bosom in a way that was far from gentlemanly.

She hid her flustered response with a determined graciousness. He would only gloat at his power over her. Little did he know, she intended to have him in *her* power.

Presiding over one end of the long table, he dominated the candlelit chamber. Vivien could scarcely believe he was the same man who had insulted her that morning in the library at Stokeford Abbey. Tonight he was all charm and smiles, trading jests with the Rosebuds and relating the scandals in London. Even Lady Stokeford had left her bed to join them, and Vivien was glad the dowager's health had taken a sudden turn for the better.

His eyes a piercing blue, he glanced at Vivien from

time to time as if to make certain she was listening. And she *was* listening, more avidly than she'd expected of herself. He entertained them with tales of the *ton*, his descriptions so sharp and clever, she could easily picture the fashion-mad ladies who agonized over the proper size of a bonnet, the glittering parties where people danced until dawn, and even a decadent gathering where a mummy from ancient Egypt had been unwrapped. He made London society sound utterly frivolous—and so very foreign.

All too soon, Lady Stokeford rose slowly from her seat at the end of the table. The marquess leapt to his feet and strode to his grandmother's side. "You've overtaxed yourself," he said, reaching for her arm. "I told you not to come down for dinner."

"I told *you,* I feel fit as a fiddle. I took a refreshing nap after you left me." Eluding his aid, she made a shooing motion. "You needn't coddle me."

The other two Rosebuds came scurrying toward them. "Olivia and I shall watch over Lucy," Lady Enid said, giving Vivien a blatant wink from behind Lord Stokeford. "You two youngsters are free to run along now. We elderly ladies must be boring you."

"Oh, but you're not," Vivien protested. "I enjoy your company."

"Nevertheless, we three shall retire to Lucy's boudoir," Lady Faversham said smoothly, taking Lady Stokeford's arm. "But don't let our departure spoil your evening. Lord Stokeford, you must keep Vivien engaged with your gossip."

"A capital notion," Lady Stokeford agreed. "Michael, I'm sure you have much more to say to dear Vivien."

The Rosebuds nodded and murmured their agreement. Then the trio strolled, arm in arm, out of the dining chamber, casting a few significant glances back at the couple.

Left alone with the marquess, Vivien was aware of the

dampness of her palms. The shadows cast by the candles gave him a sinister aspect, and her nerve wavered. Curse him, he was handsome as a devil in his fancy *gorgio* clothes, the dark blue coat and fawn breeches, the white cravat at his throat. His eyes studied her, his mouth quirked into a faintly calculating half-smile that sent a shiver racing over her skin.

"So, Miss Thorne," he drawled. "It seems we've been abandoned. On purpose."

She swallowed, her mouth dry. Janus was vain and stupid, his thoughts easy to read. Michael Kenyon, however, remained a mystery to her. He was harsh and coldhearted, and even now, when he behaved cordially, she sensed secrets in him. Did he truly still grieve for his wife?

No matter. If the Rosebuds wished her to practice her social skills on him, then she would do so. Surely he was a man like any other.

Curving her lips into the sensual smile she had practiced before the mirror, Vivien strolled toward him. "It would please your grandmother very much if we were friends."

"The question is, can a man and a woman be just friends?"

"Not so long as the man thinks he's her superior."

He laughed. "Touché. Come, stroll with me in the conservatory."

In his annoyingly masterful manner, he didn't wait for her agreement. He took hold of her arm and guided her out into the dimly lit corridor. In spite of her resentment, the firm touch of his fingers stirred a curious thrill in her. For once, he seemed easy to please and genuinely interested in her. But Vivien didn't entirely trust him. Why had he ceased his hostilities?

"This morning you made your dislike of me very

plain," she said. "What changed your mind?"

He shrugged. "There's no point to enmity. My grandmother is determined to keep you, and I must bow to her wishes."

"Or perhaps that blow knocked some sense into you."

His teeth showed in a faintly feral grin. "Perhaps."

So he didn't like being reminded that a woman had bested him. She must guard her sharp tongue and play to his masculine weaknesses.

Edging closer, she batted her lashes. "Whatever the reason, my lord, I'm pleased that you and I are finally—"

He pulled her to a halt. "Is there something in your eye?"

"Why, no."

"Then why are you blinking so much?"

Ignoring her protests, he walked her to a wall sconce. There, to her mortification, he cradled her cheeks in his large palms and tilted up her head, bending close to examine her face in the flickering light.

How novel an experience it was for a man to tower over her. His masculine scent submerged her in an awareness of him. His gentle touch on her cheeks caused a warmth that flashed downward to places that should never respond to him. He stood so near she could see the shadow of whiskers along his cheeks and jaw. She could also see the faint mark of a bruise where she had struck him.

And she felt an appallingly savage sense of satisfaction.

With his thumbs, he traced her lower lashes. "There's no speck I can see," he said. "Which eye is it that pains you?"

"Neither," she snapped, annoyed that he couldn't distinguish flirting from hurting. "It's gone now."

He held on to her, subjecting her to an intense scrutiny. His fingers stroked ever so slowly along her cheekbones.

"What beautiful eyes you have," he said in a low, musing voice. "They reveal the fire inside you."

Her heart skipped a beat, and his brooding half-smile scrambled her thoughts. She found herself staring in fascination at his mouth, at those firm and sensual lips.

"There's something you should know," he murmured.

She dragged her gaze back up to his. "What?"

"You should know that my grandmother has nothing at all to do with my being here with you."

Vivien tensed. She was very aware of how alone they were in the passageway, the house silent around them. The Rosebuds had everything to do with *her* being here. But of course, she mustn't tell him that.

"I'm here because you interest me," he said in that smooth, silken tone. "I want to know all about you, Vivien. I trust you won't mind if I address you so familiarly."

Wary, she shook her head. "No, m'lord."

"You must call me Michael," he went on. "There's no need to practice formality between . . . friends." The gravelly inflection of his voice hinted at another meaning, though Vivien had no time to ponder it.

He leaned closer, and with a shock she realized he meant to kiss her. A pulse of heat seized her, and she couldn't move or speak. Never before had she had the slightest interest in feeling a man's lips on hers. But she did now. Now, she felt intensely curious to taste his inviting mouth, to learn how to kiss from an expert seducer . . .

Abruptly, the unfamiliarity of her yearning struck cold sense into her. She stepped back, clinging to her composure by a thread. It wouldn't be easy to charm him without giving him the wrong idea. She wanted to make this *gorgio* lord fall in love with her, not to invite his physical attentions. She wanted to see him grovel.

For all that she had thwarted him, he had the nerve to

look pleased with himself, lounging against the gold-papered wall like a sultan biding his time with a potential conquest. That made her all the more determined to seize the upper hand.

Mastering her anger, she summoned a ladylike smile. "How decent of you to show an interest in me . . . Michael," she forced out. Among the *Rom,* everyone went by their first name, so she shouldn't feel a reluctance to address him so. Yet in this formal *gorgio* society, it created an unsettling aura of intimacy. She went on, "I look forward hearing more about your adventures in the city. Shall we proceed?"

"It would be my pleasure."

Somehow his words sounded vaguely indecent; then he took her arm again and escorted her into the conservatory. Coming here with him was a mistake, she realized at once. The circular room was enormous, with much of the walls and the roof comprised of glass panes, giving the illusion of being outdoors yet entirely apart from the rest of the world. The scents of earth and vegetation held a lush intensity. A velvety darkness enveloped them, the only illumination cast by a silvery quarter moon through the windows.

Vivien promptly seated herself in the middle of a stone bench too small to accommodate another person.

To her chagrin, the marquess propped one foot beside her on the bench so that his shoe rested against the folds of her skirt. Not the marquess, she corrected herself. *Michael.* If she were ever to enrapture him, to manipulate him like a puppet, she must start thinking of him by his birth name.

"Tell me more about London," she said. "The people there sound terribly elegant."

"Rather, they are elegantly terrible. They're a self-absorbed lot, concerned with fashion and gambling and amusements."

"Then why do you live there?" she asked, curious at his cynicism. "Why would you choose to stay among disagreeable people?"

His elbow on his knee, Michael leaned over her in a casual pose, a tall shadow against the black outline of a palm tree. His scent drifted to her, something dark and masculine. She wished she could discern his expression in the gloom. "It appears I've given you the wrong impression," he said smoothly. "Despite the buffleheads, there are also those who are clever and witty, intelligent and well read. In the country, one cannot attend the opera or enjoy a literary debate."

"You could if you found someone who's read the same books as you."

He laughed as if to deny any such person existed. "My friends are in London," he said with a finality that closed the subject. "But enough about me. Tell me, how do you like living in a fine house? It must be very different from traveling all the time."

How neatly he deflected her interest in him. A polite lady allowed the man to direct the conversation. Hiding her annoyance, she said sweetly, "I do like this grand house, though I was lost at first. It has too many rooms."

"There can't be more than twenty."

"Twenty-four. I counted." She had wandered around that first week, peeking through doorways, amazed at the size and number of chambers. Her entire *kumpania* could live here comfortably. "All for one person," she added, shaking her head in mingled disgust and wonderment.

"Two now, it would seem." Before Vivien could decide if he sounded resentful, Michael went on. "The Dower House is a mere cottage. Stokeford Abbey has more than one hundred twenty rooms."

She'd glimpsed a dizzying array of them that morning, on her way to and from the library. Yet she'd had no idea his house was so staggeringly huge. Of course, he was a *gorgio* lord, wasteful and extravagant. "How can you possibly use them all?"

"I don't. Most of the rooms are closed off with dust-covers over the furniture."

"But what is the purpose of having so many chambers?"

"It seems the ancestor of mine who built the place enjoyed entertaining." He paused, and she heard the rustle of a leaf falling somewhere. "The rooms will be used again very soon. You see, my grandmother is planning a large party. I wouldn't be surprised if the Rosebuds are writing the invitations as we speak."

"A party? They haven't mentioned any such event to me."

"I'm sure they will. You see, Vivien, they intend to introduce you to society."

Her heart faltered, then commenced a frantic clamoring. She'd hoped Lady Stokeford had given up that plan after Vivien had voiced her objections. She didn't want to meet a lot of snooty strangers. She only wanted to bide her time here until her two months were up.

But if she didn't behave as the dowager wished, her ladyship might send her away. She might never earn the two hundred guineas that would ensure her parents lived out the rest of their years in comfort.

"When?" she whispered.

"A fortnight or so from now."

"How many people will there be?"

"Everyone my grandmother knows—and probably some she doesn't know." He laughed, a curiously hard-edged sound. "She was a celebrated hostess in her day, though she hasn't done much entertaining these past few years."

Worse and worse. Vivien had only two weeks in which to prepare herself. Two weeks to learn all the customs and rules so that she wouldn't shame Lady Stokeford and be sent packing. Two weeks of freedom before she had to meet more hated *gorgios*. She couldn't count on any other aristocrats to be as kind and welcoming as the Rosebuds.

Plucking a frond from a nearby fern, Michael leaned down to brush it over her cheek. "You needn't look so alarmed," he said in that urbanely mocking tone. "This is your chance to shine. To be accepted by all of society."

The tickling leaves made her shiver, and she thrust his arm away. "I don't want to be accepted," she snapped without thinking. "Nor to choose a husband."

"A husband?"

"The Rosebuds . . . have some mad notion that I should be married."

Michael said nothing for a moment, and when he did speak, his voice was low and tight. "They've told you that?"

"Yes." Frustration welled up and overflowed. "*Develesa!* Why can't they see that a woman can be perfectly content without a man?"

He chuckled, toying with the frond of fern, drawing it through his fingers in long, smooth movements. "There are many reasons that women want men. For money, for children, for companionship." His voice lowered to a husky roughness. "And for those women who have known a skilled lover, the foremost reason of all is . . . pleasure."

All of her senses sprang to alertness. His masculine scent drifted through the cool, earthy darkness. The upper half of him was hidden by a pocket of shadow, the silvery moonlight illuminating only his trouser-clad leg, still propped on the bench, so close she had only to lift her hand slightly to touch him.

To *slap* him.

She laced her fingers in her lap. "You're no gentleman to make such a wicked comment to a lady."

"I beg your pardon." Removing his foot from the bench, he made a formal bow, sweeping the frond like a feathered cavalier's hat. "I must have drunk too much wine at dinner."

She doubted he was truly sorry, and she forced herself to think of what a lady would say next. "Apology accepted. Surely you'll be leaving before the party."

"That depends. Would you like for me to stay?"

She'd like for him to go away, and never mind her plan to make him grovel like a dog. "Of course," she said, injecting warmth into her voice. "Lady Stokeford would be very happy if you were to prolong your visit."

"And you, Vivien? Would my presence make *you* happy?"

Perhaps it was that sinfully masculine tone, but he could make the simplest question sound heavy with insinuation. Flustered, she chose her words carefully. "I've enjoyed talking to you this evening. It's good practice for when I meet society."

He gave a short bark of humor. "A suitable answer, and very ladylike. Perhaps in time you'll answer me more plainly."

"I can't imagine how much plainer I can be."

"Well, I can." He touched her with the frond again, this time lightly feathering it down her bare arm. Even as she tensed her muscles against a delicious chill, he added, "I do wish you wouldn't be so cautious of me."

She couldn't hold back an ironic smile. "I'm cautious for a reason. I've heard you're an infamous rogue."

Michael laughed. "Rumors tend to stretch the truth. You must judge me for yourself."

She seized the chance to feed his self-importance. Men liked to talk about themselves. "Then you must tell me more about yourself."

"What do you wish to know?" he asked.

His secrecy intrigued her, and a hundred queries sprang to her mind. She settled on the most important question of all. "I'd like to know why you keep your daughter from Lady Stokeford."

He didn't move, though she sensed that every muscle in his body went rigid. "I won't discuss Amy. Find something else to ask me."

There was something odd going on with his little daughter that Vivien didn't understand. "Is she deformed? Is that why you're hiding her?"

"No! She's perfect in every way." He sounded as if he spoke through gritted teeth.

"Then bring her here," Vivien urged. "It would ease her ladyship's mind. She worries about you—and her great-granddaughter."

"Grandmama shall have to console herself with circumstances as they stand. I don't owe anyone any explanations."

"*Develesa!* You owe her respect as your elder. And more than that, for taking care of you and your brothers all those years when your own mother and father neglected you."

He inhaled a deep breath. "So the Rosebuds have been telling you tales, have they? Here's a rule to add to all those you've been taught: men don't like to be the subject of prying female gossip."

"Gentlemen shouldn't talk about women, either."

"Have you been around so many gentlemen, then, to know their conversations?"

"Of course not. You know I grew up with the *Rom*."

"Yes, the Gypsies." Michael leaned a little closer, again touching the tip of the frond to her cheek and making her shiver. "I'm curious about your life before you came here. Was there a particular man who interested you?"

She edged away. "Why should it matter to you?"

"Because you interest me, Vivien. I want to learn all about you." He lowered his voice to a caressing murmur. "I want to learn everything."

Her heart beat faster, and she reminded herself not to respond to his seductiveness. "You wouldn't answer my question. So why should I answer yours?"

"Because if ever you expect me to be honest, then you must first set a good example for me."

"Bah. A man like you knows naught of honesty."

"Just answer me."

"Very well," she said, deciding to bend the truth in the hope of making Michael jealous. "I was to marry a man named Janus."

Through the darkness, Michael stared intently at her. "Has he bedded you?"

She pressed her lips together. The pig! It took a moment to leash her anger. "Among the *Rom*, it is considered to be *moxado*—impure—for a man to even brush the hem of a woman's gown as he walks past her."

"A roundabout answer is no answer at all."

He wouldn't believe the truth, so there was no point in arguing her innocence. "You have your secrets, my lord, and it seems I shall have mine."

He was silent for a long moment, the only sound the drip of water somewhere in the conservatory. Then abruptly he asked, "Do you ride?"

"Only the men of the *Rom* ride."

"That isn't what I asked."

"I . . ." Half glad of the change in topic, Vivien confessed, "Once in a while, I would sneak out at night and ride bareback. Until. . . ."

"Until what?"

"Until I was caught."

She cringed to remember her father's angry, mournful expression. Pulika had appeared through the predawn mist as she picketed the horse at the farthest edge of the herd. Though she'd taken scrupulous care to be quiet and to rub down the animal, she hadn't realized a man could tell the next morning if his horse had been ridden, or that her father had been suspicious for some time. He had subjected her to a stern and unforgettable scolding. She could still remember the painful sting of remorse, and the shame she'd felt at having disappointed her parents.

"There will be riding," Michael said, "during the week my grandmother is entertaining. You'll need the proper attire."

"I won't accept any more gowns from Lady Stokeford. She's given me more than enough already."

"You'll also need instruction in the correct form," he said, continuing as if she hadn't spoken. "We'll start your riding lessons tomorrow morning."

"We?"

"Yes. I intend to teach you all you need to know." Again, his voice held that hint of a double meaning.

Why was he so aggressively seeking her company? There could be only one reason—he wanted her in his bed. Even as the thought stirred her anger, she felt the reckless urge to tantalize him, to make him suffer.

He stepped closer, into the moonlight. From her seat on the bench, she looked up at him, struck by his splendor. A silvery shimmer created an aura over his dark hair and wide shoulders. The clean angles of his face held a confidence bred by untold generations of nobility. Discreet gold buttons glinted on his waistcoat, drawing the eye to the magnificent breadth of his chest and downward to places no lady should look.

Chiding herself, Vivien met his direct gaze. He was all she despised in a man, arrogant and proud and . . . *gorgio.* She didn't want to do as he asked. Yet how fine it would be to bring him to heel.

"Where shall we meet?" she asked.

"The stables at Stokeford Abbey, nine o'clock." He tossed away the frond and held out his hand to help her to her feet. His manner was gentlemanly, yet his fingers pressed warmly around hers, his thumb stroking her palm in a most distracting way. "Unless, of course, you turn coward."

Awareness of him heightened her senses, and Vivien knew she played a dangerous game. A game she relished. The notion of besting this *gorgio* lord was like a fire burning in her blood.

Coolly, she drew her hand from his. "I'll be there."

Chapter eight

Stolen Goods

A week later, Michael stood with his shoulder propped against the open door of the cottage. He watched in cynical silence as Vivien knelt beside the old man lying on a low bedstead in the corner. She didn't fuss about the rough brick floor or the likelihood of soiling her fine blue riding habit. She took a dose of comfrey powder from the leather pouch at her waist and administered it to the ailing tenant.

"There now," she said, stroking Owen Herrington's age-spotted hand. "Take one pinch of the powder each morning and evening, and you'll soon feel well enough to dance jigs at the harvest celebration."

"Will ye promise to be me partner?" the old man asked, a twinkle in his rheumy eyes, a toothless grin splitting his leathery face.

"It will be my pleasure," she said, laughing. "But only if you tell me more tales of giants and witches."

" 'Tis a bargain, and I'll get the best of it. I'll squire the comeliest girl in the county."

"Owen Herrington, bide yer tongue." His stoop-shouldered wife left her spinning wheel to shake a gnarled finger at him. "His lordship will be thinkin' ye're flirtin' with the lady."

Michael concealed a grimace. These simple folk couldn't see past Vivien's pretense of philanthropy. But he could. Her actions were designed to make him view her as a worthy person so he would sing her praises to the Rosebuds. It would be a cold day in Hades before that happened.

To his immense satisfaction, he had learned that very morning of evidence that the Gypsy was stealing from him. He had only to procure the tangible proof when they returned to the Dower House.

Hiding his impatience, Michael fixed an affable expression on his face as he strolled to Vivien and extended his hand to her. "Miss Thorne may flirt as she wishes," he said. "She's free to choose the partner of her liking."

He could tell by the flare of fire in those velvety brown eyes that she'd caught his meaning, that he intended for her to come willingly to *his* bed. As he helped her to her feet, she flashed him a little taunting smile. "You're right, of course," she murmured. "I won't be bullied by any man."

Her brazen look had a searing impact on his body. It was an effect he had experienced many times this past week. With the finesse of a seasoned temptress, she'd trifled with him, teasing him and yet keeping him at arm's length, cleverly avoiding his ploys to corner her alone. She had eluded even the Rosebuds' obvious attempts to push them together.

The Rosebuds wanted her to marry a gentleman. That was why they'd planned the house party for a week hence. But Michael had the ugly suspicion *he* was their man of choice. Little did they know, he had a very different plan for her.

As Vivien strolled across the one-room cottage with its

stone walls and thatched roof, he turned his attention to Owen Herrington. No longer beefy and robust, the old man looked shrunken, his knobby fingers clutching at the patched coverlet. Something twisted inside Michael, a regret that he had been so long out of touch with his tenants.

"When did you take ill?" he asked.

"Nigh on a month ago, m'lord," Herrington said, with a respectful bob of his gray head. Unlike the ease of manner he'd shown to Vivien, he lowered his eyes deferentially. "With m'lady's potion, I'll soon be back to work."

"You needn't labor in the fields. You've more than earned your rest."

"I'm strong yet, m'lord," he protested almost fearfully. "These old hands can still mend harness and sharpen tools and such."

Michael held back an order to desist all work. Herrington clearly had too much pride to consign himself to a rocking chair by the hearth. Leaning down, he gripped the old man's bony shoulder for a moment. "You'll always have a home here. No matter what happens."

Herrington worked his shrunken mouth as if unable to find the words to express his appeciation. He slid a glance up at Michael, then looked down again at his hands. "Thank ye, m'lord," he mumbled. "Ye're most kind."

Michael noticed the old man's hesitation, and wondered if there was another topic he wished to broach. Then he spotted movement out of the corner of his eye, and he saw Vivien walk to the single window, where she admired a length of cream-colored homespun. Little Mrs. Herrington twisted her fingers in her apron, glanced over at the two men, and then whispered something to Vivien.

Clutching the fabric, Vivien leaned closer to the old lady, listening intently, offering a muted comment now and then. The misty light of late morning etched her fine features. At first glance she looked like a gentlewoman in her elegant riding costume, yet closer inspection revealed a disdain for convention from her ungloved hands to her careless coiffure.

If the Rosebuds insisted she wear a bonnet, Vivien would discard it the moment they were out of sight. She didn't seem to mind that the sun had tinted her skin to a golden sheen. He could see a trace of copper in her black hair, unusual for a Gypsy, yet somehow it suited Vivien. She simply didn't fit any mold.

Michael resented her ability to charm the farmers, the villagers, the servants, everyone they met. Though they must have heard the rumors, people warmed to her friendly manner, and she soon had them believing in her sincerity. They seemed to forget she was a Gypsy so long as she dressed like a lady. At times, Michael too found himself lulled into enjoying her companionship, trading witticisms with her or discussing the latest book she'd read.

Every morning for the past week, they had taken a ride on his estate. And every morning, she had insisted on stopping at each cottage and hovel they passed. In her saddlebag, she carried a pouch of herbal medicines and always had a remedy for any ailment. As if determined to win over his people, she encouraged them to confide their personal woes and joys—and other tales, too, fairy stories and old legends. She would sit raptly listening until he'd had enough of her chicanery and marched her out the door.

As he would do now.

Michael stepped toward the two women. "I'm afraid Miss Thorne and I must be leaving."

Vivien shot him a fierce glower; he must have interrupted a choice bit of gossip. He lifted an eyebrow, daring her to disobey. Almost to his disappointment, she did not.

After laying the cloth on a chair by the spinning wheel,

she hugged Mrs. Herrington. The spontaneous gesture was typical of the Gypsy. No true gentlewoman would embrace a minion, but Vivien must not have learned that nuance of proper behavior.

"Come back soon, m'lady," Owen Herrington called from his bedstead. "I'll tell ye the tale of the piskie threshers."

A smile lit Vivien's face. "Piskies?"

"The wee fairy folk. They like to play tricks, they do."

"I'll look forward to returning, then," she said, as if she really meant it. "If you don't mind, I'll bring paper and pen so that I might take notes—"

"You can't return until first you depart," Michael quipped.

With a pleasant smile that concealed his gritted teeth, he took her arm and escorted her out of the gloomy cottage and through a small flower garden, where pinks bloomed along with a few late roses, beaded with mist. Pewter clouds scudded across the sky. The scent of impending rain flavored the air, and thunder grumbled in the distance. With any luck they'd make it home before the storm broke. Then he would find the proof of her theft, present it to his grandmother, and oust the Gypsy once and for all.

Or perhaps first he would confront Vivien. Yes. It might be gratifying if she tried to use her body to dissuade him from turning her over to the magistrate . . .

Under a hard push of his hand, the rickety wooden gate squeaked, then tilted askew on its rusty hinges. Pausing to straighten the gate, he muttered, "Remind me to send a man here. This damned thing should be repaired."

"That isn't all that needs fixing," Vivien said tartly.

"What the devil does that mean?"

"Come away from here and I'll tell you." Hips swaying, she minced toward the towering elm tree where their horses were picketed.

Michael stalked after her. He shouldn't let her irritate him. Better he should concentrate on his favorite fantasy . . . lowering Vivien to the grass, reaching beneath her skirts, coaxing her wildness into passion, a passion for him alone. Once he'd had her, he'd be rid of this seething frustration.

Her manner disdainful, she waited by her gray mare for him to boost her into the sidesaddle. Like a gentleman, Michael allowed her to place one dainty half-boot in his linked fingers as she mounted. Unlike a gentleman, he slid his hand beneath her hem and up the smooth length of her silk-stockinged calf.

Vivien inhaled a quick breath that lifted her lush bosom. For an instant, she stared down at him and her eyes widened, mirroring his desire. She felt soft. Warm. Willing.

Then she slapped the reins, and the mare danced away. "Don't *do* that," she said sharply.

He laughed, pleased to elicit a genuine reaction in her. "This is my land, and I'm the master here. I can do as I please."

"That doesn't give you the right to abuse people."

"I never abuse my women," he said in a honeyed tone. "In truth, they've been known to beg for my attentions."

"Then the women of London are silly sheep, bleating in stupidity."

"They're well-satisfied cats, purring with contentment."

"You delude yourself. You, with your elegant clothes and *gorgio* manners." Sitting straight in the saddle, Vivien cast him a severe look. A look that bore an eerie resemblance to the inimitable Miss Harriet Althorpe.

Banishing the unlikely thought, Michael mounted his bay gelding. The horse shook its mane and snorted as if eager to go. "If your waspishness toward me is a delusion, then I'm a happy man."

Her fingers tautened around the reins. For once, she didn't respond with a saucy remark designed to entice him. "You are a pig," she stated, narrowing her eyes and glaring fiercely. "No, that would be an insult to pigs. You're a *snake* for the way you treat people."

What had wrought this change from coquette to carper? "Out with it now," he said easily. "Who do you imagine I've wronged?"

Vivien didn't reply at first. Leaning down, she spoke a soft command and the mare trotted along the narrow, winding lane that meandered across the windswept moors. When Michael drew up beside her, intending to demand an answer, she asked a terse question of her own. "How many years has Owen Herrington worked for your family?"

"All his life," Michael said a trifle impatiently. "As a lad, I remember seeing him laboring at the haying and threshing. He's one of my most loyal tenants."

"Then may the crows pluck out your eyes for what you've done to him. That sick old man has sweated and toiled in your service, yet you would deny him a pension."

Stunned, he reined to a halt. "What the devil are you babbling about? I've done no such thing."

"Oh?" Fury flashed in her dark eyes. "You've been living like a king in London while the Herringtons and other poor folk on this estate struggle to survive. Then after they've slaved to feed your rich tastes, you leave them to starve in their old age."

Anger gripped him. "That's a lie. Who told you this?"

"Mrs. Herrington. Her husband dares not cease working because your steward told him there will be no pension."

"Impossible. Herrington must have misunderstood."

Her expression murderous, she walked the mare closer to the gelding. The two animals snuffled at one another, then began to crop the grasses alongside the path. "So tell me why he's received nothing these past weeks," she hissed. "Their only income is the pittance that Mrs. Herrington earns from her spinning. If not for that, they'd be begging for pennies at the crossroads."

Frowning, Michael glanced back at the picturesque stone cottage with its wisp of smoke drifting from the chimney. He remembered the impression of hesitancy in the old man. Had Herrington been wanting to ask about his pension?

No. Certainly the Herringtons lived in humble quarters, but he provided for all their basic needs. Turning back to the Gypsy, he snapped, "You're making all this up. If there was a problem, they would have brought it to my attention. Not yours."

"They were reluctant to speak out of fear of losing what little they have." Vivien regarded him as if he were sheep dung. "You see, m'lord, they don't trust you. You've abandoned them for a life of leisure. They see you for what you are: a pleasure-seeking nobleman without a care for their needs."

He felt a moment's guilt. He'd neglected his tenants, but not for the reason she'd thrown in his face. As their horses clopped side by side, he struggled to rein in his temper. "The quarterly reports from the estate always include a generous sum for annuities. Perhaps Herrington was overlooked. I'll investigate the matter with Thaddeus Tremain."

Her lip curled. "Tremain. He's the one who carries out your dirty deeds. I spied him walking on the moor yesterday afternoon. He's a mole-faced man who picks his teeth when he thinks no one is looking."

How like a woman to judge a man by his appearance.

"He's a skilled accountant and business manager. If he made an error, it will be his first."

"This is no error, but proof of your *gorgio* greed," Vivien said heatedly. "The Dunstans and the Keasts have little stores in their larder. The widow Bowditch has no wood for the winter. And the Jelberts' children were dressed in rags. Because you steal their hard-earned coin and squander it on extravagances."

Even as his hackles rose, he thought back to the cottages they'd visited. He was chagrined to realize he'd been too busy watching the Gypsy to take more than cursory notice of his surroundings. He'd been too distracted by her ability to beguile everyone around her.

Michael rejected her wild accusations, for the only logical explanation could be that Thaddeus Tremain was skimming the profits at the expense of the tenants. By God, Michael trusted the man too much to leap to such a conclusion at the word of a Gypsy. Tremain had seen to the smooth running of the estate for as far back as Michael could remember. A confirmed bachelor, the steward was married to his work. His deft handling of the day-to-day responsibilities had enabled Michael to live in London.

Michael always took care to examine the accounts that the steward delivered in person four times per year, and he'd seen nothing suspicious. Thaddeus Tremain was dependable, honest, and discreet. In addition to his other duties, he'd provided monthly letters detailing the activities of the dowager countess. Those reassuring reports had eased Michael's conscience.

No, the Gypsy had to be concocting this tale for a reason. This was a smoke screen, that was all. She must have realized that he'd found her out.

He urged his mount forward and stopped in front of her, forcing her to a halt. "You would accuse me of robbery," he said in a harsh tone, "when it's you who are a thief."

Her black brows clashed together. "*Develesa!* How can you bring up those stupid accusations when your people are starving?"

Lightning flashed closer now, but he paid no heed. He watched intently for a sign of guilt, a shifting of her gaze, a faint blush. "I'm not referring to the letter you forged in order to swindle my grandmother. Or the hundred guineas a month you've wrung from her. I'm talking about the things you've stolen from my house."

That stopped the Gypsy's tirade, but only for a moment. In a show of innocence, her eyes widened and her lips parted. "I've taken nothing of yours," she said indignantly. "Any books I've borrowed, I've returned within a few days."

A brusque laugh grated from his throat. "This past week, Mrs. Barnsworth has been tallying the contents of the Abbey. It seems quite a few valuables are missing. A medieval icon from Russia. Several pairs of gold candlesticks. A number of silver serving utensils that have been in my family for generations."

Clutching the reins, she shook her head, stirring the wisps of black hair that had escaped her chignon. "Look for your thief within your own walls, m'lord marquess. I've no use for your *gorgio* things."

"They can be sold for a small fortune in gold." Crisply he added, "We will return to the Dower House. You'll show me where you've hidden the goods."

The Gypsy proudly sat the sidesaddle, viewing him with scorn, never once averting her gaze. She said nothing more in her defense, only stared at him until *he* felt the annoying urge to lower his eyes.

Abruptly she snapped the reins, and the mare launched

into a trot. Over her shoulder, she called, "I'll gladly race you home, then."

Her eyes sparked a challenge at him. She bent low over the silky gray mane, and the mare launched into a full-out gallop, veering off the path and onto the rough moorland.

"For God's sake, Vivien!"

If she heard him, she gave no sign. With the firm seat of a born horsewoman, she went tearing over the hills, the wind snatching at her hair.

Michael acted on instinct. Applying his boot heels to the bay's flanks, he went charging after her.

"Damned fool," he muttered, not knowing if he meant her or himself. His muscles tensed at the tooth-jarring pace. Didn't the wench realize it was suicide to gallop over such rugged terrain? Not that he should concern himself with her safety. If the mare caught a hoof in a rabbit burrow and Vivien broke her neck, it would be her doing, not his.

Then, just like that, he experienced a swell of savage joy, an aliveness he hadn't felt in a great many years . . . perhaps never before. He reveled in the wind whipping his hair and coat, the pelting of cold droplets against his face, the flicker of lightning in the distance. He craved the chance to catch Vivien, to tame her brazen spirit.

It was the thrill of the chase, he knew. She had teased him and taunted him for days. The game had strained the boundaries of his control.

The moorland flew past in a blur, then the stubbled fields shorn of wheat and rye. Ahead, she crouched low, one with the beast. Michael was gaining on her, though he admitted that was due more to his powerful mount than to any superior skill as a horseman. Even hampered by the sidesaddle, Vivien rode as easily as a force of nature.

She hadn't needed lessons in sitting a horse, except in the rules of proper equestrian behavior.

Rules she ignored on a whim.

A flash split the skies, chased by a roll of thunder. Energy crackled in the air, prickling over his skin. Danger added an edge to his frenzied determination, and without warning he remembered another storm, another mad chase through the countryside, that time in the dark of night. He remembered his fury and his anguish over Grace's betrayal . . .

In a burst of speed, he brought the gelding beside Vivien's mare so they galloped in tandem. The rain fell faster now, stinging his hot skin. He could see the chimneys of the Dower House in the distance. Not that he intended to go there yet. He wanted her all to himself.

"We need shelter," Michael shouted over the pounding of hooves.

Her eyes blazed with willful defiance. Despite the fury of the ride, he felt a surge of wild heat, the provocation to bring to fruition his plan to seduce her.

Amid the landscaping of lakes and trees that formed a vista from the house, Michael spied a blur of white along the riverbank.

Cutting Vivien off, he urged her mount toward the small building. She made a face at him; then a closer bolt of lightning caused the mare to rear. His chest tightened with the dread that Vivien would fall, and there would be nothing he could do to save her.

But she clung to the gray mane, her lips moving as if to comfort the animal, though the wind snatched her voice from him. The horse calmed, and this time, Vivien let Michael guide her to the refuge.

In a clearing through the trees, the Grecian temple rose in lone splendor. The white columns were overgrown with ivy, and a peaked roof extended out over broad stone steps. Though open on all sides, the structure would protect them from the elements.

They reached the temple in the nick of time. Gusts of cold damp air buffeted them. Lightning stabbed and thunder complained. The heavens opened, and rain poured from the eaves in a silvery curtain.

Beneath the broad overhang, he dismounted and saw Vivien slide unaided from the saddle. Her chignon had come partially undone so that several long, dark hanks hung down her slender back. The damp riding habit clung to her curves. She snatched a towel out of the saddlebag and began to rub down the mare, crooning words too soft to be heard.

With a jerk, he knotted the reins around a pillar. No woman had ever caused such a furious tumult in him, not even Grace.

Glancing over at him, the Gypsy gave him that provoking smile, a blend of superiority and sensuality. "Don't look so angry, m'lord. A little wetness never hurt anyone. Or do you melt in the rain?"

His temper snapped. He forgot all about his resolve to charm her into trusting him. He forgot everything but the need to master this tempestuous woman.

"No," he said, stalking toward her. "But by God, you'll melt for me."

Chapter nine

A Fire in the Heart

She had pushed him too far.

The rag dropped from Vivien's nerveless fingers. One hand resting on the mare's silken mane, she felt her heart thudding with alarm and something darker, something wild and shameful.

In the moment it took for Michael Kenyon to stride across the temple, a flicker of lightning carved his features into sharp relief. He looked like a god from ancient Greece in the book she had borrowed from his library. An angry, vengeful god who frightened her.

A handsome, powerful god who enthralled her.

Catching her by the arm, he marched her up the marble steps and into the dimness of the temple. The drumming of the rain and their footsteps intruded on the peace of the sanctuary. In one swift glance, she took in a stone bench and a statue of a robe-draped goddess in the gloom of an alcove. Dried leaves scattered the floor, crunching beneath their shoes.

His harsh breathing brought her gaze back to his face, to the tautness of his cheekbones and the thinning of his lips. His nostrils flared like a stallion scenting its mate. A fervent intensity glittered in his blue eyes, an emotion she couldn't quite fathom. Awareness of him ignited a flame of yearning in her breast.

A fire in the heart.

A fire that had never burned for any man of the *Rom.* A fire she must never feel for this domineering *gorgio* lord who called her a thief. He had been relentlessly pursuing her for a week now. And she was horrified by the ungovernable response of her body to his.

She attempted a low, husky laugh. "Michael, I didn't mean to insult you—"

Before she could finish, he hauled her against him, clamping her to the hard length of his body and lowering his mouth to hers. She squirmed against his embrace, but he held the back of her head firmly in his palm so she could not turn away. Then she no longer wanted to turn away. His kiss made her weak at the knees, and she clung to him, aware of the sculpted muscles beneath her fingertips, the stimulating scents of rain and man, the compelling taste of his mouth.

Dear God, *his mouth.*

Hard and hungry, it moved over hers as if to consume her. She wanted to be consumed by him, to give herself up to the appalling pleasure of a man's lips on hers. And not just any man. *Michael.*

Alone in her bed, she had dreamed of his embrace, tame fantasies in which he held her close, declaring his adoration, his manner tender and worshipful. She would refuse him, of course, and he would grovel at her feet. She would laugh to see him reduced to abject misery over the woman he regarded as far beneath his exalted self.

But never had she imagined that reality could plunge her into an abyss of passion.

Her breath caught in something halfway between a gasp and a moan, and he took advantage, thrusting his tongue into her mouth. That startling stroking sent heat down to the deepest, most intimate part of her. His kiss demanded, seduced, aroused, but somehow didn't satisfy. She wanted something more from him, something that eluded her.

Then he performed an act even more outrageous. He put his hand on her breast, cupping her over the riding habit, circling his thumb over the peak until she almost swooned from waves of delirious pleasure. In a rational part of herself, she knew she ought not allow him such liberties. Yet he touched a madness in her that defied all common sense.

Giddy, she was aware of him tilting her backward onto the cold stone bench, never breaking the ravenous contact of their mouths. Before she knew quite how it happened, he'd pushed up her skirt and opened her legs so that her feet slipped to either side of the bench. He promptly settled himself atop her, his heavy weight trapping her in place. Through his breeches, she felt a distinctively hard ridge press against her most vulnerable place. And for one riveting moment, she experienced a rush of carnal desire more powerful than anything she had ever known. He moved his body against hers and she arched to him, wanting, craving, desiring him with mindless fervor.

Then his hand went to her hip, stole beneath her hem, and fondled her bare thigh. Even as she nearly swooned with wanting, the realization of his intent pierced her sensual haze.

This *gorgio* intended to take her innocence. To dishonor her. To use her for his own pleasure.

Slapped by repugnance, she turned her head from his kiss and thrust her hands at his shoulders. "No!"

"Yes. You want this. You want *me*."

He caught her face and kissed her again, a dominating kiss that only increased her panic. Though she bucked and twisted, she couldn't dislodge his solid body. She felt as if she were suffocating. He would take her against her will. He would *force* her.

Frantic with fear, Vivien reacted with a vengeance. She sank her teeth in his lower lip.

He reared back, roaring in outrage, his hand clapped to his mouth. "What the devil—!"

She scrambled out from under him and stood up unsteadily, backing away and catching her balance by flattening her palm against a stone pillar. Her shaky legs threatened to buckle. Rain splashed musically from the roof, and a gust of cold damp air cooled her overheated skin.

Her breath shuddering, she burst out, "Stinking *gorgio*. How dare you treat me so!"

"You bit me, dammit." Michael shot to his feet, drawing back his hand and grimacing at the blood smeared there. He whipped out a handkerchief and dabbed gingerly at his mouth. "What the hell's wrong with you?"

"I told you to stop. I won't be your whore."

"You liked what we were doing. You even spread your legs for me."

Vivien flushed at his crude insult. "Curse your conceit. I didn't realize your intentions—not at first."

"You did, indeed. No innocent girl kisses the way you just did." His hair mussed and damp, he lowered his lashes slightly, all sulky, sinful man. His chest heaved with heavy breaths. In a menacing murmur, he said, "You were wild for me, Vivien. You were moaning with pleasure."

Was that true? Had her lewd behavior encouraged him?

Mortified and confused, she felt the pulsebeat of passion deep within her. The memory of his kiss burned in her, a shameful reminder of her ardent response. She had craved the pressure of his body against hers. She had wanted his hands on her breasts and between her legs. She still desired his masterful touch . . .

No! Her only mistake had been to think it would be easy to manage Michael Kenyon, to tease him into falling in love so that she might have the pleasure of spurning him. The overconfident ass had no right to take from her what she refused to give. To steal what belonged to her husband someday—if ever she could respect any man enough to marry him.

"You'll never find out how wrong you are," she snapped. "Because you will never again touch me."

Michael watched her, his gaze bold. As if even now he were plotting ways to seduce her. "You don't mean that."

With despicable confidence, he sauntered toward her. Panic seized her by the throat. He would ravish her again!

Pivoting, Vivien dashed for the mare. She hiked up her skirt, but couldn't quite vault herself into the awkward sidesaddle. Curse these *gorgio* trappings! She would ride his horse instead.

She started to turn. Too late.

His approach sounded on the marble steps behind her. "Where are you going?" he said sharply. "It's still raining."

She ducked past the mare and ran onto the moor, her only thought to reach the safety of the Dower House. Cold droplets wet her face. Mud sucked at her half-boots. The long skirts hampered her, tangling in her legs.

His heavy footsteps pounded behind her. He called out her name, his voice brusque, angry. In desperation, she increased her pace, slipping and sliding on the spongy turf. She shoved a strand of hair out of her eyes. The breath seared her lungs. *Develesa!* He was closing in on her.

Pushing herself harder, she neared a grove of oaks. But his strong fingers grasped at her arm. In a frenzy, she yanked herself free. If she couldn't outpace him, she could fight.

Snatching up a stout stick from the ground, she swung toward him, brandishing the weapon. "Don't!" she gasped out. "Don't come near me."

The marquess stopped, breathing hard, his chest rising and falling. He watched her warily as if her seriousness finally had broken through his male arrogance. "You're afraid of me."

"Curse you! I'll fight you to the death."

"For Christ's sake. I'd never harm a woman."

"You'd force me to lie with you." She tasted a bitter fear in her throat. "But I'll kill you first. I swear it!"

Michael regarded her without moving. A lock of damp hair had slipped onto his brow, giving him the aspect of a pirate. The downpour had slowed to a drizzle, and lightning flickered far in the distance. A spatter of cold rain struck her back, and she shivered as much from awareness of their isolation as from the chill. Her teeth chattered, but she clamped them together to hide her fear. She should never have chanced being alone with this *gorgio.*

Then, to her amazement, he made a formal bow, right leg thrust out, one hand tucked behind his back. "Pray forgive me for alarming you. Your beauty tempted me beyond all rational judgment."

Michael thought her beautiful.

Resisting an insidious softening, Vivien stared suspiciously at him. The almighty marquess was apologizing to her. He was insincere, of course, but at least his gentlemanly effort gave her a small sense of satisfaction.

She could still taste his kiss. She could still feel his broad, hard body covering hers. His mouth had moved hungrily, his hands caressing, arousing an unsatisfied yearning for more. Even now, knowing his base intentions, she experienced the treacherous weakness of desire.

She didn't understand herself. How could she feel anything but contempt for this despotic lord who used women and then discarded them? The man who believed her a thief?

When he took a step toward her, Vivien pointed the branch like a spear. Her arms quivered, and she fought to hold them steady. "Stay back," she snapped. "Do you think I trust your apologies?"

"I think you're a high-spirited woman with a penchant for violence. Now put that down."

She shook her head. "Beware, m'lord. I know many ways to subdue a man. Gypsy ways." Fixing her gaze on him, she sent him the menacing look that always worked on troublesome *gorgios* who tried to cheat the *Rom*.

His mouth curved into a sardonic grin; then he winced, no doubt pained by his puffy lip. With the slow movements he might use around a skittish filly, he shrugged out of his charcoal-gray coat. "Put this on," he said. "You're wet and shivering."

It was a trick. An excuse to come nearer.

As he closed the distance between them, she held the stick up in warning. "No! I want nothing of yours."

"You're getting it anyway," he said, and draped the garment around her shoulders.

As he stepped back, she automatically reached up with one hand to catch the lapels and keep the coat from sliding off. The cloth carried his heat and scent, and she was hard-pressed not to snuggle her face into it and breathe deeply, to rub her cheek against the smooth texture. She had the uncanny sensation of being enveloped in a loving embrace. *His* embrace.

He could not have calculated a more effective way to steal past her guard.

"There now," he said, those blue eyes bewitching her.

"I want you to remember that I desire you. I'll dream of your soft lips."

Stupefied, Vivien watched as he turned around and started back toward the temple. The damp white shirt was molded to his magnificent physique, and buckskin breeches and knee-high boots outlined his powerful legs. Against all sanity, she felt her fear and anger dissolve beneath a stirring of warmth.

I'll dream of your soft lips.

She should walk to the Dower House. She didn't want to be anywhere near Michael Kenyon. But if he'd wanted to overpower her, he could have done so. Besides, if he was on horseback, it made no sense for her to be on foot and vulnerable. So after a moment's hesitation, she dropped the stick, clapped the dirt from her hands, and marched after Michael.

Vigilant for any false moves, she let him boost her up onto her mount. He acted the perfect gentleman, his touch impersonal, his manner polite. He refused her attempt to return his coat. The misting rain cooled her hot cheeks. But nothing, not even the uncomfortable sidesaddle, could cool the furtive excitement that burned in her blood.

I'll dream of your soft lips.

She hid her flustered confusion behind an aloof expression as they rode over the wet earth. Michael Kenyon didn't need to know how he'd bewitched her with that one remark. Nor did he need to know she felt an appalling attraction to the man who had tried to force her to his will. The *gorgio* lord she could never, ever love.

The mud pulled at the mare's hooves, and Vivien concentrated on guiding the animal around the worst puddles. She kept a prudent distance from Michael, fearing the dangerous effects of his charm. Like the aftermath of lightning, the memory of his kiss glowed within her, and for the first time, she wasn't indifferent to a man's body.

His form felt so different from hers, hard and brawny, capable of pleasuring a woman. She couldn't help wondering how he looked beneath his clothing, if his chest was smooth or furred with black hair, if his skin was pale or the same bronzed hue as his face and hands. To her shame, she wanted to gush with admiration like all those silly girls of the *Rom,* gazing moon-eyed at their suitors.

I'll dream of your soft lips.

She must never forget his true opinion of her. Michael Kenyon thought her a common thief. He had almost ravished her, and she had almost succumbed. She didn't understand why such a man could arouse a woman's longings in her.

Before she had time to sort through the quagmire of her feelings, Vivien heard Michael utter a muffled curse. Reining in the bay gelding at the top of a hill, he frowned past Stokeford Abbey, its large stone façade visible through the dripping trees, and toward the winding river and the Dower House.

She stopped nearby, regarding him uneasily. "What is it?"

He made no response. Following his gaze, she saw a stately black coach trundle along the curved drive leading to the Dower House. The driver sat hunched on the top seat, and two crimson-clad footmen clung to the rear of the vehicle. Even from a distance, the servants looked drenched.

"Bloody damn," Michael snarled in an undertone. "*Damn* her."

"Who?"

"My grandmother. By God, she'll pay for this." He flashed Vivien a look stark with fury and something else, something dark and fearful. "Stay here. I won't have you involved in this." Then he took off like a shot, thundering down the hill toward the bridge, clods of earth flying in his wake.

Chapter ten

The Motherless Girl

Vivien had no intention of obeying his order to stay back. The tyrant might very well upset his grandmother. And that, Vivien wouldn't tolerate. She would earn every pence of her hundred guineas a month by protecting Lady Stokeford from her bossy grandson.

She urged the mare to follow him. What could her ladyship possibly have done to deserve his bitter denunciation? What visitor did this traveling coach bring? Unless she'd misunderstood, the guests for the party wouldn't begin arriving for another week.

She rode over the little stone bridge and through the garden, reaching the Dower House right behind Michael. The coach pulled up before the portico, and the footman leapt down, sliding on the wet gravel. Recovering himself, he lowered the step below the door and grasped the ornate handle.

"Stop!" Michael called out.

He swung down from his horse, flung the reins at a waiting groom, and stalked toward the frozen footman. Vivien followed suit, though staying a little behind until she could assess the situation.

"M'lord?" the footman said with a visible gulp.

Michael ignored him. Hands on his hips, he aimed a glower at the stout coachman, who sat hunched on his high perch. "Keep going, Pritchard," the marquess said. "You're returning to London immediately."

"But m'lord," the coachman sputtered, doffing his tall hat, "we need a change o' 'orses. An' like as not, 'er ladyship could use a bit o' fresh air along wid a 'ot meal."

Her ladyship?

Vivien's heart squeezed with a ferocity she didn't care to examine. Had one of his women come to call? But why would his doxy come here to the Dower House? And what had his grandmother to do with it all?

A muffled thumping came from the interior of the coach as the passenger banged on the door. In the rain-wet window appeared the pale oval of a face. A rather small, woeful face plastered against the glass.

"Proceed to the Abbey, then," Michael ordered, stepping forward to block her view. "I'll be there in a moment."

Even as the footman released the handle, the door flew open. Out tumbled a little girl dressed in blue silk with a white pinafore, a blue bonnet tilted askew on her copper curls. Splashing through the puddles, she launched herself at Michael, who crouched down to catch her to him.

Her lower lip wobbled. "Papa! Why do you wish to send me away? Don't you want me anymore?" Then she burst into tears.

Vivien's heart melted, and she was barely conscious of the misting rain. His daughter. This adorable girl was the Lady Amy, the only child borne by his beloved wife. The seldom-seen great-grandchild of Lady Stokeford.

"Amy," he said in a gentle tone she'd never heard him use before. "Of course I want you with me. We'll see each other up at the Abbey. Now get back in the coach."

She turned off her tears like a spigot. "I won't. I been stuck in there with Miss Mortimer for*ever*."

"We departed yesterday morning, my lord, and spent the night at a very pleasant inn near Shaftesbury," said the plump, aging woman who had emerged from the coach. She had merry brown eyes and a contented countenance, though she looked a bit worried at the moment. "Lady Stokeford wrote to convey your request that Lady Amy come here immediately. If I was wrong to bring the child . . ."

"Never mind. What's done is done." Holding his daughter in his arms, Michael stood up, looking incongruous and yet so masculine carrying a bundle of ruffle-skirted little girl. "We must go, sprite. Perhaps you'd prefer to ride with me on my horse."

"Let me *down*. I wish to see my grammy."

"Later. We'll invite Great-Grandmama for dinner."

"Now," she said, ruining her imperious tone with a pout. "If you don't let me, I'll weep again. I'll kick and scream and throw a tantrum."

Surprisingly, her father didn't explode with anger. He gave her a look of mock sternness and straightened her bonnet. "Silly girl," he teased affectionately. "If you don't watch out, I'll tickle you into smiling again."

"Oh, do let her down," Lady Stokeford called from the porch. Trailed by the other two Rosebuds, she glided down the steps. "Please, Michael, you mustn't take her away."

Vivien tensed. What a selfish, vile man he was for keeping his child from Lady Stokeford!

Michael shot a glare at his grandmother. At the same moment, Amy gave a twist of her miniature body and slid out of his arms, her skirts flying up to her knees. Heedless, she scampered across the pebbled drive and threw herself at Lady Stokeford.

"Grammy, Grammy! I'm *here*!"

The dowager would have been bowled over had not Lady Faversham planted her cane and grabbed onto her while Vivien rushed to her other side. "So I see," Lady Stokeford said, bending down to hug Amy. "Oh, my dear girl. How wonderful it is to hug you again."

"I 'member you," Amy declared. "Papa said I wouldn't, but I *do*. You keep sweets in your pocket."

Lady Stokeford laughed, her blue eyes sparkling with happy tears. "Yes, indeed, and here you are." A tremor of emotion in her hands, she rummaged in her pocket and gave the girl a lemon drop, then leaned down to touch her cheek. "My darling, how you've grown."

Sucking on the sweet, Amy said, "I'm four. I had my birthday last month."

"You're quite the young lady now. And your copper hair glistens so prettily."

"You have your mother's delicate features," observed Lady Faversham, cocking her graying head to the side.

"And look at those lovely hazel eyes," cooed Lady Enid. "I do believe Lady Grace had blue eyes, but yours are every bit as beautiful."

Amy basked in their admiration. As they murmured and fussed over her, Vivien couldn't help smiling, momentarily forgetting her own troubles. Amy had inherited a good deal of charm from her father. Then Vivien glanced over at Michael, and her sentimental mood vanished.

His jaw was clenched, his hands fisted at his sides as he glowered at the crooning Rosebuds. Clearly, he begrudged his grandmother even a few moments with her great-granddaughter. Why was he so cruel?

Vivien marched to his side. In a whisper meant for his ears alone, she said, "Lady Stokeford was right to summon Amy. You're wrong to keep her in London. What reason have you to hide her?"

He swung on her, his expression fierce. "Stay the hell out of what you don't understand."

The naked pain in his eyes silenced her as much as the emotion that vibrated in his voice. She couldn't fathom the depths of his savagery. How could a man deny his child her family? And why did she sense a deep-rooted torment in him, and a mystery at odds with his arrogant nature?

Despite her anger, she felt a softening inside herself, and the appalling impulse to lean forward and kiss his swollen lip. She scorned the weakness in herself. Considering his despicable treatment of her, it was humiliating to feel even the slightest attraction to him.

He strode toward the group and took Amy firmly by the hand. "I'm afraid we're leaving," he said in a voice that brooked no nonsense. "I'd like the chance to visit with you myself, Amy."

"But Papa, I *can't*. I need to go. *Now*." When he started to draw her toward his horse, she crossed her legs, wriggling her bottom in an unmistakable dance.

He halted, looking uncharacteristically confounded. Before Miss Mortimer or the Rosebuds could react, Vivien hastened forward and took the little girl's hand from him. "I'll show you to the convenience," she said. "That is, if you don't mind the company of a stranger."

Amy looked up, her small features screwed into a frown. "Who are you?" she asked around the lemon drop stuffed in her cheek. "Why are you wearing my papa's coat?"

Vivien had forgotten about the heavy garment draping her shoulders. The Rosebuds twittered and giggled. A blush stung her cheeks, as if she'd been caught in an illicit embrace.

But she mustn't show embarrassment. They couldn't know about that kiss. That intense, passionate, shattering kiss.

She shaped her lips into a smile. "I'm Vivien. Your papa and I were caught out in the rain, and he was kind enough to lend me his coat." Slipping it off her shoulders, she handed the garment back to Michael. "Now, shall we go into the house?"

As they started toward the porch, the little girl continued to stare up at her. In a loud voice, she said, "Are you one of Papa's doxies?"

"No," Vivien choked out.

"Amy Kenyon," Michael snapped. "That's rude and improper. Apologize to Miss Thorne."

"I'm sorry," Amy said, looking bewildered as she sketched a curtsy.

The Rosebuds were smiling in fond enjoyment. "My dear child," Lady Stokeford called out. "Wherever did you hear such a naughty word?"

"Nanny says I see and hear too much. And I oughtn't talk so much." Her face framed by the blue silk bonnet, Amy returned her wide-eyed gaze to Vivien. "Do you think I talk too much?"

"Of course not, darling." Touched by tenderness, Vivien bent down to her level. "I confess, my parents told me the very same thing when I was your age."

Amy smiled, her hazel eyes sparkling. "I like you lots, Miss Vivi. I think p'rhaps you can be my new mama."

The day had gone from bad to worse, Michael thought darkly.

He paced the length of his grandmother's boudoir, striding from a pink-upholstered chair to a gold-tasseled ottoman. First, the matter of Vivien's thievery, which he had yet to prove. Next, the perplexing state of his tenants.

Then that ill-timed kiss which had very nearly upset his scheme to rid himself of the Gypsy. Worst of all, Amy's unexpected arrival.

Like a flock of magpies, Vivien and the Rosebuds gathered in the bedchamber, and he could hear their chirping and cooing through the closed door. They were fussing over Amy as if she were a porcelain doll. As if she required four guardians to help her answer a call of nature.

He fumed over his grandmother's audacity in finagling this visit. She knew Amy was to stay in London. He'd told her so many times in no uncertain terms. Yet like the quintessential female, she'd plotted behind his back. She had brought Amy here without his permission, where the Rosebuds might find out the truth . . .

An ice-cold fist clamped around his chest. He sucked in a breath, expanding his lungs with air. He must take Amy away from here as soon as possible. It was the only way to protect her.

Yet he remembered the tears in his grandmother's eyes when she'd embraced Amy. She truly loved his daughter, and he had deprived her of that joy. But it couldn't be helped. If she discovered his secret, she'd blurt it out to the other Rosebuds, and that he could not endure. He had to place Amy's welfare above all other considerations.

Bloody hell, what was taking them so long?

He took two strides toward the door, intending to knock, when the white-painted panel opened and the women tiptoed out. Three old crones, but no ravishing young Gypsy. And no little copper-haired sprite.

Stepping forward, he demanded, "Where's my daughter?"

His grandmother held a forefinger to her lips and quietly closed the door. "Sshh. The little darling is asleep."

"Asleep! Why the devil is she sleeping?"

"She's taking her nap," Lady Faversham murmured,

leaning on her cane. "All young children need to rest in the middle of the day."

"I tucked her into my own bed." His grandmother's mouth curved in a soft smile. "Such a dear child she is. I always wanted a little girl."

"She snuggled right down and closed her eyes," Lady Enid added with a nod, her yellow turban bobbing. "She was up before dawn, and the long drive must have tired her."

"Where's the Gypsy? I don't want her anywhere near my daughter."

He reached for the door handle, but the three Rosebuds arranged themselves like guard dogs in front of the door. "You can't go in there," Lady Faversham said in a scandalized whisper. "That is a lady's bedchamber!"

"It would cause a scandal for you to be there with an unmarried woman!" Lady Enid said stoutly.

Taking firm hold of his arm, Lady Stokeford propelled him toward the outer door. "Don't get yourself in a dither, my boy. Amy is quite safe. Vivien is lying down with her."

He told himself not to worry. They would have pestered him with questions and accusations if they'd stumbled upon his secret. Yet still he didn't trust them. He trusted no one with his daughter but himself. Not even Vivien, who knew little of his past.

Especially not Vivien.

P'rhaps you can be my new mama.

The notion brought a grimace to his lips, along with a stinging ache where Vivien had bit him. Bit him! As if he were a ravisher and she an innocent maiden. Remembering her slim, strong body arching beneath his, the softness of her mouth, the fire of her response, he felt an almost painful surge of lust. Never before had one kiss caused him to lose control. He'd been in such a fever that he'd ignored her protests. Because he'd believed her to be merely willful, defiant.

Then she had run from him because she feared he would force her to his will. Self-disgust churned in him. He'd never treated any female so shabbily. Better he should forget her and concentrate on Katherine, his long-time mistress and intended bride. She suited his discriminating tastes in a way Vivien Thorne never could.

"I'll sit with Amy," he said. "She shouldn't be left in the care of a stranger. A Gypsy."

"Pish-posh," Lady Stokeford scolded. "Amy has taken to dear Vivien quite admirably. It's important for children to be with those they trust."

"She trusts *me. I'm* her father."

Lady Faversham stepped forward, steadied by the ivory cane. "But Lord Stokeford, you should never disturb a slumbering child."

Irritated, he swung toward her. "Why not?"

"Because they're sweet little angels when they sleep," Lady Enid put in, clasping her hands to her pillowy bosom. "Why, when my own grandchildren, Charlotte and Dominic, were babes, I would tiptoe in just to take a look at them—"

"We needn't look in on Amy since Vivien is present," Lady Faversham cut in. "Once Miss Mortimer freshens up belowstairs, she'll resume her duties."

"And while the children sleep, the adults have time to discuss adult matters," his grandmother said, tugging on his arm again. "Now come along, Michael. We've things to settle."

He shot one last frustrated glance at the closed door. His grandmother barely came to his shoulder, yet he found himself obeying her imperious command and escorting her downstairs. The other Rosebuds lagged close behind, whispering to each other. When they would have followed him and his grandmother into the morning room, he blocked the doorway.

"This is a private matter," he said bluntly. "Lady Stokeford and I will speak alone."

Lady Enid's pudgy face formed a moue of disappointment. "Oh, dear, I suppose you do have that right."

Lady Faversham gave a crisp nod of her graying head. "You will not badger Lucy," she said in an austere tone. "She isn't well. And remember, she loves Amy as you do." Then she reached out and drew the door shut.

Annoyed by the reprimand, Michael stalked into the small chamber. Like the boudoir, the morning room sported frills and furbelows in a fussy yellow and white decor. The dainty tables and flower-sprigged chaises made him vaguely uncomfortable, and he wished for a sturdy leather chair where he might lounge in contentment, propping his booted heels on the fender of the hearth and enjoying a stiff drink.

Hell, he'd like to down an entire decanter.

He walked toward the bellpull. "I trust you've a bottle of port in this godforsaken house."

He knew his grandmother was distracted when she didn't chastise him for cursing. "I'm afraid there's only my cream sherry," she said, staring at him. "You may order a bottle brought up from the cellar if you like."

He lowered his hand without touching the bellpull. The day was going from worse straight to Hades. "Never mind," he muttered, shaking his head. "Let's get this over with quickly."

His grandmother glided across the floral rug, raised herself on tiptoes, and peered up at the lower portion of his face. "Michael, dear, I've been wanting to ask you. What happened to your lip?"

He touched it gingerly. "I bumped into a door this morning."

"But are those not *teeth* marks?"

"I bit myself in the doing," he snapped, then shifted the conversation away from that ill-fated kiss to the subject uppermost in his mind. "About Amy. I wish to know why you brought her here against my command."

Lady Stokeford arched an indignant eyebrow. "Are you saying you aren't happy to see her?"

Happy? He'd felt a throat-tightening joy to feel her small form in his arms again, to smell her little-girl scent and see her bright smile. *Papa! Why do you wish to send me away? Don't you want me anymore?*

Entombing his regrets, he paced the confines of the morning room. "That's beside the point, Grandmama. You lied to Miss Mortimer, convinced her that you had my approval, and dragged my child away from her lessons in London."

"Amy is scarcely four years old. A holiday will do her no harm, and she does need to know her blood relations."

"I promised to bring her to visit at Christmastime."

"But you're here now. Such a tiny mite should not be left all alone in that dreadful city."

"I've a well-trained staff to care for her. Miss Mortimer is more than capable of providing for all her needs. She's like a mother to Amy."

"Or a surrogate great-grandmother." In a show of dramatics, the dowager sank down on a chair and pressed the back of her hand to her brow. "Oh, your coldness and disapproval pains me. If only you knew how many times I've wept these past three years. Why don't you want me near her? What have I done to earn your distrust?"

The sheen of moisture in her eyes discomfited him, hitting him hard in the chest. It wasn't her he distrusted, it was her Rosebud friends who might jabber the truth all over England. But he dared not say so to her. He'd stayed in London all these years in order to avoid such a sticky morass.

Crouching beside her chair, he patted her frail, blue-veined hand. "Please don't weep, Grandmama. I care very much for you."

"Care," she said scathingly. "The word I wish to hear is *love*. But never mind, you're like all men. You cannot voice that sentiment without flinching."

"I love you," he muttered.

"Bah, you don't speak from the heart. You mean only to placate me."

Women, he thought in disgust, springing to his feet and prowling the room. He should have known the impossibility of holding a rational conversation with a female. "I merely want you to accept the fact that Amy is *my* daughter. That I alone have jurisdiction over her."

"So you think me ill-fit to raise her. I, who raised you and Joshua and Gabriel. And did a fine work of it . . . at least with them."

He froze. "Surely you're not suggesting that *you* raise Amy."

"Why not? I'm an experienced mother. The child would be better off with the guidance of a woman, her own flesh and blood. Of course, Miss Mortimer could stay on as her governess."

"That's impossible. I won't be separated from Amy."

"Then the two of you should move home together." She eyed him with heartfelt sentiment shining in her eyes. "Oh, darling, I know you grieved for Grace, and that you needed time to adjust to her loss, but three years have passed. It's time for you to live again, for Amy's sake if not your own."

"I'm living quite well enough in London," Michael said stiffly.

He pivoted away, striding to the window to scowl

blindly into the wet garden. God help him, the situation was more dangerous than he'd feared. His grandmother would dig and dig until she unearthed the distasteful truth about his marriage. He couldn't allow that, couldn't let any taint of scandal be cast upon Amy. But how much longer could he keep up this pretense of the grieving widower?

He turned around, crossing his arms and affecting a casual stance. "Forgive me for speaking so sharply," he said. "But I won't burden you with raising another child. You should enjoy a well-deserved retirement. Play cards with the Rosebuds and talk about old times. Make jests about the vicar and his dry-as-dust sermons. Hold court with the neighbors and send baskets to the poor. That's more than enough activity to fill your hours."

"You're suggesting I should waste my time with gossip and idle pursuits?" She tilted up a regal chin. "Family is far more important to me. Though *you* have yet to realize its importance."

"Nevertheless," he said with forced pleasantness, "so long as I live in London, Amy stays with me. And that is that."

Lady Stokeford's mouth quivered, and he feared for a moment that she would weep again. Then she pursed her lips and stated, "Since you won't leave Amy with me for good, you'll at least permit her to stay here for a nice long visit."

"No," he said. But he admitted to himself that he couldn't bear to send her back to London just yet. "She'll go to the Abbey with me. As soon as she awakens from her nap."

"Where will you put her, pray tell? The nursery will be filthy with cobwebs and dust."

She had a point, one that he hadn't considered. "She

and Miss Mortimer can occupy another bedchamber, then."

"Really? The place has been closed up for years. Has the housekeeper begun her cleaning for the party?"

"There have been scores of maidservants dashing about, scrubbing this and that. Footmen dusting chandeliers and such." It had been a madhouse of activity, and he'd escaped at every opportunity. "But I'm sure I can find a room for her."

"Find a room? She isn't a dog to be kenneled just anywhere."

"You're exaggerating, Grandmama," he said testily.

"I most certainly am not. I very much doubt that the bedchambers have undergone a thorough cleaning as yet. The mattresses must be aired, the linens freshened, the woodwork polished, the chimneys cleaned, the rugs beaten—along with untold other details. I won't have my great-granddaughter housed in any but the finest surroundings." Lady Stokeford eyed him with iron determination. "So you see, my boy, you've no choice in the matter. Amy *must* remain right here with me."

Chapter eleven

The Rosebuds Revealed

Giving her eyes time to adjust to the dimness, Vivien walked slowly into the third-floor nursery at Stokeford Abbey. In the center of the long chamber loomed a table with three inkstands and three straight-backed chairs. Shelves crammed with books and knicknacks filled one entire wall. On the mantelpiece stood a clock that had long since ceased ticking.

Harriet Althorpe had ruled here many years ago. Closing her eyes, Vivien tried to feel the presence of the woman who'd given birth to her, some lingering spirit in this forgotten chamber. But she detected only the odors of dust and neglect, the cool mustiness of air too long shut up.

And the presence of Michael Kenyon, the Marquess of Stokeford, behind her.

"As you can see, the schoolroom needs an airing," he said crisply. "However, a team of housemaids should have the place ready by tomorrow."

He stood close to her. So close the warmth of his breath stirred the fine hairs on her neck. Skittish, she spun around to face him. "Her ladyship asked me to examine these rooms. To confirm that your nursery isn't suitable. She's perfectly happy to keep her great-granddaughter with her."

"If Amy is to stay for a brief visit, then she'll live here with me at the Abbey."

Vivien frowned at his implacable expression, superior and confident in the murky light. Bunching her fingers in her skirt, she said, "I don't understand why you wish to keep Amy from your grandmother. They love each other, and they belong together."

"Grandmama may visit Amy as often as she likes. I'll say no more on the matter."

Pursing her lips, Vivien had another flash of intuition that he was hiding something. Whatever it was, he wanted to keep *her* away from Amy, too. That, at least, she could comprehend. A snob like Michael Kenyon wouldn't think a woman of the *Rom* respectable enough to associate with his daughter.

Or perhaps he had a more nefarious purpose. Perhaps he saw another opportunity to seduce her.

Keeping a vigilant eye on him, she edged toward the table, tracing her fingertip over the webwork of scratches in the wood. She couldn't imagine how a cold man like him could have sired such a wonderful little girl. Back in Lady Stokeford's bedchamber, she had told Amy a story about a magical land where trees could talk and flowers could sing, and afterward, she'd cuddled the girl close while she fell asleep, her thumb stuck in her mouth. Vivien had marveled as she always did at the beauty and innocence of youth. She'd missed having the children of the *Rom* gather around to listen to her tales. Holding Amy had brought her a poignant pleasure, the ache for a child of her own.

P'rhaps you can be my new mama.

Amy didn't know it, but nothing could be less likely to happen. The Marquess of Stokeford would never offer marriage to a woman raised by Gypsies. And *she* would never want as a husband the most offensive, arrogant, depraved, and sinfully handsome *gorgio* lord who had ever walked the earth.

When she'd tiptoed out of the bedchamber, leaving Amy sound asleep with Miss Mortimer quietly tatting lace, she'd gone downstairs to find Michael quarreling with Lady Stokeford. The dowager had asked Vivien to accompany him here, and Vivien hadn't argued. She was drawn by the chance to view the place where Harriet Althorpe had once reigned. And in a secret, loathsome, foolish part of herself, she had yearned to be alone with Michael.

Walking briskly to the windows, she drew back the draperies and sneezed from the dust that filtered down from above. She tried to push open the casement, but it wouldn't budge.

"Allow me."

Michael brushed against her, and she quickly stepped aside, her heart fluttering like the wings of a sparrow. *Develesa,* she mustn't let him fluster her so. She mustn't remember that glorious, carnal embrace or the disgraceful lust he stirred in her. He was an amoral nobleman who wanted to use her. And to her shame, she didn't quite trust herself not to let him.

With a raucous squeaking of hinges, the window opened. Cool, damp air poured into the nursery and she breathed deeply, relishing the freshness. She didn't know how these *gorgios* could bear to be shut up all the time.

"Library paste," Michael said, his dark head bent low to examine the windowsill.

"Pardon?"

"One of my brothers put library paste in the crack. That's why the window wouldn't open easily."

Vivien ventured closer to him, picking up a piece of

the gray stuff and crumbling it between her forefinger and thumb. "Are you sure you didn't do the deed?"

"Quite. It was Gabe, most likely. He was the youngest, the last one to leave the schoolroom."

Brimming with questions about Michael's childhood, she said, "He's exploring in Africa, isn't he? Lady Stokeford has mentioned him."

Michael nodded. "Gabe is charting jungles that have never seen a white man, drawing flora and fauna and strange beasts."

"Her ladyship has a picture he sent her framed on her wall." Vivien recalled the tall spotted creatures with their long, slender necks, nibbling at the tops of the trees. *Giraffes*, the drawing was labeled.

"Every now and then, Gabe sends me a lion's skin or a warrior's spear or some such. I've a room at my house in London decorated in his souvenirs."

Vivien felt an odd pang as she realized that she would never see the place he called home, never touch the things he treasured, never observe his daily routine. It was purely curiosity, of course, about a man who defied her comprehension.

Clapping the dust from her hands, she said, "Her ladyship mentioned that your middle brother is in the army."

"The cavalry. Joshua has worked his way up to the rank of captain, and he'd take great offense to hear anyone call him a mere foot soldier."

"Do you ever see your brothers?"

"Josh sometimes stops in London on his leave before coming here to visit Grandmama. Gabe has been gone for two years, but he writes whenever he's near a trading post or a mail packet."

"Do you miss them?"

"Of course." A smile of rueful affection made Michael

look unexpectedly human. "We were all so eager to grow up. We never stopped to think about leaving behind the people we held dear."

"How true," Vivien murmured, surprised that he could feel any depth of emotion. She, too, missed her parents and the bustling familiarity of the Gypsy camp. She yearned to smell the smoke of the campfires, to chat with the women, to hear stories told by the elders. How odd to think of the haughty Michael Kenyon having his own fond memories.

As if he regretted revealing so much, he prowled across the schoolroom to a low chest, where a battalion of toy troops were arranged in precise lines. His back to her, he scooped up a tin soldier, turning it over in his long, capable fingers.

Vivien watched him a moment, picturing him as a small black-haired boy, studying his lessons at the desk or playing a prank on one of his brothers. How different his upbringing had been from hers. She'd had much freedom, little education, and few rules, for the *Rom* were indulgent parents who loved their children to distraction. Yet she envied Michael his brothers, for she'd always wanted the special closeness of siblings.

Going to the chest, she picked up a toy soldier, finding it surprisingly heavy. "Did these belong to Joshua?"

Michael frowned slightly as if just remembering her presence. "Yes. We held many a mock battle in this room. Oftentimes real ones, too."

She set down the figure, then touched an open tin box with its pots of dried-up paints. "And these must have been Gabriel's."

"He liked to draw and paint ever since he could first wrap his fingers around a pencil or a brush."

Moving a few steps away, she examined a grouping of

broken birds' eggs arranged in several nests on a shelf. "And these? Who collected these?"

"I did."

His laconic response discouraged further questions. But she asked one anyway. "The rocks, too?" she said, pointing to the neatly labeled rows of stones on another shelf.

He gave a curt nod. "They'll need to be tossed out with all the other rubbish."

"No! Amy will want to see the things that interested you as a boy."

"I doubt that. She prefers dolls and other girlish toys."

"All children like to hear stories of when their parents were young. And these things"—Vivien touched a yellow finch's feather—"show that you love the land and nature. Or at least that you did at one time."

He raised a disdainful eyebrow. "You read a lot into a boy's shabby keepsakes."

"Perhaps. Or perhaps not." Impatient with the worldly scorn on his face, she voiced the half-formed observation that was taking shape in her mind. "The odd thing, m'lord, is that both of your brothers are still following their childhood interests. While you idle away your time in London."

For an instant, his eyes narrowed on her. Then that indulgent expression returned, and he caught her hand, his flesh heavy and warm. "Quite the contrary. I'm doing what interests me the most. Seducing women."

His wolfish smile caused a melting sensation in the pit of her belly. Yanking her hand free, she quickly stepped back. "I can't claim to understand your *gorgio* need to own so much property. But I do know that if you cherish this land, you should return here for good, and so should Amy."

"That isn't for you to decide." A dangerous edge to his smile, he approached her, forcing her to retreat or risk his embrace. "But enough of your badgering. I'd rather talk about us."

She stepped backward. "There's nothing to say."

"Surely you've wondered why I allowed a thief to enter my house. A very lovely thief."

"I've stolen nothing!" she asserted, though bitterly she knew he wouldn't believe her.

"That remains to be proven. In the meantime, perhaps you and I should become better acquainted."

Like a stalking wolf, he advanced on Vivien, herding her backward, alarming her with his transformation from amiable man to tempting seducer. When she bumped into the wall in between a sturdy desk and an oak cabinet, she thrust up her fists. "I warn you, don't touch me."

"As you desire." His eyes slumbrous, he braced his palms on the wall behind her, his broad chest mere inches from her bosom. "I don't mean to frighten you, Vivien. I only wish to have a few words with you."

She didn't trust that honeyed tone. Her heart thudded fast from a combustible mix of fear and longing, and she cast about for a way to distract him. "Then I'll tell you why *I* came here," she said. "To see if I could find out more about Harriet."

He frowned. "Miss Althorpe."

"My . . . mother," she said, her voice catching. "You knew her, Michael. Will you tell me what you remember about her?"

His eyes turned cool and skeptical, but he answered her anyway. "She was tall and thin as a post. She wouldn't abide any nonsense like botched papers or rude messages passed under the table. When we were too rambunctious, she would send us down to my father to be punished."

"What did he do to you?"

"Gave us a stern scolding—and then offered us a glass of gin to make up for it."

"Gin! To a child?"

He regarded her with cynical aloofness. "Miss Althorpe didn't know about that part. However, you'll be pleased to hear I was too young to appreciate gin, and I'd always refuse it. As did my brothers."

Appalled nonetheless, Vivien shook her head. "A father shouldn't corrupt his sons. You ought to have told your mother. She would have put a stop to it."

"I did tell her," he said with a shrug. "But she believed a wife was subordinate to her husband, and so she never questioned his judgment. She merely ensconced herself in the chapel and prayed for us."

What a peculiar, sad family; the poor children could not trust their parents to protect them. It made Vivien yearn for her warmhearted foster parents who had always made her feel loved. Their times together had been boisterous and warm and full of laughter. "Then you should have told Harriet Althorpe—or your grandmother. They would have protected you."

Impatience flitted across his hard features. "It was long ago and best forgotten. Besides, my experiences in life have enabled me to see the truth about people. And made me realize exactly what I want."

He lowered his head ever so slightly, watching her with the lazy interest of a tomcat toying with a mouse. She was keenly aware of his arms bracketing her, as close to an embrace as possible without touching her. His masculine scent enveloped her, as did the heat radiating from his body.

"About Harriet Althorpe," she began, her voice entirely too breathy. "I wondered—"

"Enough about her." His brooding gaze dropped to her lips. "I'm more interested in you, Vivien. In this attraction between us."

"It's all in your imagination."

He chuckled. "One kiss, and I could disprove that. However, I've no intention of giving you the opportunity to savage me again."

To her shame, Vivien knew that she would like his roguish kisses. "Step away. I won't be trapped by a man."

"Nor, it seems, will you give him the chance to redeem himself."

"If you want redemption, then go to your *gorgio* church."

He laughed again, reaching out to brush a tendril from her brow, his hand disturbingly tender. "You're far too pretty to spout such malevolence. Tell me, Vivien, why do you dislike men so much?"

It's only you I despise. She swallowed the acid retort, remembering her somewhat unraveled plan to charm him into falling in love with her so that she could spurn him when she returned to the *Rom.* With effort, she shaped her lips into a mysterious smile. "Perhaps I've yet to meet a man who knows what a woman really wants."

His caressing gaze moved up and down her body. "And that is . . . ?"

"Why, my lord," she said on a husky note. "You surely can't expect me to reveal all to a man who has yet to prove himself worthy of my trust."

"How, pray tell, would a man go about winning your trust?"

"By courting me, of course."

His eyebrows lowered, giving him the hooded look of a hawk. "You mean by showering you with gifts—or more specifically, expensive jewelry."

She shook her head. "I mean by treating me with gallantry and politeness, not with grabbing and pawing."

His frown deepened. "I haven't pawed you."

"What would you term that episode in the temple?"

"A pleasurable interlude. Until you changed your mind."

"I was never given a choice. But you're too pigheaded to see any fault in yourself."

"There you go again," he said. "You're carping about men. This Janus of yours must be a rough, slovenly fellow."

Vivien tensed. Why would Michael bring him up? Could he be . . . jealous? Her lips curved into a smile designed to torment him. "Do allow me to correct your mistake about Janus," she said, letting her voice caress the name. "He's a fine man of excellent character. In truth, he's far more a gentleman in his behavior than you could ever hope to be."

A muscle hardened in his jaw. "Is that so?"

"Yes," she said recklessly. "You *gorgios* know little about true chivalry."

"And Janus does."

"Certainly. You don't think *I* could ever have any interest in a man who mistreated me, do you?" There. Let him realize that he should revere her, not ravish her.

His heavy-lidded eyes studied her with faint calculation. "So you think a Gypsy is better than a gentleman at wooing a woman."

"Yes, I certainly *do.*"

Quite unexpectedly, Michael took her hand and brought it to his mouth. He kissed the back, his lips tender and tickling, making her melt all over again. Though, of course, she concealed her reaction.

When he straightened to his superior height, his half-smile held the promise of wickedness. "If you wish to be wooed, then you shall be. But in the end, darling, I shall expect my reward."

* * *

"Ah, youth," sighed Enid. "Such vitality they have. It makes me wish I were eighteen again."

The Rosebuds sat in the sunlit garden of the Dower House, wrapped in shawls against the cool morning air while they watched Vivien play hide-and-seek with Amy. The chime of their laughter filled Lucy's heart with contentment.

"When you were eighteen," Olivia said rather dampeningly, "you were foolish and impulsive."

"So were you," Lucy said tartly, turning to regard her friend, whose wrinkled features still held a haughty elegance. "Myself as well. Remember the Landsdownes' ball?"

Olivia sniffed. Enid giggled. Lucy knew they too would never forget that wonderful, romantic, mortifying night.

"Ooh, we were naughty girls, were we not?" Enid said, her plump face alight with pleasure. "We were also the most beautiful young ladies of the season."

"Everyone admired us," Lucy agreed. She leaned forward to clink glasses with the others; then they all sipped their sherry.

"That wasn't why everyone stared at us," Olivia pointed out. "We made spectacles of ourselves. How I ever let you talk me into that vulgar scheme, I'll never know."

"Oh, don't be a crosspatch," Enid said. "None of us have ever again looked at a pot of rouge in quite the same way."

"Nor have we ever lived down the disgrace."

"Now ladies, no quarreling," Lucy said, tapping her glass on the iron arm of her chair. "Granted, we were silly to put rouge on our nipples. But none of us knew the ballroom would be hot and we would perspire."

"Indeed," Olivia said with a huff. "If we'd had the

sense to wear our corsets, the color wouldn't have seeped through our white gowns."

Lucy smiled. "And we wouldn't have become known as the Rosebuds."

Enid leaned forward, her eyes dancing. "Charles was the first to notice, remember? He immediately proposed marriage to you, Lucy. On bended knee in front of the entire assembly."

"Yes," Lucy murmured, that long-ago joy mingling with the awareness of sorrows to come later. "We all had success in love that night."

Enid's bosom lifted in an extravagant sigh. "I had my first dance with Howard. He was quite a timid man and had never worked up the courage to approach me"—she giggled again—"until he saw my rosebuds."

"He was hardly timid," Olivia scoffed. "You were with child by the morning." But her stern mouth eased into a smile. A smile not of ridicule, but of fond remembrance.

"You fell in love, too." Lucy reached over to pat the gnarled hand curled around the cane. "With the dashing Lord Faversham, who had professed never to marry because no woman was fine enough to please him."

"Roderick did have more than his share of charm," Olivia said, her gray eyes going soft and unfocused as if she were gazing into the past. Yet there was sadness there, too, a sadness that broke Lucy's heart.

With determined cheer, she held up her glass in another toast. "I must say, I'm quite pleased with the way life has turned out. Why, if that night had gone differently, I might have married someone else, and then I wouldn't be sitting here, watching my darling great-granddaughter."

Olivia's thin mouth quirked into a rueful smile. "You always could see the silver lining in every cloud, Lucy."

The Rosebuds fell silent a moment, savoring their wine while gazing at the small child and young woman romping in the grass. Now they played a twirling game that soon had them collapsing in a giggling heap.

Enid's expression sobered as she turned to Lucy. "Amy is such a lovely little girl. What a pity she lost her mother at so tender an age."

"All the more reason for Vivien to wed Michael," Olivia avowed. "How is their romance progressing?"

"Quite well, I think," Lucy said. "They've been riding every morning. And today, he sent her several books—not a very passionate gift, but she was charmed. Oh, and she bit him, too, so he must have tried to kiss her."

"Or perhaps he attempted something even more improper," Enid said, all agog. "You don't suppose he's already bedded her, do you?"

Olivia thunked her cane on the paving stones. "If the rake dares to do so, he'll marry her immediately. I will see to that."

"My grandson is an honorable man," Lucy stated sharply. "Should he discover Vivien's innocence, he'll do right by her."

"Where is the boy today?" Enid asked.

"Tending to estate business," Lucy said. "But he left his guard dog on duty." She waved her glass of sherry toward Miss Mortimer, who sat tatting lace on a bench at the other end of the garden. "Oh, I should like to hate the woman, but she is so . . . so *agreeable.* And Amy is terribly fond of her."

Olivia arched an eyebrow. "It seems odder than ever that Stokeford discourages you from keeping the child for a visit."

"I always thought it was because Stokeford Abbey held so many sad memories for him," Enid said.

"Surely in three years he's recovered," Olivia said, logical as ever. "We've all been widowed, and we've picked up the pieces of our lives. That is what one does in the face of tragedy."

"I quite agree, it's unnatural for a man to grieve so long," Lucy said slowly, remembering the way Michael had turned away from her yesterday when she'd asked him about Grace. "For some time, I've had a peculiar feeling about his marriage, that perhaps there was something he wasn't telling me. Something very wrong."

Enid leaned forward, her brown eyes widening. "Why, Lucy. Whatever do you mean?"

"Well, we all know that even when marriages begin like a fairy tale, sometimes they don't continue in so happy a manner." Lucy and the other two Rosebuds nodded sagely at one another. "Michael and Grace did have a very romantic, whirlwind courtship . . ."

"He won her from Brandon," Olivia said, her mouth twisting wryly. "My grandson dallied too long in making his offer."

"Michael loved her to distraction," Enid said. "When Lady Grace walked into the room, his face would light up."

Lucy nodded, troubled all the more. "Then why does he always seem angry now when I bring up her name? Why does he turn away from me as if he has something to hide?"

"Men often hide their pain with anger," Olivia stated. "In truth, men prefer to hide *all* sentiment."

"Michael used to confide in me," Lucy mused in frustration. "But this tragedy has utterly changed him. He's shut out everyone except Amy."

"Then the question is," Olivia said, "why would he have stayed away from here, if not out of grief?"

"And why has he kept Amy from you?" Enid added indignantly. "Why, it isn't to be borne."

Her heart twisting, Lucy took a sip from her glass,

turning her gaze to the little girl with the shining copper curls, who laughed and jumped while Vivien attempted to brush the grass from her white pinafore. The two joined hands and skipped toward them, Vivien's face glowing as much as Amy's.

"I don't know," Lucy said in anguish. "But I do wish to find out. In the meantime, I'll make certain Amy stays here with me."

"How?" Olivia asked. "Stokeford is quite adamant about keeping her all to himself."

With a steely smile, Lucy motioned for her two friends to lean forward. "For that, dear Rosebuds, listen closely. I have a plan."

Chapter twelve

A Handful of Stardust

Michael despised being played for a fool. He despised facing the fact that he'd shirked his duties. Most of all, he despised losing his chance to incriminate the Gypsy.

Fists on his hips, he stood on the front steps and glowered after the dogcart that disappeared into the gloom of twilight. There was an autumn chill in the air, but he scarcely noticed. A pair of his strongest grooms drove Thaddeus Tremain, bound in irons, to the village gaol, where he would be held until trial by the magistrate.

Vivien hadn't stolen from him. His steward was the culprit.

Michael had scrutinized the account books that morning, after sending Tremain off on a fabricated errand to settle a minor dispute with a neighbor over a property boundary. Then Michael had ridden around to his tenants, assessing their needs, making a list of their grievances, and arranging for restitution.

As the day went on, his fury grew.

The Herringtons were only one family of many who had been cheated. His people had been robbed of their justly earned coin, a bit here and a bit there, enough to impoverish them without pushing them to rebellion. Thaddeus Tremain had supplied them with inferior tools, refused to do repairs on their cottages, inflated their rents, and reduced their wages. Then he'd cleverly manipulated the ledgers to conceal all traces of his embezzlement.

By the time the steward returned, Michael had more than enough proof with which to confront him. Tremain denied everything, his squat nose twitching with indignation. Until Michael brought out the hefty sack of gold coins he'd found secreted beneath the floorboards of the steward's bedchamber. Only then did the mole-faced steward collapse into a blubbering heap of remorse. Begging for mercy, he'd claimed to have needed the money to provide for his sick old mother in Wales.

Michael scorned the story. There had been other things he'd discovered while searching the steward's austere chamber—the silver serving pieces, the icon, the heavy gold candlesticks. All the missing items he had accused Vivien of stealing.

He had also found a new gold pocket watch, a trunk packed full of stylish garb, and a much-thumbed pamplet about the United States of America, land of opportunity.

Thaddeus Tremain would go to Australia instead.

A rustling sounded behind him. Pivoting, he saw his staff crowding the open double doorway. Footmen, maidservants, cooks, and grooms stood wide-eyed in the light of the torches. Several servants shrank back into the shadows as if to escape notice. Heads ducked, eyes shifted, and voices muttered uneasily.

He frowned. Surely they weren't afraid of being sacked, too.

"You've naught to fear," he said. "Only Tremain is at fault."

Mrs. Barnsworth ventured a few paces forward, her hands folded over her stout middle. "We heard the news, m'lord," said the housekeeper. "And we all wished to say . . . good riddance to bad rubbish."

The others murmured their assent, heads bobbing and fists waving.

On a hunch, he asked, "Did Tremain mistreat any of you?"

"He was a mean 'un, m'lord. He cut our wages, he did."

Michael swore under his breath. "You should have informed me."

"We thought ye wouldn't believe us, m'lord," piped a young maid who couldn't have been more than twelve. When the attention shifted to her, she blushed red and fell silent, lifting her apron to hide her face.

The balding butler cleared his throat. "What Daisy means, my lord, is that Mr. Tremain told us he was acting on *your* orders."

The news struck Michael with as much chagrin as anger. It was the same bald-faced lie Tremain had told to the tenants, thereby destroying their trust in Michael. Was he truly so much a stranger to his people that they could believe him capable of such cruelty? "It seems Tremain has told many untruths," he said. "I want all of you to know that your former wages shall be restored and you'll also receive whatever has been taken from you. Plus an additional sum for your inconvenience."

Excited murmurings rippled among the servants, along with a few hearty cheers and a spate of applause.

"We're grateful to ye, then," Mrs. Barnsworth said, bobbing her mobcapped head. "Might I add, we're pleased ye're back for good."

For good? This must be his grandmother's doing, spreading rumors about his permanent return. Because she wanted . . .

Amy. During the events of the day he'd nearly forgotten about his daughter. He wouldn't feel at ease until he brought her here, where he could keep a close eye on her.

As the servants returned to their duties, Michael motioned the housekeeper to remain on the porch. "Has the nursery been prepared?"

The housekeeper stared at him in obvious consternation, her beefy hands grasping at her apron. "Aye . . .'tis bright as a new penny. But ye mustn't bring the little lady here yet."

"Why not?"

"Because when her ladyship inspected it—"

"My grandmother came here today?" he asked sharply.

"Aye, while ye were off makin' yer calls on the tenants. She and her two lady friends trooped upstairs and checked the nursery. Then I heard a screechin' and a hollerin' loud enough to wake the dead." Mrs. Barnsworth lowered her head, peering up at him as if expecting his wrath to descend at any moment. "I swears, I don't know how it happened, m'lord, but there was mice runnin' about everywhere."

Mice? When he'd gone up there with Vivien, he hadn't noticed any sign of an infestation. What damnable bad luck. Or perhaps, Michael thought in dawning suspicion, it wasn't luck at all. "I trust you've taken measures to remove the rodents."

"Aye, the footmen trapped a few, and I set out the rat poison meself." Her shoulders slumped as she worried the folds of her apron. "I swears on me mam's grave, there's never been mice upstairs afore today. I keep a clean house, I do."

"Don't give the matter another thought," Michael said with grim resolve. "I'll personally make certain it shall never happen again."

* * *

"Miss Vivi! Miss Vivi!"

A small body barreled into Vivien as she opened the door of her bedchamber. Alarmed, she reached down, her arms automatically surrounding Amy in a protective embrace. She could feel the girl's heart pounding like the beating wings of a frightened sparrow. "What is it, darling? What's wrong?"

"I had a scary dream," Amy sobbed, her hazel eyes watery and her lower lip quivering. Unruly copper curls framed her elfin face. A ruffled white nightdress was buttoned to her little chin, and she clutched a tattered rag doll.

Vivien was ready for bed, too. As was her custom, she'd wrapped a shawl around her nightdress and slipped outside to escape the confinement of the house for a while. Only this time, she'd heard a tapping on the door of the bedchamber. She brushed back a strand of Amy's hair from her brow. "My sweet little dove, you're safe now. What did you dream about?"

"I was running and running and I couldn't find my papa, not nowhere. I couldn't find *you*."

"You're safe with me now." Enfolding her in an extra big hug, Vivien glanced down the darkened corridor. "Where is Miss Mortimer?"

"She's snorin' terrible loud," Amy confided. "So I came to see you, Miss Vivi. Can I stay? Please?"

Seeing the trust on that young face, Vivien felt her heart melt. Yet she hesitated. She ought to take Amy back to her own chamber. Michael had left strict orders that only Miss Mortimer was to care for his daughter, and Vivien had no wish to antagonize him, and possibly risk losing her place here. "Your father wants you to stay with your governess."

Amy squeezed her arms around Vivien, pressing her

small cheek to her bosom. "Please don't send me away. Pleasepleasepleaseplease*please*."

Curse his rigid rules. "Of course I won't send you away. Come in."

Her tears vanishing with mercurial swiftness, the little girl fairly bounced into the bedchamber, which was lit by a single beeswax candle on the bedside table. Gloom lay thick in the corners where the light didn't reach, and the fire on the hearth had died down to glowing red embers. "It's spooky in here," Amy whispered. "But not as spooky as my room."

"Then you shall stay right here for now," Vivien assured her. "Hop into my bed where it's warm and comfortable."

She drew back the pristine white counterpane, but Amy balked, looking suspiciously from the plump, unused pillows to Vivien. "Why weren't you sleeping?"

"I was standing out on the balcony for a bit, that's all." It was ten o'clock, and Lady Stokeford had retired already, distressed by the most recent quarrel with her grandson. Earlier in the evening, he'd come stalking into the Dower House, shouting for his grandmother. The despot had accused the dear lady of releasing mice into the nursery. Mice! As if the dowager were as crafty as he was.

"Why?" Amy asked.

Vivien pulled her attention back to the little girl. "Why what?"

"Why were you outside?" Amy wagged her finger in imitation of a stern governess. "You ought to be sleeping."

Vivien laughed. "I like being outdoors. The stars are especially lovely tonight."

"Oooh, I wanna see." Without waiting for permission,

Amy snatched Vivien's hand and towed her toward the partially opened door to the balcony.

"Wait," Vivien said, laughing again. "The air is chilly. Let me fetch a blanket."

Dancing with impatience, Amy hovered by the door while Vivien stripped the eiderdown coverlet from the bed and carried it outside. The balcony was a mere jut of stone with a low railing dark with twining ivy. There were no chairs or benches, so Vivien made a pallet out of some folded blankets and then wrapped herself and Amy in the fluffy eiderdown. Cozy and warm, they sat with their backs to the stone wall as they gazed up at the sky, the stars like diamonds strewn across black velvet. Vivien held the tiny girl snuggled in her arms. Oh, it did feel wonderful to embrace a child, she thought. Especially one as sweet and lively as Amy.

"Miss Vivi?"

"Yes?"

"Why are there stars?"

Vivien smiled, remembering what her father had told her. "Each star is someone's soul sparkling down upon us."

"What's a soul?"

"It's the part of you that thinks and feels. The part that never, ever dies."

Staring upward, Amy fell quiet for a long moment before whispering, "My mama must be one of those stars, then. 'Cause she's an angel in heaven. Papa said so."

Vivien's heart twisted. According to Lady Stokeford, Amy had been not quite a year old when her mother had died in a tragic carriage accident. Michael's beloved noble wife. Had her loss caused the great, angry hurt she sensed in him? Feeling a curious wistfulness, Vivien said, "I'm sure your mama is one of the most beautiful stars of all."

"Really?" Amy asked, her voice hushed with awe. "Which one do you s'pose she is?"

"I believe you could find her more easily than I. Look for one that twinkles at you."

With an expression of rapt concentration, Amy peered up at the sky, her fine features washed in a pale white glow. A sleepy bird twittered in a tree nearby, then fell silent. "That one," she said finally, pointing with the indomitable confidence of a child. "The big one right over Papa's house."

"Yes, I do believe you're right," Vivien said, gazing up at a star that glowed brightly. "So you see, my little dove, you're never alone. If ever you miss her, you can look up into the night sky and she'll be watching over you."

The girl made a happy sound and nestled closer to Vivien, her eyelids drooping a little. "Tell me a story now," she said, wriggling against Vivien. "Please, Miss Vivi."

"Lie still, then," Vivien said, "and I'll tell you about the boy who thought he could catch a star."

Lowering her voice to a soothing murmur, she began the old Gypsy tale, relating how the boy wanted to present his poor widowed mother with a star so that her every wish would come true. He built a long, long ladder and set it upon the top of the highest mountain in the world, climbing and climbing, up and up, but all he could reach was a handful of stardust. His feet dragging, he returned home dejected, only to be greeted with hugs and kisses by his frantic mother, who declared that his safe return was the greatest gift of all. And her tears turned the stardust into diamonds so that she and the little boy became rich and lived happily ever after . . .

Vivien looked down to see Amy draped against her with her eyes closed, her thumb in her mouth, the rag doll tucked beneath her chin. Her breathing flowed soft and even. In the white gown, she might have been a tiny angel come to earth.

She sighed in her sleep, and Vivien felt a rush of affection so intense it was disturbing. How could she love the child of an arrogant English lord? How could she feel any contentment here among the *gorgios*?

All her life, she had encountered their mistrust. She'd seen mothers pull their children away whenever the wagons of the *Rom* passed by. She'd been shunned by ladies in the street and spat upon by shopkeepers. Worst of all had been the ghastly day when a mantrap on the Duke of Covington's estate had crippled her father. Vivien had found him herself, moaning in agony, the jagged teeth of the trap clamped around his leg . . .

Shuddering, she hugged Amy closer, breathing in her sweet scent and willing the nausea to recede. That horrible event had naught to do with the little girl in her arms. Nor with Lady Stokeford or the servants or the tenants she'd met. With a lurch, Vivien realized that her hatred toward the *gorgios* had mellowed. She had found many things to like here—the books and the learning, the companionship of the Rosebuds, the comforts of hot baths and delicious food. To her shame, she'd even enjoyed sparring with Michael. He made her feel alive in a way she'd never before known.

A fire in the heart.

No, she denied fiercely. He was the first man to awaken her womanly needs, that was all. Though her blood was *gorgio,* her heart belonged to the *Rom.* In a little over a month, she would leave here forever. She would take her two hundred guineas and return to the wandering life she'd always known. The life she loved.

Shutting her eyes, she could almost see the campfires glowing, smell the smoke upon the wind, hear the hoot of an owl through the darkness. She and her parents would eat a simple meal seasoned by laughter and talk. Then she would make a bed for the night beneath a canopy of stars. She'd hear her parents whisper as they, too, settled down for the night. And she would know that she'd done her best for them.

A pleasant weariness washed over Vivien. Though the night air was chilly, the eiderdown enclosed them in a snug nest. She knew she must carry Amy back to her bedchamber, but not yet. Michael would be furious if he learned his daughter was here. Vivien couldn't sanction his strictness, though she could see by his devotion to the child that he loved her.

Why *did* he guard his daughter so jealously? Drowsy, she couldn't make sense of the matter. She could only envy him having the gift of this precious little girl, and indulge her own jealous desire to claim Amy for herself, if only for a few moments.

Just a few moments . . .

Chapter thirteen

An Uneasy Truce

Michael knew he'd gone mad. Like some idiot Romeo, he fought his way up the trellis beneath Vivien's upper-floor chamber. He hadn't climbed a wall since he was ten—and certainly never in pursuit of a woman.

A short while ago, he'd been drinking a fine bottle of port without tasting it, pacing the library in the Abbey, unable to rid himself of an innate restlessness. His tenants, his grandmother, his daughter . . . all these worries had nagged at him. Aside from that, he knew he'd wronged Vivien. He had accused the Gypsy of a crime perpetrated by Thaddeus Tremain.

Michael had gnawed that bitter truth until finally, hoping to clear his head, he'd gone for a walk in the cold night air. His wayward steps had carried him across the bridge and to the Dower House, where he'd spied the gleam of white on Vivien's balcony.

For an instant, he'd stood blinking his bleary eyes in disbelief, certain he was fantasizing. Sitting there on the balcony, swathed in a blanket and quiet with slumber, was Vivien.

Now, halfway up the wall, he cursed the lunatic impulse that had sent him on this Byronic mission. His shoes groped for toeholds in the rough stone. His fingers grasped the thick stalks of ivy that had thrived there for untold generations. His teeth anchored the stem of a hastily plucked rose.

He grimaced. Romantic tales seldom mentioned that roses had thorns, that the stem tasted nasty, or that the pollen prickled one's nose.

But if Vivien wanted to be courted, then by God, he'd court her. He'd succeed at that goal at least. He would seduce the Gypsy and be rid of her, once and for all.

Lascivious thoughts lured him upward. Was she naked beneath those blankets? She would be soft and warm with sleep, all her insolence and resistance gone. She would arch toward him, sinuous as a cat eager for a petting. He would touch her . . . all of her . . . and this time, she would wrap herself around him while he kissed her and caressed her—

His foot slipped and Michael cursed, his fingers tensing around the ivy. Out of the corner of his eye, he could see the ground far below, but he clamped down harder on the rose and looked up instead. To his relief, the balcony nearly brushed his head. He stretched up one arm and grasped a stone post, then raised his other hand to do likewise. With a mighty heave, he hoisted himself up and over the railing, his feet landing with a scuffling noise on the narrow escarpment.

Vivien's head shot up. Her eyes flew open. She gasped.

He started to speak, remembered the rose, and gingerly removed it from his teeth. Turning his head, he spat out a leaf. So much for romance. "Don't be frightened," he murmured. " 'Tis I, Michael."

"I know who you are," she whispered indignantly, scooting back further into the shadows. "But I didn't invite you into my bedchamber."

"I haven't been in your chamber. I came up the wall."

"The wall?"

"Yes. I climbed the ivy so that I might catch a glimpse of your breathtaking beauty." He paused a moment, and when she didn't respond, he added curtly, "This is where you compliment me on my prowess and strength."

"Why should I?" she hissed. "You manage to strut aplenty all by yourself."

Unable to discern if she wore a nightdress, or if all that pale fabric was the blanket, he stepped closer. "But I don't wish to be all by myself, darling. That's why I'm here."

Vivien snuggled down further into the oversized coverlet. "Go away."

She wasn't making this easy, but when had she ever behaved like his other women? "You can't mean that," he crooned in his most charming voice. "Look what I've brought you." Hunkering down beside her, he held out the rose. "A beauty for a beauty."

She stared, and he thought her eyes softened a bit, though she sat too deep in darkness for him to be certain. Then she shook her head, her loose, dark hair drifting around her shoulders. "We of the *Rom* do not believe in plucking flowers," she whispered as if afraid for anyone else to hear. "They belong in nature, where they might grow and thrive."

"Then nature should worship a goddess like you."

Determined not to be thwarted, Michael leaned forward slightly, brushing the velvety petals across her cheek. He saw her shiver, saw her eyelids droop with unmistakable sensual enjoyment. A breathy little sigh escaped her lips. Triumphant, he knew he'd caught her at a moment when she was vulnerable to his touch.

Before she could don her armor, he brought his mouth to her face, kissing her temple and her cheek. Aroused by her sleep-warm scent, he traced the whorls of her ear with his tongue. She trembled again, making a halfhearted attempt to turn her head away. "Michael, don't . . ."

"I want you, Vivien. I need you so." Inching closer, he continued his seduction, hot for the feel of her naked skin. He drew back the coverlet, anticipating the heaviness of her breast in his palm—

Through the darkness, he spied a small form cuddled against her.

His blood cooled instantly. He jerked his hand back, staring in momentary befuddlement at Vivien. Then he pushed the coverlet farther down to see the faint shape of a child nestled in the crook of Vivien's arm.

"Amy?"

"Hush," Vivien whispered, tenderly rearranging the covers around his daughter. "You'll waken her."

A sour taste in his mouth, Michael sat back on his heels and ripped the petals, one by one, off the rose. He couldn't shake a sense of sordidness. In another moment, he'd have groped Vivien and encountered his daughter instead.

"Bloody *hell.*" He kept his voice down, though vehemence edged his words. "You should have told me she was with you."

"You hardly gave me a chance."

"You could have spoken up at any time."

"You could have ceased distracting me."

He crushed a petal between his fingers. In a tersely silken tone, he said, "So I distracted you, did I? That means you like for me to touch you."

She blew out a breath. "You have a way with women, m'lord. And I *am* a woman."

"So I've noticed," Michael said with great irony. He peered through the gloom, but he could discern only the pale oval of her face and not her expression. "Why the devil are you out here, anyway? More to the point, why is my daughter not in her bed?"

"She had a frightening dream, and she wanted someone to hold her."

That twisted his gut. He should have been the one Amy had run to, not this Gypsy. *His* daughter belonged in *his* home. "Where is Miss Mortimer?"

"Sleeping soundly. Amy asked me to tell her a story."

He sent the denuded stem sailing over the railing. "It isn't good for her to sleep out here in the damp chill. She'll catch a lung fever."

"On the contrary, the night air will invigorate her." Vivien raised her chin. "You forget, I've slept outside almost every night of my life."

Of course, you're a vagrant. Just as quickly, he was ashamed of himself. She had comforted his daughter, however unorthodox her methods, and he owed her his gratitude for that.

"Amy can't stay out here all night," he muttered. "I'll carry her back to bed."

On his knees, he pulled back the covers and slid his hands beneath his daughter. His fingers inadvertently brushed Vivien's nightgown, and for a flash he was aware of her breasts, heavy and unbound beneath the thin cloth.

Banishing her from his thoughts, Michael concentrated on his daughter, carefully settling her small, sleep-warmed body against him. She mumbled a protest, and he had to smile. How sweet she was, how innocent. The faint starlight touched her button nose and tumbled curls, and as always, he felt a fierce thankfulness that she belonged to him. Amy was the one blessing in his life, and he would allow no one to take her from him.

Rising to his feet, he glanced down at Vivien. She scooted to her knees, then turned to gather up the eiderdown. As she stood up, clutching it like a downy cloud to her bosom, he said, "Show me the way."

He already knew the location of his daughter's chambers, of course. But he meant to keep the Gypsy with him.

Vivien led him into her dimly lit bedchamber, where she laid the coverlet on the bed. At the bedside table, she picked up the guttering candle that sat beside a pile of books. Conscious of his precious bundle, Michael kept his gaze firmly averted from the wide four-poster with its pale yellow hangings.

It wasn't so easy to keep his gaze averted from Vivien. She glided ahead of him out into the corridor, a tall, slender wraith carrying the candle held high to light their path. Her long dark hair danced with the sway of her hips. Her feet were bare, of course; she seemed to dislike the restriction of shoes. He had to admit he preferred her brazen immodesty. No unwed lady would allow a man to view her in her nightclothes, yet Vivien walked proudly, without a care for propriety.

At the end of the passageway, she opened a door and stepped aside to let him in. The glow of her candle guided him to Amy's bed, a diminutive four-poster trimmed in lace and ruffles that he knew his grandmother had kept prepared for the visits that had never come to pass. Until now.

From a trundle on the other side of the bed, the rise and fall of snoring emanated from Miss Mortimer. The sound continued unabated as he settled Amy beneath the rumpled sheets and drew the pink coverlet up to her chin. She wriggled into a comfortable position, but didn't open her eyes. With a tiny sigh, she curled up on her side, her favorite rag doll nestled to her cheek.

As he tucked her in, Michael felt an unmanly rush of love. He kept his face averted, for the meager light of the candle told him Vivien stood close to him. Too close. He didn't want her to witness any private softness in him.

"Wait by the door," he muttered.

She didn't move. He glanced up to see her watching

him, her eyes tender in the candlelight. "You truly do love her."

Tightening his mouth, he said nothing.

But Vivien didn't seem to expect an answer. Brushing past him, she bent down to place a gentle kiss on his daughter's brow. In a hushed tone, she said, "Good night, little dove."

Amy stirred, smiling, her eyelids fluttering. " 'Night, Miss Vivi," she mumbled, then promptly fell deep into slumber again.

A whipcord tension strangled his chest. Vivien had no right to assume a mother's role. Amy needed only her father. She needed *him*.

Seizing Vivien's arm, he marched her out the doorway and into the gloomy corridor. He shut the door with a quiet click. Keeping his voice down, he stated, "It isn't necessary for you to coddle Amy."

"Coddle?" Her black brows arching in a scowl, Vivien held up the candle to regard him. "She's a little girl who needs to be loved."

"Quite so. And since you'll only be transient in her life, I'd prefer that you not solicit her affections. Else she'll be hurt when you leave."

"When *you* leave. It's *you* who insists upon taking her away from her great-grandmother. For reasons you continue to hide."

Curse her! With effort, he controlled his rage. He wouldn't let her draw him into a quarrel where he might let something slip. Deliberately mellowing his voice to a seductive murmur, he said, "Let's call a truce. I didn't mean to lash out at you. I've been troubled by something else."

"A guilty conscience, no doubt."

She was right, damn it. How he loathed admitting the truth. "I owe you an apology. I found out today that Thaddeus Tremain stole those things from my house." He proceeded to tell her about the account books, the stash of gold and valuables, all the wily ways in which the steward had squeezed money from the tenants.

"Send *him* to Australia," she said murderously. "He belongs there. No one should take advantage of people who can't defend themselves."

"For once, we're in complete agreement."

Her fierce expression gentled, and she regarded him with approval. Her eyes glowed like dark velvet in the candlelight. "I'm glad of that, Michael. I'm surprised to say . . ."

He glanced at her pouty, kissable lips, and said hoarsely, "Go on."

"You appear to be a cold man. But sometimes . . . I sense that you really do have a heart."

Her observation made him uneasy. He should exploit the softness he saw on her beautiful face. Yet he hesitated, aware of how young and guileless she appeared to be. She was far from innocent, he reminded himself. He must never forget that she'd forged that letter from Harriet Althorpe, pretending a connection so his grandmother would take her in. He must never forget she'd talked Grandmama into paying her a hundred guineas a month. She was a Gypsy, raised by swindlers and thieves.

"Come, there's another matter we need to discuss." Grasping her arm, Michael guided Vivien down the corridor to her chamber. She cast him sidelong glances, suspicious looks tinged with the curiosity he wanted to stir in her. Let her wonder what he intended; it would atone for all the times that he had faced the frustration of guessing *her* thoughts.

"If you think to keep me from getting to know Amy," she said as they reached her door, "I warn you, I won't be threatened."

He affected a casual laugh. "You misunderstand me. I'd merely like to see you in private."

Pushing open the door, he started to steer her into the bedchamber, but she dug in her heels. "Whatever it is," she whispered, "you can say it right here."

Out of the corner of his eye, he could see the bed cloaked in shadows, a bed big enough for two. "I'd rather we were alone," he said silkily. "My grandmother's chamber is only two doors down."

"She's asleep. Which means you oughtn't even be here."

"I want to be here," he said in a cajoling murmur. "I want to be with you, Vivien. And therein lies my dilemma. I can't stay away from you." Without touching her, he inched closer, and her faint musky fragrance heated his blood. "You haunt me, Vivien. When I sleep, I dream of you. When I awaken, I think of you and only you. You're fast becoming an obsession with me." That was no romantic embellishment, he knew to his chagrin.

"Don't say such things to me. I don't want to hear them." But she made no attempt to move away; she merely leaned back against the doorjamb, her breasts rising and falling, the candle held out to her side.

"I'll tell you anyway," he said. "Tonight I couldn't keep my mind from you. I was pacing my library, unable to govern my own thoughts, before I decided to take a walk—"

"You were drinking, too."

"Yes, but I'd sooner get drunk on you, darling." His gaze on her lips, he bent nearer, his fingers giving in to the temptation to touch the velvety skin of her throat. He wanted to taste her all over, to strip off that damned nightdress and feast himself on her beauty.

She turned her head to the side. "Don't."

"Afraid of a kiss?"

When Vivien looked at him again, he could swear there was coyness in her glance. "Yes, I am. Because that isn't all you want from me, is it, m'lord marquess?"

"Until you ask for more, I'll touch you only with my lips." Seizing his chance, he brushed his mouth over hers.

She drew in a breath, yet she didn't turn away. With a soft exhalation, she let him kiss her tenderly, sensually, a kiss unlike the practiced ones he gave to his mistresses, who were less clever women than Vivien Thorne and easier to please. He made his kiss all honey and delicacy, a feathery lightness that aroused him to hard, aching lust.

Yearning to caress her all over, Michael dug his fingers into the wooden doorjamb above her. It was torture, but he would court her slowly and deliberately until she lowered her guard. He savored the pliancy of her lips, the minty taste of her mouth, the throaty little sounds she tried to hold back, but couldn't. She wanted him, he knew with triumph. He would ensure that she succumbed to temptation.

Redoubling his effort, he turned the kiss into a work of art, his tongue making brushstrokes on the canvas of her mouth. They stood so close he could feel her radiant warmth with every muscle and every fiber in him. It was an odd experience not to indulge himself, to take what he wanted, when he wanted. He burned to caress Vivien, yet he must show her he was in control; he must use only his mouth to make her melt with desire. If it took him half the night, he would hear her beg him to bed her . . .

Her lips left his. One moment he was sipping the nectar of her mouth, and the next, she ducked beneath his arm, leaving behind only a whiff of her womanly fragrance.

His eyes opened, his arms fell, and his brow lowered into a scowl. She swooped into her chamber, the white gown swishing around her bare feet. As she spun around, her dark eyes met his. They were knowing eyes that saw his physical discomfort. "That was quite pleasant, m'lord. Good night."

Pleasant? "Don't shut me out. We aren't through—"

"Yes, we are."

Even as Michael took a step toward her, the door closed in his face and the key rattled in the lock. Leaving him alone with his frustrated passion.

Chapter fourteen

The Duchess of Covington

"Tonight will be your triumph," Lady Stokeford declared, flitting around Vivien and straightening a seam here and a hairpin there. "You'll enchant everyone."

Standing by the long mirror, Lady Enid nodded vigorously, the egret feather on her green turban bobbing. "As one of Lord Stokeford's guests, you're sure to be accepted as a member of the *ton*."

Lady Faversham sat primly upright on a nearby chair, her fingers gripping the ivory knob of her cane. "I cannot say I've always approved of your schemes, Lucy, but it was sheer brilliance to move back into Stokeford Abbey and bring Vivien with you."

"I could hardly allow Michael to keep me from my only great-granddaughter, could I?" Lady Stokeford dabbed a faintly musky perfume behind Vivien's ears, then handed the crystal phial to a waiting maid. "Besides, it will suit our plans perfectly to have Vivien right here, too."

As the Rosebuds fussed over her, Vivien stood in front of the tall, gilt-framed mirror and listened to their chatter with only half an ear. The glass reflected the vastness of her new bedchamber, its magnificence lit by the soft glow of candles. That very morning, a covey of servants had transported the contents of her wardrobe to the huge dressing room, right down to the last silk stocking and confining corset. She had protested the move, of course, uneasy with the notion of living under Michael's roof, but Lady Stokeford had been adamant. Wherever Amy went, she said, there, too, they would go.

In the end, the desire to stay close to the little girl had persuaded Vivien. She had told Amy a bedtime story just an hour ago in the nursery, kissing her good-night before a maidservant had guided Vivien back here.

If she'd believed her room at the Dower House to be grand, this one struck her speechless with awe. The high ceiling had been painted like a blue sky with naked nymphs cavorting with coy goddesses among the clouds. Pale blue hangings draped a canopied bed large enough to accommodate an entire family of the *Rom*. In addition to the chaises and chairs—far too many for one person—there were tables decorated with porcelain vases and a dainty desk containing a plentiful supply of embossed cream paper and assorted quill pens. Not that she'd had time to record any stories of late.

The past week had flown by, a happy interlude with Amy . . . and Michael. Ever since that tender kiss outside her bedroom at the Dower House, when she had been tempted to melt in his arms and let him do with her as he willed, they had played a dangerous, exhilarating game of chase. He'd continued his relentless pursuit, and she had only just managed to avoid being caught alone with him again. He'd showered her with gifts, too: pens and pots of ink, a collection of leather-bound books, even an exquisite little bird made of crystal that sparkled in the sunlight.

Lady Stokeford had assured her it was perfectly proper

to accept a gentleman's offerings. Vivien wanted to keep them, for she had never owned such splendid things in all her life. She treasured each item, saving even the pretty paper wrappings, carefully folded in the drawer of her bedside table. The gifts belonged to her, though she felt a certain dismay at the intensity of her greed. Was she becoming like the *gorgios,* coveting material possessions?

No. She didn't feel an attachment to the fine gowns Lady Stokeford had bestowed on her. Oh, the silks and muslins felt deliciously soft to her skin, yet she would leave them behind without a qualm when she returned to the *Rom.* She liked having a steaming pot of tea delivered to her in bed each morning by a smiling maidservant, and she had been spoiled by the rich meals prepared by Monsieur Gaston. But those comforts were not what she treasured the most.

She loved the simple joys of life: walks in the woods, the warmth of the sun on her face, the burble of the river as it flowed beneath the stone bridge. She delighted in introducing Amy to the wonders of nature, smiling at her excitement when she found a shiny rock on the pathway or spied a trout swimming downstream.

When she watched Michael and Amy together, laughing and playing, her emotions twisted into an aching knot. At such times, she could almost forget that her father had been lamed by a *gorgio* trap, or that Michael had almost seduced her in the temple on a stormy afternoon.

With Amy, at least, he showed a tenderness at odds with his usual ruthless charm. Vivien wondered if, after the death of his beloved wife, he could ever again regard a woman with affection. She sensed a fire in him, but it had long since died to cold ashes. Or were there embers that could be stirred to life again? And why did she feel compelled to find out?

"Don't look so anxious, my dear. You'll be the loveliest girl at tonight's fête."

Vivien blinked at Lady Stokeford's kind face with its tracery of fine lines. On a rush of fondness, she hugged the dowager, inhaling her lavender scent. "My lady, I'm glad to meet your friends and neighbors."

A smile bloomed on that dainty, aged face. "The pleasure will be mine when they see how charming you are. After all, you've been practicing this past fortnight on my grandson."

"To excellent success," Lady Enid added with a knowing smile. "Why, judging by his attentiveness toward you, Stokeford regards you as a true lady, worthy of a gentleman's courtship."

Vivien compressed her lips lest she blurt out that Michael only wanted to seduce her. Lust wasn't the reaction the Rosebuds wanted her to inspire in men. They intended for her to choose a husband from their *gorgio* world. They had fussed over her for hours, instructing the maid on how to curl her hair, deciding which scent to put in her bathwater, even discussing in minute detail which undergarments she ought to wear.

Vivien hadn't had the heart to spoil their fun. They needn't know she was counting the days—twenty-one exactly—until she could leave the *gorgios* forever and return to her parents.

Still, a confusing welter of excitement and apprehension clutched at her breast. Her palms felt icy inside her kid gloves. If truth be admitted, she was more nervous about seeing Michael in his glittering world than facing a roomful of snooty, aristocratic strangers. Would he find her pretty?

His opinion didn't matter, she told herself. Michael Kenyon was a prideful lord with too much confidence in his own superiority. Nevertheless, she studied her reflection in the mirror, smoothing the simple white muslin with its modest neckline and cap sleeves. She felt half-naked without the gold bracelets that usually decorated her arms.

"Don't I look too plain?" she asked. "Couldn't I wear my bangles?"

"Rest assured, you're lovely just as you are," Lady Stokeford said comfortingly. "You're the perfect débutante."

"White is the color of purity," Lady Faversham said. "It's suitable for innocent girls."

"Oh, my, you do look splendid," Lady Enid added, her hands clasped to her enormous green bodice. Then she nudged Lady Faversham. "Though 'tis a shame you hid the rouge pot, Olivia."

Leaning on her cane, Lady Faversham rose to her feet, tall and formidable in gray silk. "Vivien is far too young to wear rouge," she said in a severe tone. "There will be no more mention of it."

"She's exactly the age we once were," Lady Stokeford said, her blue eyes dancing with glee. "But of course, we bow to your wisdom."

She winked at the other Rosebuds, and they shared an intensely private glance, Lady Enid snickering behind her plump hand and even the dour Lady Faversham allowing a brief smile.

Puzzled by their secret jest, Vivien stated, "I've no wish for cosmetics. The *Rom* do not use such false enhancements."

Lady Faversham thumped her cane. "Here, now. You mustn't speak of those *Romany* tonight. It's bad form."

Vivien bristled, and for once she couldn't hold her tongue. "I'm not ashamed of my past," she said, her voice choking with emotion. "Nor of my mother and my father who raised me well. If you expect me to deny them, know that I will not."

"Of course you mustn't, my dear." Lady Stokeford shot

the countess a warning glance. "Olivia only means it would serve no purpose to *invite* the disdain of small-minded people."

"I shan't tell lies, either," Vivien said recklessly. "If anyone asks me a question, I shall reply honestly."

"Yet I'm certain you're clever enough to turn the conversation to other topics," Lady Enid said.

"Vivien can manage any circumstance. She's a diamond of the first water." The dowager slipped her birdlike hand into the nest of Vivien's arm. "Come, we mustn't keep your future admirers waiting."

Vivian took one last look in the mirror. What would her *dado* and *dye* think of her all dressed up in fancy clothing? Where were they now? Did they miss her as much as she missed them?

Subduing her melancholy, she drew a deep breath for courage. The time had come. She must enter the exclusive society of the *gorgios*. She must do her best to earn that two hundred gold guineas.

As they left her new chambers, Vivien looked around her with interest. An extravagance of candles flickered in the wall sconces, and other guests strolled ahead of them. She marveled at the rich oak paneling and the plush carpeting, the labyrinth of corridors and staircases and rooms. One hundred twenty chambers, Michael had told her. It was disturbing to think that one man laid claim to so much splendor.

They reached the grand staircase that curved downward to the vast foyer with its archways of chiseled stone. The lofty ceiling and intricate carvings of the Abbey always inspired a sense of awe in her, as if she were entering a church. Tonight, the place had the merry atmosphere of a celebration.

In the foyer below, enormous pots of colorful roses bloomed on every table. The crystal chandelier blazed with candles, casting a glittering light over the guests who milled and conversed. Crimson-liveried footmen stood at attention by the massive front door.

The magical sense of being a princess in a fairy tale swept over Vivien. She felt a traitorous longing to absorb every fantastical sight and sound. Her heart soared like the voices rising to the high ceiling, and the distant lilt of music called to her wild spirit. Dancing was a tradition among the women of the *Rom,* a dance of a far more unrestrained type than the sedate steps she'd learned from the Rosebuds.

"Oh, I do adore parties," Lady Enid said, a smile dimpling her cheeks. "I vow, my heart is all aflutter."

"Wouldn't Harriet Althorpe be proud?" Lady Stokeford whispered, her small fingers touching Vivien's arm. "Indeed, I'm giddy at the prospect of achieving our plan at last."

"Do have a care lest you both swoon," Lady Faversham returned dryly. "You wouldn't wish to spoil Vivien's grand entrance."

Then they were gliding down the wide marble staircase, and Vivien had to concentrate lest she stumble in her dainty *gorgio* slippers. Clinging to the wrought-iron railing, she saw gentlemen resplendent in formal suits and ladies in every color from primrose to moss. As they conversed in small, intimate groups, she gawked at them in fascination.

Then, when she was halfway down, everyone turned to gawk at *her.*

The din of conversation diminished to a low buzz. Gentlemen stared up with bold interest in their eyes. Ladies whispered behind their fans. She was a curiosity to them, she knew. An upstart Gypsy who dared to enter their exalted world.

Vivien held her head high. She wouldn't let their bigotry ruin her fun. Instead, she scanned the throng for Michael's dark hair and tall form.

"He's over there," Lady Stokeford murmured in her ear as they reached the bottom step. "In the doorway to the drawing room."

Vivien couldn't stop a blush. "Who?"

The white-haired dowager cast her a shrewd glance. "My grandson, of course. Just look at him. Isn't he the most magnificent man you've ever seen?"

Vivien turned her gaze toward the drawing room, and the impact of his masculine beauty struck her senses. He was resplendent in a pewter waistcoat with silver buttons, a charcoal-gray coat and breeches, and a snowy cravat at his throat. As he spoke with several guests, his handsome smile made her feel flushed with warmth. But it was more than fine garb that made him stand out like a king among his subjects. Michael had . . . allure. She could feel it pulling at her, drawing her like a magnet.

"Who is she?" Lady Faversham asked.

"Why, it's Lady Katherine Westbrook," Lady Enid said, peering through her quizzing glass.

"His mistress," Lady Stokeford hissed sharply. "How dare he bring her here."

Stunned, Vivien stared at the lady clinging to Michael's arm. The dainty blonde wore a gown of rose silk with a neckline that revealed too much of her bosom. Smiling up at him, she stroked her fingers over his sleeve as if to tell everyone present that he belonged to her.

He had a mistress. She oughtn't be shocked, for she'd known he was a rogue, that he engaged in all manner of wickedness in London. Nonetheless, a queasy fury coiled in her belly like a snake waiting to strike.

"Oh, my stars!" Lady Enid rattled on. "I'll never forget the scandalbroth! A decade ago, Katherine wed Baron Gibbons when he was ninety-two years of age, and she but eighteen. He died six months later, leaving her a wealthy widow. Since then, she's been"—she glanced at Vivien—"a favorite of the gentlemen."

Lady Stokeford tightened her mouth. "The brazen baggage was not on my guest list."

"Perhaps your grandson invited her," Lady Faversham said in a voice heavy with disapproval.

The dowager arched a thin white brow. "Hmph. We shall see about that." Then she sailed off toward him.

Burning with anger, Vivien hastened after the marchioness. The wretch shouldn't be allowed to flaunt his women. He would spoil the evening that his grandmother had planned for weeks.

A number of guests glanced curiously at her as she brushed past them. "The Gypsy," one of them hissed, loud enough for her to hear.

She flashed the evil eye at a pair of gossipy grandes dames, who promptly hushed. She had no tolerance for their prattling prejudice. Nor for arrogant lords who paraded their sins. She cared only for Lady Stokeford.

Vivien caught up to her just as a burst of laughter eddied from the marquess's group. Lady Stokeford modified her swift pace to a stroll, shaped her mouth into a smile, and joined the gathering.

"Good evening," she said. "I trust my grandson is behaving himself?"

The gentlemen bowed to her. "Quite so, my lady," said a dandified man dressed entirely in green with huge gold buttons on his waistcoat. "He is a model of manners."

"Indeed," added a thin man with a mop of luxurious brown curls, lifting his wineglass in a salute. "Stokeford's an impeccable host."

Michael grinned. "You two would have your heads knocked together if you said otherwise."

Graceful as a serpent, Lady Katherine sank into a

curtsy, the candlelight shining on the delicate curve of her neck. "If I may be so bold as to say so, my lady, Michael is always the perfect gentleman."

She was even more beautiful up close, Vivien thought, aware of a smothering pressure in her breast. Small and fragile, the golden-haired woman exuded an aura of inbred hauteur. Her diamond-and-ruby necklace sparkled in the candlelight, and a diamond ring winked on her finger. She looked exactly like Michael's type of woman: sophisticated, polished, worldly.

The intimacy Vivien sensed between them made her feel like an intruder. She felt a wild wrath to imagine Michael lying with this woman, his body hard and masculine, his mouth kissing hers. She curled her fingers to stop an appalling urge to shove Lady Katherine into the nearest gutter.

Then, with a lurch of surprise, Vivien saw that he was watching *her.* His blue eyes hooded, he scanned her plain white gown as if comparing her to his beauteous mistress. Vivien wanted to spit at the two of them. Unwilling to risk her position with Lady Stokeford, she curtsied, all the while returning his stare, challenging him to find her lacking.

With languid elegance, Michael said, "Grandmama, Miss Thorne, this is Lady Katherine Westbrook."

The blonde cast a cool, dismissing look at Vivien; then her expression warmed as she turned to the dowager. "It's a pleasure to meet you, my lady. I do hope you don't mind my intrusion. My cousin invited me to attend her."

Lady Stokeford smiled politely, though her blue eyes were like chips of ice. "Your cousin?"

"Yes, my lady. Hillary, the Duchess of Covington."

The room seemed to tilt and sway. A frigid wind slapped Vivien, chilling her to the marrow. Covington.

That name represented to her all the cruelties and injustices of the *gorgios.*

The previous year, while crossing the Duke of Covington's estate, her father had stepped into the sharp maw of a mantrap.

Chapter fifteen

Hidden Scars

"Ah, Hillary," Lady Stokeford said, her smile altering subtly with a certain calculation. "The premier hostess of the *ton*."

"She was speaking to Lord Effingham in the drawing room." Lady Katherine inclined her fair head toward the doorway. "There she is now."

A rather stout young woman with a headful of elaborate brown curls made her way toward them. Clad in an evening gown of frilly lilac crêpe, she cradled a small, fat white dog in the crook of her arm. The duchess held her nose in the air, now and then nodding to someone as if she were a queen acknowledging a subject.

Viven's head throbbed painfully. She wanted to fly at the duchess in a rage, to condemn her with a savagery equal to the pain her father had suffered. Just in time, wisdom prevailed. Denouncing a duchess might cause her to lose her position here—and the promise of two hundred gold guineas.

Lady Stokeford dipped the required curtsy, but the duchess stopped her with an imperious wave of the hand. "My dear Lucy," she said in a patronizing tone. "You needn't show obeisance in your own home. Or rather, your grandson's home."

"You honor us with your presence, Your Grace," Lady Stokeford murmured. She stepped back to draw Vivien forward. "I'm delighted to introduce you to my very dear ward and companion, Miss Vivien Thorne."

Vivien's limbs felt wooden. She stood stiffly, her fingers crushing the soft folds of her skirt. Never had she expected to come face-to-face with the wife of the nobleman who had ordered that mantrap set—as if a *Romany* trespasser were no better than a wild animal.

Stroking the dog in her arms, the duchess haughtily looked Vivien up and down. "So you're the Gypsy girl."

"Her mother was governess to my grandsons for ten years," Lady Stokeford said smoothly. "Harriet Althorpe had impeccable bloodlines, the Althorpes of Yorkshire. The family has died out, so I'm sponsoring Vivien."

With a striking similarity to the dog's snout, Her Grace's lips curled into a grimace. "Speak up, miss. What have you to say for yourself?"

"Where's your husband?" Vivien blurted out, her voice dry and raspy. "Is he here?"

The duchess blinked. "No, he remained in London. Why do you inquire about him?"

Vivien couldn't trust herself to respond, so she said nothing.

Giving Vivien a baffled glance, Lady Stokeford said, "Do forgive her, Hillary, she's never seen a duke. La, this is such an exciting event for Vivien, taking her rightful place in society, meeting the most illustrious members of the *ton*. Now, you and Katherine must tell me all the latest gossip. I hear that Montcrieff has wed a coal merchant's daughter, Theodora Blatt."

As the three women launched into a discussion of the scandalous event, Vivien was relieved to have the attention directed away from herself. The remnants of shock had been thawed by the fire of rage. If the Duke of Covington had been present, she didn't know what she would have done. It was horrid enough to realize that for the coming week, she must live under the same roof with his duchess.

A hand touched her arm. She looked up to see Michael at her side, frowning at her. Testament to her agitated state, she'd forgotten his presence. "You're pale," he said in a low voice. "Are you ill?"

She felt ill to think that his mistress was cousin to the Duchess of Covington. "I'm fine."

He kept his fingers tucked into the bend of her arm, his flesh firm and warm on her bare skin. "No, you're not. A moment ago, you looked as if you'd seen a ghost."

"I'm overwhelmed by all the jewels here," she whispered. "It's a thief's paradise."

Predictably, Michael scowled. "Don't be a featherbrain. If so much as one gold ring goes missing, you'll be blamed."

"And you'll be first in line to point your finger at me," she retorted.

He had no time to reply, for Lady Katherine strolled to his side and whispered in his ear, her generous bosom pressing against his arm. Michael devoted his attention to her for a moment before bowing to his grandmother and the duchess. "If you'll excuse us, I promised to take Katherine on a tour of the house."

Lady Stokeford glared. "You shouldn't leave your guests."

"Nor should I ignore a promise."

As they walked away, he flashed a penetrating glance at Vivien, a look she didn't understand. Of course, the rogue would pursue easier game. Lady Katherine would go willingly to his bed. Those two deserved each other!

Vivien swallowed her bitterness like a dose of bad medicine. She wouldn't yearn for him. She would see Michael as the *gorgio* lord he was: amoral and arrogant.

Out of her reach.

The Duchess of Covington strolled away, too, no doubt to favor some other lucky soul with her snobbish presence.

"Thank goodness that hurdle is over," Lady Stokeford said under her breath. "As for my wayward grandson, you must make him jealous by charming the other gentlemen." Before Vivien could protest, the dowager introduced her to a crowd of men.

"Oh, rose among weeds, thy name is Thorne," proclaimed stout Sir George Rampling, the man clad in green, his brown eyes shining with fervor. "I'm struck dumb by your beauty."

"Then do hush," said Lord Alfred Yarborough, his beautiful curls bouncing as he sprang forward to kiss Vivien's hand. "You've flown to me straight out of a dream, Miss Thorne. Where have you been all my life?"

With effort, Vivien focused on her goal of pleasing Lady Stokeford. She must think of nothing else. Forcing a coquettish laugh, she withdrew her hand. "I've been here and there."

"Really?" Sir George drawled. "And where would 'here and there' be? Where do you call home?"

From the gleam in their watchful eyes, she knew they'd heard the rumors. "I call England my home. The greatest kingdom in the world."

Smiling, Lady Stokeford clapped her gloved hands. "A fine answer, my dear. You gentlemen should applaud her patriotism."

Hearty male cheers rose into the air. "Hear, hear!" Several other guests gathered around, drawn by the commotion.

Lord Alfred caught Vivien's gloved hand and reverently kissed the back. "You, Miss Thorne, are a true nonpareil. All the other débutantes of the season pale beside you. They are nothing but silly, tedious girls."

"Why, Alfred, I'm crushed," said a female voice from behind Vivien. "You spoke the same words to me last year."

A pretty girl with rich chestnut hair and leaf-green eyes sauntered into the group, her long-sleeved yellow gown swishing. A lively interest on her fine-boned features, she surveyed the gentlemen, smiling jauntily at Vivien.

"Ah, my godchild, how good to see you!" Lady Stokeford said, kissing the newcomer's cheek. "Please meet my ward and companion, Miss Vivien Thorne. Vivien, this is Enid's granddaughter, Lady Charlotte Quinton."

"I'm honored," Vivien said, spying a trace of Lady Enid in Charlotte's impish smile. "I do like your grandmama. She's very kind."

"The honor is mine," Charlotte said. "And the dishonor belongs to Lord Alfred if he cannot appease my outrage."

"My esteemed Lady Charlotte," Alfred said, bowing. "I wouldn't have said the same thing to you. I'm not so dull-witted as to repeat myself."

"Then you *don't* think me a nonpareil?" Charlotte asked with a sly wink at Vivien. "Am I no better than all those other silly, tedious girls?"

"Why, of course you're different," he blustered. "It's simply that . . . you are unique in your charms. As is Miss Thorne."

"Well, Vivien," she said. "Shall we be satisfied or not?"

Vivien liked her at once. "He ought to say which of us ranks first."

"A capital notion." Charlotte aimed a wicked stare at the young dandy. "Alfred, we await your decision."

A sheen of perspiration on his brow, Alfred fidgeted with the lace at his cuff. "I could never make such a choice," he said. "Why, it would be impossible to choose between two such radiant and ravishing roses—"

"If you cannot make up your mind," Charlotte said, "then there's no point to us remaining here. Do excuse us, Lady Stokeford."

The dowager smiled fondly at them. "Run along, my dears, and amuse yourselves. I must see to the dinner arrangements."

Leaving Lord Alfred with his mouth agape, Charlotte twined her arm with Vivien's, and they strolled away into the throng. "What a bore men can be," Charlotte said. "They must think us ninnies to believe their flattery."

Vivien smiled. "Men are the same everywhere, thinking themselves our superior. Yet though the cock may crow, the hen lays the eggs."

A peal of laughter came from Charlotte. "You *are* an original. I do believe we shall be fast friends. What do you say?"

Vivien had never had a *tésorthene,* a friend of the heart. Of late, she'd grown distant from the girls of the *Rom*, who cared only for doing domestic chores and attracting a husband. Yet in the space of a few moments, she felt a connection with Charlotte Quinton, perhaps because they were both linked to the Rosebuds. "I would like that," Vivien said.

"Then let's find a quiet place in which to become better acquainted."

Charlotte steered a path through the milling throng. Bypassing the formal drawing room where the musicians played, they headed down an unfamiliar corridor and ducked into a deserted chamber. Hushed and dim, the room had high arched windows and rows of pews facing an altar of heavy, carved oak, where thick candles flickered against the darkness.

Charlotte draped herself on a pew and leaned back. "Ah, peace," she said, her voice echoing. "I vow, this is one of my favorite rooms in the Abbey."

"The chapel," Vivien murmured, sinking down beside her and looking around in interest. "This must be where Michael's mother came to pray."

Charlotte grimaced. "Now there was a peculiar soul, the marchioness with her prayer books and psalms. However, my fondness for this chapel is rather secular. I like the pageantry of baptisms and marriages, the Easter and Christmas services." She sent Vivien an oddly piercing look. "Michael and Grace were wed here, you know. What a glorious celebration that was."

Vivien's heart beat faster, and she succumbed to a morbid curiosity. "Did you know Lady Grace? Was she pretty?"

"Like an angel. But then, Michael has always preferred dainty blondes. Did you notice how swiftly he went off with Katherine Westbrook?"

Aware of a hollow pain in her heart, Vivien struggled to keep a calm expression. "He intended to show her the house."

"In particular, the bedchambers." She turned a naughty grin on Vivien. "Do I shock you?"

"Yes," Vivien admitted. "I don't like the easy morals of English nobles. Girls must be chaste, yet men and older women take their pleasure as they choose."

"I quite agree. Oh, I do wish I'd been born male. Dom is allowed to travel all over the Continent—Rome, Athens, Paris." Charlotte thrust out a pouty lower lip. "While *I* languish at home with my four sisters and brothers who are still in the nursery."

Vivien sensed a deep-rooted bitterness in her. "Who's Dom?"

"My younger brother, Dominic. I'm three-and-twenty years and he's one-and-twenty, yet no one tells *him* he's in danger of being left on the shelf."

"What shelf?"

With a tinkling laugh, Charlotte cocked her head and studied Vivien. "It's an expression meaning 'old maid.' You *are* new to society, aren't you?"

"Very."

"Forgive my boldness, but is it true you were raised by the Gypsies?"

Vivien knew she should cleverly change the subject. But she disliked glossing over the truth. "I was given to the *Rom* as an infant, yes. *Miro dado* and *miro dye*"—she paused, her heart sore—"my father and mother are wonderful, kind people, and I miss them so very much."

"Who are your real parents?" Charlotte leaned forward, her green eyes intent and inquisitive. "Tell me, are you half sister to Michael Kenyon?"

Vivien gave a start of surprise. "Oh, no! No, most certainly *not*. I'm the daughter of a lady governess named Miss Harriet Althorpe. She once worked for Lady Stokeford."

"And your father? Who is he?"

"I don't know," Vivien said fiercely. "And I don't *want* to know. He tore me from my mother's arms, and I curse him for that."

"What drama you've experienced." Her lovely features taut with something like envy, Charlotte sat back, her slim arm draped over the back of the pew. "Life among the Gypsies sounds wild and different. Why ever would you give up all that freedom to live here in the confinement of the *ton*?"

Because otherwise, I'd have had to wed Janus for his

money. "We women of the *Rom* are no more free than *gorgio* ladies," she said cautiously.

"We? You speak as if you're still one of them. Will you return to the Gypsies one day soon?"

Vivien lifted her shoulders in a noncommittal shrug. "I would like to, yes. I miss the traveling, seeing new places, sleeping beneath the stars. Most of all, I yearn for my father and mother."

"But the Rosebuds want you to marry. They're giving you a dowry."

"Pardon?"

"Didn't you know? They're each contributing a thousand pounds for your marriage portion."

"A thousand . . . *three* thousand . . ." Stunned, Vivien tried to absorb the news. For a moment, she was torn between disbelief and eagerness, the thought of giving such riches to her parents. Then disgust filled her. Not even for a vast fortune would she wed a *gorgio*! "Michael will be furious."

Interest sharpened Charlotte's features. "Michael?"

"He believes me a thief already," Vivien said heatedly. "He thinks no one of the *Rom* is to be trusted."

"How devilish of him. Well, that would explain why he was staring so intently while you descended the stairs."

Vivien's mouth felt parched. Michael had been watching her?

Charlotte gazed at her with a faintly secretive tension. Then she changed the subject with mercurial ease. "Will you tell my fortune?"

Vivien knew Michael despised such deceptions. The devil take him. "If you wish. Show me your palm."

Charlotte slowly peeled off her glove, and Vivien scooted closer, considering what this carefree, impetuous girl wanted to hear. But as she reached out, she froze, staring down at Charlotte's hand. A mass of whitened scars covered her skin, twisting over her palm and fingers. The hideous, ridged flesh extended up her wrist and vanished inside her long sleeve.

"Oh, Charlotte," she whispered, raising sympathetic eyes to the girl's face. "What happened?"

Charlotte stared coolly back. "My right arm was burned in a fire when I was thirteen. Ugly, isn't it? Prospective suitors are especially horrified."

Vivien saw a bitter pain in her eyes. Though she sensed Charlotte would spurn pity, her heart went out to the girl. No wonder she'd never married. Men would be drawn to Charlotte's vivacious beauty, only to be repulsed by her scars.

But why had Charlotte shown her? Did she use her disfigurement to determine who were her true friends and who were not?

"Give me your other hand," Vivien said, deciding it was best to play her game rather than express compassion. "I'll read that palm, instead."

Charlotte regarded her with an understandable suspicion. Then, as she removed her other glove and extended a slim, flawless hand, a deep male voice echoed through the chapel.

"So here's the entertainment. May I be next in line for the Gypsy fortune-teller?"

Chapter sixteen

Vurma

Vivien swiveled around on the pew to see a tall, lanky stranger filling the arched stone doorway.

Gasping, Charlotte seized a glove and tugged it on over her scarred hand. "Brand! What are you doing here? I'm sure you weren't invited."

"I live to plague you, Char."

He sauntered into the chapel, a long-limbed man of about thirty who moved with an easy elegance that was almost canine. He had harsh features, thick dark hair, and the alert gray eyes of a wolf. A thin scar shaped like a half-moon quirked up one corner of his mouth.

"If Michael finds you here, he'll kill you." Charlotte's gaze raked him scornfully. "Though of course, that would be no great loss."

He chuckled. "I appreciate the warning," he said, sounding not in the least concerned. "Why don't you introduce me to your lovely friend?"

Charlotte hesitated, then pulled on her other glove. "Miss Vivien Thorne, lately of the *Romany* tribe. Vivien, this is Brandon Villiers, the dastardly Earl of Faversham."

The force of those penetrating eyes stirred an uneasy

feeling in Vivien. He was the grandson to whom Lady Faversham had written to give the news of Vivien's presence in Lady Stokeford's house. He'd promply told Michael.

Recalling her manners, Vivien rose from the pew and curtsied. "I'm pleased to meet you, my lord. Your grandmother has spoken of you."

He bowed sardonically. "Badly, I fear. She doesn't approve of my choice of companions."

What did that mean? Vivien wondered. "I'm certain she'll be happy to see you, though."

Charlotte remained seated, her arms crossed sulkily. "Don't fawn before him, Vivien. You'll only feed his conceit."

"Pay her no mind, Miss Thorne. She has an appalling lack of breeding." Lord Faversham paused as a hollow ringing sounded in the distance. "There's the dinner gong. Run along, Char, and find the unlucky fellow who's been assigned to you. I'll escort Miss Thorne."

Charlotte made a face at him, looking surprisingly childish for all her sophistication. "I'd sooner leave her with a cobra."

"The choice belongs to Miss Thorne." The earl strolled forward and held out his arm to Vivien. "Do you mind my company? I would consider yours an honor."

Though the scar made him appear sinister in the flickering shadows, he could not have acted in a more gentlemanly fashion. She did feel an intense curiosity to know all of the Rosebuds' grandchildren. Still, she paused, glancing in confusion at Charlotte. She could sense an attraction between her and Lord Faversham, though Charlotte appeared far from ready to admit to it. Had he ever recoiled from her scars? Surely not, for he was scarred himself.

"Why don't you walk with us?" Vivien suggested.

"With that devil?" Charlotte snorted. "You'd do well to come with *me*. Brand is a notorious rake. He wants to have his way with you."

The earl chuckled. "You're only jealous because I've never showed a depraved interest in you."

"Why, you self-admiring dolt. I'd sooner welcome the attentions of a . . . a sewer rat." The brunette sprang to her feet and flounced to the door, where she swiveled to make one parting comment. "Vivien, I'll see you later." With a twitch of her yellow skirts, Charlotte vanished out the chapel door.

The earl stood in the shadows, one eyebrow arched in covert amusement. "Don't mind her, Miss Thorne. I fear we've been at loggerheads ever since our youth. You see, Michael and I wouldn't allow her to tag along whenever we went rowing on the lake or spying on the neighbors."

With only a slight hesitation, Vivien took Lord Faversham's proferred arm. His muscles were strong and wiry beneath his smooth black coat. She might have pursued the topic of Charlotte's animosity toward him, but a greater interest burned in her. "You and Michael were once friends?"

The earl led her to the door and out into the passageway. "As children, yes. My boyhood home is some three miles from here."

"Did you see each other often?"

"Every day, rain or shine. Ah, we did have some escapades. Once, we smuggled a sack of frogs into the village church and freed them during service. Another time, we sneaked away and camped out for two nights before we were found by a search party."

"Your parents must have been frantic."

"Our parents were in London for the season. But the Rosebuds made certain we received our just rewards. Neither of us could sit down for a week."

"But what happened, then? Why would Michael shun you now?"

Lord Faversham chuckled, a faintly ominous sound that echoed down the deserted corridor. "We once quarreled over a woman. I carry a daily reminder of that." He stroked the curved scar beside his mouth.

Vivien shuddered. "He made that mark?"

"We fought a duel with swords. Alas, he was the first to draw blood." As they rounded a corner, the earl slowed his steps. "But enough about the past. I would rather learn my future by the fine art of palmistry."

She wanted to ask him more about the duel, most particularly, the name of the woman involved. But she could ascertain by his flinty expression that the subject was closed. "Michael has forbidden me to tell fortunes."

"Michael needn't know. Besides, when I walked into the chapel, you were reading Charlotte's palm."

"You interrupted us. I hadn't yet told her anything."

"Now don't put me off, Miss Thorne. I would like to know my destiny."

He drew her into an alcove near the stairs, where a lamp cast a soft glow over a pedestal bearing a bust of some long-dead Roman. After a momentary hesitation, she took the earl's hand in hers, its weight heavy and warm. Lord Faversham certainly didn't make her tremble and soften the way Michael did. She felt discomfited to stand so close that she could smell his spicy cologne. She sensed something dangerous in the earl, a recklessness she couldn't define.

Opening his hand wide, she ran a light fingertip over his thick skin. She could feel him watching her. Fortune-telling was pure artifice, she wanted to confess. Yet she could never divulge the secrets of the *Rom*.

"You've a long lifeline," she said, tracing its curving path around the base of his thumb. "I can see, too, that you have the ability to love deeply, although you've yet to find happiness in love. When you do marry, you'll enjoy a lifelong contentment." There, she wouldn't give him a prediction of wealth to be won at the gaming tables or any other selfish *gorgio* desire.

Faversham grunted, sounding half amused and half disbelieving. "Who is this woman who would leg-shackle me?"

"Leg-shackle?"

"Entrap me. End the carefree days of my bachelorhood." Edging closer, he watched her. "Could she be you, Miss Thorne?"

Revulsion twisted in her stomach. Collecting her wits, she gazed down at his palm again, slitting her eyes as if in great concentration. "No, she's someone you've known for a long time. Her name is . . . Charlotte Quinton."

He snorted. Quick as a blink, he turned his hand, seizing her fingers. "I do believe you're trying to bamboozle me."

His grip pained her, and she glimpsed a darkness in him that made her afraid. "Release me," she stated.

"Tell me something first," he said. "Are you the reason why Michael has stayed here for more than a fortnight?"

"He and his daughter are visiting his grandmother."

"Strange that he's so seldom brought little Amy here before now."

"He prefers to live in London. Now, I'd like to join the others for dinner."

He continued to gaze at her, his eyes narrowed, as if he were thinking, plotting, weighing some riddle. Abruptly he said, "Come along. It should prove interesting to see Michael's reaction when you arrive late. With me."

Vivien thought it would be interesting, too. She might enjoy the chance to rankle him, to show a fascination for another man.

Faversham loosened his hold, moving his hand to her upper arm as he guided her out of the alcove. It was on the tip of her tongue to ask why he'd come to the Abbey, and why he would purposely stir up trouble. Then she spied Michael striding toward them, followed a short distance behind by old Lady Faversham.

Vivien's heart lurched. A stark fury tightened Michael's face as he halted to block their path. His wintry blue gaze moved from her to the earl. "What the devil's going on here?"

"Michael," Faversham drawled. "It's good to see you, too. I presume Charlotte told you where to find us?"

Was that true? Vivien wondered. Had Charlotte been so worried about her? "His lordship was kind enough to escort me to the dining room," Vivien said quickly, hoping to diffuse the tension. "I'm lost in this enormous house."

Michael flicked her a scathing glance before returning his hard gaze to the earl. "Take your hand off her. Then get out."

Faversham maintained his hold on her arm. "Miss Thorne and I were just enjoying a little conversation. Surely you wouldn't imply that anything untoward happened between us."

"Miss Thorne is a guest in my house. You are not."

"That isn't very neighborly of you, old chap. Perhaps we should let the lady decide whether I stay or go."

They were like two dogs, growling and snapping. "Stop it, both of you," Vivien said sharply, trying to free herself. "I won't be a part of your quarrel."

Michael clenched his fists. "Release her, Brand. Now."

Before he could take more than one threatening step forward, Lady Faversham reached them. She swooped past Michael, raised her cane, and smacked her grandson hard on the shin. "Brandon Villiers, how dare you try to sully an innocent girl!"

"Damn—!" Lord Faversham bit off the curse and slackened his hold, bending down to rub his leg. "For pity's sake, Grandmama. I'm not ten years old anymore."

"Indeed?" she said, glaring down her nose at him. "Your actions leave much to be desired. At times I wonder where you learned your morals."

He straightened to his superior height. "There's no law against charming a lady. Ask Miss Thorne if I behaved badly."

Vivien shook her head. "We were merely talking, my lady. Until a few minutes ago, Lady Charlotte was with us."

"I should hope so." Lady Faversham turned her disapproving gaze on Vivien. "It was foolish of you to leave the party. Lucy has been frantic with worry."

Nothing else she could have said caused as much concern for Vivien. Catching up her skirt, she started past the others. "Then I must reassure her. If you'll excuse me."

As she rushed down the passageway, sharp footsteps sounded from behind, and Michael caught up to her, capturing her arm. His hard face might have been chiseled from stone. "You're not to wander around my house alone," he said in a harsh undertone. "I'll escort you to the dining chamber."

"I'd rather ask a servant for directions."

"No," he said firmly. "Tell me what Faversham wanted of you."

"Our conversation was private. It's rude to expect me to repeat it."

His fingers flexed around her arm. "If he made any carnal advance toward you, I demand to know of it."

"I already told you and Lady Faversham the truth. May your man parts shrivel for not believing me."

He continued to glower a moment; then he burst out laughing. "I can assure you, my man parts are quite the opposite of shriveled," he said, his voice easing into a smooth tone, rich as cream. "And no wonder. You're the most desirable woman I know."

Her heartbeat surged. She sidestepped his embrace, though the lingering feel of his hard masculine body disturbed her. "What of your mistress, Lady Katherine Westbrook?"

He grinned. "Jealous, are you?"

"I've no interest in becoming part of a . . . a love triangle."

"If you'd invite me to your chamber tonight, I'd forget all other women. I'd be yours alone."

Vivien hid her foolish longing behind a cool expression. "Cross my threshold, m'lord marquess, and I shall slit your throat."

"Such a fierce one you are." Michael looked amused by her threat. "Come, I'd rather you slice your meat than slit any throats."

The gabble of voices came from an arched doorway. As they entered an immense dining chamber, Vivien forgot her animosity in a rush of awe. Candlelight cast a soft glow over an immensely long table set with fine china and silver on snow-white linen. Guests talked and laughed in cultured tones, and footmen moved around, pouring wine into crystal glasses. The elegant scene looked like something out of a dream.

Michael started to guide her to an empty chair in between two middle-aged women, but Lady Stokeford swooped forward to intercept him. "There you are, my dear Vivien. I've saved you a place beside me."

She took hold of Vivien's arm, and they strolled toward the opposite end of the table. "My grandson can be so masterful at times," she murmured. "But I'm pleased to see you two are getting on better."

Vivien didn't want to disappoint her by revealing the truth, so she took advantage of the chance to bring up a more pressing issue. Bending close to Lady Stokeford, she whispered, "Charlotte told me about the dowry."

"Oh, that girl. She gossips just like Enid."

"One hundred guineas a month is quite sufficient," Vivien said firmly. "I won't accept any more."

"That's very admirable of you, my dear." With a benevolent smile, Lady Stokeford patted her hand. "But never fear, we're merely using the dowry as bait."

"Bait?"

"Why, to draw the men, of course." Her blue eyes lively, the old lady added in a low voice, "And if you don't want the dowry, the answer is simple. Marry a rich nobleman who has no need of it."

With that outrageous statement, Lady Stokeford guided Vivien to a chair at her right hand. The murmur of conversation and the clink of glasses resounded. On Vivien's other side sat a moustachioed man with the narrow face of a fox whom Lady Stokeford introduced as Viscount Beldon. His eyes swept her with a haughty admiration, and he launched into a rhapsody about the joys of country life and his own grand estate where he kept a pack of hunting hounds. From across the table, the Duchess of Covington glowered in grumpy disapproval.

Vivien fought the urge to glower back. So the duchess disliked having to share a table with a Gypsy. Or perhaps she was irked at the prospect of Vivien marrying one of these stupid *gorgio* gentlemen.

Irritating the woman was small revenge, but Vivien reveled in it, making herself charming and flirtatious. When she let her napkin flutter to the floor, Lord Beldon almost knocked over his soup bowl in his haste to fetch it. The dunderhead had heard about the dowry, of course.

Marry a rich man, indeed. She would never spend her life in this exclusive *gorgio* world, where people would always regard her with suspicion.

So why did her gaze stray to the far end of the table, where Michael sat talking and laughing with the beautiful Lady Katherine? Why, Vivien wondered, did her heart leap for a man she could never have?

"Come inside," Katherine invited. "The night is yet young."

Pausing outside her bedchamber, Michael was aware of a disquiet in himself. The corridor was deserted, the other guests having lingered in the drawing room or gone off to bed already. No one would know if he enjoyed a tryst with his mistress. Nevertheless, he took hold of her arms and set her away from him. "I won't carry on our affair while Amy is under this roof."

Katherine pursed her lips. "Your daughter? She's three years old—"

"Four," he corrected tersely.

"Four, then," she said breezily. "The point is that she's asleep in the nursery. There's no chance she'd walk in on us."

"Amy sometimes has bad dreams. She comes to me for comforting."

"Then you needn't stay all night. Please, darling, just for a little while."

The offer should have tempted him. Having been a fortnight without a woman, he should take advantage of Katherine's willingness. Especially since Vivien had tied his loins into a knot.

Vivien. His blood surged with the memory of her, dressed in a pure white gown, gliding down the staircase with the wide-eyed innocence of a débutante. But the garb of a lady couldn't disguise her true nature—her bold dark gaze, the defiant tilt of her chin, and the sharp wit that both amused and annoyed him.

Gritting his teeth, he focused his attention on the lady in his arms. Blessed with beauty, poise, and breeding, Katherine would make the perfect wife. Yet he didn't want to deal with her now. "I'm sorry," he said. "You oughtn't have come to the Abbey. I asked you to wait for me at your estate."

"But it was so dull there without you. Haven't you missed me, too?" Sulky and sensual, Katherine kissed him, her lips moving with the practiced strokes of a courtesan.

For once, her seduction left him cold, and he ended the kiss. "Of course I've missed you. But we'll have to bide our time until later."

Her blue eyes narrowed, a sign of her pique. "It's that Gypsy, isn't it?"

"I don't know what you mean."

"I saw you staring at her tonight. You're drawn to her."

Michael silently cursed himself. He must be more careful in the future. "I'm worried about her influence on my grandmother, that's all." The chatter of voices approached from around the corner. Seizing the distraction, he gave Katherine a swift, placating kiss, and then pushed her inside the chamber. "Sleep well, darling. I'll see you on the morrow."

Quickly, Michael strode down the passageway. An odd sense of relief dogged his heels, as if he were making an escape. He called himself every kind of fool. By refusing a night of passion with his intended bride, he had damned himself to long, dark hours of lusting for that willful Gypsy vixen.

* * *

The next day dawned balmy and bright, the air more like summer than early autumn. The Rosebuds promptly announced a picnic to entertain the houseful of guests. A few chose to stay back to play billiards or cards, but everyone else piled into carriages that bore them the mile's journey to a grove of oaks overlooking a lake.

Preferring to walk, Vivien set out at a brisk pace with Lady Charlotte Quinton. The dappled sunlight made the air cool in the woods. They talked about the other guests at dinner the previous evening, laughing at the pompousness of some and the vanity of others.

Vivien stepped around a fallen branch lying on the rutted lane. She would have liked to remove her shoes, but knew better than to ruin her silk stockings. "I must say, the Rosebuds introduced me to so many men that my head is spinning to remember them all." She looked curiously at Charlotte. "I saw Lady Enid maneuvering a few men toward you, too. Is your grandmother trying to find you a husband, as well?"

Charlotte's laugh held a razor edge. "The Rosebuds have given up on me! Though Grandmama still chides me to bat my lashes and flirt."

"She gave me the same advice," Vivien said. "But when I did so with Michael, he thought I had a speck in my eye."

Charlotte's green eyes looked fathomless in the sunshine, enhanced by the deep forest hue of her gown and the large straw bonnet that framed her creamy features. "The Rosebuds wish you to marry Michael?"

Uneasy, Vivien shrugged. "They merely told me to practice my charms on him. He's the last man I would ever marry."

She was the last woman *he* would ever marry. Michael, curse him, wanted only to lift her skirts.

"I'm glad you're a woman of sense," Charlotte said

with a toss of her head. "Michael is a rogue, and rogues do not make suitable husbands. They gamble and drink and whore. I would far rather be independent."

Vivien suspected her breezy attitude hid a bitterness due to her scarred arm, always covered by long sleeves. Impulsively, she touched Charlotte's gloved hand. "You *are* beautiful, you know. Any man who can't see that isn't worthy of you."

A fierce pain flashed in Charlotte's eyes, disappearing so swiftly Vivien might have imagined it. "Fie on men! I vow, I'm chafing at the bit to leave home. But I lack the means to set up my own household."

Knowing that Charlotte preferred not to speak of her disfigurement, Vivien said lightly, "I can't imagine living alone. All of my life, I've been surrounded by people I love."

Charlotte grimaced. "With five brothers and sisters, I long for peace and quiet, and a chance to order my life as I please. Instead, I'm expected to help the governess with the lessons." Bending down, she plucked a daisy from alongside the path, touching the golden center. "So you see why I must find a way to escape my lot."

Vivien sympathized with Charlotte. She knew what it was like to yearn for something more. Of late, she had felt a restless disquiet in herself, and a traitorous liking for *gorgio* life.

As they neared the edge of the woods, she spied a bit of blue cloth that was snagged on a bramblebush. The sight riveted her, driving out all other thought. With a low cry, she caught up the fabric and held it to her nose, breathing deeply, inhaling the faint smoky scent of a campfire . . .

"What is that cloth?" Charlotte asked, her lip curling in disgust. "Why are you smelling it?"

"Was I? I was lost in thought." Vivien let the scrap

flutter to the ground. Unwilling to give voice to the clamor of her emotions, she turned her gaze to the clutch of vehicles in the distance. A column of footmen carried tables and chairs and hampers under the direction of the Rosebuds. "Look, there's our picnic," she said by way of a distraction. "I believe Lord Alfred is waving at you."

Charlotte shaded her eyes against the sunshine. "Or perhaps the buffoon is waving at *you*. Come quickly now. If we hasten to the lake, we can elude him." She veered off through the meadow of tall grasses, heading toward the shining streak of blue water.

Vivien followed more slowly, glancing back at the woods. Had there been other scraps of cloth or broken twigs that she'd missed?

Excitement and impatience tangled inside her. She had found *vurma.* The tiny piece of material was a sign that the *Rom* had passed by here recently, deliberately leaving a trail for another *kumpania* to follow. But who? Who were they?

Her heart skittered over a beat. *Develesa!* Were her parents camped nearby?

Chapter seventeen

The Gypsy Visitor

Vivien stared into the forest, transfixed by the possibility that her *dado* and *dye* might be so close. How she longed to see them again, to hear the cheerful sound of her father's laughter, to feel her mother's warm arms encircling her. She wanted to savor Reyna's wild onion stew and listen to the elders tell tales around the fire. She yearned to travel again, to ride in their colorfully painted *vardo*, to hear the comforting rattle of wheels and the clip-clopping of the horses' hooves over the rutted roads. The pull of nostalgia was so strong she started to turn.

Then, out of the corner of her eye, she spied a small figure barreling down the hill where the picnic was being set up by a bevy of servants.

"Miss Vivi," Amy called, her short pink dress revealing the skipping motion of her chubby legs. "Miss Vivi, wait for me!"

Her heart melted, and then another sight banished all thought of the *Rom.* Carrying a small net attached to a wooden pole, Michael strode down the grassy slope after his daughter. He had shed his coat in the warmth of the day, and he looked sinfully handsome in his white shirt and blue waistcoat. Buckskin breeches and black boots enhanced his powerful legs. When his teeth flashed in a grin, Vivien almost forgot to breathe. She could not understand this enfeebling effect he had on her. She could think only of falling into his embrace and feeling his lips meet hers. How could this *gorgio* rogue overwhelm her just at the sight of him?

Amy ran straight to her. Vivien bent down to catch her close, enjoying her childishly exuberant hug. "Good day to you, little dove. You must like picnics very much."

"I do! Come, look what Papa gave me." She tugged on Vivien's hand, drawing her toward the marquess. "See?"

Michael's gaze did a slow sweep of Vivien's saffron-yellow gown, lingering on her bosom and making her warm all over. Then he took the pole from his shoulder and held it out to his daughter. "Here you go."

"What is it?" Vivien asked.

Amy brandished the net, her hazel eyes bright. "It's my flutterby catcher."

"Butterfly, love," Michael corrected.

"Flutterby," Amy insisted with a faintly quizzical frown. "Come watch me, Miss Vivi. You, too, Papa."

The little girl marched off into the tall grasses, her bonnet dangling by its ribbons and her coppery curls shining in the sunlight. With the air of a hunter stalking prey, she held the net poised to pounce as she scanned the meadow near the wooded area.

"The hunt awaits us," Michael said, his eyes lazily scanning Vivien again. "Shall we proceed?"

"If you're certain your other guests don't need you," she said tartly.

His grin widened. "The ladies do, and they'll mourn the loss of me. But it'll show them that I don't belong to any female."

He placed his hand at the back of her waist, a seemingly courteous gesture that made Vivien wonder if the butterflies resided in her stomach. Fie on him! Michael Kenyon was a noble rake who would use a woman for his pleasure. He'd proven as much that stormy day in the temple when he had nearly overpowered her.

When, in a fit of madness, she had nearly let him have his way.

As they strolled into the meadow, she kept her gaze on Amy, refusing to feed his conceit by watching him. Yet she was very aware of him, the brush of his leg against hers, the heat of his palm on her back, the scent of his masculine cologne.

In the distance, the lake glistened. She could see several guests rowing a boat across the glassy surface while others on the shore played a game of hitting a shuttlecock back and forth with paddles. The Duchess of Covington stood chatting with Charlotte.

Tense and angry at the sight of Her Grace, Vivien sought to distract herself. "Charlotte Quinton is so very lovely. It's a pity about her scarred arm. I'd think many men would enjoy her lively character."

Michael snorted. "It's her acid tongue that drives them away."

"Then men are shallow creatures," Vivien declared. "I've wondered if a man once spurned Charlotte because of her disfigurement. Do you know?"

He cast her an irritated glance. "How the devil would I? I'm too shallow to notice such things."

"She's your neighbor, the granddaughter of Lady Enid. You ought to remember when Charlotte became a woman and entered your *gorgio* society."

Michael shrugged. "She flirted with a lot of men, I suppose. Myself included. But I don't know if she ever settled on any man in particular. Why do you care anyway?"

"Because she seems so unhappy inside. I can't help but think she'd wed if the man she loved wanted her." Vivien braced herself for his wrath. "Do you suppose . . . that man is Lord Faversham?"

Michael's affable expression vanished, a muscle tensing visibly in his jaw. "Brand and Charlotte? What the deuce gave you such a notion?"

"I sense there's something between them. An awareness." *Like the fire I feel for you.*

"Charlotte would be a fool to go after Brandon Villiers," he said harshly. "Irksome as she is, he isn't fit to kiss her feet."

His virulence shook her. "His lordship told me what happened, but still, I don't understand this hatred you have for him. It's wrong of you to harbor a grudge."

Michael's fingers stiffened against her back, and his eyes narrowed. "What exactly did he tell you?"

"That you fought a duel over a woman, and you cut his face. That should be the end of it."

"You know nothing of it," he bit out. "So keep your judgments to yourself."

Fury shimmered from him in almost visible waves. His eyes were like blank blue mirrors, reflecting nothing of his thoughts. His mouth thinned to a strict line that she ached to soften with a kiss. A kiss—when she should hold on to her anger as a shield against his masculine allure. Why did she have the feeling there was more to the story than he was willing to tell? That his anger masked the pain inside himself?

"Papa! Miss Vivi! Come quick! Watch me catch a flutterby."

Amy's excited voice pierced the thickness of tension. A tiny yellow butterfly swooped over the meadow grasses at the edge of the forest. Amy brought the net down with a whoosh, missing the insect by at least a foot.

His hostility dissipating like smoke in the wind, Michael clapped his hands. "Excellent, sprite! You almost had that one. Keep trying." Leaning closer to Vivien, he whispered, "I daresay the butterfly population is in little danger today."

She was in danger, though, Vivien knew with a bone-deep quiver. She was in danger of surrendering to the longings inside herself. Just like that, Michael had changed from churl to charmer. His breath tickled her ear, stirring the hairs at the nape of her neck. His fingers idly caressing her back, he returned his gaze to her mouth.

She tried to move away, but he held tightly to her. "I'm starving for you," he murmured. "It's been forever since I kissed you."

"Two days," she said breathily. "You cornered me outside the stable after our morning ride. Have you kissed so many other women that you forgot one more?"

Smiling seductively, he moved closer, his body brushing hers, so that she felt giddy and light-headed. "An eternity has passed since then," he said in that silken voice. "I'll tell you what I'd like to do right now."

"I'll hear nothing of it."

"I'd like to lay you down right here in the grass. Have you ever made love with the sun warm on your skin?"

Mutely, she shook her head.

"Nor, I confess, have I," he admitted with a crooked grin. "But we will, I vow. When we don't have forty of my grandmother's guests in sight."

She glanced at the lake, where elegant people strolled and conversed. Somehow, she found her voice. "Your vanity will defeat you, my lord. I'm not like your other women. I won't be another conquest for you."

On that, Vivien caught up her muslin skirt and hastened

after Amy. She could hear Michael's footsteps as he strolled after her, whistling. Whistling! As if he had enjoyed their banter and was confident of his success.

If only she could be so confident of resisting him.

Amy stood stock-still at the edge of the woods, the net held tightly in her little hands. "Look," she said in a hushed tone. "Do you see it?"

She stared into the shadowed forest, and Vivien's breath stopped in sudden alarm. For one dizzying moment, she feared the girl had spied a circle of Gypsy wagons camped beneath the trees.

But Vivien could see only the brown trunks and the spreading branches of the trees, the autumn leaves beginning to turn yellow and orange. "What is it?" she asked.

"Sshh." Amy put her forefinger to her rosebud lips. Her eyes were wide with wonder. "There's a bunny. Over there."

Slowly lowering herself into a crouched position, Vivien peered into the underbrush. A short distance away, a small brown rabbit nibbled on the tender shoots of a sapling. "Ah," she whispered. "He's eating his luncheon."

"I want to catch him." With all the brash faith of a child, Amy crept closer, darting from tree trunk to tree trunk, the net held at the ready.

Michael hunkered down beside Vivien. An indulgent expression on his face, he watched his daughter, then glanced at Vivien, and an awareness seemed to radiate between them, the bond of shared love for his little girl. Despite all his other faults, he did love his daughter. Again, Vivien felt that vexing tug of attraction, along with something deeper and richer, something she yearned for with all her heart and soul. Resolutely, she turned her eyes to Amy, who tiptoed with exaggerated patience toward the rabbit.

Sensing danger, the rabbit ceased eating, its nose

twitching and its eyes watchful. Amy darted the last few feet and swung the net downward. The small animal bounded toward the underbrush. Aiming at its original position, Amy overshot her target and the net fell straight over the rabbit.

She froze, a look of stark amazement on her impish face. "Papa! Miss Vivi! I caught him!"

"You did, indeed," Vivien said, hastening toward her. "What a clever girl you are."

Michael carefully turned the net to lift the squirming animal. "What an amazing feat," he said, smiling. "When I was a boy, it once took me an entire week to trap a squirrel."

Amy's eyes shone with pride. "Please may I keep him?" she asked, reaching up to stroke the rabbit. "He can sleep in my bed. I don't mind."

Vivien laughed. "Miss Mortimer will mind. Besides, a wild animal would be happier living outdoors." *Like me,* she thought, *raised in the sunshine and wind . . .*

"I do want Nibbles to be happy," Amy said, her expression thoughtful as she petted the rabbit's fur.

"Nibbles?" Michael asked.

"That is his name," Amy said with a firm nod. "Could we make a little house for him outside? Please?"

"An excellent idea," Michael said. "For now, we'll put the beast in a crate and sneak some lettuce to feed him. Then we'll build a proper hutch when we go home."

"Oh, thank you, Papa."

She threw her arms around him, almost overbalancing him. With a chuckle, he pretended to lose his hold on the rabbit. Amy squealed and he showed her the animal was quite safe, nestled in the crook of his arm.

Vivien felt a sudden, aching sense of isolation. Biting her lip, she glanced into the silent woods. When she returned to the *Rom,* she'd never see Amy anymore. She would never delight in her smiles or watch her grow into womanhood. And she would never again see Michael . . .

Father and daughter started toward the picnic. Clinging to his hand, Amy swung back. "Miss Vivi, aren't you coming, too?"

"In a short while. I want to walk among the trees for a bit."

"But you'll miss our luncheon." Her eyes grew big as saucers. "Grammy said there are strawberry tarts with cream."

Vivien tucked a stray lock of copper hair behind Amy's tiny ear. "Then you must save one for me. I'll return soon, I promise you."

Michael sent her a penetrating, quizzical look, but he didn't try to persuade her otherwise. Carrying the rabbit, he and Amy walked through the meadow together.

Vivien watched them for a few moments, listening to the sound of Amy's excited chatter drifting on the breeze, noticing the way Michael bent closer to listen to her. She had to admit, he was a fine father. She admired his attentiveness to his daughter when he might have abandoned her to the care of nursemaids. It was peculiar and disturbing the way these *gorgio* aristocrats often ignored their children.

Then her gaze was caught by a lady who left the throng of guests idling by the shore of the lake. The fair-haired woman strolled toward Michael, her hips swaying, a parasol shading her dainty features.

Lady Katherine.

As the woman joined Michael and Amy, Vivien experienced a burning intensity in her breast. Lady Katherine reached out to stroke the rabbit, smiling up at Michael. Together, they started up the hill to the place where the footmen arranged the food for the picnic under Lady Stokeford's eagle eye. The sight of those two filled Vivien with the fire of anger and another, increasingly familiar and noxious emotion. Jealousy.

She was jealous of the woman who fit so easily into Michael's world.

Quickly, Vivien turned her back and marched into the woods, heading toward the lane. Curse the *gorgios.* More than anything, she hoped to visit her parents and see to their comfort.

Keeping her eyes alert for *vurma,* she walked slowly along the lane where their wagons might have passed. The air was cooler here, and she shivered, drawing her silk shawl closer around her shoulders. She felt an odd prickly feeling between her shoulder blades, as if someone were watching her. But when she looked around, she saw only the natural movements of the forest, the flutter of leaves in the breeze, the swaying shadows caused by the sunshine, the flight of a wren from one branch to another.

A tall granite boulder stood at a crossroads where the lane led back to Stokeford Abbey and a path veered off deeper into the woods. A dark streak on the rock caught her attention. The sign was low to the ground. When she leaned down to touch the *vurma,* her finger came up black.

Seemingly random, the mark had been made by a charred stick. On closer inspection, it was an arrow that pointed down the narrow dirt path.

In a turmoil of excitement, she strained to see through the trees. Were her parents camped there? Or was it another *kumpania*? It surely couldn't be coincidence that a band of the *Rom* would venture onto Stokeford land.

Then, as she started down the path, a man stepped out from behind the boulder. She gasped in recognition. She knew those angry eyes and the sweeping moustache, the muscled oxlike form clad in a red vest and dark blue breeches, a yellow *diklo* tied jauntily at his throat.

"Janus!"

He thrust his hands onto his hips. "So, Vivien," he said in the Romany tongue. "I wondered if you would find my trail."

"*Your* trail?" Answering him in her native language, she swallowed the dryness in her throat. "Are my parents not here?"

"Pulika will arrive here on the morrow with your mother. One of his horses threw a shoe, and they were forced to lag behind the rest of us."

Vivien's spirits fell. So they weren't camped just beyond the trees. Perhaps a delay was for the best. If she were seen visiting the Gypsies, Lady Stokeford would be upset, and Vivien might jeopardize her place.

Janus's scornful gaze raked her gown. "You look like a *gorgio*. If Reyna were to see you now, she would weep all the more."

Vivien's stomach tightened as she thought of her mother's kind eyes and warm smile. "*Miro dye* . . . she has been weeping?"

Janus gave a cold nod. "Your father misses you, too. He seldom laughs anymore. This is what your headstrong actions have caused."

Develesa! She ached to see her parents, to make them understand that she was living with the *gorgios* out of love for them, and that she really would return. "Why are you traveling with them?" she asked Janus. "Your *kumpania* was to make its way to the winter campsite in the east."

"I go with your *kumpania* for now—until you come to your senses."

"What I choose to do shouldn't matter to you."

His eyes as black as a raven's wing, Janus shook his fist at her. "Impudent girl! You promised yourself to me. But I saw you making eyes at the *gorgio* nobleman."

Vivien stiffened. "What nonsense."

He took a step toward her. "Don't try to deceive me. I was watching from behind a tree. You let him touch you."

Michael had placed his hand at the base of her spine, nothing more. No one else could know that his words had been erotic, arousing. *I'd like to lay you down right here in the grass. Have you ever made love with the sun warm on your skin?*

"So you'd stoop to spying on me," Vivien said scornfully. "That tells me you have no honor."

Janus struck his broad chest with his fist. "When I'm your husband, you won't behave in so bold a manner. You'll be a respectful, obedient wife."

Disgusted, she spat at his feet. "No. I was right to change my mind about marrying you."

Loosing a growl of anger, he stepped toward her. Vivien realized how alone they were. Janus could abuse her as he willed.

In a panic, she whirled around and dashed down the lane toward the lake. She heard him shouting after her, but with her long legs, she had always been more fleet than any man of the *Rom*. The breath stabbed her lungs. She ran until she could hear only the pounding of her own feet, the rush of the wind, and the roaring of her pulse in her ears. When she reached the edge of the woods, she slowed, glancing back over her shoulder.

The road was empty; no ox of a *Rom* thundered in pursuit.

Weak with relief, Vivien slumped against the rough bark of an oak tree, taking in gulps of air. Shading her eyes against the bright sunlight, she gazed into the distance at the *gorgio* picnic. In twos and threes, the aristocratic guests walked up the gentle slope to the tables that had been set with the lavish trappings of silver and crystal.

Like a dainty general, Lady Stokeford directed the people to their seats for luncheon.

Nearby, Michael settled Amy into a chair. Then he turned his gaze to the woods, his hands on his hips, and it seemed to Vivien that he stared straight at her.

A traitorous warmth stirred inside her, chasing away the cold and filling her with a longing she knew she oughtn't feel for him. Her loyalty belonged to the *Rom,* she fiercely reminded herself. Even if she dared not visit her parents for fear of encountering Janus again.

Chapter eighteen

Something Dreadful

The following afternoon, Michael stalked through the Abbey in search of Vivien. She had vanished again, damn her.

Rain spattered the windows of the long gallery where monks had once bent over their copywork. Now the cavernous chamber held groupings of chairs and chaises, and the oak-paneled walls sported portraits of long-dead Stokeford ancestors. Not even the two blazing fireplaces could dispel the chill in the air.

A blast of wintry weather had swept in during the night, canceling all outdoor activities. Confined to the house, the guests had amused themselves with games of billiards and cards and charades until they grew restless halfway through the afternoon. That was when the Rosebuds had put forth the notion of a treasure hunt.

In swift order, teams had been organized and a list of items compiled. The Rosebuds had assigned Michael the task of helping them oversee the hunt. Any team he joined would have an unfair advantage, they declared, since he knew the house and its contents too well. Gallantly, he had gone from group to group, giving hints as to where they might find a long list of miscellany such as a ball of string, a wooden cross, a fiddler's bow, and a tricorn hat.

He had sent bands of five or six guests off in various directions, upstairs to the attic or downstairs to the cellars. Katherine had teasingly attempted to lure him off alone into a deserted bedchamber, but he'd firmly repeated what he'd told her before, that he wouldn't take her to bed with his daughter in the house. It wasn't like him to spurn the advances of a beautiful woman, especially one so well suited to him. But to his chagrin, he could think only of Vivien Thorne.

He burned for her. Thoughts of the Gypsy dominated him, day and night. He desired more than her lush body; he enjoyed matching wits with her, teasing her just to see those large brown eyes flash with fire. Damn it, he needed to seduce her and end this obsession. Then he could oust her from his house.

He'd prowled after Vivien's team, but a befuddled Lord Alfred told him she had disappeared not ten minutes earlier while they were hunting for a brass farthing in the servants' quarters. Then Michael had sought out Charlotte Quinton's group, but she, too, had no knowledge of Vivien's whereabouts. He had declined Charlotte's offer to help him search. More suspicious than alarmed, he intended to find Vivien himself.

The ancient Persian carpet muffled his footfalls. Though a fortnight had gone by without an incident, he didn't trust Vivien not to steal from his grandmother. The Gypsy might dress like a lady, she might have befriended his daughter, but she was as deceitful as any woman—likely more so since she had learned her morals at the knees of her Gypsy parents. She had cleverly forged that letter from Harriet Althorpe, winning herself a place in his grandmother's household—and now his. She had tricked his grandmother into paying her one hundred guineas per month.

But *he* would not be duped. Yesterday, Vivien had melted into the woods for the better part of an hour, and he intended to find out why. Today, the treasure hunt would give her the perfect opportunity to poke around his house.

He was heading for a back corridor, intending to search the music room, when he spied her at the far end of the gallery. Half hidden by a swath of green draperies, she sat curled up in a window seat, gazing out at the rainswept garden. At his approach, she turned her head sharply, and her dark velvet eyes shimmered with tears.

She was weeping. The shock of it struck him like a blow. Quickly she lowered her gaze, wiping her wet cheeks with a corner of her shawl.

He should excuse himself and bow out of the room. Now that he knew she wasn't up to mischief, he should leave her alone. Weeping women were a plague to be avoided.

But in a far gentler voice than he'd intended, he said, "Forgive me for intruding. I've looked everywhere for you—the kitchens, the conservatory, the library."

"There were too many people trooping in and out of the conservatory looking for a geranium petal, and in the library, seeking a book of psalms." Her small white teeth sank into her lower lip as if to stop its quivering.

"Why did you leave the treasure hunt?"

She shrugged, and her copper shawl slipped to expose the sun-burnished skin of her throat and shoulder. To his disappointment, her modest gown of olive-green muslin concealed the swell of her breasts. How he would love to undress her, to lower her clothing inch by inch, to taste her warm flesh. How he would enjoy parting her legs and sinking into her . . .

"It didn't interest me," she said.

Michael scowled, confounded for a moment before

picking up the thread of their conversation. Though her cool manner indicated she didn't welcome his presence, he sat down beside her on the wide, padded window seat. She edged back, hugging her knees and scrupulously avoiding any contact with him.

"Has someone been unkind to you?" he asked.

"Only you, m'lord marquess."

"*I* drove you to tears?"

"Of course not!" she said scathingly. "You mean nothing to me."

He doubted that. No woman could feign the passion he had aroused in her. "Then why were you crying?" he persisted.

"Stop bothering me. Go away."

Firming her lips, she turned her gaze out the window. Rain tapped against the paned glass, coursing downward in long rivulets. She'd been staring outside when he'd entered the gallery, and she hadn't heard his approach until he was upon her. Curious, for usually she had keen instincts.

He frowned out the window at the drenched pathways of the garden and the wild woodland beyond it. Through the trees, a rutted lane led to the lake where they'd had their picnic the previous day. Where she had disappeared into the forest for too long.

"Why did you go off into the forest yesterday?"

Vivien swung her attention to him, her eyes widening for a telltale moment. Then she ducked her chin and regarded him through her thick lashes. "I took a walk. Is that not an appropriate act for a *gorgio* woman?"

"That depends on what you were doing in the woods. You were subdued when you returned."

"Bah! I don't have your liking for gossip and idle talk."

"Something happened there to upset you," he said on

a hunch. "Something that made you weep just now. I wish to know what it was."

"I regret robbing one of your tenants of his last ha'penny. There, are you satisfied, m'lord marquess?"

Her sarcasm only proved she wished to distract him from her true purpose. Had a man tried to molest her? With her Gypsy heritage, she would be viewed as fair game. Michael couldn't remember if any of the male guests had disappeared from the picnic at the same time as Vivien. But he would thrash the man who dared to touch her, be he common or noble.

"If someone has been bothering you, I demand to know of it."

"Go away," she repeated. "You're the only one annoying me."

"You're hiding something." He leaned forward, his gaze intent on her. "Tell me, Vivien. Did you meet a man out there?"

She said nothing. She stubbornly looked away, her fingers tightening in the folds of her skirt.

"You leave me no choice, then," he said. "Henceforth, I'll attend you wherever you go. You'll venture nowhere without me present as your guard."

As if he'd poked her with a red-hot prod, she sat up straight. Anger blazed in her eyes. "*Dosta!*" she burst out, slapping her hand down onto the cushion. "Enough. If you'll cease your prying, I'll tell you what's weighing on my mind. I miss my parents."

"Your parents?"

"Yes! I haven't seen them for weeks. I went off into the woods so that I could be alone to think about them. So you may take your cursed suspicions and leave me be!"

Tears welled again in her eyes. Her lower lip trembled as Amy's did when she was sad. Hugging her knees,

Vivien hid her face, her shoulders shaking in silent weeping.

Michael sat unmoving. Never had he imagined she might be distraught over something so innocent as a longing for her family. He hadn't spared a thought for her feelings at all. The hard knot inside him loosened, casting him adrift in a treacherous sea of tenderness.

Though his intellect told him to walk out, he placed his hand on her back, absorbing the deep shuddering of her sobs. Unsure of how to console her, he rubbed lightly between her shoulder blades.

"Tell me about them," he said gruffly. "What sort of people are they?"

She gulped several unsteady breaths before speaking. "My mother, Reyna . . . is all that is good and kind and gentle. My father, Pulika . . . is brimming with stories and love and laughter. Or at least they were thus before I left." Vivien lifted her head to look at him, her eyes glossy with grief in the dismal gray light from the window. "I fear," she added in a quavering voice, "they didn't like for me to accept money from the Rosebuds."

He frowned. So her parents were opposed to her trickery. Had she acted entirely on her own? Or was she aided by her suitor, Janus?

Michael no longer knew what to think, except that he couldn't bear to see her so unhappy. Cupping her cheek in his palm, he caught a tear with his thumb. "You'll see them again. They'll forgive you."

Seeking to comfort her in the only way he knew how, he pulled Vivien onto his lap and into his arms. He shouldn't take advantage of her in her vulnerable state. But he didn't give a damn if it were a mortal sin.

For once, she didn't fight him. She welcomed his embrace with a desperate, inarticulate cry. Her arms looped around his neck, her fingers delving into his hair and her breasts pressing to his chest. A surge of passion shut out the rest of the world, narrowing his focus to Vivien . . . only Vivien.

Their mouths met in a stormy kiss that went on and on, deep and drowning, making him tremble with an urgency he'd never before known. Her scent, her taste, her softness, fed the beast inside him. He touched her everywhere, face and bosom and waist. He reached beneath the hem of her gown, up her slim legs and past the garters that held her silk stockings.

When he cupped her, she cried out and he feared she might resist him. Then she opened her thighs in sweet invitation, burying her face in his cravat. Her swift surrender drove him down the path toward madness. She was hot and silken, ready for him. By God, he would give her a pleasure so intense she would never again refuse him.

Ignoring his own raging need, he used his expertise to caress her until she arched and moaned, her hands clutching at him. So fiery she was, so eager for him. All too soon, he sensed the gathering tension in her. He heard the catch in her breathing and the long keening cry that heralded her climax.

Her features alight with dazed wonder, she slumped against him, murmuring in her Gypsy tongue. She pressed kisses to his jaw and throat, her soft eyes still clouded with ardor. Her exultation increased his desire to violent heights, and he might have taken her right there on the window seat if not for the nudging of sanity.

Guests roamed the Abbey. At any moment, a group of treasure hunters might walk in here in search of some damn-fool trinket. He would not have his pleasure interrupted. Nor would he let anyone else see Vivien in her gloriously carnal state.

Her hair was mussed, the black tendrils drifting around her face and neck. Her mouth was reddened from his kisses. She looked like a woman who had been thoroughly satisfied. He wanted to pleasure her again. But this time, he'd be inside her, sharing the ecstasy.

He lifted her from his lap, snatched up the shawl that had slipped to the floor, and draped it around her shoulders. She leaned against him, rubbing her cheek against his shoulder like a kitten in want of affection. Distracted by her allure, he kissed her again, deeply and thoroughly.

Lust, he told himself as he drew her toward the door, pausing to claim another kiss. Lust was all he felt for the Gypsy. His blood blazed out of control because she had refused him, taunted him for weeks. Until now.

At last he would have Vivien in his bed. He couldn't think beyond satisfying the painful demand of his loins.

Near the carved archway of the door, the chatter of voices intruded on his feverish state. Quickly he pulled Vivien back into the gallery, holding her flush against his body, out of sight of the corridor. He recognized Alfred's bragging voice along with several ladies of his grandmother's generation.

Wriggling against him, Vivien made a soft mewling sound. He put his finger to her lips, and she blinked slowly like someone awakening from a long slumber. He didn't want her to awaken, so he kissed her again.

The laughter and talk had faded away by the time he could drag his mouth from hers. Only then did he guide Vivien to the empty doorway.

"Where are we going?" she asked drowsily.

"To my chamber."

Awareness dawned on her slumberous face. "To . . . your bed?"

"Yes," Michael said, tortured by the knowledge that she alone could transport him to paradise. Taking care not to overwhelm her, he gently stroked her breasts. She was a wild filly who might bite and kick to escape her taming. "I'll give you more joy. Just let me love you, Vivien."

Her eyes widened, expressive with wonder. "*Could* you truly love me, Michael?"

Her literal interpretation mystified him. He couldn't imagine how an experienced woman could mistake his intent. "Come upstairs with me, please," he urged, not caring that she'd reduced him to begging. "I'll love you as I did a few moments ago. I'll do so again and again until we're both satisfied." As he spoke, he drew her out into the dimly lit corridor and toward a narrow stone staircase, one of many that honeycombed the house.

Abruptly, Vivien tore herself free, backing up until her spine met the newel. Her eyes stark, she put her palms to her cheeks. "No," she said, a catch in her voice. "Curse you, Michael. I'm not like Lady Katherine. I won't be your whore."

"Vivien—"

He reached out, but she darted down the passageway, leaving her shawl in his hands and his loins caught in an iron fist of frustration. Wild to release the pressure boiling in his blood, he sprang after her. Just as swiftly, he halted. He couldn't—wouldn't—force a woman to his will.

Cursing, he swung his fist blindly and connected with an arrangement of figurines on a side table, sweeping them to the stone floor. The porcelain shattered with a loud crash, and pieces spewed in all directions.

Michael leaned his forehead against the cold wall and breathed deeply. The hammering of his heart gradually slowed and the grip of unslaked passion began to abate so that he could think coherently.

Damn the Gypsy! She had enjoyed her rapture and left him to suffer. The scent and taste and feel of her lingered to taunt him. So did the memory of her tears.

Vivien had been troubled about her parents. For all his anger, he couldn't banish her forlorn face from his mind. He didn't like thinking of her as vulnerable, yet the more he came to know her, the less he understood. How could a woman who was capable of deep, genuine emotions also lie and steal? How could he, who knew better than to trust a female, allow himself to be drawn into the spell of a Gypsy fortune-teller? Even now, he burned to hold Vivien, to kiss her, to talk with her, to learn all her secrets.

"Dear heavens!" someone exclaimed.

Michael's eyes snapped open. He pivoted, porcelain crunching beneath his shoes. To his annoyance, Lady Charlotte Quinton stood poised on the bottom step of the staircase, one gloved hand on the newel. Her eyebrows raised, she stared from him to the shards littering the floor.

"What happened here?" she asked, her anxious green eyes scanning him. "Are you all right?"

"I bumped into the table, that's all."

"But . . . I heard upraised voices a few moments ago. Were you quarreling with someone?"

"No," he said flatly. "There are guests roaming all over this house. You must have heard someone else."

"Then whose wrap is that?"

Glancing down, he felt like an ass to realize he still gripped Vivien's copper silk shawl. "I don't know," he said, fumbling for an explanation. "I found it lying on the floor."

Charlotte ventured closer, careful to step around the sharp pieces, and examined the fringed shawl. Then she frowned suspiciously at him. "Why, this belongs to Vivien. Did you find her, after all?"

"No," he said, snatching it back from her. "But I'll have this returned to her. If you'll excuse me, I must ring for a servant to clean up the mess."

"Wait!" Charlotte caught hold of his coat sleeve. "I came to find you, Michael. Something has happened. Something dreadful."

"What is it now?" he asked, remembering how as a girl she'd plagued him, forever dogging him and Brand on their adventures, always poking her nose where she wasn't wanted. "Did someone else win the treasure hunt?"

"This has nothing to do with that silly game." She leaned closer, her bosom pressing lightly against his arm, her eyes alight with both alarm and a certain excitement. "You see, while we were all on the hunt, someone robbed one of your guests. I'm afraid there's a thief on the loose."

Vivien raced blindly through the maze of corridors. She was frantic to escape the confinement of the house and the appalling reality of her actions. Again, she'd allowed Michael a liberty that should belong only to a husband.

This time was so much worse. This time, he hadn't needed to force her to his will. This time, she had abandoned herself to him without so much as a whimper, letting him lift her gown and stroke her intimately.

Despite her shame, a thrill flashed through her. *Develesa!* No wonder such caresses were forbidden. Now that she knew the stunning glory of his touch, she craved it again. She wanted so fiercely to lie with Michael that she'd had to run from her own foolish weakness.

She intended to go outdoors into the rain to clear her head, to recoup her strength of will. But all the passageways looked alike, gloomy and long, barren of people. The treasure hunt must be over. Everyone would be gathered in the drawing room to determine the winner. How unreal that seemed compared to the splendor she'd found in Michael's arms. How frivolous beside the yearning that thrummed in her breast.

God save her! In another moment, she would have let the rogue unbutton his breeches and have his way with her.

Hopelessly lost and sick at heart, she turned a corner

and ran into someone. Lady Katherine Westbrook. Michael's mistress.

Staggering backward, the elegant older woman touched the paneled wall to catch her balance. "What on earth—" she exclaimed. "Miss Thorne?"

"Pardon me," Vivien said, panting. "I wasn't watching where I was going."

"What is the meaning of your haste? Is aught amiss?"

"Nothing, truly. I . . . was just looking for an outside door."

"Don't be ridiculous," Lady Katherine said, looking her up and down. "You can't mean to go out into this storm."

In a cloud of rose perfume, she took Vivien by the arm and marched her down the corridor to an arched window, dribbled gray with rain. There, she pressed Vivien into a sturdy medieval chair that stood against the wall.

"Now," she said crisply, "take several deep breaths to calm yourself."

Not knowing what else to do, Vivien complied, inhaling draughts of cool air. She didn't understand why Lady Katherine showed kindness to her. The woman was a self-centered snob who until now hadn't deigned to speak to one of the *Rom*. Worse, she was cousin to the Duchess of Covington, whose husband set mantraps to cripple innocent passersby.

Vivien knew she ought to turn her most evil glare on the woman, but she felt too limp and scattered to do more than gaze at all that refined beauty. Lady Katherine was as small and dainty as a goddess, draped in gold silk with ribbons artfully woven through her fair hair.

Through narrowed blue eyes, she watched Vivien. "Now. You'll tell me what has you dashing pell-mell through the house."

"Nothing."

"All right, then, perhaps you'll answer another question. I was looking for Lord Stokeford. Have you seen him?"

"No!"

"The truth now. You've been with him, haven't you?"

Vivien lowered her gaze, for the first time noticing the wrinkled state of her gown, the untidy tendrils of hair hanging down her back, and the way her lips felt swollen from his kisses. Mortified, she blushed. Surely Lady Katherine with her sharp eyes saw all that.

She probably even guessed what they'd been doing.

Then let her, Vivien thought, mustering anger from the chaos of her emotions. No one else need know she felt ashamed of her actions. Least of all, this harlot who wanted Michael for herself.

Raising her chin, she returned the woman's stare. "Perhaps I have."

As cool and serene as ever, Lady Katherine showed no reaction. "My girl, you're no match for such a rake. You're a virgin, I believe."

"That is for no one to know but Michael."

Lady Katherine thinned her lips. "Indeed. I feel it my duty to pass along a warning, then. He won't marry you. Men like him live for pleasure. He's only interested in bedding you."

Her bluntness hurt, but Vivien refused to acknowledge it. "You don't speak out of duty, m'lady. The truth is, you fear he prefers me to you."

For an instant, Lady Katherine froze, her milky features taut as a mask. Then she inclined her head in a nod. "Well, Miss Thorne. Perhaps you're more clever than I'd thought. But heed this: Michael is a lord and you're a commoner raised by Gypsies. When it comes to marriage, he'll ask me, not you."

"Then take him and be gone."

"I intend to do just that." Dignified, she started to turn,

then glanced back. "By the by, you wouldn't happen to have been lurking about the upstairs corridors this afternoon, would you?"

"No. I was . . . otherwise engaged."

The slight tensing of those slender fingers gave the only indication that Lady Katherine caught her meaning. She went on tersely. "A diamond ring has been stolen from my chamber. I noticed it was missing when I went to change for dinner."

Distracted, Vivien rose to her feet. "Perhaps you misplaced it."

"Hardly. I saw the ring this very morning in my jewel case." Her gaze bored into Vivien. "The ring was given to me by my late husband. With Lord Stokeford's aid, I shall make certain the thief is found and punished." On that pointed statement, she glided away down the corridor.

Vivien watched stiffly until the fine *gorgio* lady disappeared around a corner. Raindrops pattered a lonely melody on the window. Caught up in a flurry of anger and alarm, she felt shaken by Lady's Katherine's implication.

Clearly, she believed Vivien was the thief.

Chapter nineteen

Meeting with a Spy

"I don't trust that woman an inch," Lady Faversham muttered. With angry flicks of her bony fingers, she dealt out the cards for another round of whist. "Katherine Westbrook must have misplaced that ring. Yet she dares to insinuate that Vivien is a thief."

Lady Stokeford leaned closer so the other guests in the drawing room couldn't eavesdrop. "I should like nothing better than to toss her out of this house. But Michael is too pigheaded to consider it."

"I vow, the hussy has been fawning over him all evening," Lady Enid whispered. "What do you suppose they're saying to one another?"

While the Rosebuds glowered at the couple, Vivien kept her gaze fastened on her cards. She could hear the trill of voices and laughter from the noble guests who gathered after dinner in the huge drawing room with its Gothic arches and gold-striped chairs.

Ever since Lady Katherine's diamond ring had disappeared the previous day, Vivien had endured the speculative stares of the aristocrats. She'd seen them whispering among themselves, though at least these *gorgio* lords and ladies hadn't accused her outright. They respected the Rosebuds, Vivien knew. For that reason, she'd vowed to bridle her anger and make Lady Stokeford proud. Not for anything would she let these snobs drive her away before she completed her two months here.

"Look at how she's behaving in full view of everyone," Lady Faversham said in a low tone. "Why, it's disgraceful."

"It's scandalous, that's what," Lady Enid hissed. "No wonder I've heard so much gossip about the woman."

Lady Stokeford huffed out a breath. "It's clear that I must have another talk with my grandson. Later, in private."

This time, Vivien couldn't resist stealing a peek. The handsome couple sat on a chaise at the far end of the chamber. Michael looked sinfully appealing in his dark blue coat and fawn breeches, and Lady Katherine dainty as a princess with her flaxen hair and filmy gown of pale blue. She rested her hand on his knee and flirted with a practiced ease that Vivien could never quite master.

Pretending a ladylike calm, Vivien arranged her cards. But inside she felt a wild fury that urged her to storm across the drawing room and thrust that spell-casting *chovihani* away from Michael. Forbidden though he was, Vivien wanted him all to herself, to experience again the pleasure of his mouth on hers and the caress of his hands, arousing her to a shameful glory. Over and over, she'd remembered that starburst of rapture, the stunning sense of belonging to him, body and soul.

It was disgraceful, this passion she felt for him. She shuddered to think how horrified her *dado* and *dye* would be if they knew the liberties she'd permitted him. The Rosebuds, too, would be aghast. If they found Lady Katherine's behavior scandalous, what would they think of

Vivien's? What would they say if they knew how she longed to lie with him?

At that moment, Michael looked straight at her, and the fire in her heart blazed hotter. He gave her a keen, speculative scrutiny as if he could read her wicked thoughts.

Or perhaps because he, too, thought her a thief.

Though her skin felt rosy and her pulse drummed, Vivien refused to look away. She met his penetrating gaze until Lady Katherine touched his sleeve and brought his eyes back to her.

Vivien returned her attention to the card game. Thankfully, the Rosebuds weren't looking at her; they gazed at one another in that peculiar, silent communication they often shared.

The lighted candles at the corners of the table cast a golden glow over their wrinkled, aging faces. Lady Stokeford's dainty white brows were winged together in a frown, Lady Faversham's gaunt features appeared as thunderous as a storm cloud, and even Lady Enid's cherubic face held a fretful expression beneath her russet turban.

With a snap, Lady Faversham placed the last card faceup in the center of the table. "Diamonds," she said sourly, regarding the pasteboard rectangle with its eight red markings. "How appropriate."

"Speaking of diamonds," Lady Stokeford said, spreading her thirteen cards into a tidy fan, "I've been pondering the identity of our thief."

" 'Tis likely to be Katherine's lady's maid," Lady Enid whispered. "One can never trust those Frenchies."

"No," Lady Stokeford said, shaking her head. "Colette is a sweet girl, and I refuse to believe she's the culprit."

Lady Faversham's frown deepened. "You should have let me question her, Lucy. At times you're too trusting."

"Michael and I were there, too," Vivien said, reaching

across the table to touch Lady Stokeford's thin hand in support. "The three of us interviewed all the servants. I'm sure none of them stole Lady Katherine's ring."

But did Michael agree? He'd been noncommital this afternoon, his face impassive. She had always believed herself adept at discerning the thoughts of the *gorgios.* From fortune-telling, she'd learned enough of physical mannerisms to make a fair guess at a person's emotions and opinions. Michael, however, was the one man whose mind she couldn't read.

"How can you be so certain?" Lady Enid asked doubtfully.

"Some of the servants looked nervous," Vivien said, "but no one shifted their eyes away in guilt. Nor did they hesitate to give their whereabouts during the treasure hunt."

"Then it's just as I suggested—Katherine misplaced the ring," Lady Faversham said, tossing down a jack. "Perhaps it rolled off her dressing table."

Lady Enid perked up. "That happened to me once, when my favorite emerald earbobs fell behind the desk in the library while Howard and I were—" Glancing coyly at Vivien, she giggled. "But never mind that."

Vivien absentmindedly put down a queen. "Colette swears she locked the ring in Lady Katherine's jewel case."

"Who keeps the key?" Lady Faversham asked.

"Katherine put it in the bedside table," Lady Stokeford replied. "She insists it was there during the treasure hunt."

"Careless chit," Lady Faversham said with a snort. Glancing around the drawing room, she made her voice even lower. "I hesitate to propose this, but . . . do you suppose one of the guests stole the ring? Someone who knew Vivien would be blamed?"

Vivien faltered in the act of collecting up the winning

hand. The dowager countess had voiced the suspicion that had been hovering at the edge of her mind. Someone here wanted her to be branded a thief, to be discredited and humiliated, perhaps even carted off to the gaol.

"Who?" Lady Enid whispered, sounding both shocked and intrigued. "Who would do such a vile deed?"

"We shall find out," Lady Stokeford said, her voice soft yet steely. "Come closer, ladies. We must make a list of suspects."

Clutching their cards, the Rosebuds leaned into the table, their gazes occasionally flitting over the company of aristocrats. Laughter and chatter mingled with the crackling of the log fire on the hearth. Footmen moved about the long chamber, offering refreshments of wine and other spirits.

"Sir George Rampling," Lady Enid murmured. "He's been sulking because Vivien is clever enough to spurn his suit."

"Lord Alfred Yarborough," said Lady Stokeford. "What a prig he is."

"Viscount Beldon," Lady Faversham pronounced. "Though his grandfather was in trade, he thinks himself superior to Vivien."

Surreptitiously, Vivien surveyed the drawing room. Sir George and Lord Alfred played cards with two other gentlemen who had paid court to her over the past few days, presumably drawn by rumors of the large dowry. Then her attention moved to the table where Charlotte and the vicar shared a table with the fox-faced Viscount Beldon, who groomed his little moustache with his forefinger and thumb. Opposite him, the pinch-mouthed Duchess of Covington gazed down her snooty nose at her cards.

Feeling a spurt of anger, Vivien wished she could point the finger of blame at the duchess. Just then, Lady Katherine and Michael rose from the chaise. When he made a move as if to walk away, she took his arm and spoke to him a moment, standing so close that her bosom brushed his chest. Then the cad strolled with her toward the pianoforte.

Before seating herself on the bench, Katherine glanced directly at Vivien, her aristocratic features showing a hint of triumph. She sat down, arranged her skirts, and began to play a lilting melody with effortless ease. All the while she chatted with Michael, who leaned against the pianoforte and turned the pages of the songbook for her.

That look of victory burned Vivien like a hot coal. Lady Katherine was determined to keep Michael for herself. She regarded Vivien as a rival to be bested . . .

The cards spilled from her frozen fingers. Though she sat close to the hearth, she felt cold in every part of herself. Interrupting the Rosebuds, she said in a thready whisper, "Perhaps the ring wasn't stolen."

"What?" Lady Faversham demanded. "Do you know where Katherine lost it?"

"No." Her mouth dry, Vivien looked at each of them in turn. "I believe she hid the ring. Then she announced the robbery in hopes I'd be thrown out of this house. I wouldn't be surprised if she and her cousin plotted together."

"Mercy me!" Lady Enid gasped out. "We hadn't considered that."

"It's fiendishly clever," Lady Faversham said grimly.

"And precisely what that scheming Katherine would do," Lady Stokeford said, her blue eyes narrowing. "I must alert Michael immediately."

"Not yet, m'lady. He won't believe you without proof." Caught up in a rush of wrath, Vivien pushed back her chair. "First, I'll search her chamber and find the ring. Will you come upstairs and show me which room is hers?"

"Patience," Lady Stokeford said in a soothing whisper. Rising, she rounded the table, took Vivien's arm, and added in an undertone, "Smile, my dear. People are watching. We'll quell the gossip before we stroll out into the corridor where there are not so many listening ears."

Vivien forced her lips into a pleasant expression. Though itching to hurry, she made herself walk slowly, matching her pace to Lady Stokeford's graceful steps, while the other Rosebuds followed close behind them.

She glanced at Michael and found him broodingly watching her progress through the drawing room, though he made no move to leave his paramour. He'd scarcely spoken to Vivien all day, not even when they were interviewing the servants. Now, the intensity of his regard caused a flurry of goose bumps over her skin. Against her will, she felt a softening inside her, a yearning she shouldn't feel for this *gorgio* man who would never view her as any more than a lying, cheating vagabond.

The Rosebuds stopped to exchange pleasantries with Lady Charlotte, Viscount Beldon, the fawning vicar, and Hillary, the Duchess of Covington, who promptly dominated the conversation. The duchess had elaborately styled brown hair, a thick form, and a small nose that twitched like Nibbles the rabbit's. Her hand stroked the pug dog nestled in her lap. Pointedly, she ignored Vivien, addressing only the elderly ladies.

Charlotte rolled her eyes at Vivien and pretended to yawn behind her gloved hand. But Vivien spared her friend only a glance. She seethed with resentment of the duchess. Who was this *gorgio* lady to regard her as a peasant unworthy of notice? Worse yet, a criminal, when likely she herself had plotted with her cousin to brand Vivien a thief.

Unable to stop herself, Vivien stepped forward to command the duchess's attention. "That's a lovely necklace, Your Grace."

With undue haste, the duchess clapped her hand over the magnificent jewels at her throat. "It's a Covington family heirloom."

"The emeralds and diamonds must be worth a fortune," Vivien said, letting her realize that two could play this game of burglary. "You must take care to keep them locked up, lest you lose them to our thief."

"How thoughtful of you, my dear girl," Lady Stokeford said, her sky-blue eyes bright with approval. "Indeed, we must all be watchful."

The duchess's pale eyes turned frosty. "You should have called in the magistrate, Lucy. Never before have I attended a house party where a vicious robber stalked the guests."

"You exaggerate, Hillary," Lady Faversham said crisply. "I've no doubt your cousin's ring will turn up soon."

"Hmph. I wish to know what's being done to find it."

"You may trust that I have the matter well in hand," Lady Stokeford said breezily. "If you'll excuse us now."

Vivien and the Rosebuds strolled out the arched doorway, leaving the hum of conversation behind them along with the sprightly music from the pianoforte. She caught one last glimpse of Michael watching her exit the drawing room. A footman stood on duty by the front door in the foyer, so they headed in the opposite direction.

"My stars," Lady Enid murmured, "didn't Vivien give the duchess a well-deserved tease?"

"It was hardly the way to win her approval," Lady Faversham said, her hands folded around the knob of her cane. But her gray eyes twinkled and she didn't look terribly displeased.

"She'll be even more miffed when we find Katherine's

ring and prove her story a fraud," Lady Stokeford declared. "Vicious robber, indeed!"

"Aren't we going upstairs?" Vivien asked as they passed the curving grandeur of the main staircase.

"We Rosebuds shall proceed by way of a back stairway," Lady Stokeford said gently. "You, Vivien, must return to the drawing room."

"No!" Vivien whirled around to face the Rosebuds in the empty passageway. "*My* honor is at stake. *I* must find that ring."

Lady Stokeford patted Vivien's hand. "I'm afraid not, my dear. Think of how damning it would look if you were discovered in that woman's bedchamber, rifling through her possessions. If you did find the ring, you'd be called a thief the moment you appeared with it in your hand!"

"The maid is likely to be there, anyway," Lady Faversham added. "While we can send Colette away on an errand, your presence would arouse her suspicions."

"Go to my granddaughter," Lady Enid suggested. "You and Charlotte can plan your costumes for the masquerade ball. You've only two more days until then, you know."

"An excellent notion," Lady Stokeford said. "Now come along, Rosebuds. Time is of the essence."

The three old ladies hastened away down the corridor, clucking and whispering amongst themselves.

Vivien stood there until they vanished around a corner. She could understand their concern. It made more sense that they should search for the ring. Yet she despised being left behind. A restless energy drove her to pace back and forth, her footsteps echoing in the deserted corridor.

She considered returning to the drawing room and fetching Charlotte, who'd be happy for an excuse to leave the party of card players. But that would mean seeing Michael again. It was enough to hear the faint notes of the pianoforte and know that he still fawned over Katherine Westbrook.

Fuming with discontent, Vivien felt a need to escape the confinement of these *gorgio* walls, where intrigues and jealousies abounded. She ventured into a darkened chamber and found a door that opened onto a long terrace overlooking the formal garden.

The night air held the nip of autumn, and she hugged herself, wishing for a shawl but reluctant to go back for one. She darted lightly down the stone steps and into the shadowy garden, pausing only long enough to remove her slippers and wriggle her toes. Though the ground was cold and damp from the previous day's rain, she left her shoes on the steps and kept to the paving stones that meandered through the beds of cultivated roses.

She halted at the very edge of the moonlit garden, where the forest began, gloomy and impenetrable. Breathing deeply, she savored the fresh scents of earth and wind. A hint of woodsmoke in the air stirred nostalgia in her. It was only the hearth fires from the Abbey, she knew. Yet she wanted to believe the scent emanated from somewhere deep in the woods, from the campsite where her parents would now be staying.

The ever-present ache inside her grew sharper, stronger. She wanted so desperately to go to them, to bask in their love and protection. She wanted to hear her mother's wise advice and feel her father's bear hug. The desire was so powerful, she took several steps toward the trees, tempted to plunge into the gloom and keep walking.

But she wasn't a little girl anymore. She was a woman of eighteen, and she needed to care for her parents now. She needed to bring home two hundred guineas so that her father and mother could enjoy comforts in their old age. That knowledge stopped her like an insurmountable wall.

Behind her, the Abbey rose like a black monolith against the starry sky. A row of darkened windows marked the picture gallery, where yesterday Michael had taken her to the heights of rapture. It seemed almost like a dream now, a magical, wondrous moment that couldn't have been real.

Yet it *had* been real. In his arms, she'd found bodily joy. *Gorgio* rogue or not, he had made her feel fully a woman.

Her gaze shifted to the candlelit windows of the drawing room, but she could see only the shadows of movement. She shouldn't long for a man who thought himself her superior. She shouldn't allow herself to be ruled by the natural yearnings of her body.

Turning her back to the house, she shut her eyes. When she opened them again, she saw her worst nightmare.

Janus!

A few feet ahead of her, his hulking dark shape emerged from the woods. She had no time to run, no time to do more than cry out in alarm. Bounding forward, he seized her by the arms. "I knew you'd come to me, *juvali,*" he said gruffly in the Romany tongue.

"I'm not your betrothed," she snapped, tugging at his grip. "Release me, else I'll scream. You'll spend the rest of your days in a *gorgio* prison."

He laughed, a cocksure sound that grated on her nerves. "Don't fight me. Lest Reyna and Pulika find out what you've been doing."

His feral scent made her stomach queasy. So did her guilty conscience. But he couldn't possibly know about that. "Have my parents arrived, then?"

He grunted an assent.

"How do they fare?" she asked anxiously. "Are they well? Has my father's leg been hurting him?"

"They pine for you, that's what. Come, let me take you to them."

He started to pull her toward the woods, but she balked. "I'm not yet ready to go back. But do tell them I miss them very much."

"Bah. You haven't given them a thought. You've kept company with Lord Stokeford." In the moonlight, his mastiff features held a look of resentful fury. "I've been watching you. Both of you."

Again, that uneasy fear slithered through her. "You've no right to spy. This is Lord Stokeford's land."

"He's a *gorgio* dog," he said in a guttural tone. "I saw the two of you yesterday. Pawing each other in the window."

A sick revulsion soured her throat. Janus had witnessed that kiss? She shook her head in denial. "No," she whispered. "You saw nothing."

"Liar! You let him fondle you. I should tell Pulika you've given your maidenhead to that devil."

Horrified, she stared at his dark eyes, the flaring nostrils, the sweeping moustache over his bared teeth. *He* was the devil, not Michael. She wanted to beg for his silence, but stopped herself. As much as she feared shaming her parents, she also felt an intense desire to guard that special, private memory.

Think, she told herself. *Trick him.* "Where were you standing?" she asked mockingly. "All the way out in the woods?"

"Yes," he said. "But I have eyes. I know what I saw."

"The rain poured down all day, and there are many guests in the house. It must have been one of the other women you saw."

"I know my betrothed," he insisted, though a hint of doubt crept into his voice. "It was you in the window."

"I've not given myself to Lord Stokeford. That's the truth. Let go now, you're hurting me."

Janus stared suspiciously. "You're pure?"

"*Haisheli!* I swear it."

His hold eased, though he didn't release her. To her disgust, he dragged her closer. "Your virginity doesn't matter, anyway," he muttered. "I'll still take you to be my wife."

"And I *told* you, there is no betrothal."

He went on as if she hadn't spoken. "We'll wed, and you'll stay here for as long as I say. You'll give the hundred guineas a month to me."

Outraged, she shook her head. "The money is for my parents."

"Then trick those old ladies into giving you more gold. Or steal it. You must have plenty of opportunities, eh?"

Vivien stared at him through the darkness. No wonder he was so persistent in his suit. He was as greedy as the *gorgio* gentlemen who had courted her for her dowry. "I wouldn't give you a farthing," she snapped.

"Willful girl." His grip tightened on her arms. "You'll do as I say, else I'll tell your father you lust for a *gorgio* lord."

His garlicky breath blew on her. She was frighteningly aware of his strength and how alone they were here at the edge of the darkened garden. Even as she recoiled, ready to strike him, she heard footsteps on the terrace.

A familiar deep voice called out her name. "Vivien!"

With a weakening wave of relief, she saw Michael's shadowed form dashing down the steps and into the garden.

Janus uttered a curse and released her. She ran headlong down the path and met Michael halfway. Flinging herself against him, she pressed her cheek to his smooth waistcoat, absorbing the reassuring beats of his heart. She felt cold to the core, ashamed and afraid, in desperate need of his heat.

He held her close for a moment, his arms tight and bracing. His lips brushed her hair, and his hands moved over her back. "Did he hurt you?"

"No . . . I'm f-fine." To her vague surprise, her teeth were chattering. Then a greater shock jarred her. *Did he hurt you?* He had seen Janus.

"Stay here." Setting her aside, Michael raced toward the woods.

Vivien ran after him. She could think only that he would fight Janus, that the commotion would attract the attention of the guests, and she would disgrace Lady Stokeford for certain. "Michael, come back!"

But her worries were for naught. Janus had melted into the woods. The moonlit grass showed only the faint flattening of his footprints.

Michael pivoted to face her. "He's gone, dammit. I'll get some men with torches. We'll flush him out—"

"No!" she cried out, catching hold of his arms, absorbing the power in him, the tension of fury. "It's too dark. You'll never find him. He's gone."

His face shadowed in the moonlight, he stared down at her. "Who is he? Who are you protecting?"

"I'm not protecting anyone."

He seized her shoulders. "Tell me his name, Vivien. It was someone you knew. Your lover."

"No!" Sickened, she couldn't let him think that. "Janus is not my lover."

His fingers tightened on her. "Janus," he growled. "He's the Gypsy man you intend to marry."

She shook her head. "He asked, but I've refused him." Realizing Janus could be out there watching them, she tugged on Michael's arm. "Let's go inside. We can talk in the house."

"You're afraid of him."

"I'm cold, that's all." Vivien shivered, proving she didn't lie.

"You ran to me for protection."

"No, I—I wanted to stop you from following him."

He made a disbelieving sound and escorted her toward the terrace, his strides long and angry. Her disquiet increased as she sensed a dangerous purpose in him. Would he listen to her? Or was he still bent on chasing Janus?

He opened the door and motioned to her. "Go in."

"Only if you come with me. You can't go after Janus."

"The devil I can't. He's trespassing on what belongs to me."

Did Michael mean . . . *her*? Even as Vivien thrilled to his possessiveness, she felt the chill of a shadow. If he organized a search party, he might discover the campsite of the *Rom*.

She took urgent hold of his arms again. "He's taken nothing of yours. He's gone now, and that's all that matters."

"You and I have a difference of opinion, then."

Michael gave her a little push toward the doorway, but she pressed her fingers against the iron muscles of his arms. In a panic, she blurted out, "Please, you mustn't go! You mustn't search. You'll find my parents!"

That caught his attention. His keen eyes glittered through the darkness. "Your parents."

"Yes," Vivien said, prepared to throw herself at his feet if necessary. "I beg you, don't drive them off your land. They've come to be near me, that's all. They're good people, kind and decent. They'd never harm anyone."

"This Janus, he wanted to take you to them."

Her eyes stinging with tears, she nodded jerkily. "I would have gone, but . . ."

"But?"

"But I need the money your grandmother is paying me. To help my parents in their old age. My father can no longer work at odd jobs."

Michael stood silent, unmoving. The moonlight silvered his hair and cast his features into shadow. She sensed a wildness in him, a struggle with disbelief. What had made him such a harsh, cynical man? Was it a hateful prejudice against the *Rom*? Or the loss of his beloved wife? More than ever, she sensed pain in him, the ashes of a cold fire. Could he ever feel the warmth of love again?

She knew only the answer to the last question, for he had displayed tenderness and affection toward his daughter. He had punished Thaddeus Tremain and shown justice to his tenants these past weeks, raising their wages and repairing their cottages. And he could touch a woman gently, too. Even now, in the midst of her fear for her parents, his nearness aroused in her a passionate need to soothe the hurting heart he kept hidden. She wanted so badly to lean forward and press her lips to his, to feel his arms close around her in a loving embrace . . .

"Come inside," he muttered.

Vivien drew a shaky breath. "First, promise me that you won't approach my mother and father. You won't expel them from your land."

"I've no quarrel with them."

She wanted to trust him. But in this, she would take no risks. "You gentlemen make much of your honor. So give me your word that you won't go near them."

He cast a final, penetrating stare at the woods. Then he nodded. "If it pleases you," he said, "you have it."

Michael ushered her inside a shadowy antechamber, closing the door behind them. His blood ran hot with the urge to punish Janus for laying his hands on Vivien. Initially, he'd gone out onto the terrace in search of her, directed by a footman who had chanced to glimpse her leaving the house. Already suspicious of her purpose, he'd been struck with rage by the sight of the entwined couple. Then as now, he wanted to kill the bastard. For a fraction of a moment, the blood lust overwhelmed Michael with the need to charge outside and track the Gypsy like a dog.

But he had given her his vow not to send out a search party. Bloody hell! He'd have some answers at least. For once, he'd have the truth from her.

Vivien hastened ahead of him, her slippers whispering over the stone floor. Before she could reach the passageway, Michael caught her by the arm and swung her around to face him. "So you've been meeting that Gypsy."

"No, I haven't—"

"Don't deny it. You saw him in the woods at the picnic, too."

She drew in an audible breath. "By mischance, that's all."

"I see. Your betrothed just happened to be strolling through the woods on my property. Then again at night near my house."

He could feel the fire that always leapt between them, the short fuse of anger . . . and passion. "He is *not* my betrothed," she burst out. "Why can't you accept that?"

"Then why did he come here tonight?"

"I told you, to let me know that my parents are nearby."

But a slight hesitation in her voice hinted otherwise. "That isn't the whole of it," he said harshly. "Tell me the real reason."

She must be having an affair with Janus, damn her. A woman so beautiful and fiery had to have lovers. It was unthinkable that no man had ever touched her. But he had no time to pursue the thought, for she went wild with fury, lashing out with her fists, battering his chest.

"Devil! You think I gave Lady Katherine's ring to Janus!"

He caught her flailing arms. "I never said that."

"*Sheka!* You believe me a thief. I curse you!"

Michael pushed her against the wall, imprisoning her with his body, her softness arousing him even now, in the heat of their quarrel. She wriggled and fought, and the strength of her outrage took all of his wits to control. "Calm yourself," he snapped. "You can't get away, so you may as well listen to me."

She struggled for another moment, then went limp, her bosom heaving. Her scent enticed him like a siren's call. Determined to finish his inquiry, he eased back a little, forcing his mind away from the demands of his body.

He *had* suspected Vivien at first. But she was too clever to jeopardize her place here with petty thievery. The more he'd mulled over the problem, the more his suspicions had turned to Katherine Westbrook. She had ample reason to discredit Vivien. Better than most men, he knew that women used tricks and artifice to get their way.

"I wasn't thinking about the ring when I went outside tonight," he admitted. "I thought you were meeting your lover."

"Is that meant to comfort me? That you believe me a whore?"

There was a certain breathy catch to her voice that belied her angry tone. Curbing the violent need in himself, he stroked his knuckles across her cheek and over her lips. "I believe you're a passionate woman," he murmured. "*My* woman."

Vivien expelled a sharp breath. "I'll never belong to such a man as you. A man who looks down on me as a beggar and a thief."

"The question of who took the ring remains to be seen.

Katherine agreed to look again, to make certain she didn't misplace it."

"To look—" Vivien went very still.

He could discern her fine features in the shadows, the soft lips he wanted to kiss. The need was so powerful, he lacked the inclination to resist it. As he lowered his head, she caught hold of his coat and said in a rather alarmed tone, "Where's Lady Katherine? Has she gone to search *now*?"

"When I left the drawing room, she was chatting with her cousin. But yes, she meant to retire to her chamber shortly."

He tried again to kiss her, but with a gasp, Vivien turned her head away. "Oh, no! The Rosebuds!" She ducked beneath his arm and hastened toward the corridor.

Annoyed, he stalked after her. "What about the Rosebuds?"

In the doorway, she spun back toward him, her eyes large and luminous in the shadows. "I must warn them. They're searching Lady Katherine's bedchamber right now!"

Chapter twenty

The Sinister Monk

From the moment she entered the crowded ballroom two nights later, Vivien heard the whispers and saw the stares. A Gypsy these aristocrats could accept out of respect for Lady Stokeford. But a Gypsy who would steal from one of them was another matter entirely.

Tonight was the masquerade ball, the grand finale to her ladyship's house party. Neighbors from miles around came in carriages that poured down the front drive in an endless stream. In the midst of the noble guests, Vivien walked straight and proud. Rather than array herself in the stiff, pearl-encrusted gown of a *gorgio* princess as the Rosebuds had wished, she had decided on an act of bold defiance. She wore the traditional garb of the *Rom.*

The full turquoise skirt swished around her bare feet. The saffron-yellow bodice dipped fashionably low over her bosom. Gold bangles chimed at her wrists, and a wide sash cinched her waist. How natural and free she felt in the familiar raiment of her upbringing. Sewn by her ladyship's personal seamstress, the costume was made of the softest silks and satins.

She thought guiltily that *dado* and *dye* couldn't afford

to purchase such fine fabrics, though her parents had always bestowed on her the riches of their love. It was for their sake that she was here, pretending to be a lady. Scandalized murmurs swept in her wake, but she kept a disdainful façade. Let these small-minded noble folk see that she had done nothing wrong. Let them know she scorned their suspicions.

Despite the best efforts of the Rosebuds, Lady Katherine's diamond ring had not been found. Vivien had told Michael about their plan to search her chambers, and together they'd rushed upstairs to warn his grandmother. He'd been furious, of course. Escorting his grandmother to her boudoir, he'd chastised her, and Vivien had defended Lady Stokeford with heated words. In the end, he'd admitted to the possibility of wrongdoing on the part of Lady Katherine Westbrook, and he'd agreed to look into the matter. Vivien had heard no more about it.

Only later had another suspicion occurred to her. What if Janus *had* stolen the ring? He'd admitted to skulking in the bushes outside the Abbey. Perhaps he'd entered the house during the treasure hunt. The thought of encountering him in a deserted corridor made Vivien shudder. She'd kept a sharp watch, but thankfully he seemed to have vanished like a puff of smoke.

Taking a deep breath of air flavored by a score of fine perfumes, she willed her worries to vanish, too. For tonight, she'd ignore the gossips. She would enjoy the evening to its fullest, her first real ball in the *gorgio* world.

The long, high-ceilinged ballroom glowed with the light of a thousand candles. Vivien felt as if she'd stepped into a fairyland full of fantastical creatures. There were queens and courtiers, nymphs and knights, Turks and Greeks and costumes of other nationalities she did not know. Most people wore half-masks, as she did. But a keen scrutiny revealed the identity of quite a few guests.

The Rosebuds, clad as the Three Graces in classical white robes, flitted hither and yon through the crowd. She didn't see Lady Katherine anywhere, but she recognized the Duchess of Covington by her mousy brown hair and superior smile, a red Japanese kimono draping her thick form. The duchess chatted with a king in a white periwig and cavalier's clothing, and by his small, bristly moustache Vivien knew him to be Lord Beldon. Deliberately she turned away from those two.

She caught herself searching for a tall, powerful man with dark hair and a sensual smile who made her toes curl and her heart race. What disguise had Michael chosen? She could imagine him as a hero in the legends and stories that she had read avidly over the past few weeks: St. George who slew the dragon; Apollo, the most handsome of the gods; King Arthur with his knights of the Round Table.

No, he'd be nothing so glorious. He'd be a seductive rogue, a highwayman, perhaps. He had plagued her thoughts during the day and invaded her dreams at night. Lying alone in bed, she would toss and turn, her body flushed and aching for his touch . . .

"Hsst, Gypsy!"

Near the dais where the orchestra tuned their instruments, a woman motioned to her. She wore the flowing green gown of a medieval princess, and her thick chestnut hair streamed loose, crowned by a gold circlet. As always, long sleeves and gloves hid her scarred arm. A green domino concealed her features, but Vivien knew Lady Charlotte at once.

The man standing beside Charlotte gawked at Vivien. That gangly Roman senator with the large front teeth, olive-branch crown, and shiny purple mask could only be Lord Alfred.

He bowed to her. "Who is this loveliest of maidens?

Remove thy mask and show us thy full beauty."

Not even Lord Alfred could be so stupid as to mistake her identity. "Nay, sir," Vivien said demurely. "You're too bold."

Charlotte prodded him in the chest with her gold scepter. "Knave. You said *I* was the loveliest of maidens. You must stop repeating yourself."

His mouth opened and shut and opened again. "Pray do not take offense, my princess, for both of you are ravishing. Perhaps the Gypsy can foretell if I will be lucky in love tonight."

He turned to Vivien, and the slits of his mask revealed the avid gleam of his eyes. His gaze lingered on her décolletage, and his open interest made her hackles rise. Like all the others, he believed her a thief, and a thief surely possessed easy morals.

Taking his hand, she bent low to study his palm. She muttered nonsense in Romany while he shifted from one sandaled foot to the other. "What do you see?" he asked.

"Something very odd . . . something unusual . . ." She gasped dramatically, then dropped his hand and took a few steps backward as if in horror. "Oh! I cannot tell you."

"Tell me what?" Lord Alfred demanded.

"It is the curse. *The curse.*"

"Curse?" His leer changing to alarm, he peered down at his palm. "W-what do you mean?"

"Do not ask. It's best you not know." She spun away, giving Charlotte a secret wink. Charlotte bit down hard on her lip, her green eyes dancing behind the domino.

Lord Alfred stepped in front of Vivien, his palm outstretched like a beggar's. "Enlighten me! You cannot hold me in suspense." He gulped visibly. "Am I . . . to die soon?"

"Rather, you're doomed to live," she said cryptically. "To suffer a terrible loss."

"Loss? I beg you, speak plainly."

"Very well, then. You're doomed to be made a eunuch." She made a slashing gesture. "Cut off in your prime."

He jumped, and his hand made an involuntary move toward his groin. Then he scowled, crossing his arms over his senatorial robe. "By Jove! You are funning me, Miss Thorne."

"Actually," Charlotte said slyly, "Vivien didn't need to look at your palm to make her prediction. You're certain to lose your family jewels if you continue to provoke the ladies."

Through her mask, Vivien gave Lord Alfred the evil eye. "*Bengui!*" she said, pointing her finger in a menacing gesture. "Beware the angry woman."

"Stuff and nonsense." He took a step toward her, his face threatening, his lips thinned. "You would dare to ridicule a lord of the realm. Perhaps the duchess is right. Perhaps you did steal her cousin's ring."

Vivien stiffened. "That's a lie."

"You can't say such a thing to her," Charlotte huffed.

Ignoring Charlotte, he stuck his face in front of Vivien's. "You're nothing but a pretty trickster. You should leave here before you're arrested."

"*You* should leave before you're thrashed within an inch of your life," said a hard, male voice from behind Vivien.

She whirled around to see Michael garbed as a pirate in a billowy white shirt, black breeches, and knee-high boots. A brace of long-barreled pistols protruded from his belt, and in lieu of a mask, he wore a rakish patch over one eye. When she caught a trace of his scent, something intoxicatingly male, she wanted to put her face to his chest and breathe deeply.

Charlotte strolled to his side. "Now here's a handsome buccaneer," she said. "He'll rescue us from this dullard."

Michael paid her no heed. His one-eyed gaze drilled into Lord Alfred. "Apologize to Vivien."

"What? The Gypsy tried to bamboozle me—"

"Apologize. Else you and I shall step outside to settle this affair."

"S-settle?"

Michael caressed the ivory butt of a pistol. "The trouble is, only one of us shall return to enjoy the party."

Lord Alfred stood with his mouth working like a fish's. Then he sank to one knee before Vivien, his bent head revealing a bald spot within the circle of his olive-leaf coronet. "A thousand pardons, Miss Thorne. I don't know what came over me. I meant you no disrespect."

Though she knew he lied, his groveling satisfied her. "Rise," she commanded. "Be gone from my sight."

Hastening to his feet, he caught his sandal on his senatorial robes and stumbled over a chair to the sound of ripping fabric. Trailing a piece of his hem, he slunk away into the crowd.

"Pea-brained plebeian," Michael said. "He deserves a fist in his face."

Vivien told herself not to feel thrilled by his defense of her. The room shouldn't sparkle just because Michael stood near. Her breath shouldn't catch in her throat, and her body shouldn't quiver with awareness of him. She shouldn't see anything worthy in this *gorgio* rogue.

Coolly, she said, "I'd already dealt with Lord Alfred. Your assistance wasn't necessary."

"She told his fortune," Charlotte put in. "I know you don't approve of such Gypsy tricks, Michael, but she did so very cleverly, indeed."

"She's a clever girl. Quite adept at avoiding the company of those whom she cannot bend to her will." Focusing one brilliant blue eye on Vivien, he extended his hand to her. "I trust you'll grant me the first dance."

He would choose her as his partner? Her mind whirled with confusion and excitement. Vivien stared at his hand, the tanned flesh with a sprinkling of dark hairs and the long fingers that could arouse her to such pleasure. He had neatly trapped her, she knew. If she accepted, he would have his way. Yet if she refused, it would be tantamount to admitting she couldn't manage him.

What did it matter anyway? she thought in a rush of recklessness. She *wanted* to dance with him.

Their eyes were locked. Ever so slowly, she reached out to him. Warm and firm, his fingers closed around hers, and she glowed with a giddy awareness of the life force that surged between them.

"You mustn't dance the first set with him," Charlotte protested. "He's a rake. People will talk."

"They're already talking," Vivien said, flashing a smile at her friend and scarcely noticing that Charlotte didn't smile back.

Then Michael swept her away through the throng of people. Heads turned, voices whispered, fans waved faster, yet Vivien could think only of the man at her side, their linked hands drawing her along. He looked every inch the pirate, looter of gold and ravisher of women.

Anticipation bubbled like champagne through her veins. She wondered again why he'd bestowed on her the honor of the first dance. Did she mean more to him than a conquest to be won? Had she sparked a fire in the cold ashes of his heart? Those were dangerous questions, she knew. She mustn't wonder; she must simply enjoy the moment.

As they neared the dance floor, she saw the Rosebuds

gathered in a group, smiling and waggling their fingers at her. That gave her a sudden suspicion. "Did Lady Stokeford tell you to dance with me?"

His mouth twisted in a wolfish grin. "Hardly. I choose my own partners."

It was amazing how his smile could warm her insides. They joined the other dancers forming two lines down the center of the ballroom, the men on one side and the ladies on the other. Taking her place opposite Michael, she stood between a dumpy Queen Bess with a stiff ruff circling her neck and a thin woman in a mustard-yellow Indian sari. Both of them eyed her askance as the orchestra launched into a formal melody, but Vivien saw only Michael.

He bowed to her and she curtsied; then they commenced the steps that she'd practiced for weeks under the tutelage of the Rosebuds. She took care to perform each action with perfection, giving Michael her hand again as she gracefully moved around him. They switched hands and he repeated the steps. After a few moments of concentration, she felt at one with the *gorgio* melody, gliding as if she'd been born to it.

"You dance well," he said.

"Surprised, m'lord marquess?" She cast him a saucy look. "Perhaps the music of the *gorgios* is in my blood."

"Or perhaps you have a natural gift for mimicry."

"As you have a natural gift for skepticism."

His teeth flashed in a pirate's grin. He guided her around him, then asked, "Tell me, how does this compare to your Gypsy dancing?"

"Our songs are much livelier."

"I'll tell the musicians to play a reel."

"But these formal steps would still restrain us. We of the *Rom* dance with feeling, with freedom. And the women do most of the dancing."

His unpatched eye gleamed with interest. "They dance for the men?"

"Yes. Sometimes in groups and sometimes alone."

He bent nearer, his warm breath caressing her cheek. "You must dance for me, then," he murmured in her ear. "When next we're alone."

Her blood quickened, making her light-headed. She should rebuff him, yet no clever words sprang to her mind. She was caught up by the vivid image of Michael reclining by the campfire, his smoldering eyes fixed on her as she twirled and dipped, enticing him with the sinuous movements of a woman for her beloved . . .

The steps momentarily separated them, and in a daze, she linked arms with a portly knight whose armor clanked as he stiffly circled her. Then she did the same with the next man, a king in cavalier's garb and long curly wig.

Viscount Beldon. His little moustache twitched as he stared up into her face, for he was a few inches shorter than she. Yet not even his sneer could mar the magic of the night.

She rejoined Michael as the two lines of dancers lifted their arms to form a long archway. One by one, the couples dipped beneath the arch and stepped fleetly to the other end. Then the music drifted to a close and he grasped her hands for a moment, devouring her with a look of hunger, a rawly sexual intent that both alarmed and enticed her.

She felt the leaping of flame inside her, and an almost painful yearning for his embrace. People swirled past them, chatting and laughing, assembling for the next dance, but Vivien was only vaguely aware of their curious eyes. Her entire awareness concentrated on Michael in his buccaneer's garb, his sinful half smile making her bare toes curl.

If in that moment he had invited her to leave the ballroom with him, she might have succumbed to the weakness inside her. She might have done his bidding, danced for him alone, let him touch her as he willed . . .

But he merely squeezed her fingers, then let go. In a low, guttural tone, he said, "I'll see you later."

Transfixed, she watched him stride off like a swaggering corsair into the milling crowd. What did he mean? That he would ask her to dance again? Or perhaps . . . perhaps he would come to her bedchamber?

Her bosom rose and fell with quickened breaths. *Develesa,* would he be so bold? *Yes.* She felt an imprudent desire to open her door to him . . . and her heart. She wanted to believe his regard for her went deeper than mere bodily passion; she wanted to disregard all the reasons he was wrong for her.

Then the crowd shifted and she spied him again. He went straight to an Egyptian princess in filmy gold robes with a serpent-adorned crown on her blond curls. She slithered as close to him as manners allowed.

Lady Katherine.

Vivien's skin went cold from a flood of icy pain. So much for his serious regard for her. The knave kept a mistress, and she was angry at her own foolishness in forgetting that fact. Michael Kenyon was a *gorgio* lord who took his pleasure where he willed.

Turning her back on them, Vivien stalked through the crush of guests, picking up a glass from the tray of a passing footman. While she drank the champagne, the bubbles tickling her throat, she searched in vain for a friendly face. But the Rosebuds and Charlotte were nowhere to be seen, and these noble folk edged away from her, shutting her out so that she wanted to hurl curses at them. She knew that to them, she would never be anything more than a sly Gypsy thief.

"Found you!" A stout man clad in the bright red and

gold garb of a court jester sprang into her path. Despite his harlequin mask, his barrel shape and springy brown curls gave him away as Sir George Rampling. He swept a dramatic bow, the bells jingling on his lofty hat. "Fair Gypsy, I've been seeking you all evening. Will you honor me with a dance?"

She almost refused the buffoon. But why should she spoil the ball by brooding over Michael and his noble friends? "Fie, sir, of course I'll dance."

As Sir George partnered her, she had to bite back a laugh at his foolish prancing. Then the armored knight approached her for the next set, and with guarded surprise she found herself much in demand by the masked gentlemen, some dull and others amusing. The few insulting ones she took pleasure in besting with a sharp quip or a Gypsy hex.

From time to time, she saw Michael squiring other ladies, and Katherine twice more. But Vivien refused to wonder why he didn't approach her again. She would find her own enjoyment in the festive atmosphere, and he could go to the devil.

After a time, she looked again for Charlotte, but her friend seemed to have vanished. Charlotte jokingly called herself an old maid, with a certain bitterness in her tone, but surely she wasn't sitting out the dancing with the matrons who gossiped at one end of the ballroom. Perhaps she'd gone outside. It was almost midnight, time for the fireworks display in the garden. Already a few people were strolling in the direction of the glass doors that were opened to the chilly night. Afterward, there would be an elaborate supper and then more dancing.

Remembering the promise she'd made to Amy, Vivien headed toward the archway that led into the corridor. She must go up to the nursery. The little girl had begged to be awakened for the fireworks, and Vivien's heart had melted at her pleading. In truth, she was delighted that Amy preferred her company over all the other fine ladies present.

As she went out into the passageway, Vivien removed the bothersome domino and tossed it onto a nearby table. Then she spied Charlotte by the staircase. She stood with a tall, lean man in the rough brown robe of a monk.

A loose cowl draped his head, casting his face into shadow. He wore a black domino that further concealed his features. There was something furtive in the way he glanced toward the ballroom. As if he were watching for someone.

Though his stance was casual, the two appeared to be quarreling. Vivien could tell by the rigid way Charlotte crossed her arms and thrust out her lower lip.

As Vivien approached, the man looked up, straight at her, and she noticed the half-moon scar bracketing one side of his mouth. A sharp breath seared her. No wonder an aura of stealth surrounded the monk. He was Brand Villiers, the Earl of Faversham.

Stopping before him, she curtsied as the Rosebuds had taught her. "Charlotte! And Lord Faversham, I'm surprised to see you here."

His mouth curled into something halfway between a grimace and a grin. Pushing back his cowl and taking off his mask, he ran his fingers through his hair, ruffling the dark brown strands. "Devil take it. I thought this an excellent disguise."

"You, a monk," Charlotte mocked. "How preposterous."

"Don't think I have it in me, eh?" He made the sign of the cross over her. "Bless you, my child. Your sins are forgiven."

Snorting, Charlotte pushed his arm away. "You're the sinner, not I."

Worriedly, Vivien regarded him. "Michael was very angry to find you here a few days ago, m'lord. Do you think it wise to come back?"

"He wasn't invited, of course," Charlotte snapped spitefully. "This ball isn't for ne'er-do-wells."

"Nor for sour old spinsters," he said in amusement.

Charlotte stiffened all the more. "Michael will be furious," she hissed. "I've a good mind to tell him you're here."

He shrugged. "Do as you wish. You always have."

"Then I shall. I'll find him and he'll throw you out of here." Whirling around, she flounced off toward the ballroom.

Stunned by her malice, Vivien turned to Lord Faversham. "I'm sorry. It isn't like Charlotte to be so ill-mannered. I'll have a talk with her."

His chuckle echoed down the long corridor. "Let her go. She's on a fool's mission."

"What do you mean?"

"Not ten minutes ago, I saw Michael go upstairs with Katherine Westbrook."

A sword of shock plunged into Vivien's breast, driving out all thought of Charlotte's rudeness. He would take his mistress to his bed in the midst of a party. He would caress her with his skilled fingers; he would hold her close and kiss her passionately. A savage pain throttled Vivien. Curse him! Curse herself for hoping he might care for her.

Lord Faversham took hold of her arm. "You're pale. I didn't mean to distress you."

A keen curiosity lit his eyes. Did he guess her feelings for Michael? With effort, she subdued her wild emotions. "I'm fine. If you'll excuse me, I must go upstairs. I promised Amy I'd awaken her for the fireworks."

"Michael's daughter." Lord Faversham made no move

to release his hold on Vivien. He stared at her through narrowed gray eyes, and she was uneasily aware of a coiled tension in him. The sensation was nothing she could have defined or wholly understood, but it was there nonetheless. "I've never had the chance to meet the girl," he added. "I'll go with you."

Why would a rake like him bother to meet a four-year-old child? "But Amy will be asleep. She'll be frightened if she awakens to anyone but me."

"I'll stay back, then. She knows my grandmother, so I'm almost like an uncle to her."

"Michael won't like you wandering through his house."

"But he won't know." That scarred mouth curled into a smirk. "Come, Miss Thorne, you cannot stop me. I know where the nursery is. I spent enough time here as a boy."

Still holding her arm, he drew Vivien up the stairs. There was a determination in him she couldn't quite fathom. She thought for a moment that he'd heard the rumors about her, and like some of the other men, he wanted to get her alone. But she swiftly rejected the notion. His attention was focused up the stairs and away from her, on something vital to himself.

Was he determined to thumb his nose at Michael? Or did he simply enjoy courting danger?

In any case, there could be no real danger in allowing Brandon Villiers to visit the nursery. He was Lady Faversham's grandson, not a dastardly stranger. Besides, Michael was occupied in a bedchamber with Lady Katherine. The reality of that fact hurt so deeply Vivien had to cling to the railing for support.

"He's a damned fool," Lord Faversham said abruptly.

In the dimness of the stairwell, her eyes flashed to his. "Who?"

"Michael, of course. Spurning you in favor of that . . . wench."

His eyes were penetrating, seeing too much, so she turned her gaze to the steps. "Michael may do as he pleases. It matters naught to me."

"That doesn't make him any less the fool. But then, he was always a fool when it came to women."

The bitterness in his tone caught her attention, and she would have asked him to explain himself, but they arrived at the door to the nursery. The schoolroom was dark, the embers of a fire barely glowing on the hearth. The sound of Miss Mortimer's snoring came from her bedchamber.

Picking her way past the shadowed lumps of furniture, Vivien led the earl down the short corridor to Amy's chamber. Just outside the doorway, she whispered, "Wait here."

He nodded, his expression hidden by shadow. Again, she wondered what he was thinking, why he wanted to spite Michael. Clearly, there was bad blood between them, and the resentment persisted despite the duel that had left a scar beside Lord Faversham's mouth. Proceeding into the doorway, she stopped short.

A faint sheen of moonlight illuminated the four-poster bed with its frilly hangings. Clutching her tattered rag doll, Amy lay soundly asleep. But that wasn't what sent Vivien's heart stumbling over a beat.

A man leaned over the bed, his hand outstretched as if to awaken Amy. The white of his pirate's shirt gleamed through the shadows.

Michael.

A stunning relief surged through her. So he wasn't with Lady Katherine!

Pivoting on his heel, he stared from her to the earl. He had removed his eye patch, she noticed nonsensically. The dueling pistols were also gone from his waistband. He looked more like a fiercely protective father than a pirate of the high seas.

Until he uttered a low snarl and charged at them.

Chapter twenty-one

After the Fireworks

Gasping, Vivien stepped forward with the half-formed notion to stop him, but Michael was already surging past her. He caught Lord Faversham by his monk's robe and shoved him against the wall of the corridor.

"Cur!" he said in a low voice. "What are you doing here?"

The earl regarded him coolly. "I merely wish to meet your daughter."

Michael said nothing for a moment, and his breathing sounded strident in the quiet corridor. A powerful darkness emanated from him, a violence that mystified Vivien. Through the gloom, the two men stared at each other. They were of equal height, though the earl was lean as a whip while Michael was broader, more muscular.

"You'll roast in hell for coming here." His fist flashed out, clipping the earl in the jaw and knocking him sideways.

"Michael, stop!" Vivien hissed in horror. "Amy's in the next room!"

He gave no indication of having heard her. Like feral dogs, he and the earl circled each other. Lord Faversham landed a blow to Michael's ear. With lightning swiftness, Michael returned the strike.

Vivien stood in shock, her hands clasped to her throat. The brawl was almost unreal, enacted in near silence, the only sound the sickening thud of flesh on flesh. She had to stop them before they awakened Amy.

Remembering what her mother had once done to two fighting men, she dashed into the bedchamber. Amy was still sound asleep, thank the heavens. Looking wildly around, Vivien spied the porcelain pitcher by the wash-basin.

She snatched it up, and water sloshed inside the vessel. Carrying the pitcher into the shadowed corridor, she hurled the contents at the men.

She'd meant for Michael to take the brunt, but in the last second, he saw her and ducked, and Lord Faversham caught the water smack in the face. Liquid poured down, soaking his hair and his robe. As he cursed and shook the water out of his eyes, she stepped in between the men.

"That's enough," she said in a low, stern voice. "You're behaving like bad-tempered children."

Panting, Michael glowered through the shadows. "Move out of the way."

"Will you strike me, too?" she mocked. "*Develesa!* And you call yourself more civilized than the *Rom.*"

"Vivien, I'm warning you—"

"Papa?" came a small, fearful voice from the doorway. "Why are you talking so mean to Miss Vivi?"

As one, they whirled around to see Amy hovering in the doorway, clutching her doll. The little girl looked like a tiny ghost in her pale nightdress. She gazed in perplexity from her father to Vivien to Lord Faversham.

As one, Vivien and Michael headed toward Amy, but he reached her first, hunkering down to block her view of the earl. "You misunderstood, sprite," he said in a far gentler tone than he'd used with Vivien. "Nothing's wrong. Go back to bed now. I'll be in there in a moment."

The little girl looked at him uncertainly, then peered around him. "Who is that man?" she asked, her expression changing to wonderment as she stared at the earl in his dark, rough robe. "Is he Jesus?"

Despite the tense circumstances, Vivien smiled. "Lord Faversham is a guest at your grandmama's masquerade party."

Michael swung up his head to glare at her. "He's not a guest—"

"I'm your uncle Brandon." Lord Faversham strolled closer, his gaze keen on Amy. "You're a very pretty girl, Lady Amy. We should light a lamp so that I might see you better—and you can see me."

"No," Michael said coldly. "You were on your way out the door."

"Was I?" the earl said, looking diabolically amused. "I don't recall saying so."

"You're all wet, Uncle Brandon," Amy piped up.

"So I am." He gazed down ruefully at himself. In the moonglow, the dampness of his hair and robe was more evident. "I'd like to stay and visit—"

"But he had an unfortunate accident with a water pitcher," Michael interrupted. "He's leaving. *Now.*"

The two men exchanged an intense stare. Tension radiated from both of them, thick enough to slice with a knife. Why could they not set aside their differences? Vivien wondered. They had dueled once over a woman. Was that not enough?

Lord Faversham grimaced, gingerly rubbing a faint discoloration on his jaw. Then he bowed. "It seems I am cast out. *Adieu,* Lady Amy. Vivien." With one last glance at them, he strode out of the corridor and through the schoolroom, and there came the faint sound of the door closing.

Seething with questions, Vivien turned to Michael. Though forced to bide her tongue in front of Amy, she sent him a determined look. He returned her gaze with a stony stare. But she would have her answers, she vowed silently.

Amy tugged on his sleeve. "I thought I only had two uncles, Papa."

"That's correct," he said, gazing into her small, bewildered face. "There's your uncle Gabriel, who's off exploring in Africa, and your uncle Joshua, who is commissioned with the cavalry."

"Then who is Uncle Brandon?"

His mouth firmed as if he'd bitten into something rotten. "He's not really your uncle, darling. He's Lady Faversham's grandson."

Seeing the little girl's bafflement, Vivien sank to her knees and took Amy's small hand in hers. "What your father is trying to say, little dove, is that even though you're not related by blood, Lord Faversham is *like* an uncle. Because your grammy and Lady Faversham are such fast friends."

"Oh!" Amy said, nodding sagely. "He's my *pretend* uncle."

"Yes, that's right."

Michael scowled, though he didn't gainsay her. Vivien arched an eyebrow to show him that she didn't care what he thought. Let him grumble. She wouldn't allow his petty feud to affect his daughter.

"Amy asked me to watch the fireworks with her," Michael said abruptly. "Perhaps you'll join us."

"But she already asked me—"

Vivien fell silent, frowning at Michael. He frowned back, and she glimpsed on his shadowed features the same dawning awareness she felt. Together, they looked at Amy.

"You invited both of us," Michael said. "Why didn't you tell me?"

"Grammy said it must be a secret. She said you'd like being surprised." Amy smiled innocently at him. "*Are* you pleased, Papa?"

To his credit, he hugged her without hesitation. "I'm very pleased, sprite. You did an excellent job of keeping the secret."

Over Amy's head, he aimed a wry, unexpected smile at Vivien. She couldn't help smiling back. So this was another scheme devised by the Rosebuds. But with the house party nearly over, there was no need for her to practice her flirting. So why were they still finding ways to throw her together with him? Did they want him to learn to trust her?

Or perhaps there was another reason. A suspicion had hovered at the edge of her mind, and for the first time she allowed herself to examine it. Perhaps they wished to encourage a romance. They wouldn't approve of her having an affair, so their scheming could only point to . . . marriage.

The Rosebuds wanted her to wed Michael.

Her heart beating faster, she clutched the empty pitcher to her bosom. Their praise of him, their maneuverings, even their lack of effort in encouraging other suitors, made perfect sense. All this time, they'd been plotting her betrothal. To Michael.

He didn't appear to notice her stunned silence. Standing up, he caught his daughter's hand in his. "Come along, darling," he said without a hint of his earlier rage. "We mustn't miss the fireworks."

They went into Amy's bedchamber, where he threw open the casement window to the chilly night air. Slowly, Vivien trailed after them. As she set down the pitcher, her attention remained fixed on Michael.

He could be her husband. It was impossible, of course. She could never live in his *gorgio* world, where cruelty and prejudice abounded. In a few weeks, she must return to her parents and their simple life on the road.

Yet her heart clenched with a sweet yearning that couldn't be denied. Never before had she felt this way about a man. She wanted to discover all his secrets, to share in his life. She wanted to possess him, to be possessed by him. She wanted to be his *wife.* The giddy thought almost made her sway.

Amy peered out the window, half hanging over the sill, her bare feet dangling a few inches off the floor. "I don't see any fireworks, Papa."

He snatched her up into his arms. "Whoa there. The fireworks will be in the sky, not on the ground."

"Where are they? What's taking so long?"

"Patience, sprite. The show will begin soon."

The moon glowed a misty white in the starry sky. On the terrace, guests milled in clusters, huddled in cloaks and pelisses and overcoats. Vivien felt a sense of impatience, too. In Michael's library, she had read about fireworks in one of a series of books called an encyclopedia. But this would be the first time she witnessed such a wonder herself. It could be no finer than the excitement she felt when she looked at him.

"See those men down there?" he told his daughter. "They're about to light the first fuse."

To the side of the lawn, several shadowed figures gathered in a clump. A tiny flare of light glowed in their midst. As one, they stepped hastily back. There was a whistling noise that had Amy squealing, clinging to her father's neck. An instant later, an explosion of red and yellow sparkles burst in the sky and then rained downward and winked out.

Then another flare shot up, this one casting out a dazzle

of white crystals that lit the darkness for a moment before descending like a shower of falling stars.

Enchanted, Vivien oohed and ahhed along with Amy, clapping at the more magnificent displays. Michael was very attentive to his daughter. He cheered and smiled, cuddling her close, touching her face now and then or brushing back her hair. Yet several times, when Amy wasn't looking at him, his eyes would narrow with a grim intensity, as if he were so wrapped up in his private thoughts that he didn't really see the fireworks.

He was brooding about that fight with Lord Faversham, Vivien knew. A bruise darkened his cheekbone, and his knuckles surely stung. She burned to know what he was thinking, but her questions would have to wait. For now, she rejoiced in the perfection of the moment, in this chance to be with him and Amy, watching the vivid flashes of color across the night sky.

Without conscious intent, she found herself leaning against his arm, seeking his warmth and vitality. "How exquisite," she murmured. "I've never seen anything so beautiful."

Bending closer, he whispered in her ear, "I have."

His mouth slanted into a pirate's smile, and for a moment his gaze held the look of a starving man. A forbidden hope sparkled inside her. Did he truly find her beautiful? Again, she sensed the bond between them strengthening into something warm and good, not shameful in the least.

"Papa, Miss Vivi, look!" Bouncing in her father's arms, Amy pointed outside. "That one is a dragon."

"I believe you're right," Michael said as a brilliant pattern flared across the night sky. He tapped her small nose. "What a clever girl you are."

Vivien's heart ached. How tender and loving he was with Amy. For the first time, she dared to imagine them as a family, a fantasy that suddenly seemed real and possible, a dream within her grasp. But she would have to live here among the *gorgios* forever. How could she abandon her parents?

The fireworks came to a spectacular conclusion, the darkness alight with color and magic before all faded to black. The guests on the terrace began to drift back into the house for a sumptuous midnight supper. Amy's head drooped onto her father's shoulder. "Do you s'pose Nibbles saw the fireworks?"

"Absolutely," Michael said. "No doubt he had a grand view from his hutch outside the stables."

"May we go visit him and see?"

A chuckle rumbled from deep in his chest. "You shan't wheedle me, sprite. It's off to bed with you."

As he bore the grumbling girl to the four-poster, Vivien reached out to close the casement window. Her senses felt fully alive tonight. She reveled in the coldness of the air, the acrid aroma of smoke from the fireworks, the lilt of faraway music resuming in the ballroom. She was keenly aware of Michael as she followed him to the bed.

He leaned down and kissed Amy. The girl reached up to hug him tightly, and he held her close, murmuring gruff words of affection.

Vivien blinked back the sting of tears. All the longing inside her crystallized into an even more spectacular perception. She loved him. She loved Michael Kenyon, the Marquess of Stokeford. She loved his strength and his softness, the tenderness he hid from the world. With one look, he could warm her insides. With one touch, he could dissolve her resistance. With one kiss, he could melt her defenses. She had felt the force of his allure from the first moment she'd seen him, fierce and windswept, standing in the doorway of Lady Stokeford's boudoir, a powerful *gorgio* lord determined to protect his grandmother. *A fire in the heart.*

She shouldn't love him, Vivien thought uneasily. Love was built on a foundation of trust, and Michael regarded her with suspicion. Even as his wife, she wouldn't be accepted by his noble circle. Yet she couldn't deny the fact that he made her spirit dance with joy, even as questions bedeviled her mind. Why were he and Lord Faversham rivals? They had dueled over a woman. Who was she? Lady Katherine?

More to the point, did that woman own Michael's heart?

He stepped back from the bed, and as if it were the most natural thing in the world, Amy held out her arms to Vivien. Still shaken, Vivien sank onto the edge of the bed and cuddled the little girl in a warm embrace. Oh, how she yearned to protect Amy against the harshness of the world, to enjoy her accomplishments and console her when she was sad. How she longed for the privilege of being a mother . . .

"Miss Vivi, will you tell me a story?"

"It's past midnight," she murmured, smoothing back a lock of curly coppery hair from the girl's brow. "I'll tell you one tomorrow."

"Promise?" That Amy didn't beg gave testament to her sleepiness.

"I promise." Brimming with love, Vivien bent down to kiss the girl's velvety cheek. "Good night, little dove."

Amy sighed, her eyelids drooping. " 'Night, Miss Vivi." In the next moment, she was asleep.

Michael's hand closed around Vivien's, drawing her up from the bed. He gave her that look again, the forceful regard of a pirate for his captive. Her skin tingled with a desire that was enriched by love. Was he aware of the newfound depth of emotion in her? Did he feel anything for her but lust? She could read nothing on his shadowed face, and his enigmatic nature maddened her.

In silence, he led her to the doorway. They stopped to look back at Amy, who lay in innocent slumber, the rag doll nestled in her arms. "How sweet she is," Vivien whispered. "You're very blessed to have her."

"Yes."

Michael fought to keep his voice steady. He told himself Vivien had made an innocuous remark, nothing more. She couldn't know about the knot of fear in his chest. Nor could she fathom his dedication to keeping his daughter safe. He loved Amy with an unshakable intensity that left him vulnerable. He would let no one exploit that weakness in him.

No one.

As they left the nursery, he turned his mind to Vivien, walking beside him in the dimly lit corridor. The gold bangles at her wrists chimed faintly. In her natural garb, she looked as wild and free as a Gypsy princess. The yellow blouse dipped low over her bosom, and the flowing turquoise skirt swished around her small bare feet. Not for the first time, he wondered if she wore any undergarments, or if he could lift her skirt and caress her.

He welcomed the desire that gripped his loins. All evening, he'd watched her dance with other men. He'd waited to get her alone. At last he would have his chance—

"Why did you fight Lord Faversham?" Vivien asked point-blank.

The question poisoned Michael's mood. She should never have witnessed that brawl. "The subject is closed. I'd rather kiss you, anyway."

He stepped closer to her, but she nimbly eluded him. "Tell me why you were so desperate to get rid of him."

"Desperate?" If she had impaled him with a sword, she couldn't have stunned him more. *Why had Brand come up here tonight?* Fearing the answer, Michael took several deep breaths. "I won't let that riffraff anywhere near my daughter. Better you should tell me why you brought him to the nursery."

"I didn't *bring* him. He came of his own accord."

"You were in his company." Prodded by red-hot jealousy, he took hold of her arm. "What the devil were you doing with him, anyway? Did he seduce you?"

As if he'd struck her, her eyes widened with pain. *Pain.* Odd that, for she was no innocent. Yet he wanted to kick himself for hurting her.

Shaking off his hand, Vivien stepped back. "You insult me. The earl isn't so ill-mannered as you are."

"He's a cad who uses women."

"You're two of a kind, then. You should be the best of friends."

He battled his smoldering rage. "Stay out of what you don't understand, Vivien."

But she didn't stay out. She gazed at him with a relentless concern. "You attacked the earl without provocation. Who is the woman who still comes between you two?"

An icy sensation slid down his spine. His palms felt cold and sweaty. Vivien was too damned persistent. He knew only one way to distract her.

Sauntering toward her, he lowered his voice to a sensual undertone. "Enough questions. Let's talk about us."

Clearly recognizing the value of retreat, she backed down the corridor. "This *is* about us," she said in a throaty murmur. "I must know why you won't speak of her. What does she mean to you, Michael?"

"The past is best left buried."

"But *you* haven't left it buried. What happened tonight proves that."

He remembered the shock of seeing Brand standing in

the doorway, gazing at Amy. A wild rage jolted Michael again, but he kept his face impassive. "It was a stupid brawl, nothing more. Forget about it."

Reaching the stairway, she descended the steps, still facing him, keeping one hand on the wall for balance. "I can't forget. You knew Amy was nearby. Yet not even that stopped you."

He cursed himself for letting Vivien see too much. Stepping down the carpeted risers, he said bluntly, "It's over with and done. But you and I are far from done. I want you, Vivien."

She paused at the base of the stairs. The flickering light from a wall sconce gilded her parted lips, her dreamy eyes. From out of nowhere came a yearning more potent than lust, the urge to hold her close and never let go. Ruthlessly, he crushed the feeling. He wouldn't allow any woman to have such power over him ever again.

"Do you love her?" she asked.

"Who?"

"The woman you're protecting. I can only think . . . that your heart still belongs to her."

"You think too damned much, then."

He leapt down the last two steps. Determined to stop her questions, he trapped Vivien against the wall, letting her feel the force of his passion. She caught her breath in a little moan that fed the tumult inside him. She wanted him; he could feel the desire softening her, making her as pliable as butter.

He bent to capture her mouth, but she turned her head to the side so that his lips grazed her cheek instead. "Please, Michael." She gave him a sidelong, soulful look that somehow wrenched his gut. "You must tell me what she means to you."

"Nothing," he snarled. "She means *nothing*. She's dead."

Vivien reared back to stare at him. Then her dark velvet eyes widened with the light of revelation, and he realized his mistake—or perhaps deep down, he'd wanted her to know, for he felt a strange relief.

"She was Lady Grace," Vivien whispered. "Lord Faversham seduced your *wife*."

Chapter twenty-two

In the Linen Closet

Awash in a stunned awareness, Vivien read the truth in Michael's grim features. He had been cuckolded by his childhood friend. Betrayed in the most despicable way possible. No wonder they'd fought a duel. No wonder he still loathed Lord Faversham.

Then her mind made another shocking leap. Her mouth went bone-dry, so that she could barely speak. "Amy—"

He said nothing, though the stark of anguish in his blue eyes spoke volumes. Dear God. *Amy had been sired by Lord Faversham?* "Are you certain?" she whispered.

He looked away from her, staring fiercely down the deserted corridor. "It can't be proven. So don't repeat it."

She drew in a shaky breath, then expelled it slowly. "I would never speak of this to anyone. Please believe that."

Michael brought his gaze back to her. His anguished, skeptical gaze. Heartsore, she stared at him, letting all of her love shine in her eyes. A faithless wife explained his mistrust of women. His mistrust of *her*.

No wonder he'd barred Lord Faversham from his house. No wonder he'd lashed out with his fists. He feared losing his beloved daughter. Vivien felt his torment as if it were hers, too. The threat of another man laying claim to Amy must be eating at him like acid.

And she had so blithely ignored Michael's wishes and led Lord Faversham upstairs.

Feeling inadequate to comfort him, she put her arms around him, pressing her cheek to his clenched jaw and reaching up to stroke his hair. His body felt rigid with tension. "I should have stopped the earl," she murmured. "Oh, what have I done?"

"It isn't your fault. Brand does as he damn well pleases."

Remembering the earl's interest in Amy, Vivien lifted her head. "Do you think . . . he knows, then?"

A muscle worked in his jaw. "She was nearly a year old when I realized the truth. For the three years since then, I believed he didn't know," he said, the words sounding dragged from him. "Until tonight. The way he looked at her . . ." His voice broke off, and his gaze pierced her with an almost frightening intensity. "Vow on your life you will tell no one of this."

"Of course," she said. "I would never, ever betray you or Amy."

He regarded her with a cynical aloofness, and she knew with despair that it would take time and patience to prove to him that she wasn't like his late wife. But she would convince him. She *must* convince him.

And perhaps he already *did* trust her, at least a little, for he had allowed her to befriend his daughter, a right he had given to only a select few. The thought filled her with a hopeful warmth.

The sound of voices came from the far end of the corridor. Several ladies in costume rounded the corner. Their giggling conversation echoed down the long passageway with its Gothic tables against the stone walls.

Michael hissed out a breath from between his teeth.

Sheltering her with his body, he thrust open the nearest door and urged her inside. Vivien had the swift impression of a rather small room with shelves full of linens, and a large worktable holding neat stacks of bedsheets. Then he closed the door, plunging them into total darkness.

He held her close so that she felt the steady beating of his heart. Out in the corridor, the ladies strolled past, probably on their way to freshen up before the midnight supper. As their chatter faded into the distance again, she leaned into Michael, letting his heat radiate into her.

How she wanted to heal him, to help him forget—at least for a short while—the dreadful burden he bore. And deep down, she admitted she also craved a memory to take with her when she returned to the *Rom*. Sliding her arms around his waist, she smoothed her palms up and down his muscled back, tilting her head to kiss his throat and jaw.

The tension in him altered subtly. His hands skimmed over her shoulders and down to her waist, where he gripped her tightly. "Vivien," he muttered.

He lowered his head, but she needed no encouragement. Eagerly she lifted her face to meet his questing mouth. He kissed her hard and deep and long, and she surrendered to the rush of passion. The darkness heightened her other senses. The faint scent of soap clung to his flesh, along with his alluring masculine musk. He tasted of wine and wickedness, of all the sins she ached to learn from him. From Michael alone.

He tugged down her bodice and cupped her breasts, weighing them in his hands, his thumbs stroking the tips. Pleasure jolted her so that she shuddered in his arms. Then he did something even more extraordinary. He bent down and suckled her, tasting her with his tongue and teeth until she almost swooned.

With a whispery moan, she writhed against him, trying

to press herself as close as possible to him. Her hands moved restively over the smoothly hewn muscles of his shoulders and chest.

"Tell me you want me," he said gruffly in her ear. "Say it."

"I want you," Vivien murmured readily. She no longer cared if loving him was right or wrong. She knew she couldn't live another moment without him. Without *this*. "Oh, Michael, I'm yours. Only yours."

He made an unintelligible sound of satisfaction in his throat. Then he undressed her quickly, stripping off her bodice and sash and skirt until she stood naked before him. Cloaked by darkness, she felt only a twinge of modesty. How gloriously decadent to feel his large hands on her, touching places no other man had ever touched.

His fingers glided over the globes of her breasts, brushed the indentation of her waist, and roamed downward to her hips. She arched to him, impatient to experience again that wondrously intimate caress. As if he'd read her mind, he touched her exactly where she ached, and she gasped from the ever-increasing torment of arousal, burying her face in his throat to muffle the little cries she uttered. The skillful stroking of his fingers made her twist and moan from a maddening swell of passion.

He took her right to the verge, then withdrew his hand without satisfying her. Kissing the protest from her lips, he guided her a few steps backward through the darkness until her thighs met softness. There, he pressed her down onto something cool and smooth. She smelled the freshness of starched linen.

The bedsheets. The table.

In a daze, she sank back, her legs too weak to support her. Through the shadows came the rustle of his clothing, the tiny ping of a button that rolled away on the floor, his curse of impatience. A faint light seeped in from beneath the door, enough for her to see the dark shape of him looming over her. Then he came down onto her, his body strong and hard, as naked as hers but oh, so wonderfully different.

She explored him with her hands, admiring the texture and contour of muscle and flesh. On a dim level of rationality, she was amazed at herself. He was a nobleman. But she felt no misgivings, no panic, no shame, only a burning desire to become one with Michael Kenyon. He was her *bokht,* her fate and her fortune. The man who was destined to ignite a fire in her heart.

His male member lay thick and hot between her legs. Yet still he didn't join their bodies. He stroked her and kissed her until she murmured incoherent words of pleading in a mixture of English and Romany.

"I've dreamed of this," he said, his voice rough and low. "Of you, Vivien."

She touched his cheek, faintly bristly against her fingertips. "I've dreamed of you, too, *vestacho*."

"Vestacho?"

"Beloved," she translated, pressing a kiss to his chest and tasting the saltiness of his skin. "You're my beloved."

He said nothing to that, and despite the darkness, she felt his brooding disbelief in the faint glittering of his eyes. He didn't love her, she knew. Yet Vivien felt a soul-deep tenderness, for her own love ran strong and true.

Then he positioned himself over her, and it seemed the most natural act in the world to open her legs to receive him. From nature, she knew the way of mating, yet the reality of it surprised her. She hadn't expected him to be so large, like a stallion. Nor had she anticipated the stabbing pain of his entry or the whimper it wrested from her.

He went utterly still. "Vivien?"

Incredulity underscored his raspy tone, and she sensed that even faced with the proof, he doubted her virginity.

She answered his question before he asked, saying fiercely, "*Yes.* You are my first, my only."

His harsh breaths broke the silence. Braced on his elbows, he regarded her through the darkness. After a long moment, he bent his head to her, his lips nuzzling her hair, a curious roughness to his voice. "Are you . . . still hurting?"

"No," she whispered, closing her eyes. "You feel wonderful. We were made for each other." It was true. As the discomfort subsided, she undulated her hips, marveling at the way he filled her so completely.

He uttered a tortured sound deep in his throat. He withdrew a bit, then slowly pushed back in, his movements incredibly sensual. Again and again he did so, each time increasing the fervor inside her. When she caught the rhythm of his thrusts, he quivered and a groan of pleasure tore from him. She knew, then, the power she wielded over him. She belonged to him, and whether he admitted so or not, *he* also belonged to *her*. Their joining was an act of mutual possession.

He kissed her with gentle savagery, arousing her with his mouth and his hands until Vivien thought she might die of need. She writhed and twisted beneath him, gasping from the urgency inside her. Just when she feared she could bear no more of the torment, she fell headlong into ecstasy, into a pulsating pleasure more brilliant than a thousand stars. His body shuddered from the force of his climax, and she sensed him right there in heaven with her, making her joy all the sweeter.

It was done.

In the quiet aftermath, Michael came to a gradual awareness of his surroundings. His chest heaved, and the sweat began to cool on his skin. He felt wrung dry, yet supremely satisfied.

Vivien was *his*. His alone.

She lay beneath him, her face tucked into the crook of his neck, her breath warm and ragged. They were still joined, and he felt no inclination to disengage himself as he did with other women. In truth, he should have withdrawn in the moment before spilling his seed; he had taken a serious risk. Yet oddly, he felt no regrets.

He wanted to crow like a barnyard cock. He had been her first. No other man had known the wildness of her passion. No other man had aroused her to the ultimate pleasure. No other man had heard her whisper ardently in the darkness.

Vestacho.

Beloved.

Something very tender clenched in his chest. He swiftly discounted the feeling. Her fervent declaration made him uneasy, that was all. Being an innocent, she would believe herself in love. She had yet to learn they shared no more than an uncommonly intense lust.

He only hoped he could trust her with his secret.

He grimaced to recall his original plan to dishonor her and present the evidence to his grandmother. What a blind fool he'd been not to see her naïveté. But Vivien belonged to him now. He would kill the man who dared to touch her.

The darkness surrounded them in intimacy. He could see the faint glow of her skin, the curve of breasts and hips. When he shifted to get a better view, the table creaked, and he couldn't help chuckling.

"Why do you laugh?" she asked sleepily.

"We're in a damned linen closet, that's why."

"Your linens are soft, m'lord." She stretched sinuously, sending his temperature soaring. "And truly, I desire nothing else to be soft."

He smiled, stirred by the gentle kisses she strewed

across his chest. It was madness to stay here. The table was too small for his large frame. They would be far more comfortable making love in his wide bed. But he balked at separating himself from her, at donning clothing when her naked flesh tempted him like a pagan offering.

It was far too soon for him, of course. That wild release had consumed him. Yet he couldn't resist moving in her again, his thrusts slow and easy. Her velvety channel hugged him like a tight glove. She moaned softly, her hips rising to his. How responsive she was, how perfectly formed. An exquisite creation of womanhood, all ripe curves and sensual nature. Now that he'd had her once, he could take his time enjoying her.

Bending his head, he lapped at her nipple, and instantly it contracted into a taut bud. She sighed out his name, that one breathy sound delivering an amazing rush of vigor to his loins. With effort he held to his unhurried pace, taking pleasure in kissing the satin warmth of her skin, caressing her breasts and thighs, drinking the honey of her mouth. Like an erotic dream, she locked her legs around his waist, drawing him deeper into heaven. She whispered to him in her exotic tongue, and more than once she spoke that endearment to him.

Vestacho . . .

Her soft utterances excited him to a fever pitch. Never had he felt such a forceful need. Never had he desired a woman as fiercely as he desired Vivien. Never had he become aroused again so quickly. It was like a wild infatuation, his craving for her. He fought for control, fought to keep from climaxing before her. Desperate, he reached between them and stroked her. She cried out at once, her body convulsing around him, and in the throes of a powerful pleasure, he emptied himself into her.

This time, he knew he would want her again, so he rolled onto his back and brought her over onto him. He was far from done with her. For timeless minutes, she lay sprawled over him in charming exhaustion, her legs hugging him, her head nestled under his chin. Idly he stroked her, enjoying the creamy texture of her skin and the feminine curves of her waist and backside. Her bosom was pressed against his chest, but he could still caress the plump globes.

She stirred, her bottom wriggling delightfully.

He stirred, too, when he'd thought himself drained.

"Temptress," he growled. "You make me feel like a randy adolescent instead of a man of one-and-thirty."

In a throaty purr, she said, "Men do not make love so often?" Then she undulated her hips . . . to spectacular results.

He sucked in a breath. "Men," he said, taking firm hold of her teasing backside, "learn to control their base urges. To take their time in pleasuring a woman."

"You've pleasured me well, m'lord marquess. I trust you'll do so again."

She brushed a tender kiss over his mouth, and with unsteady hands, he cupped her head, leisurely tasting her with his tongue and lips. He could not get his fill of her. Already he felt the hot rise of lust.

Voices intruded from the outer corridor. Lifting her head, Vivien broke the kiss. *"Dosta!"* she whispered, a note of alarm in her voice. "The guests."

He, too, had forgotten about the party, though he wouldn't admit so to her. No one else had existed for him but Vivien. Wrapped in the intimacy of darkness, he had only a rough idea of how long they'd been at their pleasure.

"It's late," he said gruffly. "The party must be ending."

"Sshh." She put her finger to his lips. "Someone will hear us."

Her sudden attack of modesty amused him. On a devilish whim, he sought out her cleft, stroking slowly in the way she liked.

Vivien muffled her gasp against his throat. *"Stop,"* she moaned, her voice a wisp of sound. "Oh, *please*."

"I thought you liked this."

"I *do*." She caught her breath. "Oh, yes . . . *there* . . ."

Then it was no longer so amusing when she reached down and explored him with delicate fingertips, torturing his exquisitely sensitive flesh. He clamped his teeth to suppress a groan. "Seductress," he hissed.

"Seducer," she breathed in his ear.

The footsteps stopped right outside their door. A man and a woman. Their voices sounded familiar.

Abruptly tense, Vivien ceased her tantalizing massage. "Viscount Beldon . . . and the duchess," she whispered, so low Michael barely heard her.

He had noticed that hint of loathing in Vivien's tone on several other occasions. For some reason, she harbored an intense dislike for the duchess. Had the shrew been rude to her? Michael wouldn't stand for it. He resolved to ask Vivien, but not now.

The muffled smacking of lips came from outside the linen closet. Clenching his muscles, he prepared himself to shield her if the door opened. Not that anyone else in their right mind would choose such a ridiculous place to make love.

The duchess giggled like a coquette, and then the pair strolled away. A few moments later, a door closed somewhere down the passageway.

"They're gone," Michael said, setting himself to the pleasure of fondling Vivien again. "The hag took him to her bed."

Vivien clasped his wrists. "But . . . she's married. The duke didn't accompany her here."

It struck him hard just how innocent Vivien really was.

He felt old and world-weary, aware of the vast differences between them. No wonder he hadn't recognized her purity. For so long, he'd known only noblewomen who schemed and manipulated. He'd used them in turn, enjoying their bodies until he tired of them. He intended to marry one of them. The notion held a sudden distaste. "That's the way of the *ton*."

"Well, I don't accept it. You shouldn't, either. Not after what happened to you."

A familiar anger smoldered in him, but he shoved it away, focusing his mind on Vivien. "If fornication is wrong," he said, caressing her backside, "then we're sinners, too."

"Perhaps," she whispered. "Yet we aren't betraying anyone else."

"A trifling detail."

He cupped her warm breast, seeking to distract her, but she firmly pushed his hand away. "No, listen to me. Marriage is sacred. A husband and wife take vows of devotion. They should cleave only unto each other."

Did she really believe that? Half of him wanted to trust in her sincerity, the other half—the cynical half—told him she was playacting in order to gain power over him. Grace had appeared just as genuine.

"Such loyalty doesn't exist," he said bluntly. "You'd know that if you had more experience."

"I know that *miro dado* and *miro dye* would never betray one another. Nor would others of the *Rom*." Her soft murmur turned challenging. "But perhaps no one in your English society possesses such honor."

He tensed. "When there are two consenting adults, there is no dishonor."

"Oh? Then you shouldn't be angry at Lord Faversham. Unless Lady Grace didn't agree."

"Hell, yes, she agreed," he said tersely. "But *I* didn't. She was *my* wife."

"Ah," Vivien said, a quietly triumphant note to her voice. "So you *do* believe in fidelity."

Damn the minx. She'd cleverly twisted his words. "I believe in protecting what is mine."

Drawing her close, he kissed her long and deep, conveying to her in no uncertain terms that she belonged to him. He felt resistance in her, but only for a moment. Then she softened and embraced him, feverishly opening her legs to mount him. As one, they were caught up in the rhythm of passion and the increasing tumult of their bodies. She came first, her delicate shivers and sweet moans sending him over the edge. The pleasure was so intense he sank into an exhausted stupor, and when he awakened later, Vivien slept in his arms, her long silken hair draping them.

An unfathomable tenderness crept through him. Touching his lips to her brow, he breathed deeply, inhaling her exotic fragrance and the scent of their lovemaking. Slowly he became aware of the lumps and bumps beneath them. The linens had shifted during their vigorous activities. One side of him rested against the hard table.

Because of the darkness, he didn't know how much time had passed, but no doubt the servants would be going about their duties soon, if they weren't already. A maid could walk in on them. He wouldn't allow Vivien to suffer the embarrassment of discovery. Her reputation would be ruined.

He grimaced. People already thought her a thief. Due to her unusual upbringing, she'd been tarred by the brush of suspicion. But his own arrogant misjudgment of her had been turned topsy-turvy. If he'd been wrong about her chastity, could he also be wrong to believe her dishonest?

Troubled, he eased out from under her and levered his bare feet to the floor. He stretched his stiff muscles, then donned shirt and breeches while rethinking his convictions. There was the forged letter from Harriet Althorpe, of course. But perhaps he'd only imagined the discrepancies in Miss Althorpe's penmanship. He'd been twelve years of age when he'd gone off to Eton, right before she'd left. He *might* be mistaken about the letter. And Vivien *might* be telling the truth about giving the one hundred guineas a month to her crippled father.

If she were *not* lying . . .

He drew a deep breath. If she was indeed Harriet Althorpe's natural daughter, she would be considered gentry. An unconventional wife, but one who might learn to enjoy society.

Wife.

The stunning prospect shook the foundations of his beliefs. A few weeks ago, he'd made a rational decision to marry Katherine, a woman bred to his world and suited to perform the myriad roles of wife to a man of his rank. Now that thought filled him with aversion. He didn't want another frivolous society lady who spent her days planning extravagant balls or indulging her whims at the shops on Bond Street.

He wanted fire. Laughter. Love.

His fingers curled into fists. Fool! Hadn't he learned his lesson from Grace? Never again would he let a woman own his heart. Nevertheless, he craved a woman who made him feel alive again, one who fit perfectly into the part of his world he kept closed off from society. His family life with Amy.

Katherine had never sought his daughter's company as Vivien had done. He was ashamed to realize that he should have put that consideration first. Vivien was a natural mother. She adored Amy as much as he did.

Gripped by a savage protectiveness, he stared into the darkness. He had loved Amy from the moment the nurse had placed her in his arms, a tiny swaddled infant, slumbering peacefully, with the most beautifully delicate features he'd ever seen. At the time, he'd had no reason to believe she wasn't his, and when he did stumble upon the truth many months later, the irrefutable evidence that explained why Grace had always discouraged him from visiting his daughter in the nursery, he could no more reject Amy than he could cut out his own heart.

Faversham wouldn't lay claim to Amy. He must never know that proof existed of his paternity. Nor must Vivien know.

And if he proved her a fraud? He would have a tougher decision to make, then. He didn't give a tinker's damn what other people thought, but there was Amy to consider. He would allow no one to hurt his daughter.

Bending down, he kissed Vivien. Her purr of protest made him wish she lay in sunlight so he could watch her come awake after a night of loving. He wanted to bed her again. The temptation was surprisingly strong, considering he'd already taken his pleasure of her so many times.

He slid his fingers down her warm hills and valleys, then lightly slapped her backside. "Up with you now," he whispered. "It's almost morning."

Just that fast, Vivien hopped off the table. "Morning! Why didn't you awaken me sooner?"

"You exhausted me, darling. We're damned lucky a maid didn't walk in on us."

"The servants," she moaned. "They'll *see* us."

She scrambled around, hunting down her clothing in the gloom, and he gallantly assisted her, stealing a touch now and then as he helped her dress. "Oh, do stop," she said breathily, when she'd pushed his hand away a dozen times. "We'll never be out of here."

"Mmm," he growled, dragging her against him, brushing his mouth over hers. "I've developed a new liking for linen cupboards."

She parted her lips for a brief, tender kiss. *"Vestacho,"* she murmured, touching his bristled cheek. "I'll always remember this wonderful night."

He felt an unmanly melting inside himself. Denying the dangerous rush of emotion, he stepped to the door and opened it. The dim light from the corridor seemed almost bright after the privacy of darkness. After glancing out to make certain the place was deserted, he beckoned to her. "Come, I'll escort you to your chamber."

She joined him in the doorway. "I can find my own way."

"No," he said, placing his hand firmly at the small of her back. "I'll make sure you arrive there safely." He couldn't let her go off alone, looking so soft and beautiful, her recent pleasuring evident by her rosy lips and rumpled hair.

She opened her mouth as if to protest, then smiled sweetly, her lashes lowering slightly. That look made him hot for another long session of lovemaking. This time, in a proper bed.

As they walked down the deserted passageway, her hips grazed his, and he found himself rethinking his day, feverishly scheming how to arrange some time alone with her. "The guests will be leaving this morning," he said, as they rounded the corner. "Perhaps after luncheon, we could meet somewhere private. My bedchamber."

Shaking her head, she laughed a little. "The Rosebuds would never allow it."

"Where, then? There are a hundred places where no one would find us. The armory. The attic. The china closet, for God's sake."

They reached the door to her bedchamber. She looked

up at him very tenderly, her eyes shining. "The library. But we shan't be alone. I promised Amy a story, remember?"

"So you did."

He wanted to watch her cuddle his daughter. He also wanted to see Vivien suckle their baby at her breast. No, he craved most of all the pleasure of planting his seed in her womb. He lusted for her now, with unabated madness, but surely she would be sore after her vigorous initiation. To use her again so soon would be selfish.

He gave her a farewell kiss that tempted the bounds of his control. She felt so warm, so willing, so right in his arms. "You're mine," he avowed fiercely. "I don't ever want to let you go, not even for a moment."

She rubbed her cheek against his. "Oh, Michael. I do love you so."

Her declaration boggled him. With a ridiculously satisfied smile on his face, he watched as Vivien slipped into her bedchamber and shut the door.

Yes. She didn't yet know it, but she would be his wife.

Chapter twenty-three

Imprisoned

The magic wand of dawn cast a glow over the pale blue hangings and the gilded chairs of her bedchamber. The canopied four-poster was undisturbed, the pillows plumped and the coverlet folded back. Although weariness dragged at her, Vivien knew she couldn't sleep yet, not while she brimmed with memories of Michael.

Never in her wildest fantasies had she imagined the intimacy they'd shared. It was as if their souls had touched, and neither of them could be the same again. Her body ached pleasantly from his loving. She had given herself to a *gorgio* lord. And there was no room in her heart for regrets.

You're mine. I don't ever want to let you go, not even for a moment.

Drunk on pure happiness, Vivien hugged herself, twirling around and around until the painted nymphs on the ceiling swam dizzily. She sank onto the canopied bed. Michael felt a fire in his heart, too, this wondrous connection of body and soul. He believed in her now, trusted her enough to tell her his secret.

They came from different worlds, but surely there was

a way for them. There had to be. Perhaps she could convince *dado* and *dye* to stay here on his estate. Would they be pleased with him? She fervently hoped so. No longer could she blame all the *gorgios* for the acts of a few. She had found warmth and love here with the Rosebuds, with Amy, and now with Michael.

Aching to hold him again, she rolled over and reached for a feather pillow to hug. As she slid her hand beneath the smooth linen casing, her fingers brushed something cold and hard. She lifted the pillow and frowned in confusion.

There, coiled like a snake on the sheet, an object glittered in the pale light. Emeralds and diamonds in a rich gold setting. A necklace. Beside it lay a diamond-studded gold ring. Both pieces looked familiar . . .

With a jolt, she recognized them. The Duchess of Covington had worn that necklace one evening. And the ring was the very one Lady Katherine claimed had been stolen.

Slapped by the chilly wind of shock, Vivien sat up. Someone had planted the gems here. Someone who wanted to discredit her, to see her thrown into prison. Someone who wanted to destroy Michael's regard for her.

Develesa! It must have been Katherine. No, Her Grace, the Duchess of Covington. She had made plain her scorn for all Gypsies.

In a frenzy, Vivien scooped up the necklace and ring. She could think only of getting rid of them somewhere, anywhere away from her bedchamber. She would drop them in the corridor outside the duchess's room, where a maid might find and return the gems to their rightful owners. Yes. She would thwart those two at their cruel game. And she must act swiftly.

Her heart thudding as fast as her scurrying feet, Vivien sped out of the chamber and down the deserted corridor. A few rays of light penetrated through a tall window at the far end. She was glad to see no servants about yet; perhaps they were downstairs cleaning up after the ball.

Cutting into her palm and fingers, the necklace and ring were a bitter reminder of the injustices practiced by the *ton*. She would never truly be accepted by some of these aristocrats. They would do everything in their power to oust her from their elite circle.

But Michael wasn't like them. She focused her mind on the marvelous closeness she'd found with him. *Vestacho*. Her beloved. How she wanted to curl up on her bed and reflect on the joy they'd found together. His touch, his tenderness, his passion had made her feel loved—

She rounded the corner, and her golden dream mutated into a nightmare.

Outside the duchess's chambers stood a cluster of women in their nightrobes: the Rosebuds, Charlotte Quinton, the Duchess of Covington, Lady Katherine. And Michael.

Dear God. Michael!

Vivien glanced wildly around for a place to conceal the stolen jewels. The stone walls stretched empty in either direction, the nearest vase on a table too far away. Her only chance was to slip away before anyone noticed her.

Too late. Even as she took a step backward, the duchess swept up her arm and pointed like an avenging angel. "There she is! The Gypsy thief!"

Michael pivoted on his heel. To his surprise, Vivien hovered at the bend in the corridor. Her face was pale, and the morning light limned her exotic garb. Her dark, mussed hair tumbled down to her slim waist. She looked startled, her eyes wide and her hands clutched behind her.

How odd that she had appeared so fortuitously. He'd

been strolling back to his suite of rooms, whistling under his breath and feeling immensely pleased with the night's events, when he'd come upon Katherine and her cousin quarreling with the Rosebuds and Charlotte Quinton. The duchess had accosted him with the news that her necklace was missing. Like a damned bulldog, she'd kept insisting on an immediate search of Vivien's chamber. He'd expressly forbidden that.

Now, his grandmother folded her arms over her ruffly white robe. "My ward isn't a thief!" she exclaimed. "You'll rue your words, Hillary."

"No, *you* will. Just you wait and see." The duchess barged down the corridor, her orange robe flapping like the wings of a chicken.

Furious, Michael stalked after her. "Your Grace, that's enough."

But the duchess ignored him. She went straight to Vivien and poked a finger at her face. "You stole my necklace and don't bother denying it."

"I've stolen nothing, Your Grace," Vivien said in a shaky tone. "I swear it." As she glanced up at Michael, a shadow of alarm touched her face from her beseeching brown eyes to her trembling lip. He breathed deeply to ease the constriction in his chest. Clearly, she expected his mistrust. He battled the fierce hunger to gather her into his arms and declare his true intentions.

Swinging toward the duchess, he said, "Your accusations are absurd. I'll hear no more of them."

"Nor I," said his grandmother.

"I quite agree," piped up Lady Enid, hugging her granddaughter, Charlotte, who for once held her tongue, apparently too shocked for words.

Lady Faversham thumped her cane. "You haven't a shred of evidence, Your Grace."

"But Miss Thorne admired my cousin's necklace one

evening in the drawing room," Katherine said. "Hillary told me so."

Michael returned her cool stare. What had he ever seen in her bloodless, perfect beauty? "Admiration is hardly proof of theft," he bit out. "Nor cause to slander Vivien."

"If Miss Thorne is so innocent," the duchess huffed, "then what is she hiding behind her back? Stolen goods, I'll warrant."

Blast the bitch. The best way to shut her up was to prove her wrong. "Vivien, show us your hands."

Vivien stood as if frozen. Her gaze flitted over the Rosebuds and Charlotte, then returned to Michael. As if he could see into her soul, he sensed a welter of emotions in her: anguish, desperation, defiance. An icy finger of foreboding touched his spine.

"Show us," he repeated.

She parted her lips as if to refuse. Then she lowered her black lashes slightly and brought her hands out from behind her back. In her cupped palms rested a gold-spun knot of diamonds and emeralds.

A collective gasp rippled from the women. His grandmother blinked in shock. Charlotte clung to Lady Enid, tangling a handkerchief in her scarred fingers.

Struck cold, Michael stared at the necklace and ring. His every instinct resisted the evidence his eyes saw. God! He couldn't believe that the loving woman he'd held in his arms a few hours ago would rob his guests. Even now, he felt her siren allure weakening him.

But the damning proof lay right there in her hands. She had stolen the jewels. Like Grace, Vivien had played him for a fool.

The duchess snatched up the necklace. "I knew it!" she crowed. She held the piece aloft, the gemstones glinting. "Look, Katherine, here's your ring, too!"

Lady Katherine hastened to clutch the small diamond-

and-gold circlet to her bosom. "Thank heavens. This ring means so much to me."

The duchess rounded on Michael. "I told you the Gypsy was guilty. She must be clapped in irons immediately!"

Fighting a bitter pain, he forced his gaze back to Vivien. Tersely, he said, "You must have some explanation."

She lifted her chin and met his angry stare. "I found the jewels under my pillow. I don't know how they came to be there. I wanted only to return them."

"A Banbury tale," the duchess snapped. She looked Vivien up and down. "It's clear that you fancy her, Stokeford. No doubt she was returning my necklace because she knew she had a chance to snare bigger game."

"That isn't true," Vivien retorted.

"Silence," Her Grace commanded. "All Gypsies are liars and thieves."

Lady Stokeford bristled. "You're the liar, Hillary. It's time someone voiced what we've all been thinking. You and your scheming cousin hid the jewels in order to discredit Vivien."

"I'd never play such games with this ring," Katherine said, slipping it onto her finger. "It was a wedding gift from my late husband."

The duchess's cheeks reddened. "Have a care how you speak to us, Lucy. Your ward will be sent to gaol at once. I, for one, won't feel safe until she's behind bars."

A small, angry cry broke from Vivien as she stepped forward to confront the duchess. "I wish I *had* stolen the necklace," she burst out. "You owe far more than that to my father."

"Your father?" the duchess said scathingly. "Lucy said you didn't know his name."

"My adoptive father. He was crippled last year by a mantrap set on your husband's estate."

The Rosebuds exchanged scandalized mutterings. Michael experienced a sudden, cold understanding. No wonder Vivien despised the duchess.

"Tell us what happened," he demanded.

"One day last autumn, *miro dado* took a shortcut through a stretch of woods. He was hunting rabbits for our stewpot." She swallowed, as if it pained her to go on. "When he didn't return to our camp that evening, I went to look for him. I found him . . ."

Lady Stokeford slipped her arm around Vivien's waist. "There, there, darling. You needn't speak of it."

"I *must* speak." Tears welling in her eyes, Vivien clamped her fingers around her turquoise skirt. "I found my father in agony on the cold ground where he'd lain all day. I couldn't open the trap, the springs were too strong. I had to leave him, to run back to the camp and fetch help. He suffered terribly. All because the Duke of Covington treats Gypsies like wild animals."

The duchess twitched her nose. "You're mistaken, Miss Thorne. *I* ordered those traps set. I've every right to guard against poachers."

Michael loathed the woman's savagery. At the same time, he realized grimly that revenge for her father's injury gave Vivien a stronger motive for stealing from the duchess.

In a flash of movement, Vivien spat at the duchess. The moist globule landed on that contemptuous nose. "There! That is what I think of you."

Her Grace squawked like a witless hen, swabbing at her face with her orange sleeve. "How dare you!" she sputtered. "I'll ruin you!"

"I'll ruin *you*," Lady Stokeford said fiercely. "Society will hear of your cruelty, Hillary. You've exposed yourself as a petty, inhuman tyrant."

"You can't touch me. You've no power in the *ton* anymore."

"But I have," Michael stated. As the duchess worked her mouth in the beginnings of alarm, he added in a steely tone, "You and Katherine have your jewelry back. You'll pack your bags and depart within the hour." Then he aimed his wintry eyes at Vivien. "Miss Thorne shall remain a prisoner in her room until I can fetch the magistrate."

"The magistrate!" Charlotte gasped. She'd been so subdued, Michael had almost forgotten her presence. Now she flew at him and grasped his hands. "You can't do that!"

Striving for impassivity, he disengaged himself. "She was caught with stolen goods. If the courts find her guilty, she'll be punished accordingly."

"Banishment is too good for her kind," the duchess snarled. "She should be hanged." On that stern note, she and Katherine swept down the corridor to her chamber.

The Rosebuds crowded around Michael. "Don't listen to that vicious woman," Grandmama pleaded. "She crippled the man who raised Vivien."

"I'd like to see the two of them swing from a gibbet!" declared Lady Faversham.

"You won't be cruel to Vivien, will you?" Charlotte asked anxiously. "Just send her back to the Gypsies. There's no need to summon the law."

But Michael ignored all of them. A frigid, unforgiving chill encased him as he took Vivien by the arm and ushered her back to her room. She spoke nothing more in her defense. A foolish part of him yearned for her to say something, anything, that would acquit her of this crime. With violent need, Michael wanted to haul her close and kiss her until he forgot how she'd gulled him.

Before he could make an even bigger dolt of himself, he shoved her inside her bedchamber and locked the door.

At first Vivien was too numb to react. For a long time, she stood in the middle of the rug, the quiet settling over her like a shroud. She felt dizzy from the effort to draw sufficient air into her lungs. Again and again, the images played in her mind.

Michael, making love to her in the darkness, so tender and wild, their passion like a living flame. Michael, relaxed and smiling, his arm around her as if he could not bear to let her go. Michael, as all the warmth and light leached from his face, leaving the stern, inscrutable mask of a stranger.

The pain of reality penetrated the fog of her disbelief. He had forsaken her. His faith in her had vanished like a will-o'-the-wisp. Their intimacy had meant nothing to him. His tenderness had been an illusion, the work of a clever seducer. She had trusted him, and he'd used her for his pleasure.

In a frenzy of pain and fury, Vivien flew into the dressing room and stripped off her clothing. She poured water into the porcelain washbasin and scrubbed away his scent and taste and touch. Yet still, she could feel Michael's hands caressing her. She smelled his masculine tang. She felt his brand upon her womanhood, for her womb felt tender and achy, her breasts sensitive, her skin rosy from the rasping stroke of his cheek. In defiance of the upheaval in her heart and mind, her body felt languid and satisfied, softened by the fulfillment she had found in his arms.

A fulfillment she would never again know with him.

Pulling a shift over her nakedness, she felt something inside her shatter. Tears poured forth, and she threw herself onto the bed in a storm of grief and rage and despair, sobbing until her emotions were wrung dry. Then she fell into an exhausted slumber. She slept until a distant awareness penetrated her uneasy dreams.

The tapping of footsteps. The clink of porcelain. The rattle of a key.

Michael.

Her heart pounding, she came fully awake, sitting up and blinking against the brilliance of the early afternoon sunlight.

She was alone in the cavernous bedchamber. But on a table near the hearth lay a tray of food. The aroma of fresh bread and meat wafted to her. Rather than pangs of hunger, she tasted the sourness of nausea.

Michael hadn't come to her, begging forgiveness. He'd sent a maidservant, that was all. Likely, he prided himself on his benevolence in feeding his prisoner.

She would starve before accepting his charity.

She sat hugging herself amid the rumpled sheets. Had he sent for the magistrate yet? Would she be transported halfway around the world to Australia? Or would she be sentenced to hang?

Fear caught her by the throat. She remembered how swiftly he'd dealt with Thaddeus Tremain. By the end of the day, the swindling steward had been carted off to the village gaol and thence to London, where he sat in prison awaiting trial.

She was bound for the same fate.

She mustn't wait like a hare caught in a steel trap. Michael Kenyon was a harsh *gorgio* lord who judged her guilty because of her Romany upbringing. She had been a fool once in giving him the gift of her body. Nay, twice a fool, for she also had given him the gift of her love.

Rising from the bed, Vivien went to the window and threw open the casement. She leaned out, looking down to the ground, the distance dizzying. There was no balcony here at the Abbey, no handy mat of ivy covering the wall. Without warning, she remembered Michael scaling the wall at the Dower House, bringing her a perfect red rose.

She breathed deeply to alleviate the sword thrust of memory. With effort, she forced herself to think, to plan. The old stones had crumbled in places, offering handy footholds. There was also a drainpipe to aid her. Yes, she could make her way down if she took care.

She hastened into the dressing room. Spurning the turquoise skirt and yellow blouse lying on the floor, she rummaged through her clothes. She wouldn't wear the garb in which she had danced with Michael, the soft silks he had stripped from her in a fever of passion.

She chose a gown at random from the many fine garments in her wardrobe and drew it over her shift. She would take only this one gown in exchange for the simple clothing she had worn on that long-ago day when she had left the *Rom* in the company of the Rosebuds.

The Rosebuds. Her heart constricted at the prospect of never again seeing them, especially Lady Stokeford. Dear Lady Stokeford with her impish smile and her staunch loyalty. How she would miss them all.

And Amy. *Develesa,* she would never again see Michael's daughter.

Weak with loss, she leaned against the clothespress. After the fireworks last night, she had vowed to tell the little girl a story today. Michael would never let her near his daughter now. In his mind he had already tried Vivien and convicted her.

But she wouldn't break her promise to Amy. Not even if it meant delaying a few more minutes and risking imprisonment.

Returning to the bedchamber, she seated herself at the dainty desk, took out a piece of cream stationery, and with trembling hands, dipped a quill pen into a silver pot of ink. *For Amy,* she wrote at the top. Focusing her thoughts, Vivien composed a quick tale about a lonely little orphan girl who through trial and tribulation discovers her papa is still alive and then the two of them live happily ever after.

Upon finishing, she sanded the ink and blew the tiny grains into the rubbish bin. She left the story on the desk. Perhaps the tale would soften the blow of her departure. It was the best she could do for the little girl.

From a drawer, Vivien removed a heavy sack containing ninety gold guineas—her wages of one hundred minus the ten that Lady Stokeford had already paid to her father. It wasn't as much as she'd hoped for, but the coins would stretch if she was careful in the coming years.

Hefting the precious sack, she contemplated the grand bedchamber. Since moving to the Abbey, she'd come to feel at home in this restful chamber with its huge canopied bed and pretty furnishings, the ceiling painted with a fanciful scene of nymphs and goddesses. She had been foolish enough to think she might belong here in the world of the *gorgios,* amid the luxurious trappings of the rich.

How wrong she had been.

Though afternoon sunlight streamed past the rich blue draperies, the chamber felt as gloomy and unwelcoming as a gilded cage. She knew the feeling originated within herself, in the anguish that ravaged her soul. She could stay here no longer.

Hastening to the window, she took a deep breath and clambered over the sill.

"This is a plot brewed by Katherine and the duchess," Lucy said for the umpteenth time as she paced her bedchamber at the Abbey. "But how can we prove it?"

Scowling, Olivia perched upright on a straight-backed

chair. "Those two connivers will never admit to their tricks, that is for certain. They would blithely send an innocent girl to prison."

Enid slumped deeper into a wing chair upholstered in gold brocade. "Oh, if only Vivien hadn't been returning the necklace and ring at that very moment."

"No doubt Katherine and Hillary would have gone to her chambers anyway, and made a great pretense of finding the jewels." Feeling every one of her seventy years, Lucy sank wearily onto a chaise. She had just spent half the day saying good-byes to the departing guests, making excuses for her grandson's absence, and pretending to be cheerful. "A woman who would set a mantrap would think nothing of framing an innocent girl."

"Blast them," Olivia said, thumping her cane on the pale green carpet. "They must have hidden the jewels sometime during the party. Are you quite sure none of the servants saw them in Vivien's chamber?"

"I've spoken to the staff. No one came forward with any knowledge, not even when I offered ten guineas as reward." Lucy took a sip of her tea and grimaced. It had gone cold, so she set down the cup with a clatter. "One particular aspect of all this disturbs me, though. If Katherine planned to tarnish Vivien's reputation, then why did she leave once she succeeded? Why didn't she stay and pursue my grandson?"

"Perhaps she thought it best to wait until he returns to London," Olivia suggested. "After all, she isn't welcome here anymore."

"Quite so," Lucy mused. Though she saw the logic in that, she could not shake the feeling that she'd missed something. Something vital.

"Oh, I cannot forget the look on Vivien's face," Enid said, blowing her nose with unladylike vigor. "She was so terribly hurt."

"I know," Lucy whispered, her throat tight with pain. "If this disaster is anyone's fault, it's mine. Had I not encouraged a romance between Vivien and my grandson, Katherine would have had no reason to pretend she'd lost her ring."

"Nonsense," Olivia said. "Michael would have been drawn to Vivien regardless."

"They were in love," Enid said, sighing wistfully. "Why, I'm sure he bedded her last night."

"Then why does he not trust her?" Olivia said with unusual vehemence, slapping her hand onto the arm of her chair. "He's no gentleman for using an innocent girl as his doxy and then throwing her to the wolves."

A small woeful cry slipped from Lucy. Though she struggled not to weep, tears pricked her eyes. When Vivien and Michael had disappeared from the ball around midnight, she'd hoped they were together. Vivien was the perfect woman to light his heart. She was warm and spirited, not cool and aloof as Grace had been.

This morning when Lucy had seen them, both charmingly rumpled, she had known instantly that they'd made love. They were *in* love, with that special, blissful glow she had longed to see in them. Once this silly business was cleared up, her grandson would offer for Vivien, and they would marry and live happily ever after with Amy here at the Abbey. He would sire a brood of great-grandchildren to fill this house with merriment again.

But in horror Lucy had watched as Vivien showed them what she'd hidden behind her back. The tenderness had faded from Michael's eyes, his face hardening to granite. Once again, he'd reverted to the cold, cynical man he'd become after Grace's death.

Olivia hobbled over to sit beside Lucy on the chaise, hugging her in a rare show of affection. "Forgive me, dearest," she murmured. " 'Twas my own bitterness toward men, I suppose. I didn't mean to distress you all the more."

"You only spoke the truth," Lucy said, groping for her friend's hand. It was as thin and wrinkled as her own. "I must face the fact that my grandson has behaved dishonorably. That he will not help Vivien."

Enid sat down at her other side. "Do you suppose Michael is still locked in the library?"

Dabbing at her eyes, Lucy nodded. "The staff has been alerted to notify me when he comes out. Though I doubt he'll listen to me."

"At least he hasn't sent Vivien to the village gaol," Olivia said. "He may yet decide in her favor."

"Bah, he's getting drunk like his father," Lucy said, aware of a piercing sense of failure. "Like his grandfather, too. That is how men solve their problems. You are right to mistrust them, Olivia."

"There, there, you must have hope," Enid said comfortingly, putting her plump arm around Lucy. "You mustn't blame yourself, either. You did a fine job raising your son, and Michael and his brothers, too."

"Quite so," Olivia stated. "But dwelling on the past doesn't help Vivien."

" 'Tis a pity we cannot get a key to her chamber," Enid said fretfully. "We could keep her company, at least. Could we fetch a locksmith?"

"That would take too long," Olivia said, thoughtfully studying Lucy. "You're certain Michael took the housekeeper's ring of keys?"

"Yes, the master key, too. If nothing else, my grandson is thorough."

"Hmph," Olivia snorted. Then a gleam of battle entered her iron-gray eyes. "We must find another way to secure her release. Let us proceed to the stables, ladies."

Lucy stood up uncertainly. "But what's your plan?"

"We'll fetch some tools. Something with which to break the lock."

Enid gasped. "What a clever notion! My stars, can we manage it?"

"We are the Rosebuds," Lucy said, her spirits rallying. "I'll take pleasure in smashing the lock myself."

As they prepared to troop out of the chamber, a soft rapping on the door caused Lucy's heart to flutter. Perhaps a servant had come to say that her grandson had emerged from the library. Had he changed his mind and realized his mistake? Or would he send for the law?

But their visitor bore no message from Michael. Instead, upon opening the door, the Rosebuds found themselves facing the real thief.

A loud knocking awakened Michael from his drunken stupor.

Blearily, he lifted his head from the table and saw the familiar rows of bookshelves in the library. He wondered why he'd fallen asleep in the middle of the day. A bar of sunlight half blinded him. On the table lay an empty decanter of brandy and an overturned glass that dribbled a few drops onto the scarred oak surface. He'd encountered Vivien here many times, perusing the shelves . . .

Memory walloped him.

Vivien.

He straightened up in his chair, wincing at the pain that stabbed his head. Vivien had deceived him. The passionate girl who had given her virginity to him was a thief. No doubt she'd hoped to secure a place in his affections. Grace had done the same, using her body as a bargaining chip. Perhaps it was best he'd found that out now before Vivien stole his heart, too.

But not even drink could make him forget last night.

He could almost taste her kisses. He could feel her arms holding him, her hands caressing him. He could hear her whispering to him in the darkness.

Vestacho . . . beloved.

In a powerful rage, he swept his arm across the table, thrusting the decanter and glass to the floor.

The knocking came again, rattling the heavy oak door, the sound reverberating in his aching skull. "Begone," he shouted.

He did not want servants bothering him with offers of food or drink. Nor did he wish to see his grandmother or Charlotte Quinton or anyone else in this godforsaken hinterland. He didn't want to hear arguments that would tempt him to trust Vivien. He wanted to be left alone to his brooding. To his drinking.

An array of crystal decanters beckoned from a sideboard. He rose, swaying a little as he started toward the promise of oblivion.

There was another hard thumping that Michael studiously ignored. Until a man's muffled voice called, "Open the door, you flea-brained idiot."

Michael stopped dead. His gaze shot to the door. *Brand?*

God help him. He'd forgotten . . .

A cold fear gripped him, followed by a hot blast of fury. If Brand Villiers had gone up to the nursery again, if he'd dared to so much as look at Amy, he would die.

Storming to the medieval archway, Michael fumbled with the key and yanked open the door. He clenched his fist, ready to strike. But Brand wasn't alone.

He stood flanked by the Rosebuds. Lady Faversham wore a grim, angry look. Lady Enid wept loudly into her handkerchief. Lady Stokeford appeared frail and shaken.

Brand's cold gray eyes held a jeering disgust. "You'll

be pleased to know that Vivien is innocent," he said without preamble. "I've found your jewel thief."

Then he turned to someone half-hidden behind him. He pushed a white-faced Charlotte into the library.

Chapter twenty-four

Letter from a Thief

The pinks and purples of dusk trailed across the darkening sky when Vivien finally walked into the Gypsy camp.

The dogs greeted her first, barking and growling, then wagging their tails in recognition. Distractedly, she patted one mangy head, then scratched another one's ears. Conscious of a tight, hurting knot in her breast, she let her gaze search the campfires.

In the clearing in the forest, some twenty *vardos* formed a rough half-circle. The tang of smoke hung in the chilly evening air. Women in bright garb bent over the fires, stirring cauldrons of stew. Men moved among the horses tethered in the woods, grooming the animals or bringing them buckets of water from a nearby stream. Children laughed and played beneath the wagons. Bits of conversation in Romany drifted like music to her ears.

She was home.

Or was she? So many weeks had passed, so much heartache, that she simply didn't have the answer.

In a welter of pain and confusion, she spied a familiar saffron-yellow caravan with tall blue wheels parked by the edge of the forest. On the steps perched a tiny woman with gray hair. She was hunched over her sewing, her needle flashing silver in the firelight. The other women chattered and laughed with each other, but she sat alone and forlorn.

Miro dye.

With a choked cry, Vivien plunged through the camp. People gasped in surprise, calling out to her, asking excited questions she did not really hear. Several children chanted her name, begging for a story. But she had eyes only for her mother. She waited anxiously for the moment when Reyna Thorne would heed the commotion and lift her head.

Then she did. Sadness haunted her dusky features, drawing down the corners of her mouth and wrinkling her brow. But the look didn't last. Her dark almond eyes alighted on Vivien. Her lips parted, moving slightly, as if she were saying a prayer—or her daughter's name. She rose slowly from the step, and the sewing slipped unheeded from her lap, falling to the dirt.

At the same moment, her father limped out of the gathering throng of people. He froze, leaning heavily on his staff, staring at Vivien as if she were a ghost. His dark weathered features held a certain wariness. Reyna stood unmoving, her hands held outstretched.

Vivien didn't hesitate. Running the last few yards, she clasped her mother in a tight embrace. Though a head taller than Reyna, she burrowed against her like a child, breathing in her familiar scent of wood smoke and spices. All her emotional tumult poured out in tears of happiness and sorrow. "*Miro dye,*" she murmured brokenly. "My mother."

Reyna wept, too, her eyes shimmering with joy. She reached up to lovingly cup Vivien's wet face in her small, careworn hands. "My not-so-little Vivi. I've so longed for this moment. To see you again."

"I should have come sooner. How glad I am to see you both!"

Then Vivien spun toward her father. He seized her in a big bear hug, twirling her around as if she were no older than Amy. "I feared you might forget us," he said gruffly as he set her down. "That you would like *gorgio* life so much you'd never wish to visit us again."

"Oh, *dado,* I could never forget you or my mother." Vivien reached out to draw Reyna closer. "I wanted to provide for you, that's all." She proudly opened the sack and pressed it into his father's hand. "There, I've earned one hundred English guineas for you. I wanted it to be more, but . . ."

He shook his head, his eyes moist. "Daughter, I don't know what to say—" he began, when a burly man stepped out of the crowd.

Vivien stiffened at the sight of Janus. In her rush to find the camp, she hadn't spared a thought for him. She hadn't even had a chance to tell her parents what had happened, that she was fleeing imprisonment, and they must all leave here under cover of night.

Janus fixed his smoldering gaze on Vivien. "It's time you came to your senses, *vestacha,*" he said. "I've been waiting for you."

His endearment struck her as blasphemy. "I am not your beloved," she said coolly. "You will not address me so."

There was a collective gasp from the watchers. A cluster of girls whispered excitedly among themselves. They were younger than Vivien, the women her age already having married into other tribes. She recognized Narilla, a shy child-woman with thick dark lashes. Ludu, a vivacious girl with a throaty laugh. Orlenda, a flirt with a sensual smile and glossy black braids. They all watched Janus admiringly, and regarded Vivien with something like shock because she would spurn such a man. She wanted to say they were welcome to him.

"You've become as haughty as a *gorgio rawnie.*" His lip curled, Janus eyed her fashionable gown and the cashmere shawl tied carelessly around her shoulders. "You look like one of them, too."

"I *am* one of them," she said, amazed to feel the pride in herself. "Their blood runs in my veins, and I won't be ashamed of that."

"You are who you are," her mother said firmly, placing her hand on Vivien's shoulder.

Smiling at her parents, Vivien felt a lightness of relief in the midst of her pain. They accepted her without judgment. No matter what happened, she could always count on their love. "My heart drew me back here."

"To me," Janus said as he swaggered toward her. "So you've finally recognized your place, girl. You will honor our betrothal."

"Enough," Pulika said sternly, stepping into his path. "My daughter will marry the man of her choice."

"You give her too much freedom. I would not—"

"Dosta!" Pulika slashed his hand downward to end the quarrel. "I've scarce yet spoken to Vivi. She hasn't even told us if she returns here forever. Or if she only comes to visit." Turning to Vivien, he gazed at her solemnly, awaiting her answer.

A lump clogged her throat. How could she explain that she might have stayed with the *gorgios* had she not been forsaken by the man she loved? That a piece of her heart would remain forever with a trio of elderly ladies, a motherless little girl . . . and a *gorgio* lord who did not know how to love. "*Dado,* I—"

A cacophony of barking interrupted her. The dogs yowled and paced at the edge of the encampment as hoofbeats thundered down the pathway. People turned to peer into the deep shadows of the forest, curious to see who would visit so close to nightfall.

Vivien's pulse surged with panic. Surely Michael hadn't discovered her absence already. Even if he had, he could not have tracked her so swiftly. The camp was hidden in a remote area of the woods, a short distance from an overgrown pathway scarely wide enough to fit a *vardo*. She herself had had trouble following the signs.

But her hopes were dashed in the next instant as a horse and rider emerged from the gloom of the trees. Atop a bay gelding sat the man whose tenderness had won her heart and whose cruelty had shattered it.

With an intensity of purpose, his fierce blue eyes found her.

Michael spied her at once.

She stood tall and willowy, her gown the color of a ripe peach, in the midst of a flock of small Gypsy women wearing deep-colored dresses, their black hair glossy, their ears and throats adorned with gold pieces. The men were short and dark and husky in blousy shirts and loose-fitting trousers. Among them all, Vivien looked like a princess. Her skin was a shade lighter than theirs, and her fine features and proud bearing lent her a distinctly aristocratic aura. It was something he had never noticed before.

The comparison shook Michael. He had misjudged her in so many ways. No doubt he would be proven wrong about her past, too.

But first he had other amends to make. He would cajole her. He'd win her back and she'd consent to be his wife.

He swung down from his horse, tossing the reins to a barefoot boy, who was joined by several other urchins in admiring the gelding. The half-wild, growling dogs bared their teeth, but kept their distance.

Michael cut between two brightly painted wagons, his

gaze never leaving Vivien. The throng parted for him. Women gathered their children close, and men made threatening grumbles. As if the devil himself walked in their midst.

He felt like a devil. Hearing Charlotte's confession of guilt had sobered him. Discovering Vivien's chamber empty had panicked him. The bone-jarring ride had awakened him to the possibility of losing her.

But now that he had found her, his confidence returned. He had only to get her alone and explain matters. She would rant at him, and then he would kiss her. As soon as he took her back to the Abbey, they could engage in another long, hot session of lovemaking. They would find accord again in the bedchamber. She would forget her anger and hold him close, whispering to him in the darkness.

Vestacho . . .

Her features cool and disdainful, she stepped forward as he approached. "You cannot arrest me. I've done no wrong."

"I haven't come here to—"

"Arrest?" snapped a short, bearlike man with graying hair. Turning to Vivien, he rattled off something in Romany, gesturing angrily.

She answered him in the same tongue, taking his hand and stroking it. A small older woman scurried closer to listen, and Vivien spoke urgently to both of them, glancing at Michael now and then. Her adoptive father and mother, no doubt. The other Gypsies listened avidly, making comments among themselves and directing resentful looks at him. He wondered uneasily if this was how Vivien had felt among the nobility, the object of scorn and suspicion.

One moustachioed young man in particular glowered darkly. Husky as a pugilist, he stood in the midst of several whispering girls who tried to catch his attention. Michael's back stiffened. Though he'd only glimpsed the man that one night in the garden, he knew he was gazing at Janus.

A savage possessiveness gripped Michael. He'd had Vivien first, and no other man would touch her. He glared until Janus looked away, speaking to the girl who tugged on his sleeve.

Michael shifted from one booted foot to the other. "Vivien, I must speak to you. Alone. I've found out—"

"Scoundrel!" Her father shook his fist. "You will never put my daughter in prison. She is no thief!"

"I know," Michael said testily. "That's why I wish to talk with her."

Vivien regarded him with scorn. "Whatever you have to say can be said right here. In front of my parents and the rest of the *Rom.*" With the perfect manners of a lady in the drawing room, she performed the introductions. "This is *miro dado,* Pulika Thorne. And *miro dye,* Reyna."

Michael bowed respectfully to her mother and offered his hand to Pulika. The Gypsy kept his thick fingers firmly gripped around his oaken staff. Letting his hand drop to his side, Michael wondered uneasily if she'd confessed to her father about her seduction. He suspected he'd be laid flat on the ground if she had. "You know who I am, I presume."

"You are not welcome here, Lord Stokeford," Pulika spat. "So begone."

The other Gypsies nodded their heads, and a few spoke curt words in their strange tongue.

Michael refrained from pointing out that they were camped on *his* land, and if there was any evicting to do, he alone had that right. One glance at Vivien's closed expression made him focus on what was important. "I'm staying. Vivien needs to know that Charlotte Quinton confessed to stealing the jewels."

Her beautiful eyes widened. Cold indifference changed to painful disbelief. "Charlotte?"

"Yes. She was jealous of you, jealous of the dowry the Rosebuds were providing you." Murmurings rose from the listening Gypsies. Grimacing at the audience, he lowered his voice. "In particular, she was jealous of the attention I paid to you. I never knew it, but she worshiped me. Because I was the one who saved her from the fire that caused her scars."

Vivien snorted. "You're making this up. She wouldn't betray me. Only you would."

Michael knew he deserved the blow. He couldn't blame her for not believing him. She considered Charlotte a friend. "Then perhaps you'll accept it when you read her letter."

Reaching into an inner pocket of his coat, he drew forth a folded sheet of parchment and then hesitated, reluctant to cause her more pain. He could turn around, ride away, spare Vivien this final disillusionment. But he wasn't so noble. He intended for her to be with him when he left here. So he placed the missive in her hand.

She smoothed her fingertips over the thin wafer seal before opening it slowly. As she read the letter, she showed no sign of relief or thankfulness, only a sadness that stirred his protective instincts.

Damn Charlotte! Michael had always regarded her as an annoying stepsister. Because of the Rosebuds, their families had always been close, often visiting back and forth on holidays. The accident had happened on Christmas Day when she was a vivacious thirteen-year-old, and he a suave man of one-and-twenty who had no time to spare for an awkward young girl just learning how to flirt.

Engrossed in a book, he'd been tolerating another dull

family party when she had popped up from behind his chair and snatched the volume out of his hands. Irked, he'd pursued her, and she had laughingly backed away.

It happened in an instant. She stepped too close to the hearth and her gown caught fire.

Flames shot up her skirt to her arm. She screamed in terror and agony. Horrified, he thrust her to the floor and smothered the flames with a rug. Yet he hadn't been able to prevent her from being badly burned.

The injury had changed a carefree girl into an acid-tongued woman. He cursed himself for failing to see just how bitter she had become. Or how much she desired his attention.

Vivien slowly looked up from the letter. Her hands shook a little, rattling the paper. Her expressive brown eyes showed a tearful anguish he'd seen that very morning, when he had damned himself by believing the worst of her.

"I must ask you to leave now," Vivien said.

Her dismissal jolted him. He needed to romance her, to transform all that frosty hauteur into the warm, loving woman who had opened her heart to him. Heedless of her parents and the watching Gypsies, he stepped closer, wishing he could take her into his arms. "Charlotte hurt you," he said in a low voice. "I hurt you, too. At least give me a chance to redeem myself."

She regarded him as if he were a leper. "Redeem?" she said, her voice vibrating with fury. "*Develesa!* You would have sent me to prison. I could have been hanged for a crime I did not commit."

"No." That image had tormented him, kept him from summoning the law. "I wanted you to flee. That's why I left you alone in your chamber."

"Bah! How can I believe anything you say? The lies flow like honey from your tongue."

"Not lies, but the truth. I'm sorry. I beg your forgiveness." Catching her hand, he brought it to his lips. He heard her father's huff of anger, a gasp from her mother, but Michael could see only the slight softening of Vivien's eyes, the merest hint of a response. Desperate, he pressed his advantage. "I miss you. Amy misses you. So do the Rosebuds. Come back to the Abbey, please."

"I won't go back," she said stubbornly. "I can't live where I'm always regarded with suspicion. Every time there's a theft, I'll be blamed."

"Not by me," he said. "I'll never doubt you again, darling. Come home now, where we can talk in private—"

A bellow of outrage echoed through the clearing. Janus. He should never have turned his back on Janus.

Before Michael could do more than pivot slightly, Janus came barreling at him. The Gypsy slammed into him, knocking him off his feet.

Michael rolled, tasting dirt, his bones jarred. Women screamed and voices chattered. Blood lust seized him. His head pounding, he sprang to his feet, his fists clenched.

As one, the other Gypsies moved back, making a wide circle in between the campfires. Vivien stood by the yellow wagon with her parents. She tried to come forward, her expression fiery, but her father gripped her arms, speaking to her in a low voice.

"Stinking *gorgio,*" Janus growled. "You will not touch my woman."

"Vivien is mine." With an uncompromising firmness, Michael added, "She will be my wife."

He saw Vivien go utterly still, staring wide-eyed at him. Good. Let her stew on that for a while. Let her realize how serious he was to state his intentions in front of so many witnesses. After she'd had time to reflect, she'd appreciate the honor he was bestowing on her.

Roaring, Janus charged again. "Pig!"

Michael feinted, hitting the Gypsy hard in the underside of the jaw. His teeth snapped shut. He staggered, shaking his shaggy head. But Michael had practiced the sport of boxing with champion pugilists.

Janus dove at him again, all brawn and no brains. He managed to clip Michael on the side of the mouth, but Michael smashed a powerful uppercut, then drove the other fist into the Gypsy's belly. The breath whooshed out of Janus. Winded, his eyes dark with rage, he seized Michael and tried to kick him in the groin. Michael twisted to the side, bringing up his palm to jam the Gypsy hard in his nose. Janus fell back, blood spurting as he staggered sideways into a campfire, scorching himself.

He yelped like a kicked dog. A woman snatched up a nearby bucket and dashed water over him. A trio of Gypsy girls ran to him, cooing and clucking as he lay moaning on the ground, his hands clutching his backside. The men gathered around, laughing and calling out jests in Romany.

It was an ignominious end to the battle. Yet Michael felt a primal satisfaction. His knuckles stinging, he walked toward Vivien. He had a metallic taste in his mouth. With the back of his hand, he wiped away a trickle of blood.

She came rushing at him in a fury. Grabbing him by the arm, she pushed him down onto the step of the wagon. "Sit! Such a big man you are, always fighting! Do you think to win me with fists?"

He watched in bemusement as she put Charlotte's letter inside the wagon and brought out a clean, folded rag and a basin of water. Dipping the cloth into the water, she leaned close to him and scrubbed angrily at the blood on his chin. Her scent drifted to him, light and pleasing, bringing hot memories. He wondered if she knew he could see down her bodice to the ripe mounds of her breasts.

He caught her wrist. "I'll win you with kisses."

"Hah," she snapped, yanking free. She scoured his jaw so hard he winced. "I'm not a prize to be won. I'm a woman with the freedom to choose my man."

"Then choose me. You know I can give you pleasure." He lowered his voice to a husky murmur. "I meant what I said, Vivien. I wish to marry you."

Her dark velvet eyes glared with disdain. She seized his hand and went to work with a fury on his split knuckles. "You know nothing of honesty. One cannot build a lifelong marriage on a few moments of pleasure."

"More than a few moments," he objected. "We made love for half the night, and I promise more when I get you into my bed—"

"Dosta!" she hissed. "Do you wish my parents to hear you?" She glanced over at Pulika and Reyna Thorne, who hovered nearby, watching them with concern. "They mustn't know about last night."

"They'll know I mean what I say." He caught her face and held her still for a kiss. For a moment he felt a subtle softening in her; then she jerked her head away, her breasts rising and falling with her rage.

"Do not touch me! I could never wed one such as you."

Pulika limped toward them. The red kerchief tied at his throat fluttered in the breeze. Though gray streaked his hair and he leaned on an oak staff, he looked tough and brawny as he glared down at Michael. "Take your hands from her. My daughter has not agreed to your suit. Nor have I."

Michael rose from the step. "I ask your permission to court her, then."

Pulika gave him a long, hard, assessing look, then did the same to Vivien. His brown eyes bored into Michael again. "I could enter your house, steal everything you own, and it would be nothing compared to what you've stolen from me."

Pulika had guessed that she had lost her innocence. Resisting the urge to flinch, Michael repeated, "I wish to court your daughter."

"Agreed. But you will abide by my rules."

Gasping, Vivien hurled the wet rag onto the step. "*I* don't agree—"

Michael ignored her. "If I do, you'll look favorably upon a speedy wedding."

Pulika grinned at that, his white teeth flashing. "It seems you must convince Vivien first. She is no docile mare to be led by a tether."

Proving his point, Vivien pushed her way in between them. "I spurn this courtship." Then she focused her glare at Michael. "You can say nothing that will convince me to marry you."

"Then you needn't fear listening to me," Michael said smoothly. He glanced at the darkened woods, thick and silent, and felt his blood rise at the thought of being alone with her. It would be so much easier to soften Vivien without using words. He caught her arm. "Come, we'll take a walk."

"No," Pulika said flatly, holding out his hand. "First rule: you will court Vivien right here."

"There are too many people watching," Michael objected. "I demand privacy."

"You won't touch her, either," Pulika went on, scowling until Michael reluctantly released her arm. Picking up a stick, Pulika drew two lines about a foot apart in the dirt just outside the circle of wagons. His movements labored, he fetched two wooden crates and set each behind a line. "Vivien, sit there. Stokeford, take your place opposite her. Should one of you walk away, there will be no more courting. And no wedding."

Resenting being treated like a schoolboy, Michael nevertheless sat on the makeshift stool. Vivien flounced to the other one and plopped down, pointedly turning her gaze to the encampment. Clearly she disliked this as much as he did.

He felt caught in the jaws of a mantrap. How the hell was he to convince her to marry him without using his persuasive touch? She wouldn't even look at him.

"Now," Pulika said, rubbing his palms in satisfaction, "you talk."

Chapter twenty-five

Grace's Betrayal

Aware of an incipient panic, Vivien watched her father walk away. He went to her mother, who waited by their fire, and they whispered together, glancing at her and Michael. Reyna nodded, and then calmly knelt down to slice cucumbers into a wooden bowl.

Her mother wouldn't come to her rescue.

Uneasily aware of Michael's gaze on her, Vivien glanced around the campsite. Janus had scuttled off with his little adoring flock. The women had gone back to cooking dinner, the men to their whittling, and all of them watched her and Michael with unabashed interest. She felt uncomfortable and exposed, yet she couldn't take offense. This was the most excitement they'd witnessed since Zurka had been pursued by an angry *gorgio* housewife after making off with a chicken.

Vivien didn't know why she sat here. She didn't want to talk to Michael. She didn't want him to court her with pretty words and tempting reminders of their intimacy. He couldn't be serious about wanting marriage.

"Look at me, Vivien."

"I would sooner gaze upon people I can trust."

He sat silent a moment. Their knees were only a few inches apart. Out of the corner of her eye, she could see his tall black boots and tight-fitting buckskin breeches. She could sense the smoldering determination in him. He smelled faintly of brandy and his spicy cologne, a scent that evoked memories of the dark of night, her mouth on his skin.

"You're right to despise me," he said. "At one time, I was planning to do worse than Charlotte."

Charlotte. The pain of her betrayal stabbed into Vivien. In the letter Charlotte had admitted to stealing the necklace and ring. She'd convinced herself that Vivien would be happier among the Gypsies. With raw candor, she'd condemned her actions and begged for Vivien's understanding, if not her forgiveness. But Vivien felt too numb to consider that now.

Realizing what Michael had said, she turned her gaze to him. "Worse than Charlotte? Certainly! You had no faith in me."

He regarded her warily. The faint glow of the campfire cast flickering shadows over his high cheekbones and noble features. His lip was puffy and bruised at one corner, his hair was mussed, and a smudge dirtied his cravat. But his slight dishevelment only made him look more rakishly handsome. And oh, those eyes. Deep and blue and seductive. In spite of her anger, she felt a lurch of longing.

Leaning forward, Michael propped his elbows on his knees. "From the beginning, I intended to charm you into my bed, Vivien. I meant to use your surrender to prove your low moral character to my grandmother."

Outrage seared a path to her heart. She clenched her fists. "You were going to *tell* her? So that she would cast me out?"

"Yes. Devilish plan, wasn't it?"

Her muscles stiffening, she started to lunge to her feet. "You are despicable—"

"Don't get up, please," he said urgently, putting out his hand. "You heard your father. He'll forbid our wedding."

"Let him." But when it came to actually walking away, she couldn't do it. She sank back down and crossed her arms, sitting as far back on the crate as possible. "Do you really think I would marry you *now*?"

He didn't answer that. Instead, he muttered, "You said I know nothing of honesty. That's why I'm telling you this. The least you can do is to hear me out."

She pursed her lips. "If you wish to further damn yourself in my eyes, then so be it."

"Try to understand, I believed you were defrauding my grandmother." When she started to protest, he held up a hand to silence her. "I examined the letter from Harriet Althorpe. It looked like her penmanship—and yet it didn't. There were . . . irregularities."

"What do you mean?"

"Miss Althorpe had a habit of writing detailed notes on my schoolwork. She formed her *r*'s and *s*'s with a certain curl. I didn't see that in the letter."

Despite her antagonism, Vivien felt a cautious interest in the woman who had given life to her. "You have papers with her handwriting on them?"

"No. But I was twelve when she left. I remember her penmanship very well."

Rankled, Vivien blew out a breath. "You remember! On such flimsy proof, you condemned me."

He looked down at his hands, then up at her. "Yes."

"I congratulate you on your success, then. You've driven me away. You must be proud of yourself."

"I beg you to see the matter from my view. A young woman appears out of nowhere, claiming to be the natural daughter of my old governess—"

"I didn't *appear.* The Rosebuds came and *fetched* me."

"Yes, well, you were a Gypsy—"

"Does that make you better than me? Better than these wonderful people who have loved me without question? *They* would never forsake me."

He winced. "Your story sounded implausible, too. Why would Harriet Althorpe wait eighteen years to contact my grandmother?"

"Because she was dying. And she wanted someone else to know I existed. I'm sure she never intended for me to be persecuted by the boy whose education she had guided."

"For God's sake," he said roughly, tunneling his fingers through his hair. "All I knew was what I saw. Grandmama was vulnerable and alone, and could be easily taken advantage of. I had to protect her."

Her heart softened, just a little. Despite his arrogance and blustering, Michael did care for Lady Stokeford. "Do you still believe I meant to swindle her?"

"No."

He didn't hesitate. Nor did he shift his eyes away. Interesting . . .

Vivien found herself tilting toward him. He looked sincere and trustworthy, a man of honor. Then he ruined the effect by glancing at her bodice. His eyes darkened, causing a tight, tingling sensation in her breasts.

Blast him! She didn't want to feel that twinge of response. The natural stirrings of her body mustn't tempt her. He had been cruel. To him, she had been nothing more than another scheming female.

Hurting, Vivien looked away again. The women were beginning to serve the evening meal. Her father sat cross-legged on the ground with the other men, and their laughter and jesting drifted on the cool breeze. How normal the scene looked, how familiar and poignant. Yet she was very aware of Michael sitting mere inches from her, his mind still a mystery to her.

"There's another reason you're mistrustful of me," she said, returning her gaze to him. "Lady Grace."

His eyes narrowed slightly, the irises turning opaque, his black lashes hooding his thoughts. "She has nothing to do with us."

"Yes she does. So tell me about her."

Michael made an impatient sound in his throat. "It can serve no purpose to dredge up the past. It's best forgotten."

"*Develesa! You* haven't forgotten. Now you will tell me about her, else I'll get up and leave." She made a move to rise from the crate.

"Sit down!" he said irritably. "What do you wish to know?"

"It's always wise to start a story from the beginning."

Scowling, he sat back, his hands clenched on his knees, displaying the knuckles swollen and cracked from the fight. He worked his mouth a moment as if preparing for a disagreeable speech. "When I first saw Grace, she was dressed in white and standing beneath a chandelier that made a golden halo on her hair. She was surrounded by men, including Brand Villiers. I fell hard for her, secured her betrothal within a fortnight, and we married six weeks later. On our wedding night, I found out she wasn't pure. It was my first warning that she was no angel."

"Nor are you the Archangel Michael," Vivien pointed out.

He grimaced. "I never claimed to be. But Grace pretended to be virtuous. She wept and begged for my forgiveness. She wouldn't reveal the name of her lover, only that he'd been in the cavalry and killed in battle—a lie, of course, I found out later. She promised never to betray me, and like a fool, I believed her. I didn't know she'd come to the altar already with child."

"Amy," Vivien breathed, feeling a smidgen of compassion.

"Yes." He appeared outwardly calm, though his fingers pressed hard into his thighs. "When I did realize the truth, months after the birth, Grace confessed that Brand had seduced her on the very night before our wedding. She threw it in my face that she loved him, she'd always loved him."

"Then why did she not marry him?"

"Greed," Michael said through his teeth. "At the time of our betrothal, he'd little hope of attaining the title. There was his elder brother George, who had a son and heir. But by misfortune, cholera took their lives not long after my wedding, and Brand became earl. Money and rank made him more acceptable to Grace."

Vivien remembered the dark turmoil she'd sensed in Lord Faversham. Was he evil as Michael clearly believed? Or was he bitter and grieving over losing the woman he'd loved? "Did you . . . find them together?"

"No, they were too clever for that. But they sought each other out at parties, at the theater, in the park. When I finally realized the truth, I forbade Grace to see him. But she would not be deterred. She made plans to run away with Brand to the Continent. By luck, I found out in time to stop her from taking Amy, else she, too, might have been killed."

Vivien shuddered. "Lady Stokeford said there was a storm."

"A tempest of heavy rain, the likes of which I'd never seen before or since." He glowered down at his hands. "Despite the danger, Grace left to join her lover. Upon discovering her gone, I went after her. But it was too late. A bridge had been washed out. The carriage had overturned, and she lay dying. Even then she asked for him. She begged me . . ."

"Begged you?"

"To tell Brand the truth. About Amy." The words sounded pulled from a dark place inside himself.

The night air had grown chilly. Vivien huddled into the warmth of the cashmere shawl. Against her will, she could understand his pain. "Oh, Michael. What did you do?"

"I went to kill him. We fought with swords. But when I pinned him to the wall, I was too much of a coward to deliver the coup de grâce." He broke off, breathing hard as if he despised himself for something shameful.

She let her fingers brush his. "Of course you couldn't murder him. He was your friend. He is Amy's father, too, the man who gave life to her."

"*I* am the only father she knows," Michael said savagely.

"Yes, and it's only right that you remain her father." Vivien paused, bothered by something. "But how can you be certain that Amy *isn't* yours?"

His gaze slid away from hers, seeking the darkness of the woods. "She takes after the old earl's family with her copper hair and hazel eyes. That's why I've kept her in London all these years, away from my grandmother. I feared she or one of the Rosebuds might realize the truth."

Why did she have the feeling he wasn't telling her everything? "But they haven't noticed, so the resemblance must be slight." Troubled, Vivien studied his harsh countenance. "Perhaps it's time to lay aside your worries and your hatred. You said yourself that the past is best forgotten."

"You don't understand," he said fiercely, returning his gaze to hers. "Amy is my daughter. I loved her from the moment I held her in my arms for the first time. Even if Brand Villiers can't take her from me, I don't trust him not to spread gossip. I won't permit anyone to cast slurs upon her birth."

The ice around Vivien's emotions thawed a little. How devoted he was to Amy, how unwavering was his love for the child of his enemy. He must be a worthy man, her heart whispered. And if he could show such devotion to Amy and his grandmother, why not to her, as well? Certainly his mistrust had been a betrayal, yet he had felt driven to protect his family . . .

Reyna Thorne scurried toward them, carrying two tin plates of food and two small knives. "You are hungry," she said. "So much talking you do." Curiosity shining in her dark eyes, she looked from Vivien to Michael, studying him as she might assess a future son-in-law.

He flashed her an engaging grin. "Ah, stew made with . . . some kind of meat. It smells delicious."

Vivien watched her mother melt before his charm. Reyna smiled modestly, her lashes fluttering. "It is but poor fare, sir."

Did he beguile every woman he encountered? "It isn't poor fare," Vivien said, picking up her knife and spearing a chunk of meat. "My mother is the finest cook in this *kumpania*."

Michael made no comment on the lack of a fork or spoon. Using his knife, he sampled a bite, then said, "An excellent flavor. What is this dish called?"

Reyna beamed proudly. *"Hatchi-weshu."*

He looked inquiringly at Vivien.

"It means 'prickly thing of the woods.' " Vivien waited until he popped another piece of meat into his mouth before adding, "It's hedgehog."

He stopped chewing. His eyes widened and his mouth puckered. Then he looked at her mother, who hovered anxiously over him. Giving her a rather wan smile, he swallowed. "It's truly a meal beyond compare."

"I will bring you tea." Smiling happily, Reyna scurried off to the fire to pour from the copper kettle that hung there.

"I'm eating a spiny rat," Michael muttered.

"You've been honored with a favorite delicacy of the *Rom.*" Vivien savored another mouthful of the sweet, tender meat, so reminiscent of her childhood. "It's no worse than you *gorgios* eating turtle soup or eel pie."

A spark of humor tempered his disgruntlement. "And I can't expect you to adapt to my world if I don't adapt to yours, too."

She arched an eyebrow. "For a *gorgio,* you're a perceptive man."

Much to her surprise, he resumed eating with gusto. He seemed determined to be agreeable. Having partaken of no food since the previous day, Vivien found herself ravenous. She ate every bite, sopping up the rich gravy with a bit of bread and licking her fingers. Michael copied her actions, his gaze intent on her all the while, making her skin tingle with awareness.

After bringing them mugs of sweet hot tea and water to wash their hands, Reyna disappeared into the caravan and emerged a few moments later, clutching something to her bosom. Hesitantly, she stepped toward Vivien. "I've kept this for you, Vivi. The blanket that wrapped you when you were brought to us."

Vivien caught her breath. Her gaze riveted to the small folded square of cloth. Slowly she put her plate on the ground and reached for the blanket. The fleecy bundle was woven of the finest cream-colored wool with a fringe on the ends. Stroking it, she realized with a coil of warm emotion that Harriet Althorpe must have touched this blanket. She had wrapped her infant daughter in it, never knowing that her lover would whisk the baby away in the dark of night. Holding it to her cheek, Vivien breathed deeply, able to detect only a faint musty odor.

Her throat taut, she looked up at Reyna. "You saved it for me all these years. Why?"

Reyna's eyes brimmed with tears. "I thought . . . someday you might like a token from your *gorgio* mother."

Vivien sprang up to hug the older woman. "*You* are my mother. The mother of my heart."

After a moment, Michael's hand curled around Vivien's arm. "Sit down before your father notices," he muttered, pulling her back down onto her crate. "Now, what are you two saying?"

She realized they'd been speaking in Romany. Quickly she related what her mother had said.

"May I see it?" he asked.

Reluctantly she gave him the blanket.

He shook it out, holding the cloth up to the light of the campfire, turning it this way and that. "It's quite ordinary," he said.

Vivien bristled, snatching back the blanket and hugging it to her breast. "Does that mean you *do* doubt the story of my birth?"

"I was looking for something that might help us identify your father. Though I suppose it's asking too much to find a coat of arms embroidered on a swaddling cloth." He regarded her thoughtfully. "If Harriet Althorpe had an affair while at the Abbey, then likely he was someone the Rosebuds knew. It's odd that they wouldn't have known."

Vivien's heart beat faster. She had refused to wonder who had sired her, for the beast had abandoned an innocent babe. But Michael had a point. Did the Rosebuds know more than they'd let on?

Turning to Reyna, he asked, "Can you describe the man who left Vivien with you?"

Reyna bit her lip, then shrugged. " 'Twas dark," she said in her accented English. "He stayed inside his coach.

But he was a tall man. I saw him kiss Vivien before the driver brought her to us."

"And the coachman? What did he look like?"

"That one came earlier in the day to our little camp, asking many questions. Friendly he was, short and fat with spots on his skin like the *gorgios* sometimes have."

"Freckles," Vivien said.

"He wouldn't reveal his name," Reyna went on. "And we did not press him. We were too happy to hear his master wished to give us a child, too afraid he might change his mind. You see . . . I had lost yet another little one from my womb. For that reason, we camped alone, while the *kumpania* went on without us."

"Where did this happen?" Michael asked.

"On a road near *Lil-engreskey gav*."

" 'Book fellows town,' " Vivien translated slowly. "It's the Romany name for Oxford. But in her letter, Harriet claimed she'd gone south to the Isle of Wight."

She and Michael exchanged a puzzled glance; then he bowed his head to Reyna. "Thank you, Mrs. Thorne. You've been most helpful."

She smiled again, touching Vivien's cheek lovingly, her eloquent brown eyes communicating affection. Then she took their plates and went to wash them in the stream.

Vivien smoothed the blanket in her lap. She resented the man who had callously left his bastard with strangers. He couldn't have been certain of her safety or happiness no matter how many questions his servant asked. Yet she had no regrets. She had been raised by the best of parents.

"Curious, that letter from Miss Althorpe," Michael mused. "I still think there's more to it than meets the eye."

She stiffened. "If you question my honesty again—"

"Calm down," he said, chuckling a little. "You're as prickly as the hedgehog that went into our dinner."

Oh, he was charming when he laughed. Aware of her

leaping senses, she drank from her mug of tea, its dark smoky sweetness refreshing. Somehow the night took on a sparkle. She could smell the smoke from the fires, the crisp autumn flavor of the woods, and Michael's elusive scent.

"I've a confession, too," she said. "I didn't intend to stay with the Rosebuds more than two months. Two hundred guineas were enough to secure my parents' future."

He winced. "I thought you wanted to be named Grandmama's heiress."

"There's more. When first we met, you were so arrogant that I wanted to entice you into falling in love with me. So that when I left, I could spurn you."

"I didn't give you much to like, did I?" He leaned forward, his eyes caressing her. "I want to make it all up to you. Marry me, Vivien."

She couldn't draw a breath for a moment. There was a tightness in her breast. Not an angry tension, but a sweet, foolish hopefulness. "I've no wish to return to your *gorgio* world," she said coolly. "Life here is simple and free. I don't have to trouble myself with intrigues and deceptions. Nor do I need to encounter people like the duchess."

His face darkened. "Everyone will know what she did to your father. Many will condemn her. She'll lose her precious standing in society."

"I don't want revenge anymore." It was true, Vivien realized, with the lightness of relief. "I only wish to see my parents live out their years in peace and comfort."

"Then let me give them all they need. As for society, it won't always be easy to face snobs like the duchess. But I'll be right there at your side."

It was wonderful to think that Michael would defend her. "This is home to me. Here, the woods are my walls and the stars my ceiling."

He inched closer, perching on the very edge of the crate, his knees brushing her gown. "I've a library full of books. And a bed big enough for both of us."

A little shiver ran over her skin. "I have a mother and father who love me. *They* would never betray me."

"I have a grandmother who misses you. And a little girl begging to hear another story."

In the midst of her softening, she remembered. "I left Amy a story on my desk. Did you find it?"

"I was too anxious to find *you.* To bring you home." Lifting her hand to his mouth, he kissed the back. "We belong together, Vivien. I want you, I need you. Marry me, and I'll make love to you every night for the rest of your life."

Michael hadn't professed to love her, only that he wanted to love her body. She wanted that, too, to be one with him if only for a few brief moments of joy. He was a charmer and a rogue, she reminded herself. She should resist the appeal in those rakish blue eyes. She shouldn't want to embrace a life with this *gorgio* lord. Yet all her hurt and anger melted away, leaving her heart lying in a puddle of longing.

Reaching out, she caressed his rough cheek. "Oh, Michael, I love you so," she whispered. "Yes, I'll be your wife."

Chapter twenty-six

Dance in the Darkness

The next day, the camp bustled with preparations for the wedding.

Floating in a cloud of happiness, Vivien helped to prepare the lavish feast. Tonight, she would be wed by Gypsy custom, then in a few days, by English law in a church. Michael had sent cartload after cartload of foodstuffs from the kitchens of the Abbey, vegetables and fruits, rounds of cheeses, and an array of cakes, hams, and flanks of beef. At the abundance of meat, Vivien felt a tweak of humor. So, Michael did not wish to be served spiny creatures at his wedding.

While she peeled potatoes and seasoned the roasting chickens with aromatic herbs, she caught up on all the news. Old Shuri's rheumatism had improved, Tesla would have another baby in the spring, Keja's son had lost his first tooth. The women in turn teased Vivien about her rich, handsome man, admiring him for besting Janus, who now courted the sensual Orlenda with a single-minded determination.

Yet for all their camaraderie, Vivien was aware of a chasm between herself and these women. She was a *gor-*

gio now. She would live in the Abbey as a fine lady with servants to wait upon her and a house with more rooms than she could count. She would entertain guests and wonder which of them were her real friends and which of them might betray her.

She took a deep, steadying breath. She trusted the Rosebuds, especially Lady Stokeford who had been like a loving grandmother to her. She longed to be Amy's mother.

Michael's wife.

That thrilling prospect overshadowed her misgivings. The previous evening, he and her father had spent a long time discussing the terms of her bride price, her father stern at first, then gradually unbending until they'd traded jests and boasts. Forbidden to partake in the affairs of men, she didn't know all that had been said, but she had warned Michael to break tradition and pay her father for her hand, rather than vice versa. At last, both men had appeared satisfied. With the formal agreement concluded, the wedding feast would take place immediately, in the custom of the *Rom*.

Toward sunset, she went inside the caravan to don the splendid white satin gown that her mother had lovingly sewn for her trousseau several years ago. The dress had wide sleeves and a full skirt, hardly the current *gorgio* fashion, but Vivien felt beautiful in it. As Reyna settled a crown of woven ivy leaves on Vivien's freshly brushed and braided hair, the clamoring of the dogs sounded outside the encampment.

"Your beloved arrives," Reyna said softly, stroking Vivien's cheek with her careworn fingers. "How happy I am that you've found love. You've found your place in the world."

"Yes." Her breast aching, Vivien caught her mother's hand and held tightly to it. "I'll miss you and *miro dado*.

You must promise to come back here often."

Tears welled in Reyna's smiling eyes. "But of course. Do you think we could stay away?" She gave Vivien a warm embrace, then drew back. "Go now, your beloved awaits his bride."

With a shiver of anticipation, Vivien stepped out of the caravan just as Michael swung off his bay gelding. He wore a dark blue coat with silver buttons, his long legs encased in tight-fitting tan breeches. The dazzling white of his shirt and cravat made a striking contrast to his black hair.

His gaze met hers across the busy camp. He smiled, a cocky tilt of his mouth that ignited a fire in her heart. How she loved him. The world took on a radiance when he was near.

She hastened to his side, glancing past him down the empty path shrouded by dusk. "Did Lady Stokeford and Amy not come with you?"

He caught her hand, stroking her palm with his thumb. "It isn't wise for Grandmama to be outside in this damp chill. And Amy will be going to bed soon."

She felt a sense of loss at their absence. "Did you tell Amy I am to be her mother?"

"To a great squeal of delight." Michael's grin broadened, his teeth flashing white in the firelight. "She asked me a thousand questions and then ran off to give the news to Nibbles."

Oh, how she wished she'd been there! "I'll go to the Abbey tomorrow and visit her."

"Beware the Rosebuds. They're busily planning our church wedding." He bent his head close so that the warmth of his breath brushed her cheek. "As for me, I must ride to Canterbury tomorrow and obtain a special license. Before the week is out, you'll wed me again and become Lady Stokeford."

His firm tone, the strength of his fingers around hers, rekindled that special glow inside Vivien. She cared little for titles or wealth, only for him. The promise in his eyes made her feel soft and womanly. He did care for her, truly he did. She would be his wife; she would show him how to love again.

At his side, she walked proudly to the long tables that had been brought from the house. By custom, the bride and groom sat apart, and the dinner seemed to go on forever. Talk and laughter swirled around her, and she smiled at comments she didn't really hear and ate food she didn't really taste. All the while, she gazed at Michael and longed for the joy of his arms around her again.

At last Pulika stood up, and a hush came over the throng. With a vibrant emotion to his voice, he gave his approval to the marriage, thus sealing their union. Toasts were raised with glasses of fine wine from the cellars of the Abbey. Everyone congratulated the newlyweds, the men thumping Michael on the back, and the women murmuring blessings to Vivien. She felt cloaked in the trappings of a marvelous dream. She was Michael's wife now. His *wife.*

Then, much to everyone's surprise, Orlenda's father stood up and announced her betrothal to Janus. Orlenda blushed and ducked her head with rare shyness while everyone cheered again. Zurka and Fonso began to tune their *bashadis,* and as the tables were cleared and put away for dancing, the lively sound of fiddle music sweetened the air.

A flock of chattering women led Vivien away. Reyna smiled through her happy tears as she unbraided Vivien's hair so that its rich, wavy mass tumbled around her white satin gown. Speculations on Michael's virility elicted envious comments from the women. Through it all, Vivien felt the beat of excitement in her blood. He was hers now, hers alone.

Once they had emerged from her parents' *vardo,* a team of men pulled it a short distance from the camp so the newlyweds might have their privacy. With much jesting and laughter, they placed a feather mattress and eiderdown quilt outside the wagon. His jet-black eyes moist, Pulika gave Vivien a bear hug, which she returned with an intensity of love. Then he presented the bride to the groom, the moment when he formally relinquished his daughter to her husband.

Michael gathered Vivien's hands in his. Bending to her, he brushed a chaste kiss over her lips. The women sighed, and the men made more ribald remarks. Caught up in a spirit of gaiety, the *Rom* returned to the campsite, where fires flickered in the distance and the fiddles resumed a merry tune that floated through the evening air.

Michael gazed after her people in bemusement. "Is there to be no ceremony, then, no vows?"

Laughing, she shook her head. "When *miro dado* announced the agreement, you became my husband then. That is the way of the *Rom.*"

A slow smile curved his mouth, and his eyes darkened with a fierce tenderness. "Then kiss me well, wife. I've been thirsting for you."

With a cry of joy, she went into his embrace, lifting her mouth to his. This time, there was nothing restrained about his kiss. It was deep, carnal, intimate, a prelude to their lovemaking. His hands glided down her back and pressed her against him so that she could feel his desire. The world slid away until only the two of them existed, two souls straining to become one.

When he ended the kiss, she clung to him as he led her to the bed on the other side of the *vardo,* where the low, boxy caravan would shield them from curious eyes.

But she was not yet ready to lie with him. First she would entice him, tease him, increase his hunger.

She stepped nimbly away, and though he grumbled, she urged him onto the eiderdown. "I promised once that I'd dance for you."

That caught his attention. Shrugging out of his coat, he lay down to watch her. To the faint, haunting melody wafting from the *kumpania,* she began to sway, moving sinuously, showing him all the love and the longing he aroused in her. The past two days had been filled with emotional highs and lows, and now she wanted nothing more than to revel in the needs of their bodies.

Michael's eyes glinted through the gloom. The woods formed a secluded bower, and stars shone through the canopy of autumn-bare branches. A chilly breeze skimmed across her skin, yet Vivien did not feel the cold; the fire within kept her warm. As she danced, she drifted closer and closer to him. She cupped her breasts like an offering; she undulated her hips in a timeless expression of desire. Then at last she drew the white gown over her head and let it drop to the ground so that she danced naked in the moonlight for her lover.

Her husband.

Uttering a feral sound, Michael lunged up from the bed, tumbling her down onto him. He rolled onto her and kissed her hard and long. His hot mouth moved down to her breasts and then to the place that ached most for him. Her gasp of surprise changed to moans of unabashed pleasure. She arched to him, her fingers tangling in his hair as the need in her heightened, taking her to the verge of madness. Unable to resist the plunge, she fell straight into rapture.

As the wild sensations slowed to a sweet lassitude, she saw Michael standing up, shedding his clothing with an intensity of purpose. The cool, clear moonlight coursed over his taut muscled form and the rampant proof of his passion. Coming down onto the bed, he entered her at once. She welcomed him with a glad cry, wrapping her arms around his neck, her legs around his thighs. How completely he filled her; how complete he made her feel. His thrusts aroused her again to a fever pitch, and this time he came with her into paradise.

They lay spent, panting for breath, their limbs tangled. Her cheek rested in the hollow of his shoulder, and she felt the strong beating of his heart against her breasts. The words rose out of the depths of her own heart. "Michael . . . *vestacho.* I love you."

He said nothing to that, but with a rough tenderness, he stroked her hair and kissed her brow. She sighed and lifted her face to him, unwilling to let his reticence mar the magic of the night. In his arms, she felt desired and secure, and that must be enough for now. His touch was gentle and caring, surely a sign that he felt the affection of a husband for his wife.

From a distance, the music played and the festivities continued far into the night. But here, in their snug warm bed beneath the stars, cloaked in the privacy of darkness, they enjoyed their own celebration. Michael knew many clever ways to thrill her, she soon discovered. He whispered to her, praising her beauty and her passion as he bestowed caresses between her thighs. He suckled her breasts until she nearly wept with need.

She, too, found ways to torture him. She found that he liked to be touched and kissed all over. He liked for her to ride him, to tease him until he groaned with pleasure. He especially liked—nay, *loved*—for her to lavish attention on his manhood, rubbing his hot length, lightly squeezing the velvety sacks beneath. She learned every part of his body, and he learned hers as well, stroking her in ways that left her gasping. He could stir her body to life when she thought for certain he'd wrung every ounce of passion from her.

The night stretched out into searing ardor and endless pleasure, with long, sweet moments in between when they lay whispering or dozing. Vivien wondered hazily if they would ever tire of each other. As weary as she felt, he could make her want him again with only a few whispered words, a compelling caress.

She slept finally in his arms, and when she awakened in the first glimmering of dawn, she was nestled with her back to his front, his heavy arm looped over her waist. Despite the chill in the air, she felt warm and cozy, drifting in drowsy contentment. By his deep breathing, she thought he was asleep until she felt him swell and harden. She shifted invitingly, and when he entered her from behind, it seemed like part of a wonderful dream. He strung lazy kisses over her neck and back, and as passion kindled in her, she closed her eyes and savored their joining. His thrusts were slow, gentle, tender, as if he, too, did not want the night to end.

By the time they found completion, the air had grown lighter, the branches of the trees visible against the pale gray sky. Michael's hand moved idly over the bare skin of her back. Enjoying his ministrations, she felt loath to stir. But in the fervor of their mating, the covering had slipped down to their waists, and though they were in a remote part of the woods, she wouldn't take the risk of being seen.

She reached for the coverlet. "We should go inside the *vardo,*" she whispered. "There is much time yet to love."

He made no response. His hand had ceased its mesmerizing massage, and his fingers lay rigid on the indentation of her waist. As she attempted to draw the quilt above her breasts, he pushed it back down.

"Michael!" she chided, laughing a little.

Smiling, she looked around, certain he was teasing her again. But his gaze was fixed on her lower back, where a blemish the size of a guinea stood out against her skin. She never thought much about the spot, which was the color of port wine. It was as much a part of herself as the brown of her eyes and the length of her legs.

"This mark," he said hoarsely, running his fingertip over its smoothness. "How long have you had it?"

"Since birth, my mother says." Vivien paused, the horror on his face making her confused and uneasy. "Does it matter to you? It is only a small imperfection—"

"My God," he grated. "It can't be true."

"What? If you find me unworthy because of a blemish—"

"No!" His quick angry answer silenced her. He sat up, his fingers plowing his hair so that he looked rumpled and rakish. "You misunderstand me. I simply can't believe . . ."

Spurred by a strange anxiety, she scooted up into a sitting position beside him. "Believe what, Michael? Tell me."

His stunned gaze scanned her features as if he were seeing her in some new and frightening way. "That birthmark," he muttered. "Brand Villiers has one exactly like it."

Chapter twenty-seven

The Secret Letters

For a moment, Vivien could not absorb the significance of what he said. "It's a coincidence, that's all."

Michael vehemently shook his head. "That birthmark is peculiar to the Faversham line. Sometimes it skips a generation. Brand's father didn't have it, though his grandfather's brother did." He grimaced. "His name was Brand, too. It's a family jest going back for generations. The first son to have the birthmark inherited the name, as well."

Her mouth went dry, and her heart thumped against her rib cage. "Then you're saying . . ." She couldn't bring herself to finish the thought.

"I'm saying that Brand's father is also your father. The old earl must have had an affair with Harriet Althorpe."

"No," Vivien whispered. Her mind shied away from taking that momentous leap. But she had to consider it. "That would mean . . . Brand is my half brother. And . . . Amy is my *niece*."

"Yes." He slapped his palm onto the bed. "God! I should have realized it before. The old earl had mistresses by the dozen. Just like his son, he could charm any woman into his bed."

Vivien clutched the coverlet to her chin. She had a brother and a niece. They were her blood relations. Harriet Althorpe seemed no more real than a ghost, but Vivien *knew* Brand and Amy. No wonder she'd been fascinated by Brand. No wonder she'd loved Amy from the moment of their first meeting. Her heart had known them.

Michael shot to his feet and pulled on his breeches, his movements stiff and jerky.

Vivien stood up, as well, holding the covers around her nakedness. "Where are you going?"

"To the Abbey. The Rosebuds have some questions to answer."

His purpose blotted out the magic of the night. She tried to gather her scattered thoughts. "Do you think . . . they *knew* Brand's father sired me?"

"Hell, yes, they knew. They probably forged that damned letter."

Her mind balked at his accusation. The Rosebuds wouldn't lie to her. Especially not Lady Stokeford with her honest blue eyes and sweet smile. "No. You must be mistaken."

"I doubt it. This is just the sort of scheme they excel at."

Dazedly, she shook her head. "We can't go now. Your grandmother will be sleeping. Besides, the other Rosebuds will be at their homes."

"No, they spent the night at the Abbey. They were planning our wedding, remember?"

His harsh tone dismayed her. Was he angry at *her*? Because Brand was her brother? Of course, she thought with piercing awareness. Her half brother had cuckolded Michael.

Then she realized another truth. She felt a pain so sharp in her breast that she had to take a deep breath before she could speak. "You lied to me, Michael. You're still lying to me."

Buttoning his shirt, he regarded her warily. "Explain yourself."

"You swore there was no proof that Brand sired Amy. But there *is.* Amy has the birthmark, too, doesn't she?" His face hardened to stone, and she knew with sinking despair that she'd guessed right. Firmly she repeated, "Doesn't she?"

Glancing away into the forest, he compressed his lips. Then he gave a curt nod. "Yes."

"That must be why it took you months to realize Amy wasn't yours. It had little to do with the color of her hair and eyes."

He looked at her, savage torment on his face. "Grace discouraged me from visiting the nursery. But one day when Amy was ill with a fever, I went to see her. The nurse happened to be dressing her, and I saw the dark spot on Amy's lower back. I knew then that she wasn't mine, that Grace had lied to me. Her lover wasn't dead. He was Brand Villiers."

The sting of his mistrust wiped out any sympathy Vivien might have felt. "Why didn't you tell me?"

"You didn't need to know." With angry movements, he pushed his shirt into his breeches. "You will not repeat a word of this to the Rosebuds, either. They don't know Brand fathered Amy. No one knows but us."

His insult stabbed Vivien. "Do you really think I'd betray you or Amy?"

He looked up, his irritated expression easing somewhat. "No, of course not. But you can't take me to task for protecting my daughter."

"I can and I will." Still shaken, she caught hold of his forearms and shoved him against the *vardo.* "You should have trusted me with the truth. *Develesa!* I might have realized sooner who I am."

He made no attempt at escape. The eiderdown slipped, and his fingers glided over the smooth blemish on her back. In a silken voice, he said, "You should have let me make love to you that day in the gallery. If I'd seen you in the light, I would have known then."

"Would you have forsaken me?" she asked, her voice raw. "Would you have refused to wed me if you'd known your sworn enemy is my brother?"

Michael hesitated a moment—a moment too long for her.

In the throes of a wild pain, she whirled around and reached for her white gown. Before she could slip it over her head, he caught hold of her waist and pulled her backward. He locked his arms around her bare middle, and his warm lips nuzzled the nape of her neck. "Vivien," he said in a low, gravelly tone. "Of course I would have married you. I was burning for you. Nothing in the world could have stopped me from taking you as my wife. Surely you know that."

She resisted the softening inside her. She wanted more from him than bodily pleasure. She wanted his devotion, his esteem, his love. But now that hope seemed farther away than ever. "What if I wished to invite Brand into our home? What would you say to that?"

His muscles tensed. "I'd say you were being quarrelsome and unreasonable. You know the sort of man he is."

"He's the father of your daughter and the brother of your wife. Perhaps it's time you forgave him."

Michael turned her around in his arms. His hard blue eyes drilled into her. "You're serious."

"Yes, I am." She swallowed, struggling to understand the tumult inside herself. "When I was a child, I longed to have an older brother. And now that I do, I can't ignore him."

His scowl deepened, erasing all signs of the passionate bridegroom. "He's a worthless devil. Forget him." Picking up his cravat, he crammed it into his pocket. "I'm going to the Abbey."

"*We're* going." Donning the beautiful white gown, Vivien no longer felt like a bride. She wished they could bury themselves beneath the quilt and find happiness again. But it was time to confront the Rosebuds.

To find out if they, too, had lied to her.

"I can't imagine why you would awaken us at the crack of dawn, Michael." Yawning, Lady Enid adjusted her nightcap, ginger tufts of hair sticking out from under it. "Why, it's not even eight o'clock."

"Indeed." His grandmother aimed a suspicious look at Michael. "I'm wondering why you aren't with Vivien. Did something go amiss at the Gypsy wedding? Surely the two of you haven't quarreled already."

"No," he said tersely. "She went to fetch Lady Faversham."

He'd knocked on Lady Enid's door and brought her here without explanation. He wanted all three Rosebuds present before he said anything else. If he gave them an inch, they'd start plotting another one of their tricks.

Going to the window, he yanked open the draperies. Sunshine poured over the pale greens of his grandmother's bedchamber. He wanted to be able to read the expressions on their faces. He'd grown weary of falsehoods and half-truths, secret motives and selfish betrayals. He was as blameworthy as they for lying to Vivien.

Recalling how she'd looked at him, with fury and pain, he felt the sharp bite of panic. After experiencing the most incredible night of his life—two nights, if he included their first time together—he had again managed to shake her faith in him. What if she left him?

His blood ran cold at the prospect. Dammit, she couldn't; she belonged to him now. He'd never been so obsessive in his affairs with the beauties of society. But with Vivien, eroticism took on a new meaning. She made him feel a wild tenderness and an unslakable desire. He'd had to have her, again and again, his passion boundless and satisfying, yet never quite sated. He needed her as he needed air to breathe.

No. This weakness for her had to be a momentary madness. He would never let a woman rule his life and lead him around like a lapdog. He would never let her dictate to him. Plead though she might, he would never invite Brand Villiers into his house.

The door opened. Swathed to the throat in a green nightrobe, Lady Faversham preceded Vivien into the bedchamber. She looked as baffled as the other Rosebuds as she hobbled to a chair and sat down. "I wish to know what this is all about," she said, bracing her hands on her cane. "Vivien refuses to answer my questions."

"I didn't refuse," Vivien clarified. "I merely said they would be answered here, with all three of you present."

Tall and slender, she glided toward the Rosebuds. She had danced for him in that white satin gown, his vibrant, sensual bride. Now she looked infinitely weary with dark smudges beneath her eyes. Without regret, Michael knew he had exhausted her. He wanted to take her to bed again, this time to hold her in his arms while she slept. The tender thought shook him, for he'd always been a man who had his pleasure of women and then went his own way.

Twisting a handkerchief in her plump fingers, Lady Enid scurried to Vivien. "I must speak to you, dear. I'm so ashamed of my granddaughter's betrayal. I know 'twill be of little comfort, but Charlotte bitterly regrets her actions. She's been banished to her uncle's estate." The old lady enveloped Vivien in a hug.

Vivien drew back. "I'm sorry, too, my lady," she said, her voice low and throaty. "I'd hoped she and I could be friends."

Rising from the chaise, Lady Stokeford joined them. "We reproached Charlotte, though it wasn't really necessary. Brandon spoke enough harsh words to set the girl to tears."

"Brand?" Vivien repeated.

Seeing her eyes light with interest, Michael stiffened. Before the Rosebuds could sing the praises of that louse, he said flatly, "Brand saw Charlotte coming out of your bedchamber on the night of the masquerade, and later realized why she'd been there. Of course, he should never have been in my house in the first place, but that's another matter entirely."

Lady Faversham pursed her lips. "I don't understand this hostility between you and my grandson. You two were once like brothers."

"He went after one too many of my women," Michael said glibly. "Now sit down, Grandmama. We've much to discuss."

Ignoring him, Lady Stokeford took hold of Vivien's hand and led her toward a chair. "Come and sit with me. You must tell me what's the matter. Has my grandson done something to upset you?"

Vivien extricated her hands. "I'd prefer to stand, my lady."

She hadn't denied his wrongdoing, Michael noted with chagrin. But surely once she'd thought about it, she'd see sense. "It's you and the Rosebuds who have done wrong this time, Grandmama." He took a breath, then launched his arrow. "You hid the truth about Vivien's father."

Lady Stokeford sank onto the chaise. Lady Enid gasped, fanning herself with her handkerchief. Lady Faversham went rigid as a board. "Here now, young man! What do you mean by such words? Harriet didn't identify her lover in the letter."

"Because she didn't write the letter. One of you did."

The Rosebuds exchanged a swift, secretive glance. His grandmother rallied to say, "Bah, first it was Vivien you accused of forging the letter. Now us? You're being ridiculous." She shook her head, her snowy hair soft around her delicate face. "I told you before, you can't remember Harriet's penmanship so well."

Michael walked to the middle of the bedchamber and gazed at the three women seated near the hearth, their faces self-righteous. "There's one thing you didn't count on when you devised your scheme," he said. "Vivien bears the Faversham mark."

The Rosebuds stared at him, then at Vivien. For once, they looked utterly flummoxed. The starch went out of his grandmother's spine. A frown pulled at Lady Enid's pudgy features. Lady Faversham clung to the knob of her cane as if she might wilt at any moment.

Standing by the window, Vivien watched the old ladies with a sort of desperation on her exquisite features. Her hands visibly shaking, she lifted them to her cheeks. She wanted the Rosebuds to be innocent, Michael knew, and he wished to hell he could have shielded her from this latest betrayal. But she had a right to know.

With a tinkling chime, the clock on the mantelpiece rang the quarter hour. The sound shattered the unnatural silence.

Lady Faversham heaved a tired sigh. Her gaze wavered and fell to her lap. "Yes, it's true. My son Jeffrey—Brandon's father—also fathered Vivien. But you mustn't blame Enid or Lucy. It was my idea to write the letter and bring Vivien here."

"We all did our part," Lady Stokeford insisted, reaching over to pat Lady Faversham's hand. "I won't allow you to take the blame, Olivia."

"Nor I," Lady Enid added.

Vivien made a little sound of distress. Alarmed by the paleness of her face, Michael went to her, placing his hand at the small of her back while addressing the Rosebuds. "Why the devil did you wait eighteen years to claim Vivien?"

"We didn't know she existed until last year," his grandmother said. "Oh, if I'd guessed Harriet was pregnant when she left here, I would have been happy to provide for both of them."

"No, *I* would have done so," Lady Faversham said. Straightening her shoulders, she glanced from Vivien to Michael. "When Jeffrey died some ten years ago, his effects were either given away or sent to the attic for storage. But last year, when I decided to have his old desk in the study refinished, the workmen found a packet of letters secreted in a compartment behind one of the drawers." She paused, the sunlight revealing every line in her gaunt features. "They were love letters. Written by Harriet Althorpe to my son. While his wife was still alive."

"I presume these letters mentioned Vivien," Michael said.

"Yes. When Harriet became pregnant, Jeffrey purchased a house for her, far enough away that no scandal could touch her."

"Lil-engreskey gav," Vivien murmured. "Oxford."

Lady Faversham arched her thin gray eyebrows. "How did you know?"

"Her mother told her," Michael said ironically. "Her Gypsy mother."

"Do relate the rest, Olivia," Lady Enid urged. "Vivien mustn't think we've betrayed her as Charlotte did."

"Quite so." Her gaze earnest, Lady Stokeford clasped her hands in her lap and leaned forward. "We acted in your best interests, my dear."

"We wanted to make up for what my son had done," Lady Faversham said, her gray eyes misty. "I couldn't rest knowing Jeffrey had given away his own daughter, my granddaughter. So I told Lucy and Enid, and we conceived the idea of finding you and bringing you here to wed a gentleman."

"I wrote the letter," Lady Enid confessed. "I've a knack for copying penmanship."

"We all contributed," Lady Faversham said. "To make it sound authentic, we put clues in the letter as to your whereabouts. Then, since we knew you'd been given to a Gypsy named Thorne, we hired a man to find you."

"A Bow Street runner," Vivien murmured.

The Rosebuds looked at each other. They seemed to be questioning each other in silent communication.

Prodded by an unpleasant hunch, Michael said, "No, you needed someone who knew the comings and goings of the Gypsies. So you hired a man named Janus."

A visible shock rippled through Vivien. "Janus!"

"Why, yes, you know him, of course," Lady Stokeford said apologetically. "A rather rough fellow, but he swore he'd convince your band of Gypsies to travel to this district."

"For a sizable sum in gold," Lady Faversham said sourly. "I still say, the man is little better than a thief."

"But he did do as he promised," Lady Enid added. "So all's well that ends well."

Michael rubbed his aching brow. "You should know, Janus tried to claim Vivien for himself. I was forced to correct his mistake with my fists."

"Oh, no!" Lady Stokeford moaned. Jumping up, she rushed to Vivien, taking her hands. "That ruffian didn't hurt you, did he?"

"No. But he thought I would steal for him."

"My dear girl, I'm so sorry. We never meant to cause trouble for you. You believe me, don't you?"

Vivien didn't speak for a moment. Her breasts rose and fell as if she were trying to control some great emotion. Then she asked a question of her own. "What happened to her?"

Lady Stokeford blinked her watery blue eyes. "Harriet?"

"Did she die last year as the letter stated?"

His grandmother shifted her gaze away for a moment. "No," she admitted gently. "Harriet died shortly after your birth."

Vivien bowed her head, and Michael wondered if she was outraged by their audacity. *He* certainly was. His hand at her back, he could feel the tension in her. Yet she seemed unaware of his presence, even when he slid his arm around her slender waist.

Intending to chastise his grandmother, he hissed out a breath.

But before he could speak, Vivien stepped away from him, going to the middle of the rug, her gaze fixed on the Rosebuds. "So you lied about that, too? You said my father tore me from Harriet's arms, left her sick and alone, without the means to find me. You let me think she lived for many years in poverty and hardship, pining for me."

Lady Faversham sighed again. "That embellishment was mine, I fear. I was furious at Jeffrey for his philandering and, most of all, for giving you away. Scandal or not, I would have accepted you as my granddaughter."

"But when you brought me here, I came to live with Lady Stokeford."

"We thought it would put you off the scent in case you were suspicious," Lady Enid said. "We didn't mean for things to turn out like this."

Vivien kept her eyes on Lady Faversham. "Do you still have my mother's letters?"

The stately woman shook her head. "I burned them all, I'm afraid. We never thought you would find out and ask to see them."

"We wanted you to be happy," Lady Stokeford said, wringing her hands. "That's all we ever wanted for you. That, and marriage to Michael." Pausing, she added tremulously, "You will wed my grandson in a proper English ceremony, won't you?"

For the first time since she'd entered the bedchamber, Vivien turned to look at him. Anguish flooded her brown eyes. "I don't know," she whispered.

Leaving him struck speechless, she pivoted on her heel and walked out the door of the bedchamber. The Rosebuds converged on him, all talking at once.

"What does she mean, *'I don't know'*?" Lady Stokeford fretted. "Michael, what did you do to her to make her say that?"

"Did the wedding night go badly?" Lady Enid asked.

"No, it's us," Lady Faversham said, her shoulders slumped. "She'll never forgive us for hiding the truth from her. She'll return to the Gypsies, and I'll never see my granddaughter again."

No.

In a frenzy, Michael dashed out of the bedchamber and into the corridor. It was empty save for a housemaid on her knees polishing the baseboards. Then he spied a flick of white skirt at the end of the passage.

He sprinted after Vivien, startling the servant into spilling her box of brushes and rags. Heedless, he plunged down the corridor and nearly toppled over a side table as he rounded the corner. He saw her ahead of him, at the top of the grand staircase, her hand on the railing. His wife. Her dark head bent, she descended the stairs, the virginal white of her gown reminding him of all his mistakes.

"Wait!" he shouted, his voice echoing through the foyer.

Vivien didn't wait. She continued down the steps as if she didn't hear him. Perhaps she didn't. Perhaps she had so shut him out of her heart that he no longer existed for her.

Damn foolish sentiment. She was wounded, hurting. He would hold her close, try to ease the ache of the Rosebuds' deception. Although he despised female tears, he would let Vivien weep all over him.

Recklessly bounding down the slick marble steps two at a time, his shoes thudding, he reached her at the base of the stairs and stepped around in front of her. "Don't go, Vivien. Please. We need to talk."

She wasn't sobbing, thank God. But the desolate expression on her face arrowed into him. "There's little left to say," she murmured. "Except that . . . perhaps I've been deceiving myself to think I could fit in here. I was happier with my own people."

She kept walking, so he walked backward in front of her. "Don't say that," he said roughly. "I need you with me. We'll marry and go to London, get away from the Rosebuds. I can't keep Amy here any longer, anyway."

Vivien stopped, staring at him with something like distaste. "You would take Amy away from your grandmother? Don't you realize how close they've become?"

He did, and that worried him. The two of them ate breakfast together in his grandmother's bedchamber. They went on walks to visit Nibbles. They sat together at picnics and luncheons. Grandmama delighted in Amy, and he didn't like hurting either of them.

But it was only a matter of time before his grandmother happened upon Amy at her bath or while dressing.

"It has to be this way," Michael said, glancing around the corridor to make sure no one was within hearing. He lowered his voice to a harsh whisper. "Don't you see? If Grandmama finds out the truth about Amy, she'll tell the Rosebuds, and they'll tell Brand."

Vivien shook her head, her long black hair shimmering in the morning light. "I don't believe her ladyship would do anything to hurt Amy. She would know it's in Amy's best interests to keep this one particular secret. I know that, too."

"I can't take that risk," he said forcefully. "You know I can't. We're moving back to London, and that's that."

"You'll go without me," she said, her voice quivering. "My eyes are finally opened, Michael. I can no longer tolerate dishonesty in those I love."

Love. She still loved him. Grasping at the seed of hope, he slid his arms around her and pulled her close. He stroked her cheek, her hair, her throat. "I hold no secrets from you now, Vivien. I vow I never will. I'll be honest with you in all things."

Her gaze didn't soften. One dark brow lifted in questioning disbelief. "Then answer me this. Do you love me?"

He opened his mouth to give her what she wanted, but the words stuck in his throat. Vivien didn't want pap from him, or pretty praise, or false declarations or any of the other sweet nothings he might use to placate a woman. She wanted candor, and he couldn't begin to define the confusing welter of emotions she stirred in him. He desired her, craved her, dreamed of her . . . but love? Love made a man weak and spineless. After Grace, he had sworn never again to open himself to such pain and humiliation.

Her eyes swam with tears, and she pulled out of his arms. "Our Gypsy marriage isn't recognized by English law. You're free to go as you please."

Frozen by her words, he gawked as she stepped around him and continued down the broad corridor, her womanly form framed by the tall stone pillars. Her bare feet made no sound on the marble floor.

She was leaving him. Forever.

Panicked, he surged after her, caught her arm, and swung her around to face him. His breath came fast and furious. "I don't want to be free," he choked out. "I intend to honor our marriage. You should be glad of that."

"I need more than honor, Michael. I need your love—your honest love." Her face stark with painful determination, she pulled away from him. "If ever you can give me that, I'll be waiting."

Chapter twenty-eight

The New Caravan

As she leaned against the trunk of an oak, watching the dusk settle into soft shadows beneath the trees, Vivien heard the rumble of a clearing throat. Spinning around, she blinked at her father, who leaned heavily on his new cane of gleaming mahogany. "I'm sorry, *dado*. Have you been standing there long?"

"Long enough to see your unhappiness." He tilted his head, his eyes dark with concern. "You are lamenting your errant husband again."

If only he knew how much. Such folly it was to gaze toward Stokeford Abbey when the forest hid the house from view. So many times she'd debated going there, to see Amy and the Rosebuds . . . and Michael. Each day, as she visited his tenants and gave out medicinals, she expected to hear that he and Amy had left for London.

Swallowing past the lump in her throat, Vivien attempted a smile. "This land is a reminder, that's all," she said firmly. "Michael will always be a part of me, but once we leave here, I'm sure to forget him."

Pulika crossed his arms over his embroidered green coat. "We'll go as soon as I finish my work. Another week perhaps."

"A week?" Vivien said in dismay. For the past fortnight, despite his handicap, her father had filled in for the village blacksmith, who had taken ill. Each day, he hobbled off, whistling, returning at sundown. Her mother, too, seemed content to stay at their campsite on Michael's estate. Though they'd been angry the day she'd come from the Abbey and tearfully told them what had happened, now their nonchalance left Vivien confused. Couldn't they see how deep her hurt was? How desperately she needed to leave here?

With her bare toe, she nudged an acorn lying in a bed of fallen leaves. "Is there no *gorgio* who can do your job? We should be on the road, seeking a place to spend the winter."

"I'm strong enough to work now. Besides, your husband asked a steep dowry."

Her chin shot up. "No! I told him to pay *you*."

"That's a man's business, and not for you to dictate." Pulika slanted a surprisingly merry glance at her. "But I will say, it costs much to persuade a suitor to take an outspoken, impudent daughter."

Had Michael taken any of her hard-earned hundred guineas? And why was her father joking about giving his meager savings to a rich lord? "You should demand he repay you. Better yet, *I* will."

Laughing, her father said, "Sheathe your claws, little cat. Your husband didn't ask more than I was willing to give."

"He doesn't deserve even a copper farthing," she said, her voice vibrating with emotion. "I'm sorry I've caused you and *miro dye* such trouble."

Pulika caught her in a bear hug. "Trouble, bah. How can the light of my life cause trouble? That husband of yours will soon realize so, too. He has much pride, but he will humble himself in the end."

Wishing she could believe him, she blinked back tears. "Michael is a *gorgio* lord. He kneels to no one, much less a woman."

"Ah, but I've seen the way he looks at you," Pulika said. "The man is smitten. Now come, else your mother will scold me."

"Scold you?"

"For keeping you so long." His jet-black eyes glinted mysteriously. "Tonight we'll have a little party to cheer you. Zurka will play his fiddle, Shuri will tell her stories, and your mother will serve us her chicken stew."

He put his hand at her back and propelled her toward the circle of *vardos* where the campfires shone through the gathering dusk. Vivien bit her lip. She had no heart for revelry, but how could she disappoint her parents in this? She owed them so much. They had taken her in as a baby, raised her as their treasured daughter, given her all the love in their hearts.

Reyna hastened forward, wagging her gnarled finger. "There you are, you laggard. What took you so long?"

Pulika cast a droll look at Vivien. "What did I tell you? I married a scold."

"And I married a buffoon," Reyna chided. "A big bear who is always teasing." But she laughed when he enfolded her in his huge embrace.

Vivien's throat tightened. There was something else her parents had given her: the ideal for a happy marriage. That closeness and love was what she'd wanted for herself. What she'd foolishly wanted with a *gorgio* lord.

Reyna motioned to her. "We must find you something more festive to wear, Vivi."

Vivien glanced down at her serviceable green skirt and gold blouse. "I won't wear my *gorgio* gown."

"You don't have to." Like a little whirlwind, Reyna bustled her up the steps and into the *vardo,* where a lantern lighted their simple belongings, a brass brazier for heat, cupboards holding dishes and pots and curios, a bed for the cold nights of winter when they could not sleep outdoors. Vivien felt more like curling up there than pretending to be cheerful.

But she would make the effort. "There's my blue skirt, though I don't see how it's any better than—"

She faltered as Reyna drew forth the white bridal gown. The gown in which she had become Michael's wife. The gown in which she had danced for him. The gown in which she had experienced such joy . . . and sorrow.

"No," she whispered. "Not that."

"Please, wear it to humor your old mother," Reyna said, helping Vivien shed her garb. "You'll look beautiful in it. Perhaps it will help you remember how happy you were."

She needed no reminder of that glorious episode. Surely her mother knew that; it wasn't like her to be so unfeeling. Then a thought riveted Vivien. Unless there was another reason for her mother's lively smile. A reason for her father's jovial mood. Perhaps he had spoken to Michael . . .

No. She mustn't hope. She mustn't let herself even think such reckless thoughts.

Outside, the dogs launched into a clamor of barking. Vivien's heart took a leap. She looked at her mother, who held out the wedding dress.

"Quickly," Reyna said, her eyes gleaming. "There is no time to waste."

"What is it? Who's here?"

"Put this on, and we'll find out." Reyna would say no more.

With trembling hands, Vivien slipped the dress over her head. The satin slithered downward, cool and caressing as a man's touch. Her hair swirled down to her waist like an ebony cape. In the small square of mirror hanging on the painted wall, she could see the sparkle in her eyes, the high color in her cheeks. If only she could be certain . . .

Her mother shooed her out the door and into the twilight. A few stars winked in the heavens. On the step Vivien paused, transfixed by an unexpected sight.

At the edge of the encampment, the *Rom* crowded around a strange *vardo*. The vehicle was large and finely built, painted a rich crimson with gold wheels. The Stokeford colors, she noted distractedly. Several Gypsy boys were busily unhitching a pair of sleek black horses. From the wide seat at the front of the vehicle, a man leapt lithely to the ground.

Michael.

Their eyes met and he went still, staring at her from across the camp. He wore the blousy white shirt and dark breeches of a man of the *Rom,* with black knee boots and a red sash cinching his waist. The very air seemed to shimmer with her awareness of him. His gaze never wavering, he strode through the throng of Gypsies who stood admiring the fancy caravan.

He stopped before the steps where she stood. His gaze moved hungrily over her, and now she was glad she'd worn the white gown. Fiercely glad. He held out his hand. "My lady," he said in his deep, silken voice, "I've something to show you."

She should not let herself be romanced by this rogue. Michael probably believed he could sweep her off her feet with pretty words. He might even be right. Not that she intended to tell him so.

Ignoring his hand, she stepped down. "What is this all about?" she asked, trying to calm her racing heart. "Where did you find that fancy *vardo*?"

"I didn't find it. I had it built. With the help of your father."

"Miro dado?" she exclaimed. "But he's spent his days at the blacksmith's . . ." Vivien fell silent, looking across the camp to see her father grinning at her. Glancing around, she saw Reyna Thorne smiling in the doorway. They had both been in on the scheme.

"Pulika's come to the Abbey every day to direct the workmen." Michael gave her a serious, penetrating look. "The deception was my doing, not his. I wanted this to be a surprise."

She was more than surprised. She was amazed, bewildered, and intrigued. "Why are you dressed like one of us?"

"You'll understand in a moment." Michael took her arm and guided her toward the *vardo.* "First, I want you to see the caravan. It has every modern comfort, the best that money can buy. I hope you'll like it."

The crowd parted to let them pass, murmuring in admiration and excitement. She could think only of the man at her side. Her husband. He walked her around the outside of the *vardo,* proudly pointing out all its amenities, the windows of etched glass, the comfortable driver's seat with an overhang in case of rain, the brass lanterns to illuminate the night. The *Rom* trailed after them, oohing and ahhing.

Michael had gone through all this expense and planning for her? It seemed too much to believe. She wished he would show her the interior so that she could ask him in privacy what it all meant.

But he sat her down on the step just outside the rear door. Before her astonished eyes, in front of her parents and the entire *Rom,* he knelt in the dirt and brought her hand to his lips.

"Michael?" she whispered, her voice wavering between

awe and embarrassment. "Shouldn't we go inside?"

"No." The lamplight showed the intensity of his blue eyes. "What I have to say, I want everyone to hear. I've behaved like an arrogant ass. But if you'll come back to me, we'll travel with your family for part of each year. Amy can come along, too."

She quivered, afraid this was all a dream, and she would awaken if she even dared to breathe. "I thought you wanted to live in London."

He pressed his finger to her lips. "No. I'm not afraid to take risks anymore. I've a special license, and if you like we can be married tomorrow in the chapel at Stokeford Abbey. The Rosebuds have made all the arrangements." He drew a deep breath. "I invited Brand, too."

Michael had done even that for her. Because Brand was her brother. She scarcely knew what to say, how to thank him.

Pulika stepped forward. "For his dowry, he asked only that we spend each winter here with you, Vivi."

She was struck mute by that, too. She could only stare at Michael, unable to stop the hope that rose so sweetly in her breast.

He said quickly, "Please don't refuse me, darling. These past few weeks have been hell without you. You're a fire in my heart." An unveiled longing burned in his eyes. He brought her hand to his chest so she could feel the strong beating of his heart. "I love you, Vivien."

Sighs eddied from the women. Wives leaned against their men. Pulika and Reyna stood together smiling.

"Oh, Michael, I love you, too." Giddy with joy, Vivien threw herself into his arms, almost knocking him to the ground. Saving her from a tumble, he sat up and chuckled, brushing his lips over hers. "Does this mean you'll let me be your husband again?"

"Yes, oh yes. *Now* will you show me the interior?"

His teeth flashed in a grin. "With pleasure."

Amid cheers from the Gypsies, he helped Vivien to her feet, dusted off her white skirt, and pushed open the door. She heard her father shooing away the curious, herding them back toward the campfires. But she had eyes only for Michael.

He carried the brass lamp inside and hung it from a wall hook. The light illuminated a sight so cozily elegant that she gasped with delight, turning around slowly so she could take it all in. Near the entrance, there was a small washroom behind a partition, and opposite it, cupboards filled with fine china and silver. A plump chaise stood against one wall. In between two curtained windows sat a small mahogany desk and above it, a glass-fronted case full of books. But what snared her attention was the wide bed situated at the far end of the caravan.

Gold cord drew back the crimson draperies to display an ornate headboard that was crowned by the gold Stokeford crest. The nest of pillows and the satiny coverlet seemed to beckon to Vivien. She went toward the bed, the fine Persian rug cushioning her bare feet.

"There's a table over here that folds down," Michael said, demonstrating its operation, clearly proud of all the gadgets. "And this chaise opens into a small bed where Amy can sleep."

"Why don't you show me how *this* works, Michael?" Giving him a sensual smile, Vivien let her fingers glide over the crimson quilt.

He dropped the cushion, left the chaise half-undone, and walked straight to her. Oh, how she had missed that cocky stride of his, the way his mouth slanted with wicked promise, that scorching intensity in his midnight-blue eyes. Without a word, he caught her to him in a long, deep kiss that left her hot and aching and gasping for breath.

"Ah, yes, the bed. My *pièce de résistance*." He settled down against the pillows and drew her into the hard cradle of his body, her long white dress draped over her like a bridal veil.

"It's very comfortable," she said, snuggling against him. "But we could enjoy it better without all these clothes." She began to unbutton his shirt, kissing the skin she exposed, smoothing her fingers over his muscled chest.

Holding her close, he kissed her brow. "Vivien . . . my God, how I've missed you. I've thought of no woman but you from the moment I saw you in Grandmama's boudoir, reading her palm."

"*Kosko bokht,*" she said, smiling up at him. "It's good fortune that brought us together. Now, give me your hand and I'll tell you what lies in store for you."

He gave her that look, the seductive one that said he already knew what would happen in the very near future. But he thrust out his hand anyway, and she touched his broad palm, tracing the lines there, admiring the strength and sensitivity of his fingers.

"One true love," she murmured. "That is what I predict for you, m'lord marquess. You'll find much happiness so long as you please your beloved."

Chuckling, he took his hand from hers and let it rest on the warm skin just above her breasts. "So, my love, let the pleasuring begin."